Tales From Cannibal Isle

Order this book online at www.trafford.com
or email orders@trafford.com

Most Trafford titles are also available at major online book retailers.

Printed in Victoria, BC, Canada.

Canadian Cataloguing in Publication Data

Peck, Pamela J (Pamela Janice)
        Tales from Cannibal Isle:
        Private Journals of an Anthropologist in Fiji

ISBN: 978-1-4251-3098-5 (sc)
ISBN: 978-1-4251-3099-2 (e)

1. Biography   2. Anthropology
3. Fijian Culture   4. Fijian History
5. Hinduism   6. Christianity

*Our mission is to efficiently provide the world's finest, most comprehensive book publishing
service, enabling every author to experience success. To find out how to publish your
book, your way, and have it available worldwide, visit us online at www.trafford.com*

Trafford rev. 6/1/2010

 www.trafford.com

North America & international
toll-free: 1 888 232 4444 (USA & Canada)
phone: 250 383 6864 ♦ fax: 812 355 4082

Tales from Cannibal Isle

Private Journals of
an Anthropologist in Fiji

Pamela J Peck

To Tau

Heart for heart
Soul for soul
Let us be
Forever friends

GUIDE TO PRONUNCIATION

For native terms, standard Fijian spelling is used.

> b is pronounced like mb in timber
> c is pronounced like th in though
> d is pronounced like nd in handy
> g is pronounced like ng in singer
> q is pronounced like ng in finger

In pronunciation, each vowel constitutes a syllable.

For example,
> *cake* is pronounced tha-kay
> *mate* is pronounced ma-tay
> *Cakobau* is pronounced Tha-kom-ba-u
> *luvequ* is pronounced lu-ven-gu
> *mataqali* is pronounced ma-tan-ga-li
> *Yaciwa* is pronounced Ya-thee-wa

GUIDE TO NAMES & PLACES

The events in these Journals are true and transpired as recorded. To protect identity, all personal Fijian names have been changed, villages are unidentified, and some kinship relationships altered.

We ourselves must become the Grail Hero who will set the waters free, not only in ourselves but in others. Secretly we are all sore wounded and need that the wound be noted and the necessary words of power spoken.

—P.L. Travers

PREFACE

The universe is so vast and time so spacious that the appearance of a mere individual for a cosmic moment can only be deemed of no consequence. Yet, in its own mysterious way, the whole universe speaks through each one of us, and our words echo into the ions of time. So it is these Fiji Journals came to be written.

It was not my intention to share personal stories about my anthropological fieldwork. I imagined my impressions would pass quietly with me into eternity. But it was not to be. A Canadian friend with an instinct for a good story urged me to start recording my adventures on these islands at the outer edge of Polynesia. I had already made a number of field trips to Fiji by this time; my doctoral and post-doctoral studies were all but completed. During these forays, many a notable anecdote had gone unrecorded—like the time I narrowly escaped the ravages of a deadly hurricane. That storm made international news, and when my friend heard about it home in Canada, he sent out the Red Cross to find me … which they did! Later, he said to me—on more than one occasion, "You should write up that hurricane!".

Months later, this same friend came to visit me in the field. As fate would have it, we were sitting on a pandanus mat inside a grass hut with our Fijian hosts when a *Radio Fiji* news bulletin interrupted our conversation, warning of yet another severe storm. I leaned over and whispered to him, "Write up your own damn hurricane!"

He didn't—but his counsel paid off. As if ordained, I began recording my sojourns on these Polynesian islands in the middle of the South Pacific Ocean. I could not have foreseen that the events unfolding in those subsequent fieldtrips would be sequential, one building upon the other, inescapably leading not only to a catastrophic cultural and historical showdown but to a personal tragedy as well, the outcomes all the more heartrending because the means to their prevention were there all along. So now I offer these private Journals in the hope that they might help those who are "on the path" to transcend the boundaries of our limited and perilous cultural mindsets and realize the infinite creative potential that is our natural birthright.

THE FIJI JOURNALS

PROLOGUE

In Search of Good Teaching

December, 1993

Out of India

Life doesn't always—even usually—turn out the way we plan it. I didn't plan to spend the better part of a decade doing anthropological fieldwork in the Fiji Islands. Not that I didn't plan to do fieldwork. That is what anthropologists do. But it was going to be in—and about—India, not Fiji. I was sure India was the place that would teach me what I most needed to know.

And I did go to India—three times, in fact, during the course of my doctoral studies. I spent a full year traversing that alluring subcontinent, waiting patiently for the project I would study to begin. But, in retrospect, that is not what I was there to do. India saw to that. She taught me to speak Hindi in the marketplace and to recite the beautiful Bengali poetry of Rabindranath Tagore. She sent me to the Himalayas in the north and to Kerala in the south, to live among Sikhs and Moslems, Hindus and Christians. And she provided dwelling in everything from a mud stucco compound in rural Harayana to a Hindu mission in teeming Calcutta and a penthouse apartment on fashionable Malabar Hill in over-crowded Bombay (Mumbai).

India *did* teach me what I most needed to know, but in her own enigmatic style, she put it in the form of a quest ... a quest about what life and death are really about, and about what we as human beings can potentially be.

Human history, I learned in that ancient setting, is not a series of secular happenings without shape or pattern. It is a meaningful process. On the surface, we see only the social drama—economic trials, political upheavals, social conflicts—while the truly significant drama—the tension between the effort of human beings and the purpose of the universe—is playing out silently in the depths below.

That was the lesson of India. But true to ancient teaching, it was only the assignment. For intellectual knowledge, they told me, is easily acquired, and, intellectually, the answers have always been there. Intellectual knowledge, as I would painfully discover, must be transformed into personal and emotional experience in order to be permanently imprinted on the subconscious mind.

That was the *real* lesson—and a bitter lesson it would be, for the human drama that played itself out during my decade in these exotic South Sea islands challenged me in a manner I could not have foreseen. Much more than an intellectual exercise, it tested body, mind and spirit before it would give out its subtle but deadly secret.

For the Love of Tau

1978 to 1988. That was my decade in Fiji. Now it is the final month of 1993, and I'm aboard a *Qantas* 747 somewhere between Hawaii and the Fiji Islands. I'm returning because of a young Fijian man named Tau, and I am bringing something with me for him.

During the ten years I lived and worked in Fiji, Tau was my faithful research assistant. It was strange, if not ordained, how that came to be. I remember it as though it were yesterday. I arrived in Fiji straight from India to begin my doctoral research on a foreign aid program funded by the Canadian International Development Agency (CIDA). The aid project was operating in many parts of the archipelago, and my contact in Suva, Fiji's capital, shortlisted what he deemed the best field locations. The first was among the hill tribes in central Fiji whose villages are poised along the riverways inland from the coastal towns and cities. The second was in the cane growing area where the wet and dry sides of the main island converge. The third was a more remote location, in three coastal villages on an outer island in eastern Fiji. I chose the outer island because I wanted an area where the population had less contact with, and hence less influence from, the European way of life.

The island is called Ngau, sometimes written as Gau, but the "g" has an "ng" sound so the word is pronounced more like "now". Ngau has an intriguing history. It is reputed to be the island in Fiji where cannibalism originated. According to early accounts, the cannibals on Ngau further distinguished themselves by serving the *bakolo* whole. (*Bakolo* is the name they gave to human bodies destined for the cannibal ovens.) In other parts of Fiji, they would dismember the bodies, then cook and serve up the parts. But on Ngau, they cooked the body whole. When it was "done", they removed it from the oven, covered it with black powder, dressed it up with a wig, and "escorted" it to the waiting guests. Then they all dug in. That was back in the nineteenth century.

By 1978, just over a century later, one could get to Ngau on a five-seater aircraft operated by *Fiji Air*. My Suva contact instructed me to fly to the outer island and he would arrange for someone named Tau to meet me there. A day or two later, I made my way to the Suva airport for the twenty-five minute flight.

Inside the terminal, a waiting passenger came to me and asked, "Are you the young girl from Canada going to Ngau?"

"Why, yes," I responded, "but how could you possibly have known?"

"We heard it on the radio," the Fijian woman replied.

They actually broadcast that! I figured that if they put that on the radio, there couldn't be much going on around here. But then it struck me. There were no telephones in these outer islands so people sent their messages by radio. That's the only way they could let the islanders know I was coming.

The view was beautiful from the air. The coastline of *Viti Levu* ("Big Fiji") dotted with villages—the church buildings were conspicuously prominent—the deep turquoise coral reef, fanning out from the shoreline in exquisite patterns, then the islands of Ovalau, Koro, Batiki, Nairai—tips of mountains piercing the surface of a deep blue ocean. It was like a magic ride through a South Pacific wonderland. Finally the plane touched down on a gravel airstrip and coasted to a standstill.

Ngau is everything the travel poster promises in a South Pacific paradise: a high volcanic island with a coral reef, deep green jungles, white sandy beaches fringed by swaying coconut palms, villagers living in thatched huts dotting the coastline, brown-skinned and wrapped in flower print *sulu* (lavalavas)….

There I was, transported via India from the lecture halls of academia to this little-known island in the middle of the South Pacific Ocean. I knew little of the culture and next to nothing of the language, having invested all my formal academic studies on India. Before I left Suva, my contact there had equipped me with two words in the Fijian language: *vinaka* which can pass for "good", "thanks", "fine", "well" and "okay"; and *tilou* which means "excuse-me" but only in the hierarchical sense as in when you walk beside people who are seated or reach over someone's head. I would use those two words a lot!

The door of the small plane swung open. The attendant pointed me toward a young Fijian man leaning against a coconut tree. He was half naked and was brandishing a very large machete. That, coupled with his mass of frizzy black hair and his deep brown skin, made him look every inch the warrior. With few words—he had a reasonable command of self-taught English—he helped me with my bags and escorted me to his village.

And there it was, "home" for the next eighteen months, a cluster of small thatched huts symmetrically arranged around an open green space, flanked by coconut palms on one side and a beach on the other. It was stunning and I paused to take it all in.

"Well, this is it!" Tau said to me.

"Oh," I murmured, "I could stay here forever." After six weeks, I felt like I had!

Over the next ten years, Tau worked faithfully beside me. With his help, I completed a doctoral degree in Anthropology and returned immediately to Fiji as a post-doctoral fellow to write a second book. He was the best research assistant one could possibly have. Why he was so adept, I cannot say. Having lost his father at the age of three, he grew up in poverty and had no chance at formal schooling. But he was gifted with a natural intelligence and a passion for the humanities, so much so that I eventually got him admitted to the University of the South Pacific as a mature student. As a result, he became the first person in his village to graduate from a university, an achievement that filled his clan and his village with considerable pride and joy.

I also brought Tau to Canada. He came three times during that decade, and he would still be there if I hadn't sent him home each time his visitor permit expired. In Fiji, we would record a large number of interviews on tape and collect a stack of documents in the Fijian language, then fly up to Vancouver to do the translations and analyses.

Tau loved it! He saw snow for the first time, he wore coats and boots and mittens, went skiing, drank wine and ate Nanaimo bars. Everything was an adventure to him—like the first time he shampooed his mass of frizzy hair with heated water and it shrank! These remain some of my fondest memories.

The Fiji Journals

It's after midnight now, and most of the passengers are sleeping. But sleep evades me. I feel a strange sensation … like being propelled backward in time … to 1985, seated on a similar aircraft heading for Fiji, when I took up my pen and began what became the first of a series of Fiji Journals. The doctoral and post-doctoral studies were over by this time and I was returning to "Cannibal Isle" to learn the lesson of India. Not another inquiry into the historical and present-day life in the mythical paradise of Fiji. No, a quest into the deepest roots of human culture in an attempt to crack the code, as it were, to get *beneath* culture and discover the "soul" of humankind. Perhaps then we would truly understand the dynamic that persuades us to acts of love and compassion and, by contrast, that which predisposes us to hatred and fear. The island nation of Fiji, with its mix of cannibalism, ethnic cohabitation and political turmoil should be the perfect place for the quest. It has had enough brutality and gentility to instruct a planet.

Entry by entry, the search continued and the mystery unfolded. Sometimes I found it humorous, sometimes warm and embracing, sometimes disturbing. And all the while there was that deeper drama playing out in the depths below, one that, true to the wisdom of India, turned out to be a matter of life and death.

BOOK I

Return To Cannibal Isle

March, 1985

Part I

INTO THE FIJI NIGHT

"Living in Darkness"

Midnight, March 1st—"Fiji: The Way the World Should Be" read the travel posters. An intriguing claim for a group of islands that well earned its former title as the Cannibal Isles. It's a strange blend: a Polynesian culture, a Melanesian people ... in a beautiful and exotic tropical area of the world. A mythical paradise in the heart of the South Pacific.

I'm high above the clouds aboard a *CP Air* jumbo jet bound for the Fiji Islands. Right now, we're somewhere between Honolulu and Nadi, crossing both the equator and the international dateline. It's a marginal space, a marginal time. I take up my pen at the stroke of midnight to embark upon another anthropological adventure.

My mission: not just another encounter with Fijian culture or Indian culture or European culture. The quest is nothing less than an encounter with culture itself, because there is something about culture that is very disturbing. That might sound strange coming from a cultural anthropologist, but a whole lot of awful things have been done and are still being done in the name of culture. We kill and die for our belief systems. We bring unbearable suffering to ourselves and others because of religion and ideology. We push ourselves to the brink, risking the very future of a living planet over a few outmoded ideas.

What makes us carry out such horrendous acts ... acts so barbarous they make Fijian cannibalism look like a family barbecue! That is the quest, and it's an illusive one because the very thing we need to look at is hidden from our view. Fish don't see water. Birds don't see air. People don't see culture—not their own anyway. We follow the dictates of our social systems much as we respond to post-hypnotic suggestion. Robots we are, ready and willing to do and to be all manner of human sacrifice.

Most of the passengers are sleeping. I have a window seat now because the man who occupied the one next to me disembarked in Honolulu. Before he left, he asked me where I was going.

"Nadi," I replied.

"Nadi?" he said, "Where in the hell is that? This plane doesn't go there, does it?"

I look out the window; I see only darkness.

"Darkness." That's how the 19th century missionaries from England characterized the culture they encountered in "the Feejees". They found "a people living in darkness". Interesting, when you think about it, because the culture the missionaries represented had plenty of "darkness" of its own: conquest and expansionism, crusades, religious persecution, witch burning, all manner of institutionalized inequality ... atrocities against the human spirit on a much grander scale than the dark-skinned natives of "Feejee" could ever muster. But then again, the "Feejeeans" were eating each other.

It seems to me if there is one academic discipline that might help us see through our cultural predicament it is Anthropology—because Anthropology is the study of human culture. If we could understand what lies at the root of these cultural forces, maybe we could make better choices about how to have a world.

Three hours pass. We land. The man sitting in front of me is wearing a long-sleeved turtleneck sweater. He stands up and puts on a suit jacket. I feel like telling him he probably won't need the jacket but I decide against it.

Time to disembark, and we are told to use the stairs "like in the old days" because the airport has been damaged in a recent hurricane. So down the steps we go from the front end of a 747. There are a few Fijian men drinking kava at the foot of the staircase. It's warm and muggy. It's 3 o'clock in the morning—and they are smiling.

Inside the terminal, we pass through the first check line where an elderly-looking Fijian man is collecting our landing cards.

"*Bula vinaka* (Hello), " I say to him.

"How are you?" he replies in English without expression. Yes, the British have been here.

We gather around the baggage conveyor. I see the gentleman has removed his suit jacket. It's so humid. There are birds singing inside the terminal and there's a tropical feel in the air. There's something else, something "Third World" about it. Hard to describe … a kind of plainness, an economy of convenience…I get my bags, proceed to Customs—they don't need to see what I've brought—so I move on through the opaque glass doors and step into the Fiji night.

Symbolic, perhaps, to arrive in Fiji before the dawn, darkness being the metaphor for traditional Fijian culture. The early accounts of explorers, traders and missionaries overflow with ghastly tales of cannibalism, widow strangling and human sacrifice, all sanctioned by the social system. Then, as mysteriously as the tradition that persuaded them to feast on human flesh, a sudden and wholesale conversion so pacified these same people that Fiji today is a model of interracial harmony.

So brutal … so gentle…That's what makes Fiji the perfect place for the quest.

Feeling the Heat

Friday morning, March 1st—Tau is here to meet me. It's just after 3 a.m. and he's standing there smiling. The best research assistant one could ask for! He has worked with me for seven years now. He is wearing clothes he got in Canada last year while we put together a second book about the culture of Fiji. The dress shirt is too much for the temperature despite the rolled up sleeves. He too is feeling the humidity.

As usual, he has set everything up "local" style. I will rest in Nadi for the day, Tau suggests, then take the transport to Suva, the capital, tomorrow morning. I agree with the plan.

It's a cute little hotel he has selected, sort of a miniature tourist resort. It consists of a reception and bar area, and a number of units surrounding a tiny swimming pool that sits in a courtyard decorated by palm trees. The rooms are of reasonable size but, like the pool, the beds are tiny, as is the bathroom. The walkways are lined with hibiscus flowers and there is an eating facility adjacent to the pool.

Some hours of sleep are welcome and I awake to that sudden realization that I am once again in a very different place. I find out that most of the other hotel guests are locals. The few Europeans here are straight out of the sixties, wandering the world in a spirit of adventure and curiosity. There's a quality to all this that is missing in the up-scale tourist spots—something very down-to-earth and authentic, like a genuine willingness to embrace "the cultural other".

Tau joins me to catch a local bus into Nadi town. I go right away to the public market to get some papaya. It's very hot. We make our way into the one department store that has a fan in the milk bar. I buy something to drink and get in a perfect spot to catch the breeze. I'm really feeling the heat.

"Everybody is hot," Tau says to me calmly. And then the electricity goes off!

Nadi doesn't have a lot to detain one. An hour or so and I've seen the whole show, complete with "local" handicrafts made in the Philippines. Art has become artifice.

We stop by a small Indian restaurant for lunch. I order some dhal and chapatti, daily fare from my sojourns in India. Tau chooses chicken curry. The young Indian waitress brings the dishes served with little things that I can't remember. Later I discover that all those little things are added to the bill! Very entrepreneurial! Given the land tenure system in Fiji, which favours indigenous Fijians at the expense of their Indian compatriots, Indo-Fijians have to make a go of it the best way they can.

Indeed, the legacy of British colonialism, which deposited indentured labourers from "the Jewel in the Crown" to the cane fields of Fiji, has made for a politically sensitive situation all around. Now the Indians outnumber the (indigenous) Fijians, and control the commerce and industry by competing successfully within the capitalist system. The Fijians, on the other hand, cling to their ancestral lands, and derive their well being from subsistence agriculture and obedience to their chiefs. Up to now they have managed to maintain political supremacy. But they will continue to do so only against the odds. Sooner or later something has got to give. Brutality … gentility … it could go either way.

After casing the few choices in our vicinity, Tau and I settle on dinner at the hotel. It's native Fijians in charge of the food this time. The arrangement is a bit unfamiliar. There's just one choice on the menu—you either have it or you don't. Sort of like an election in Chile. Tonight it's a barbecue and it's $6. Two guys from New York in unbleached cottons are eating it and say it's good. We take the plunge. The cook throws some lamb chops, sausage and fish on the grill. There's soup to start—no longer hot but, never mind, the liquid is good in the heat. And there's rice which you scoop yourself with a hot saucer. For dessert, there's "fruit salad". I see some pineapple cut up in a bowl so I figure that must be it. I take two portions and return to our table.

"Do you want ice-cream with that?" a dear lady asks me in Fijian. Ah, now I get the "fruit salad" bit.

"Yes," I reply and whisper to Tau, "It had better not be that artificial pink stuff!"

The waitress returns with a container of pink ice cream.

I'm to bed early tonight, lulled to sleep by the music of a jukebox in the hotel lobby that doubles as a bar. There's a Kenny Rogers and a Lionel Ritchie among the tunes. Yes, the Americans have been here too.

"A Strange and Secret Life"

Saturday, March 2nd—I am up early this morning to catch a bus to Suva. Tau is playing the ukulele and teaches me a new song he has written while we wait. The song is for a tape of Fijian music we will record professionally together.

We take a local bus. There's an air-conditioned coach leaving at about the same time—double the price—but I prefer the town stops at Sigatoka and Navua to the round of tourist resorts along the Coral Coast. We see lots of hurricane damage en route: hotels in disrepair and houses with roofs missing. It's difficult for Fijians to keep ahead of the game, especially since they rely so heavily on tourism. We arrive in Suva at noon, ahead of the tourist bus. The Queens Road, as they call it, is much faster now that most of it is paved.

"Suva. The bay is fine and spacious, surrounded by grey hills that stretch away mysteriously into a blue distance," wrote Somerset Maugham during a voyage to the South Seas in 1916. "You feel that in the farther country, thickly wooded, there is a strange and secret life. It suggests something aboriginal and darkly cruel." Maugham goes on:

The town stretches along the borders of the harbour. Here are many fine buildings … but there is still the air of a trading station that the place must once have been. The natives walk about in lava-lavas and singlets or shirts, tall strapping men for the most part, as dark as Negroes, with their curly hair, often bleached with lime, cut into a curious shape. There are a number of Hindus, walking softly, dressed in white; and the women wear nose-rings, gold chains around their necks and bangles on their arms …The air is hot and oppressive, heavy too, and the rain beats down incessantly.

Almost seventy years later, the bay is still surrounded by grey hills that stretch away into a blue distance, and the frame buildings still border the harbour. But today Suva is a bustling commercial centre and right now it appears more bustling than ever—maybe because it's Saturday and the bus stop is adjacent to the public market. Native Fijians and Indians make their way among the stalls, stocking up for the weekend, since the shops close at 1 p.m. and do not open again until Monday morning. The heat adds to the sense of congestion. We get a cab to the hotel.

The hotel! It is a plain but clean establishment right in the heart of downtown. I get a room and settle in, then ask for the room key. The Fijian lady—who speaks no English— explains there is no key to this room since the person who last stayed here took it with him. There is no recourse but to shift to another room—which I do, only to find there is no light. I bring this matter to the lady's attention and she hands me a light bulb. I discover it needs more than a light bulb and when I am able to convince her of that, she leaps outside and whips in a taxi driver from a vacant cab. Then she instructs him to fix it—which he does—after which, to show her gratitude, she cooks him dinner.

I have made a conscious choice to live in the style and surroundings of the people I study—but this place is too much. I guess it is the bed with the stack of overly soft mattresses that is the last straw. It's like a scene from "The Princess and the Pea". But I'm no princess. Matter of fact, I find kingship and monarchy abhorrent. Nevertheless, first thing tomorrow morning I'm going to move out of this place. I'm going to shift to a tourist hotel where I can enjoy a firm bed, a fine view and a cool swimming pool.

It's a standard of living of which Tau can only dream. So what should I do? Offer it to him when I know he cannot maintain such a lifestyle once I am gone? Or keep him where he is and rationalize the inequalities, pretending, as royalty does, to be genuinely interested in his welfare?

Yes, royalty smarts of institutionalized inequality in its most blatant, yet deceptive, form. But it's more than that. Somehow it is connected to that "strange and secret life" that "suggests something aboriginal and darkly cruel". But I can't put my finger on it yet.

I move from that cheap hotel … and I take Tau with me.

The Day of Don'ts

Sunday, March 3rd—Sunday: *Siga Tabu* in Fijian. Literally, "the day of taboo"; in other words, the day there are a whole lot of things you are not supposed to do. Where is it written?

Tau has arranged for us to visit his relatives this afternoon in Raiwasa, a suburb of Suva. We buy a pound of kava—the root of a pepper plant used for preparing a ceremonial drink—for our *i sevusevu* (offering), a ritual kind of permission to enter someone's premises. The shopkeeper wraps the kava in newspaper bearing the headline, "Child dies at CWM Hospital because a case of food poisoning is misdiagnosed as typhoid."

Good lord!

We take a local bus down past the university, then along the crowded subsidized housing area of Raiwaqa. So many people living in such small spaces! When we arrive at the house in Raiwasa, everyone is lying about on the mats, the usual Sunday afternoon activity for indigenous Fijian families. We present our *i sevusevu* and drink the kava until it is gone.

It is 6 o'clock in the evening when we leave to go back to Suva. As the bus makes its stops along the way, it quickly fills up with Sunday best-dressed Fijians on their way to evening worship. They look so prosperous, so going-somewhere-in-the-world. It is difficult to connect them with the stark poverty from which they emerge.

We all disembark at the same bus stop in Suva since my hotel is just up the hill from the big Centenary Church. And here they come, in droves, herding into the high temple of Fijian Wesleyan Methodism. They will sing and pray, and invest their hard-earned dollars into the institution, earnestly believing it will help to spare them the destruction of yet another hurricane.

Spirituality is simpler—and more profound—than that. The idea is to have your life and have it abundantly. Don't they know that? I mean, when you're hungry, eat; and when you're tired, sleep. Right now we're hungry, so Tau and I go to dinner at our favourite restaurant.

"The Mysterious Centre of Thought"

Monday, March 4th—The beginning of another workweek in Suva. It's fascinating to watch this capital and financial centre of Fiji slowly come to life—Indians and native Fijians, working alongside each other, setting up their fruit and vegetable stalls in the public market. They will be here the whole day. And tomorrow … and the day after tomorrow ….

The weather is changing. It feels like rain. I return to the hotel and spend some quiet time by the swimming pool. The view of the harbour is magnificent from here, and the grey hills stretch away into a blue distance.

I'm feeling an unusual despondency about things. Maybe the quest is too illusive, too far outside the scope of my field of study.

Anthropology: it began as a by-product of European expansionism when it satisfied both practicality and curiosity to understand the "primitive" life. The stories of early explorers, traders and missionaries became the fuel that fired intellectual minds back home, and their efforts to describe and analyze the unfamiliar were immortalized in classical theories and conventional ethnographies. Academics institutionalized the style until today, any anthropologist who departs from the conventional classical approach runs the risk of not being accepted within the discipline.

It's a lot like what happened to European art in the last century. In France, admission was controlled by the Academy, and artists with anything but a conventional, classical approach were generally refused entry. Those who moved away from long-established and "safe" subject matter in order to depict the contemporary scene in more realistic and increasingly experimental ways did not find ready acceptance. These were the Realists and the Impressionists, and today their works far outweigh the scores of academic paintings they once challenged. Interesting how time has a way of educating perception, and bridging the gap between the academic establishment and the *avant-garde*.

Courbet, Millet, Manet, Renoir, Monet … artists whose subject matter is no longer that of inherited traditions. It is the world of nature, and they convey their personal immediate perception of it. Their work has a ring of truth to it, the feeling of something experienced, understood and carefully recorded.

Like Gauguin in Tahiti. In his search for the primitive life and the source of human culture, he came to believe that painting should reflect inner emotions and ideas. The life of the mind and the soul would take precedence. The subject must be sought, he felt, "not in the world the eye can see, but in the mysterious centre of thought".

It's like my quest: searching for "the truly significant drama playing out silently in the depths below". If the mysterious centre of thought can be translated into pictures, it can surely be interpreted into words.

Yes, and perhaps it has something to do with what happened on Saturday … after I checked into that local hotel. I went for lunch and then stopped at an Indian sweet shop for fig ice cream. There I met a colleague from the University of the South Pacific with whom I had worked a couple of years earlier in Fiji. I was promptly invited for dinner that evening. I accepted and made my way there a few hours later.

There were other guests: a local anthropologist from the Pacific Islands and a visiting anthropologist from Europe, waiting—seven weeks now—for a permit to do what he called "grassroots community development applied anthropology" in the northern part of Fiji.

We were having a pleasant enough time together, but there was something vaguely unsettling about it. Let's see. We were sitting around a table, glasses in hand, discussing the merits of this and that policy for the South Pacific. That part was okay because, as detached as the parties really were from the outcome, it was more or less in accord with what academics do. Then the local anthropologist started talking about what it's like to be educated and have an income in this part of the world.

"It lets you have your cake and eat it too," he stated. "Like when relatives ask you for a loan, you give it to them knowing full well they can't pay it back. So then you don't have to be bothered with them again because they'll be too shy to come around a second time."

I found it unsettling … like he was offering me an important clue to something. Once again, it seemed to be about "that strange and secret life". Unwittingly, of course, for he is the son of a local missionary, and in that privileged status, he can lay claim to the morality of his native custom while acquiring all the vestiges of the west. He is one of them; he is one of us. He need not commit himself to either in order to reap the benefits of both.

It was sobering … so we sat around the table and appropriately drank too much wine.

Something Wrong with the People

Tuesday, March 5th—It is windy and raining, and there is a hurricane alert on the radio. Yet another hurricane! God does not appear to be tuned in to the beseeching Methodists.

I go to the Immigration office to extend my visitor's permit. They direct me to a second office. I enter but there is no one there—desks and papers and all that but simply no one there. I return to the first office. Someone hands me a form and tells me to come back later. Never mind that it is raining and blowing.

I retreat to the Grand Pacific Hotel next door. It is one of those majestic old structures that reveal how privileged an existence colonial administrators enjoyed during their tenure in Fiji. Inside, it has a spacious foyer with cane furniture and gilded fans. White uniformed bearers with tall turbans and deep brown skin stand at the entrance to open the door and close the door. That's their life! Natives are no longer sacrificed to grace the corner posts of a temple as in the last century. Now they have become a more obvious extension of the building and the culture it represents.

In spite of its opulent setting and appearance of five-star service, the Grand Pacific has never made it as a grand hotel. "It is a large, two-storied building," wrote Somerset Maugham in 1916,

> *… faced with stucco and surrounded by a verandah. It is cool and empty. It has a large hall, with comfortable chairs in it, and electric fans constantly turning. The servants are Hindus, silent and vaguely hostile, who go about with bare feet, in clean white suits and turbans. The food is very bad, but the rooms are pleasant,*

*fresh and cool. Few people stay there; the agent of the company
with his family, a few people waiting for ships, and some officials
from the other islands brought to Suva on business or holiday.*

More than half a century has passed: few people stay here—and
the food is still very bad.

The wind and rain have really picked up now. I take refuge a
while longer inside the hotel's spacious lobby. I ask a young Fijian
bearer why he thinks Fiji is having so many hurricanes.

"Because there is something wrong with the people," he replies
without hesitation.

"Oh, I don't think it's the people," I offer, "I think it's just the path
where the hurricane is going."

"No, there is something wrong with the Fijian people."

I head back to my hotel, shielding myself from the wind and rain
with a borrowed umbrella. But the wind changes direction without
warning and turns the umbrella inside out. I run for shelter under
the eve of the public library. Some Fijian children are here also, and
are amused at the sight of this foreigner, soaking wet with a broken
umbrella. We stand in the pouring rain and laugh together.

The hurricane is nearing Suva now and it will be unsafe to leave the
hotel tonight. Fallen electrical wires and flying sheets of corrugated
roofing iron are common dangers in this weather. Tau comes with me
to the public market to get some supplies: we will prepare traditional
Fijian food at the hotel. I choose the menu: *palusami* (corned beef in
taro leaves cooked in coconut milk), *kumala* (sweet potato), guava
juice and tropical fruits. While we are gathering our foodstuffs, the
wind and rain become so fierce the order is given to close down the
market. There is tension in the air as stall keepers cover and tie down
their goods. They have been through this before.

"Silent and Vaguely Hostile"

Wednesday, March 6th—The wind is still blowing and it is pouring rain, the aftermath of the storm. I head back to the Immigration office with my duly completed form. An Indian clerk serves me. He goes through the document, line by line, checking every item. He takes my passport and then wants proof of my financial capability. Fair enough. I lay my cards on the table: American Express, VISA, MasterCard … yes, I will be permitted to stay.

That is done—or so I think, because wonder of wonders, he now wants me to leave my passport for a few hours so they can stamp it. Just to stamp it! The wind is howling and it's pouring rain! And he wants me to come back in a few hours to give them time to stamp my passport!

In the evening I go with Tau to visit a Fijian family I met when I used to live in Suva. They are of very modest means, crowded into a few small rooms behind a corner store. It is lovely to see them again. We present our *i sevusevu* of kava. We pass around the coconut cup and drink together. We sing some of our recorded Fijian songs and reminisce of times past. It is a wonderful occasion and the sense of kinship I feel with them is indescribably lovely.

But I'm not their kin. There's a blatant reminder of that right outside the window. Barring their view to the outside world is the conspicuously spacious security-lit American Embassy whose reception area alone is larger than the total living space of this extended family. It stands there, a fitting symbol of the inequitable allocation of resources between the Fijians and the Europeans who, for whatever reason, are parked on their soil.

Enough to make one silent and vaguely hostile ….

Myth-Dreams and Cargo Cults

Thursday, March 7ᵗʰ—The sun is shining this morning and there is a light breeze. The *Oriana*, a small cruise ship, has just anchored in Suva Harbour. The *sulu*-clad Fiji Police Band is on the dock, blowing the melody of "Waltzing Matilda" through their instruments of brass. Then the shipload of Australians disembarks, revealing a deficiency of melanin and a surplus of cash equally envied by the observing Fijians.

For a few hours today, the balance will promise to shift. The streets will overflow with duty-free shoppers, and foreign exchange will jingle in the tills. To the Fijians, it's like the myth-dream of a cargo cult coming true: wealth pouring into Fiji from a ship appearing out of the horizon. But true to the failing of the cult rituals, the "cargo" never quite reaches into their hands. Once again, it goes to the Indians, those astute enough to know that the way to get the goods is not through magic or myth but by the tried and true recipe of figuring out what the customer wants or can be persuaded to buy. "For you, a special price …" rings out in an unmistakable Hindi accent.

While the ritual plays itself out, I prepare for my trip to the village tomorrow. First on the list, some cherished food supplies: bran cereal, rye crackers, peanut butter … none of which will be available where I am going. Not that the local food supply is lacking. There is a reef full of fish along with taro, yams, and cassava. In other words, fish and taro, fish and yams, fish and cassava….

Tonight, one last taste of European cuisine before the daily diet of *ika vakalolo* (fish cooked in coconut milk). Pizza! Not a lot of food value but it tastes great. The red wine too, in spite of the fact that, for some reason, they always serve it chilled.

Part II

TO THE MAJESTIC ISLE

Into the Microcosm

Friday, March 8th—Tau helps me with the bags and boxes I am taking to Ngau. There's clothing for the children, school supplies and bread for everyone, not to mention my bran cereal, rye crackers and carefully wrapped jars of peanut butter. By the time we check in at the airport, there are a few more boxes added to the pile. Fijians in the city take this opportunity to send supplies to their kin in the villages. More bread, bolts of cloth for *sulu* (lavalavas) and school uniforms, a part for a chainsaw….

It reminds me of the last time I took this flight to Ngau. All the other passengers that day were part of a funeral delegation. The tiny plane was stuffed, and I, with my boxes and bags, was packed in alongside a wooden coffin. Now, once again, high above the islands of Lomaiviti we soar. Then it's in over the coconut trees, and we touch down on the gravel airstrip.

Interesting how people in these outlying islands gravitate to the airstrip when a flight is due to arrive. Perhaps there is a relative to greet or a parcel to collect. It's no exception this time. There are lots of people here and the faces are now familiar. They greet me with wide smiles and vigorous handshakes, and the children gather about and lean forward to get their kisses. Without any noticeable cue, they gather up my bags and boxes and toss them into the back of a lorry. Then we all pile in, sitting on top of the clothing, the school supplies, the part for the chainsaw, the fresh bread—and my carefully wrapped jars of peanut butter.

It's just a short ride to the village. When I see the tiny huts surrounding the *rara*, an open green space, with the jungle on one side and the beach on the other, I feel propelled back in time. It has been three years since I was last here and nothing has changed … except for the "weathered" look. The two recent hurricanes have left their marks.

The children form a little procession and carry off the bags and boxes to my little house. Not the grass hut built for me the first time I came. That was a masterpiece of traditional artistry, complete with carved cantilevered ends to the ridgepole and hand-woven pandanus mats. In eighteen months of fieldwork, I never tired of it. When I left, I gave it back to the village.

I say "back", because it was constructed for my use, and I compensated the village generously for building it. However, there was always a sense in which it, like everything else here, remained communal property. I learned that rather abruptly the very day the hut was completed. I was all set to move in and start my research in earnest. Before I could even begin to make the move, in came some old pandanus mats and a huge kava bowl. Then came the chief along with all the men of the village. They drank kava and partied for three days while I had to go live somewhere else.

Now my house is a tiny block building with bars on the window and a tin roof. It's actually like an oversized prison cell! It used to be a cooperative store for Tau's clan but it went out of business. When Tau's grass hut caught fire and burned, his clan gave the store to him. And he "gave the store" to me.

To fix up, that is! For one's private property is never really one's own. Tau would continue to live there, as would any number of others for whatever reason or length of time. I fixed it up in any case. I patched and painted it, adding a wooden verandah with plenty of windows, and turned it into a modest but comfortable little "cottage"—so comfortable, in fact, that it became the kava-drinking centre of the village. Again!

No sooner are my things dumped into a heap on the verandah than I am called to tea with members of Tau's clan. Sai, who is wife of Mata, the spokesman for the village Chief, has prepared sweet coconut pancakes—and now, of course, there is also bread … and peanut butter.

A couple of hours later, I hear a dreadful squealing sound. I look out and see a young boy from the clan holding a pig by its hind legs.

"They're going to kill that pig," I run and protest to Tau.

"You've got to let them do it," he replies. "They're killing it because you've come back. It's their way of telling you you're a member of the clan."

I look again; the poor animal's throat has been cut. Strange, this custom of killing, as though one can enhance life by dealing in death. For dinner tonight, there's *ika vakalolo*—fish cooked in coconut milk— and suckling pig!

Late in the evening, after handing out some of the parcels we've brought, I indulge in one of the things I most enjoy about living in the village: a cool and invigorating bath at the water pipe, under the clear open sky. The stars of the southern hemisphere glisten in all their radiant splendour. They appear especially brilliant in darkness undisturbed by electricity. I feel a sense of timelessness and a oneness with Nature. A short time later, inside my cozy little house lit by a dim kerosene lamp, I fall to sleep, glad to be where I am.

"Aboriginal and Darkly Cruel"

Saturday, March 9th—In the early morning, I walk with Tau a one-kilometer distance to the district school. The compound provides primary education for the three villages in closest proximity.

The teachers in Fiji are on strike right now and this is causing quite a stir. Some of the powers-that-be are coming down hard on them. For example, the head teacher's name has been stricken from the preacher's list in church for supporting the strike. (Other reasons for dismissal are alcoholism and adultery.) Interesting how the very institution designed "so that they may have life and have it abundantly" operates to make sure they don't.

One of the teachers is married to Tau's mother's brother's daughter, and Tau has arranged for her to sew me a Fijian dress. I have no idea whether or not she wants to do it, or even if she thinks about whether or not she wants to do it. By tradition, Tau is *vasu* to this girl's family. That means he can go into their home and take anything he wants. In this case, he wants a seamstress; he lets it be known and his *vasu* complies.

The *vasu* relationship, which exists between a nephew and his uncle (mother's brother), is a great way to keep things even. For a wise man would think twice before accumulating surplus wealth knowing full well it may end up in the hands of his sister's son. This practice has served a very useful purpose in traditional Fijian society because a daughter is married out of the clan, and hence, does not get a share of the father's land, as do her brothers. Because of the *vasu* system, she can get her piece of the action through her son.

A very clever leveling mechanism! And it works fine, I guess, so long as you maintain your identity at the level of the group. But what happens if you don't! You either violate the norm and risk frustration to others, or you follow the norm, and risk frustration to yourself. Either way you lose. There is only one winning strategy: maintain your identity at the level of the group—and here's the crunch—drive the frustration underground.

Enough to make one silent and vaguely hostile! Might it have anything to do with that "strange and secret life" which Somerset Maugham intuited as "something aboriginal and darkly cruel"?

I spend the afternoon unpacking my things and handing out more of the gifts I've brought. Eight-year-old Mili had written me in Canada asking that I bring her a doll. I thought it unwise to bring just one as she has four "sisters" (her father's brothers' daughters) living right beside her. So I hand out five Raggedy Ann dolls, identical but for their different colours. One is stitched and outfitted in red, the others in orange, green, blue and violet. The little girls are so excited, and it's fascinating to watch what they do with them. Without hesitation, they take a *sulu*—a three-meter length of printed cotton—and strap the dolls to their backs. They go wandering about the village in this fashion throughout the evening. It's a good example of how very subtle is the conditioning process; they assume that maternal role and posture automatically.

It is so very beautiful tonight. Vati, who is Tau's oldest brother's wife, brings a mat and spreads it in the middle of the village green. I sit here with her, beneath the starlit sky, surrounded by lots of little children. At one end of the village, the men are drinking kava, and you can hear the sound of their ritual clapping and singing. Tensions are present, to be sure, but the thing that strikes me is that right here, right now, these people are "having their being". It is like a glimpse into the infinite, a possibility of what life could potentially be. Would that the blissfulness could last, but I sense these people will return to their "senses" come morning.

No Laughing Matter

Sunday, March 10th—Siga Tabu. Yes, they do. There is an early church service but I don't go. A report comes back to me that the little girls took their dolls to church! I hope they don't get chastised for this—like what happened early on in my fieldwork, when a number of children gathered in my *bure* (grass hut) on a Sunday afternoon. Something struck them as funny and they started laughing. And they kept on laughing. Before long, one of the village men came to my door.

"Pamela, it's Sunday," he said to me.

"Yes," I affirmed, "it's Sunday."

"The children are laughing," he continued.

"Yes, the children are laughing."

He just stood there, leaning against the doorpost. The children spotted him, and became immediately silent. Then I got it: children are not supposed to laugh on Sunday.

Imagine what happens to the psyche when you cannot give expression to a natural emotional response. Expression is forfeited for suppression or repression or depression…Like the *vasu* relationship, there is an important clue here.

On this Sunday, members of Tau's clan are eating their meals together to celebrate my return. For breakfast, the women bake buns and coconut cake. We gather in a shelter of palm fronds, constructed especially for the occasion. There are about 60 of us and it is a scene lovely to behold. In one row, handsome children sit cross-legged along both sides of the eating mats. In another row, men sit *cake* ("at the upper end") where they will eat first, and women sit *ra* ("at the lower end") from where they serve the food. The women will eat whatever is left when the men and children are satisfied.

I'm ushered to the top of the lineup alongside the chief of the clan. I don't like doing this because I resist hierarchical ranking based on age and gender. But I do feel the strong sense of kinship, and there is something about it that is so embracing that you just want to get lost inside it—a paradise of the collective psyche.

Then it's church. I find Methodist worship a laboured activity at the best of times, but a village church service can be especially taxing, as there are so many prayers and so many speeches. The hour is up long before they get to the sermon.

At the appropriate time in the service, the chief welcomes me. He says that I am now a permanent member of the village. I know that he means it and I do feel at home here, but I know that if I am completely a part of them, they are not yet completely a part of me. My inner wisdom tells me I cannot get to an inclusive unity by losing myself in an exclusive community.

Once to church on Sunday is enough for me while they go three times. How they manage to sit through it I do not know, and what they take away from it is more mysterious still.

The Cutting Edge

Monday, March 11th—Tonight there will be a *bose vanua* (village meeting). It will be a good time for me to present my *i sevusevu* (offering) to the chief and elders. There is no *waka* (the choice part of the kava root) in the village right now so I go with Tau to the neighbouring coastal village to get some.

There is a dirt road connecting the two villages but we walk the longer route along the beach. It is so lovely. Stretches of white sand are framed by coconut palms on one side and an offshore reef breaking the waves on the other. Tau saunters along, carrying a cane knife with the flat of the blade resting against his shoulder. The sun reflects from its smooth surface, creating an intense and dazzling light.

Our destination is Tau's mother's village, and Tau has many relatives there: two uncles (his mother's brothers) and another mother (his mother's sister) since whether a parental sibling is considered mother/father or aunt/uncle is reckoned on the basis of whether or not they are the same gender as that parent. So Tau's mother's brothers are his uncles while his mother's sisters are his mothers. His father's brothers are his fathers while his father's sisters are his aunts.

Here's another one. The relationship between cousins is a joking one while that between brothers is one of avoidance and respect—so the *vasu* relationship falls into the joking category. This means that when your cousin comes into your house and helps himself to your property, all you can do is laugh. First, you have to let him take it, and then you have to treat it as a joke. All this just to keep things even.

But that's strange when you think about it because Fijian society doesn't keep things even. It's a ranked system with chiefs and commoners, and those at the top get a lot more than those at the bottom. So there must be some way to keep things uneven too. That's where avoidance and respect come in. Because you can't argue about unequal distribution of labour and rewards if you can't talk to the people who allocate them. And the people who allocate them are the members of the clan (or tribe or nation) who are superior to you in rank.

So the joking relationship serves to keep things even while the respect relationship works to keep things uneven. But they both operate in the interests of the group at the expense of the individual. After all, who would choose to let people walk away with their things? And who would do more than their share of the labour for less than their share of the reward? One answer for two questions: people who have been culturally conditioned to drive their frustration underground!

Why does the individual comply? It's because these customs are accepted in their own right rather than being seen for what they really are: cultural by-products of thwarted individuality. Joking and avoidance, like dreams and slips of the tongue, are attempts on the part of the individual to deal in acceptable ways with unacceptable situations. Over time the responses become institutionalized and part of the "tradition".

They are compromise situations at best—and dangerous ones at that. Like the blade of Tau's cane knife: two opposite but identical surfaces that appear harmless until you get to the point where they share the cutting edge.

We arrive. It's a beautiful village situated beside a white sandy beach. The water inside the offshore reef is a brilliant turquoise. Commanding a central position on the beachfront is a magnificent handcrafted thatched "community centre", with tall slender coconut palms standing as sentinels on either side. Of all the villages on Ngau, this one best fits the storybook image. It is deceptively tranquil and appealing.

Nana—Tau's mother—kisses me again and again. And I see more familiar faces … Tau's uncle Momo and his aunt Nei and their sons, all of whom are married apart from one. We have tea together, get the kava root and return to Tau's village, once more along the beach.

Tonight, at the village meeting, Tau presents my *i sevusevu* and we all drink kava together. The meeting goes well. Tau is the "village chairman" now, a voluntary post that makes good use of his human relations skills. For six years prior to this, he had been in the post of community development worker on Ngau under the auspices of an international voluntary agency. It was this program I had come to Fiji to study.

That foreign aid program is now completed, but it has left its mark forever because it demanded a way of being-in-the-world that did not sit easily with the traditional culture. There was a price to pay in psychological terms, and Tau paid it—as indeed he must, instructed as he was to change the way of life of his own people. By the time the formal assignment was ended, he found himself hopelessly caught between two cultures, the one insisting on group identification, the other demanding individuality.

I saw the confusion and the frustration, and I thought it best to "finish the job" others had started on him. I took him out of the village and sent him to university, where he was rewarded with a (European) critical view of things. Tonight here he is, confident and self-assured, chairing a meeting of more than one hundred people. He keeps a steady pace and encourages every voice to be heard. Somehow he manages to keep it all in stride, weaving principles of participatory democracy around all those customary relationships of joking, avoidance and respect. He represents such a contrast to the traditional way of doing things that I wonder what quality of life can possibly be in store for him here.

Amazing Grace

Tuesday, March 12th—Today I get a great lesson in child-rearing, Fijian style. Mata and Sai are a married couple in Tau's clan who live "next door". They are childless themselves, and take care of four children ranging in age from 5 to 10 years. There are two girls, Mili and Mimi, and two boys, Samu and Solo. Tau also takes his meals with this family, and when I am in the village, I eat with them as well.

Early this morning Sai took Mili and Solo on the lorry to a village up the coast. They both have colds and sore throats, and Sai wants to get some medicine from the nursing station for them. Tau went to the administrative village on the same lorry. He has some phone calls to make and that is the only telephone on the island. Mata is away as well. They will all be back sometime in the afternoon.

I figure I will just find my own lunch today, but at the usual time, little Samu, age 7, comes to my door.

"*Mai kana* (Come and eat)," he says.

"*Evei?* (Where?)" I ask.

Without answering, he runs back to Mata's house so I follow. There is little Mimi, age 10, busying herself with food preparations. She has spread out the eating mats, set three places—for Samu, herself and me—and put food on the plates. She seems so little to be doing this kind of adult work, but I am reminded that in a subsistence economy such as this, there is a blurred distinction between adult work and child play. Little girls peel cassava and collect firewood, and little boys wield sizable cane knives with exaggerated gestures. It's just one version of the global assignment: culture wants us to produce and nature wants us to reproduce.

I bring some tea biscuits with me that I had planned for my own lunch, and place them on the eating mat. Now it is time for saying grace. Even in the most casual of occasions, food is not consumed before the ritual of grace, so I ask Samu to do the honours. Without hesitation, he drops his head and closes his eyes.

"Turaga, vinaka na keke. Ameni (God, thanks for the cake. Amen)," he utters.

It's not an "acceptable" grace by any Fijian standard but somehow the perfect touch for this unusual moment. It strikes me as funny and I start to laugh. Then Mimi laughs, and then Samu. It is one of those priceless moments, the three of us, sitting here laughing. I know it's not a laughing matter, but it is so funny—and so tempting to "set them free".

Children take on social roles with such willingness and in such detail. Of course, we all do. It's the enculturation process and the key to our survival. Yet I cannot help but think that something timeless, even spiritual, is being forfeited in the process … as though the more culture you take on, the more you distance yourself from nature—and then the more you search, the less you find.

Tau's Necklace

Wednesday, March 13th—I have been invited to Nana's village today, but I'm not feeling well and want some time to myself, so I stay in my little house to think and to read.

In the afternoon, when the tide is at its lowest point, I go walking along the beach. It is really beautiful: the white coral sand, the overhanging coconut palms, the deep blue ocean, the glistening coral reef forming a "necklace" around the island ... like the words in one of Tau's songs:

Sekavula na cakau ni yanuyanu ko Ngau
The glistening of the reef around the island of Ngau
Veilasa duiroka era kena salusalu
With its corals of many colours, it's like a garland
Vivili ika era dau vakatawana
Shells and fish of all kinds live in it
Ika lelevu ki na misimisi baca
From big ones all the way to the little bait-nibblers
Au druka ka noqui sarasara
I'm just amazed at its beauty.

I go to the point where the river meets the sea. The river defines the western border of Tau's land, a wonderful piece of unspoiled tropical rainforest where coconut palms fringe the shoreline. Past the yam gardens and taro patches, the hills stretch away into the distance. It is hot and the cool water of the river feels wonderfully refreshing.

Uciwai tokaitua mai vanua
Rivers and mountain ranges on the land
Veidelana drokadroka bulabula
Hills that are green and full of life.
Tivoli dalo uvi ura duna
Wild yams and cultivated yams, taro, prawns, eels
Lumi boso ko sega ni quileva
Not to forget the staple supply of seaweed

I follow the stream of the river into the ocean, then walk on toward Nana's village along the shoreline. In the distance, I see a group of women circle-fishing in the ocean. A large circumference at first, they beat and thrash the water to scare the fish into the centre of the circle.

Gradually the circle closes. Then they pull up the nets and gather the catch. Once the routine is completed, they drop the net, spread out and go through the whole cycle again.

From my vantage point, I can hear their shouting and laughing. They seem completely involved in what they are doing. When they see me on the beach, they stop and wave, beckoning for me to join them.

I gaze at them. Almost every day (except Sunday) they go through a similar routine. I wonder if they tire of it, if they would prefer to be doing something different. I wonder if they even *think* about it. If someone were to tell them they have only six months to live, is this what they would still choose to do? Or would they choose at all?

> *Nai tavi ni veisiga ra qarava*
> We attend to our daily routine
> *Marama qoli uciwai era tataga*
> Women fishing in the rivers with their nets
> *Turaga mai vanua lau na mata*
> Men planting taro on the land
> *Koronivuli ira na gone e veimataka*
> And every morning, the children go to school
> *Me ra tuberi cake kina noda kawa*
> To be educated for the good of tomorrow

Tau's music portrays nature so perfectly. It holds out the promise of living a truly natural life, free from the confines of culture. Or is the routine the very essence of the culture….

I wander back toward the village, collecting some shells to make a necklace.

People Who Live in Grass Houses

Thursday, March 14ᵗʰ—I'm feeling better today so I accept the invitation declined yesterday to visit Nana's village. Nana lives in a traditional Fijian *bure* (thatched hut), one of the few remaining here. I always find the *bure* so pleasant—cool when the summer days are hot, and warm when the "winter" nights grow "cold". They are so unlike the block houses with tin roof; floors that are hard and uncomfortable for sitting, walls and roofs that attract both unwelcome heat and chilling cold. Nevertheless, most houses in this village are now concrete block ones and those villagers who do not live in a block house long to do so. Not because of practicality—or cost—or temperature—or comfort. Rather, it's a statement about who you are and where you are going in the world. In short, people who live in grass houses shouldn't! It's another example of forfeiting the natural for the cultural….

I arrive mid-morning, and the women come to Nana's *bure* to visit me. We have the customary tea and biscuits and they have lots of questions. How many brothers and sisters do I have? What are their names? What are their ages? Are my father and mother still alive? What are their names? What are their ages? How many brothers and sisters do my parents have? What are their names? What are their ages?

In the afternoon, the men come to visit. We drink the customary kava together and they have more questions. How many seats are there in a big airplane? How long does it take to fly from Canada to Fiji? How much does it cost to fly that distance? How much money do people in Canada make? How much money do I make? They are particularly interested in this last question.

We get into a very interesting discussion about which is the impoverished ethnic group in Fiji, and about the pros and cons of the unrestricted exchange system. They acknowledge their privileged position with regard to land rights in Fiji, and praise the beauty of the landscape and the fertility of the soil.

"We are lucky, we *i taukei* (indigenous Fijians)," they say. "We can always come back to our *mataqali* (clan) land." But I get the impression there is not one of them who wouldn't sell the land and head for greener pastures if he could.

All the time, Nana sits in the corner of the *bure* preparing pandanus leaves for mat making. A common activity for her in any case but today she is busy because the village chief is dying, and the death of a chief will require a lot of mats. When the chief dies, Nana reminds me, no one will be allowed to cry. Instead, the *davui* (conch shell) will be sounded from the moment of his death until his body is placed in the grave. It should be any day now.

Woman's Work

Friday, March 15ᵗʰ—The tide is out early this morning. Some of the women walk along the beach with their babies strapped to their backs. They collect bait—worms, shellfish and prawns—for today's line fishing.

The women work continuously from morning to night. After sweeping the mats in their *bure*, preparing breakfast, washing the dishes, getting the children off to school, doing the daily laundry, preparing the midday meal, and washing the dishes again, they make their way into the sea for an afternoon of fishing. Then they bring in their catch, clean and cook it, prepare the dinner, serve it, gather up the dishes, and weave mats until sleep overcomes them. They do this every day—except Sunday—at which time they worship and pray. I wonder if this routine is frustrating to them. Or might it serve as a kind of *ora et labora* ("prayer and work"), unwittingly providing a very real opportunity for spiritual growth….

The sky clears after a tropical downpour. I clean up my little house and put the mats in the sun to dry. Later in the day, when the tide recedes again, I walk down the beach with Tau and little Mili to set a fishing-net. The shoreline looks so beautiful from this vantage point in the sea: coconut and mango trees, set against a backdrop of thick jungle greenery.

This evening, people from the north side of the island have rented a lorry and they arrive in the village to drink kava. The official reason given for the visit is to see our new "community centre". But there is no community centre! (The former community centre was destroyed in a 1979 hurricane.) There's a post and beam construction for what will someday perhaps *become* a community centre, but it has no roof, no floor, no walls…In short, there really isn't anything to see. They can't even drink kava at the site because it's raining again, so their hosts quickly construct a shelter of palm fronds to accommodate their guests who have brought gifts of kava, taro and bread. I can hear the sound of their singing from the far side of the village. When they depart around midnight, the people here keep the party going into the wee hours of the morning.

"Something Wrong with the People"

Saturday, March 16th—Before breakfast, I walk with Tau down the beach to check on the fishing net. Not much of a catch: seems we didn't set the net quite right for the direction of the wind. After breakfast, Tau goes to work in the taro plantation. He is digging a ditch to get water flowing back to the land near the road. During the construction of the airstrip, workers dug a deep trench that robbed the land of its natural irrigation. Now the garden is too wet in one part and too dry in another. Tau is trying to repair the damage by digging canals with his cane knife. His common sense is refreshing, his commitment inspiring and, so far, unrelenting.

The wind begins to pick up and *Radio Fiji* broadcasts a hurricane alert. People start at once to make preparations. First priority: secure the sleeping houses. The men run ropes over the roofs of the structures to prevent the sheets of corrugated iron from flying off in the wind.

Tau's brother Iliki walks over and gazes at the roof of my house. He says it needs to be secured and asks Tau's whereabouts. I tell him Tau is not yet back from the garden. Iliki quietly gets a ladder and climbs on top of the house to secure the sheets of roofing iron.

It is fascinating to watch the relationship between these two men. They observe the strict avoidance taboo that is traditional between blood brothers. Here they are, Tau in his late twenties, his brother in his early thirties, and in all those years they have never spoken directly to each other.

I remember the first time I encountered this custom. It was soon after I arrived on the island. I was with Tau and we were returning from the taro garden. His brother approached us on the narrow pathway. As soon as they spotted each other, their eyes fell. They passed in that narrow space without a word or gesture, seemingly unaware of the other's presence. After we had progressed a short distance, Tau asked me to run back and tell Iliki he could have some taro from his garden … which I did.

I also remember the first time I witnessed the joking relationship. It was the first Sunday of my fieldwork. I was walking with Tau to a village where, as a lay preacher, he was to deliver a sermon that afternoon. On the dirt road we met a young man. The two men exchanged the traditional *"Bula"* (Hello) and *"Lesu mai vei?"* (Where do you come from?) Then they proceeded to joke and laugh, slapping each other playfully on the back. This behaviour went on for some time, after which they parted and we continued on our way.

"You must really like that man," I said to Tau. "You have such a good time with him."

"I've never seen him before in my life," Tau replied. "He's from Navosa-Nadroga and I'm from Lomaiviti, and we have a joking relationship."

Come to think of it, that's not the only disconcerting thing that happened that day. As we approached the outskirts of the village, Tau, after rehearsing his sermon along the way, said to me, "You will also give a sermon in church today."

"Me give a sermon?" I exclaimed. "I can't just stand up and give a sermon without any preparation."

"Well, as a visitor you'll be expected to," he continued. "It only needs to be a short sermon."

"But I can't speak Fijian yet," I protest.

"You can give it in English and I'll translate for you."

This is anthropological fieldwork? No one told me that I would have to deliver sermons! I sensed, however, it was something I dare not refuse. I did some quick thinking and came up with the idea of reciting the Peace Prayer of St. Francis, which I had learned as a child growing up near a Roman Catholic university town in the Canadian Maritimes. The strictly Methodist congregation knew neither its saintly authorship nor its Catholic origin—and I gave no hint to either. They thought I wrote it! After it was over, I heard one of them comment, "Boy, can that girl preach!" And that's how I made it through my first grinding week of fieldwork!

But back to the impending hurricane. I help Iliki secure the roofing iron on the exterior of my house. I prepare the interior for villagers who might want to seek shelter here if their own sleeping houses yield to the storm. When Tau returns, he helps me gather food and water, and I settle in for a long night. Mata, Sai and the four children in their care come to stay with me because their wooden house is much less sturdy than mine. They put the children to sleep inside and join the group gathering on the sheltered verandah to keep watch during the night. Someone brings in the large *tanoa* (kava bowl) and the vigilance turns into a kava-drinking party.

The winds increase and the storm gets nearer. We drink kava and sing our Fijian songs—and we stay tuned to the weather bulletins on *Radio Fiji.*

Until the stroke of midnight, that is. Suddenly the Fijian songs stop. Not because the storm is over—or overpowering. Nor is it because people have grown tired. The Fijian songs are over because it is now *Siga Tabu* (Sunday). We switch to hymns, and continue our vigilance into the night. *Radio Fiji* usually signs off at 11 o'clock in the evening, but tonight it reaches out to us in the darkness with weather bulletins and messages in three languages. I see that the people here are really afraid.

And with good reason! During my sojourns in Fiji, I have lived through a number of tropical storms and witnessed their devastation. The most frightening was hurricane Meli in 1979, six years earlier. I vividly remember it.

When I awoke that morning in March, it was unusually windy, and the sky was overcast with dense grey clouds. Other than that, things were normal enough. People were going about their routine activities and the children headed off to the school compound about a kilometer away. By mid-day, the winds grew gusty, and seemed to be blowing from many directions at once. *Radio Fiji* broadcast hurricane warnings, instructing people to prepare for a severe storm. A delegation of men and women left at once for the school compound to bring the children home. Others secured buildings and stored up food supplies. By mid-afternoon, the winds were of such force that sleeping houses and kitchen huts began to give way. At this point, the elders directed us to move all the villagers into the three strongest sleeping houses. The place was a beehive of frantic activity.

Tau and another young man came to my *bure* to get me. Carrying my research papers and audiotapes in cardboard boxes, we stepped out of my little thatched hut. By this time, the force of the wind was so strong we could not close the door behind us. We attached a rope to the latch in an attempt to secure the door. Right beside us, the massive thatched community centre that offered a barricade from the full force of the crashing waves in an overflowing sea was bending and swaying from the assault of the wind. While the three of us tugged at the door of my *bure*, the thatched community centre collapsed and, in slow motion, fell unceremoniously to the ground. A masterpiece of traditional Fijian architecture ... reduced to a haystack. The village no longer had a community centre—and I at last had waterfront property!

Enjoyment of my real estate would have to wait, however, for we had a storm to survive. I was assigned to the house of the chief along with sixty other people. It was a small single-room wooden structure with a corrugated iron roof. There was a big double size "bed" in the upper section of the house, and I was given that area to myself. I protested and asked for a spot on the floor with the others, but the floor was so crowded there was not room for a single additional person to lie down on it. I asked then if I might share the space on the bed, so they placed the chief's two little daughters there with me— possibly the first time children were accorded the bed of a chief!

We got a direct hit in the middle of the night. The winds were so strong the frame of the small house started to collapse. Tau and some others nailed planks of wood at diagonals to keep the walls from falling in on us. The rain poured in through the wide cracks between the boards. I left my space on the bed and mopped up the water while some of the older people sighed and prayed.

Hurricane Meli killed fifty people in Fiji that night, most of them from a single village on the island of Kadavu. When their sleeping houses began to fall down, the villagers there sought shelter in the church building. Women and children congregated in the centre of the concrete block structure while the men drank kava at the entranceway. But the concrete blocks were not reinforced with metal rods and the walls caved in from the force of the wind. The men were able to escape; the women and children were not.

When the villagers on Ngau heard the news on radio next morning, they responded with their characteristic *"Welei! Welei!"* (Oh! Oh!). It was shocking, to be sure, but they were not prepared to accept it as a natural disaster. Why did the people of Kadavu suffer so terrible a fate?

"There is something wrong with the people," they uttered.

"You Eat Too Much!"

Sunday, March 17th—I don't go to church today. In fact, I'm surprised they're even having church. The winds are still very strong and we remain on hurricane alert. I bake a coconut cake in the morning and make some custard in the afternoon as a special Sunday treat. The whole process is complicated by the wind and the rain as well as a very uncooperative kerosene stove. In the evening I postpone dinner to drink kava with the villagers who are assembling once again on the veranda of my house.

The people are in a story-telling mood tonight, and they reminisce about a Canadian youth group who visited the village a year earlier on a leadership-training program. Seli tells us about the youth who stayed at his house. At mealtime, Seli wanted to tell his guest, with typical Fijian hospitality, to help himself to the food. In the Fijian language, the expression is *"Kana vakalevu* (Eat a lot)"*. Because his guest did not understand Fijian, Seli had tried to communicate in English, and the translation came out, "You eat too much!"

"Poor fellow," says Seli, "his whole expression changed. His face grew serious and his chin dropped. He didn't know whether or not to finish his dinner." It wasn't until later that the villagers figured out what Seli had said. When they did, it became the village joke, and it survives to this day. Every time someone takes the cup of kava tonight, someone else shouts out in English, "You eat too much!" Then they all burst out laughing.

During the course of the evening, the hurricane subsides. The pouring rain stops and the winds die down: we have made it through this one in good shape. The news reports say that Kadavu has once again been badly hit. Sleeping and cooking houses have been destroyed.

"There's something wrong with the people," the villagers murmur again. God, the patriarch, strict but just, demands obedience and is quick to punish. That's how they've got it. So long as they keep God in the role of father, they maintain their role as child. No opportunity here for breaking out of the confines of the repressive patriarchal system!

The kava party continues until well after midnight. By this time I am too tired to eat my dinner. When everyone has finally left, I go to the water pipe in the dark of the night to have a "bath", and then fall into bed. They have poured me so many bowls of kava I am beginning to feel sick. I guess I should have listened when they kept shouting, "You eat too much!"

The Joke's on You

Monday, March 18ᵗʰ—The weather is calm this morning and people are shifting back into their routines. The women wash clothes and scrape coconuts for cooking; the men go about their planting. I accompany Tau to the taro gardens to see how the drainage system is working. The canals have performed as they should, and there is no hurricane damage to the crops this time.

We continue to the school compound to see the head teacher. (The teachers' strike is now over.) A young boy from the village has been sent home from school today because he had no money to pay his examination fee. He was instructed by his teacher to collect copra for the day in order to come up with the funds. Poor little fellow, he's only 10 years old and is living with a grandfather who shows little interest in his schooling and has very limited means to support him. The parents are elsewhere and no longer involved in the little boy's welfare. It is really quite incomprehensible that the child would be barred from sitting his exam for this reason. Could none of his teachers have come up with a plan to get the $3 without exposing the little boy to such deprivation and embarrassment! When the lad arrived in the village with his school bag this morning, Tau sent him right back to school with a note for the teacher. Now we are at the school compound where Tau quietly contributes the $3 fee.

Just before dinner tonight, a few of us are sitting on the grass waiting our turn to bath at the water pipe. (Bathing is done in public so people wear a *sulu*.) While Mata has his bath, he tells us about something funny that happened at the kava drinking party last night. He says that Losi—an elderly man—wanted some tobacco from the village cooperative store. Since he has a respect/avoidance relationship with the storekeeper, he sent Seli to get it for him. Seli, however, has a joking relationship with the storekeeper. Instead of giving the rolled tobacco to Seli—whom he presumed to be the buyer—the storekeeper rolled up a note that read, "Fuck you, bastard!" Seli unknowingly brought back the note and gave it to the old man thinking it was the tobacco. Mata says Losi read the note and just shook his head in disbelief. The storekeeper, by kinship relation, has always treated the old man with such respect! Everyone has a great laugh about it.

But there is a bitter edge to humour—and to respect and avoidance as well.

Praise God and Pass the Carbohydrates

Tuesday, March 19th—I notice that Tau is feeling down and I ask him what is wrong. He tells me he had a meeting with the men in the village yesterday about building some new sleeping houses. The plan to do so has been "on the books" for some time now. The men said they had difficulty arranging for the timbers with people in another village and asked Tau if he would sort it out so they could start the work today. Tau agreed. Very early this morning he walked to the other village to set things up. When he returned, with everything ready to proceed, he found the same group of men preparing to go out spear fishing. They told him they would begin the building another day as they are going to take fish to the village of the dying chief.

Tau is discouraged. He has just walked five kilometers to get the building project set up for them and now they are not even going to do it. I understand his dilemma. He is living in a traditional society whose values he no longer accepts, trying very hard to help the villagers achieve the things they say they want for themselves. Meanwhile, they continue to be sidetracked by traditions he feels have long outlived their usefulness. He is dealing in life; they are dealing in death.

Sai left early this morning to go fishing, but she saw so many crabs along the beach that she collected them instead. For lunch today we have fresh crab cooked in coconut milk. A couple of hours later the men return from the reef with a lot of very big fish; we cook up a sweet-tasting *bulagi* and eat it right away. There's fresh fish again for dinner.

"*Kana vakalevu,* (Eat a lot)" they keep telling me—but I don't need this much protein!

A number of the older men go to the village of the dying chief this afternoon. They take the fish and drink kava there. The younger men stay in our village and start a kava drinking party on the veranda of my house. When the older men return, they join the party, and soon there is a very big crowd here. They strum guitars and ukuleles as they sing; the sound is harmonious and pleasing.

I don't stay at home. I go with Sai to the women's church meeting. It is being held at Vesa's house. The event is such a product of the Christian missions in Fiji that I can almost see the wife of the European missionary sitting in the prominent place now accorded the wife of the local church leader. She is neatly dressed, and sits here cross-legged on the mats, leading the worship service. The women gather around her, many of them with babies at their breasts, listening to the word of God and praying. I wonder yet again how it all translates in the Fijian mind.

"Do you have this kind of thing in Canada?" they ask me. I don't know how to answer that one.

When the worship service is completed, the women set out the eating mat for tea. Sai has baked bread and buns in the earth oven for the occasion. More than enough—or so I think. I am ushered to the top end of the eating mat and am seated beside the *Tui*, the highest-ranking woman in the village. She is the head of her clan, the only woman to occupy that lofty position on the island as far as I know. She is a very large and jolly woman in her early fifties, and she has always reminded me of the Malama in Michener's *Hawaii*. I am amazed at how much and how quickly she can eat. Before I can consume one small bun and a cup of tea, she has demolished nearly a full plate of bread and buns, washing it all down with two large bowls of tea sweetened with plenty of sugar. While I am trying to finish my modest portion, she asks to be excused from the eating-place and lies down on the mat behind me as other women come forward in turn to take tea.

"*Kana vakalevu*," they keep telling me—but I don't need this much carbohydrate! What I really need is another clue, and as it turns out, I shall need to wait only until morning.

Part III

LIFE AND DEATH

When a Chief Dies

Wednesday, March 20th—The chief in Nana's village died early this morning. The news arrives here very quickly and is communicated right around the island. The head teacher of the district school is informed as soon as classes commence, and by mid-morning the children, their uniforms still clean, arrive back in the village. Straightaway the people here start preparing their *magiti* (ritual gifts) of mats, taro, pigs, yams, tapa cloth, whales' teeth and kava.

Following tradition, each clan in the village first presents its items to the local chief. I have witnessed exchange presentations many times in the past and they always follow the same format. But this time it is a whole new experience for me since I will now take part as a member of the village. Prior to this, I was always there with my notebook and my tape recorder, at best only a participant observer. But for this visit I have been welcomed back as a full-fledged villager. After all, a pig has been killed for me. So I follow instructions to pick up the front end of a large pandanus mat and make my way in the procession to the house of the chief. Our clan goes through the ritual first, then the others follow suit.

We're all sitting here, cross-legged, in the house of the chief; the men forward, the women at the back. Appropriately positioned at the "top" of the house is Ratu (the chief) with Mata, his spokesman, beside him. In front of them are the rolled-up mats and the sheets

45

of tapa cloth, the whales' teeth and the kava. Just outside the door, bundles of taro and heaps of yams and squealing pigs....

I've heard it all many times before … "*Mana e dina,* (Supernatural power is true) *amudo, amudo, amudo.* (It is over)" accompanied by patterned and predictable ritual clapping. Above the chief, hanging from a crossbeam, are two pictures: one of Jesus as the good shepherd, the other, the Duke of Edinburgh. Taken together, they serve as a fitting metaphor for this willing-to-be-led patriarchal society.

It's time now to go to the dead chief's village. We walk the few kilometers along the road while the *magiti* is taken by boat. As we approach the village, I can hear the sound of the *davui* (conch shells) signaling the death of a chief. Young men from the designated clan— about eight of them—blow the *davui* from the moment of the chief's death until his body is placed in the grave. In this case, it will be about 36 hours, all day and all night.

When we arrive in the village, we sit together as a group until it is time for us to go to the hastily constructed shelter of palm fronds to present our *magiti.* Our turn comes; we file in—men first, then the women—bearing the gifts also hastily collected. I present a large sheet of tapa cloth.

Once the ritual presentation is completed, men and women assume separate functions. I go with the women to the chief's house, now referred to as the *vale ni mate* (house of death). Outside the house, establishing and maintaining a *tabu* (taboo area) around the compound, are eight guards with blackened faces, dressed in tapa cloth and carrying war clubs over their shoulders. Inside, the upper area of the floor is covered with about 100 new mats, many elaborately decorated, on top of which have been laid sheets of tapa cloth. In the very centre lies the dead chief. His head is resting on a pillow and his body is covered with tapa. Four women, dressed in black, from the clan of the chief's advisers, sit with the body, two on either side.

We sit inside the house while the exchange presentations go on outside the doorway. There will be delegations from every village around the island before they are done. The presentations are always the same: kava root and whales' teeth, taro and yams, pigs, mats, tapa cloth, ritual words and clapping—and from behind the house, the sound of young men blowing the *davui*. It is eerie but it helps to drown out the squealing of the pigs, bound by their hooves and waiting to be slaughtered.

These activities are repeated throughout the day and continue into the night. All the time, the women dressed in black sit with the body inside the house while the tapa-draped men with blackened faces and war clubs protect the surrounding area. I decide not to sleep the night here and, about midnight, set out on foot with Tau for our own village. Before we're halfway home, a lorry chances along and gives us a lift, so we end this ritualized day with a wild ride in the dark of the night on the back of a truck.

For the Love of the Father

Thursday, March 21st—When I return to the *vale ni mate* (house of death) this morning, the dead chief's body is in the same position but has now been placed inside a coffin which was flown in very early on a chartered plane. The large sheet of tapa cloth that draped the body is now placed on top of the coffin.

The early hours of the day are like yesterday, with more delegations arriving, more pigs and taro and yams, more mats and tapa cloth, ritual words and clapping…Throughout these activities, the men drink kava in the shelter outside while the women sit quietly in the "house of death". I remain with the women.

On one occasion, a man draped in tapa cloth enters the house and approaches the coffin. The women remove the coffin's lid so he can place a whale's tooth on the body. I now see there are mats and tapa cloth inside the coffin as well. Later in the day, the chief's youngest daughter, married into another village, arrives. She is likewise dressed in tapa cloth and is carrying a whale's tooth. She approaches the coffin. The sheet of tapa covering the wooden box is pulled back so she can view her father's face through the small glass window in its lid. She lays her head there and mourns silently for a long time. No one is allowed to cry at the death of a chief, not even the youngest child.

By mid-day the village is very crowded. The men, for the most part, remain in the palm shelter making presentations of *magiti* and drinking kava. Most of the women, now dressed in black, stay inside the *vale ni mate*. With so many of us in such a restricted space, the house gets extremely warm and some of the women have trouble staying awake. An elderly lady from our village goes to sleep and falls over onto my shoulder. The women start to snicker about it until someone nudges the old lady and wakes her up.

It's so uncomfortable. We're sitting on a single layer of well-worn mat covering a wooden floor while a huge stack of soft new mats is placed under the body of the dead man. Interesting priorities! We sit here quietly, shifting position periodically to relieve the discomfort and monotony. Outside, about 40 men and women from the host village are busy with food preparations. The men slaughter two cows and about 20 large pigs; the women cut up the flesh and cook huge pots of beef and pork stew. Served with boiled root crops, it becomes the noonday meal.

About two in the afternoon, the pallbearers remove the chief's body from the house and take it into the nearby church. The local church leader reads a scripture and recites a prayer. A couple of titled men make short speeches and we sing a hymn together. Then we follow the funeral procession from the church to the burial ground. At the head of the line is the local church leader, a Methodist catechist dressed in ministerial robes. Next are the pallbearers carrying the coffin with the body of the chief, flanked on either side by the guards dressed in tapa cloth with their blackened faces and war clubs. Following them are eight young men still blowing the *davui*. Behind this retinue are village men and women, carrying mats and tapa cloth, and mourners from every village on the island.

We walk a short distance along the road and then up the bank of a hill to where a grave has been dug. Following tradition, the gravediggers have stayed at the site the entire time to prevent any evil spirits from entering the cavity. Appointed men place a large number of mats and sheets of tapa cloth on top the vines stretching across the opening. Then they lay the coffin on top. We sing a hymn; there is a short prayer and a final scripture reading. "Ashes to ashes, dust to dust" gets translated as "soil to soil, sand to sand". And they lower the body into the grave.

Once the ceremony is done, gravediggers step forward with shovels and forks to close the earth. Others then decorate the grave with the large sheet of tapa cloth that earlier hung on a wall behind the chief's body in the "house of death". They secure the tapa with the eight *davui* that henceforth serve as a silent witness that a chief is buried here. The preacher, his job done, sits down at the end of the grave and wipes the sweat from his forehead. Soon thereafter we quietly make our way back to the village.

In this fashion, the old chief, flanked by his guards wrapped in tapa cloth, with blackened faces and war clubs, receives a Christian burial. To add to the paradox, the local church leader, standing there at the head of the coffin, dressed in his purple vestments and clutching a Holy Bible, is the dead chief's own son!

By the time we get back to the village, the mood has shifted. The gravediggers, following tradition, go at once to bathe in the ocean. The eight tapa-draped guards with their blackened faces and war clubs reappear in brightly coloured *sulu* (lavalavas) and T-shirts. One of the T-shirts reads, "Support Black Liberation".

Meanwhile, on the village green, the *burua* is in progress. The *burua* is a distribution of food to all the delegations that have attended the funeral. They shout out names; people come forward to accept their portions of slaughtered cows and pigs, of harvested taro and yams. After the *burua* is completed, the mourners depart for their own villages.

I come home at dusk with the women from our village. Soon after we arrive, I see that the women from our clan are making plans to shift to the far end of the village for the night. They say they are frightened to stay in the sleeping houses at this end of the village because the spirit of the dead chief will be lurking about for the next while. They point out to me that the sleeping houses of our clan are closest in physical proximity to the dead chief's village and our clan members are the dead chief's closest kin here. They say that if the dead man has any unfinished business with any of us, now will be the "hour of reckoning". I see they are really serious about this. They are truly afraid of the spirit of this dead man!

Sai is readying the children to go with her to sleep with a family from our chief's clan at the far end of the village. She strongly urges me to come with them since my house is at the very edge of the village and hence most vulnerable. However, after so much communal activity over the past two days, I very much want some space to myself so I decline. I do not share the beliefs and superstitions of these people and feel no need to tell them so. Instead, I simply reaffirm that I am quite okay where I am. Sai is most uncomfortable leaving me, but with four small children in her clutches, she reluctantly goes.

It is dark by now. I light the benzene lamp so I can write up details of the funeral in my Journal. Home at last, after two days of death rituals! I'm here, safely alone in this little one-room concrete house with bars on the window. I'm writing: "and they pull back the tapa cloth so she can see her father's face through the small window in the lid of the coffin …"

All of a sudden something very powerful seems to be happening inside this room. It's like someone or something doesn't like what I'm doing. And my God, it is terrifying. I muster my courage and try to reassure myself that it's just my imagination. I ignore it and keep right on writing: "She lays her head there and mourns silently for a long time …" But this dark force gets stronger, and the room becomes filled with whatever this thing is.

I put down my pen and take my benzene lamp with me out onto the verandah. It is pitch black. I hang the lamp in the doorway and stand beside it. I don't want to go back inside the house. I don't know quite what to do next because there's no one around. All the men are still in the dead chief's village and all the women and children are at the far end of this village. I just stand here, keeping very close to the light of my benzene lamp. It's not more than a minute before I see Sai with the four children hurrying across the village green. They come up to the verandah but do not enter the house.

"We are going to stay here with you until Tau comes," says Sai to my great relief.

Pressing People Down

Friday, March 22nd—I am glad to see the daylight this morning. I grant myself a quiet and reflective day. I plant some flowers along the front of the house—yellow hibiscus and sweet-smelling jasmine— which Iliki brought for me from the bush the day before the chief died.

Now I realize why the Fijians give so much attention to death rituals. It is not because they are afraid of death or even dying; rather, they are afraid of the dead! My experience last night was a sobering insight into how dangerous the spirits of the dead can be. Fijians believe that spirits depart their earthly home on the *bogi va* (fourth night). In the meantime, they wander about in the dark hours with all the vices of men. For four days and four nights, these spirits are "on the loose" and one ought not to get in their way! It is a time of reckoning, and that spirit presence in my house last night—whatever it was—served as a firm and poignant reminder to not violate the cultural norm or expectation.

Ratu, our village chief, and Mata, his spokesman, are still in the dead chief's village today, observing the *bikabika*, the "pressing down" ceremony. *Bikabika* is an example of a custom that has long outlived its usefulness but continues on anyway. In the old days, before the missionaries introduced the idea of gravesites, it was customary to bury a dead body inside the deceased person's own *bure* (grass hut). They simply removed the mats from the dirt floor, dug a hole and interred the body. They didn't use coffins. Then they put the pile of dirt on top of the body and replaced the mats. Of course, there would then be a big hump in the middle of the floor. A delegation of people would lay on top of the hump to press it down, hence, *bikabika* (pressing down)—for four days and four nights.

Nowadays they bury dead bodies in gravesites outside the village, but they still go through this wearying four-day ritual. They just lie there in the middle of the floor, doing nothing. By the end of a *bikabika*, they are suffering from headaches and backaches, upset stomach and insomnia. In this way the *bikabika* ends up pressing down the living rather than the dead!

Just Like a Dream

Saturday, March 23rd—The death rituals are almost over and life carries on. Tomorrow is Children's Sunday, and it calls for special food. Mata had previously arranged for some chickens to be sent from Suva on the *Fiji Air* flight yesterday in exchange for a carton of yams. The yams were air freighted out—but the chickens didn't come back! It will be pork instead of chicken for dinner tomorrow.

Mata is still in the dead chief's village for the *bikabika*. That leaves Tau in charge of securing the food for the feast, and Sai asks Tau to kill the pig. Tau doesn't like to eat animals, let alone kill them, but he knows he has to comply. He takes little Umi, his older brother's son, with him to fetch the pig. They catch it, and drag it by its hind legs into the village compound. The poor little pig is squealing and trying to get away. Tau asks me to get some rope so they can tie it up but I won't give him any. I just don't want to take part in the murder of that little pig. I go inside the house and watch from the window. They're trying to hold onto the animal but it manages to get away and run for cover underneath Saki's house. Little Umi crawls in after it and emerges with the little creature squealing for its life. To no avail!

I know they're going to kill it now and I cannot watch. A few minutes later I look out and see it hanging lifeless from a tree. I ask Tau if he killed it and he says no, that he asked his brother Iliki to do it for him. How, I want to know, for he and Iliki observe a strict avoidance relationship. Tau replies that he sent an "indirect" message and his brother just walked over and killed the pig right in front of him without saying a word.

Most of the men from our village are out fishing to take food to the village of the dead chief once again. In the evening, the women go with them to visit those taking part in the *bikabika*. Tau and I don't go; we mix some kava and practise our Fijian songs—like this one—on the veranda of my house.

> *Diva lesu na gauna ni noqu bula sa sivi*
> *Au kaya me'u lesu kena ca ni sa tasiri*
> *Noda bula kei gauna tawa tale vakadua …*

"If you are wishing for the past," say the lyrics, "you are wasting your time. For the past will never return. There is only today. An illusive sense of now—for life is just like a dream."

How does Tau, born and bred in a traditional Polynesian society, articulate poetically something that is more akin to the perennial philosophy of India? How does he know this? Or perhaps better stated, how is this universal wisdom getting expressed through him?

Children's Sunday

Sunday, March 24th— In church today, all the children are dressed in white and carry sweet-smelling flowers. They take an active part in the service, giving recitations and singing hymns. They are rather shy and uncomfortable in this most formal of settings, and considering the seriousness with which Fijians regard Sunday worship, their reticence is well placed.

There are a few hitches, like little Mili standing up front introducing a hymn. She gets the sequence right, announcing the hymn number, reading out the first verse, then giving the page number a second time. Pleased with herself that she gets it right, she looks down at me and flashes a big grin. Then she turns to leave, trips and falls from the pulpit.

Taku is in charge of the Sunday program. He's a man in his mid-forties, and I never cease to be amazed at how serious he takes these events to be. He has had the children rehearsing for weeks to be ready for this day. He is giving the sermon this morning as well, and he delivers it with way more energy than it deserves—or can withstand.

I cannot help but wonder what is getting done for him. Does he really have experience of this *Jisu Karisito* (Jesus Christ) he so forcefully proclaims? And what of all these people who listen? Here they sit, taking part in a ritual from Methodist England in a building to match: straight-backed, uncomfortable wooden pews for people who, on all other occasions, sit cross-legged on mats on the floor … a pulpit, a baptismal font—even a bouquet of plastic flowers—in a village of sub-standard housing surrounded by tropical flora. They just don't seem to get the connection between religion and life. There he stands, this man Taku, preaching with the cadence and intonation of an English Protestant clergyman, proclaiming to his captive audience the certainty of an eternal kingdom, a vision of which I can guess he has only heard.

Then comes lunch. Lots of pork—and people really enjoy it. I settle for yams and then head up the beach for a walk with Tau. We go to that piece of land owned by his clan—seventy-five acres of virgin property that has been set aside for his use. It is a beautiful piece of beachfront property extending inland as far as the airstrip. A portion of it looks like the jungle in the opening scenes of the film *Raiders of the Lost Ark*. Big shady trees and tropical undergrowth are bordered by swaying coconut palms along the beachfront. The most enchanting part is the river that defines one border of the property. It is wide and meandering, and at high tide, very deep. Trees and vines stretch tall and lean inward to interlace, providing a magical archway across the stream.

We swim the river inland for about a kilometer. It is cool and refreshing, somehow a special delight since it is taboo to be having this kind of enjoyment on a Sunday. Tau climbs a palm tree to get some fresh drinking coconuts. Then he tears the outer husks to tie them together so we can float them down the river. I am amazed at how he does it. Since it is Sunday, he does not have his machete with him so he uses his teeth. Sunday is likewise not a day to be climbing trees so we hide the fresh coconuts when we return to the village.

I attend the afternoon church service today as well since the children are presenting a pageant. Actually it's Taku presenting the pageant using the children as actors. I say this because they are conspicuously repeating what they've heard. Their little eyes look upward and into the distance to avoid contact with the glaring congregation. Their little choir is a miniature of the adult version. As they sing away, I can see how their lives have already been fashioned for them. It's going to be a life of more of the same. Just a short distance away is the cool river fringed with palm trees yielding sweet-tasting coconuts. What a wonderful place to be. Instead, here they are, sitting in a concrete building, having their "day of don'ts."

Tonight a few of us drink kava on the verandah and, because it is Sunday, we must confine ourselves to singing hymns. By the end of the evening I am really hungry. There is only one food choice available: I end up eating a slice of that little pig.

A Day in the Life

Monday, March 25th—Sai is cooking lunch at the school compound today so Iliki's wife Eli asks me to have the mid-day meal with them. Iliki and Tau went with most of the other people from here to their mother's village for a function connected with the chief's death. It's the *bogi va* (fourth night) and it calls for feasting. They will spend the whole day there.

I really can manage nicely on my own but Eli asks me for lunch three times so I think it judicious to accept. She lives in a "modified" *bure*: thatched walls with corrugated iron roof. I see she has prepared fresh-water prawns for me while the others are eating something else. I feel uncomfortable when I'm given special food like this and I know at the same time the appropriate thing to do is to eat some of it.

Dear Eli. I watch her daily activities and am silently perplexed. She has six children, ranging in age from 12 years to 14 months. Today, she starts at daybreak, collecting bait along the beachfront with a baby strapped to her back. Then she cleans and sweeps the *bure*, cooks and serves breakfast, and gets four children off to school. Next, she washes the breakfast dishes and sweeps the mats again. Then she gets prawns from the river and some root crops from the bush, washes (by hand) a large volume of clothes, prepares and serves the mid-day meal, cleans up the dishes, and hangs the morning wash on the clothesline. Now, with a basket strapped to her back, she heads out for an afternoon of line fishing. She returns near sunset, cleans the fish, then prepares and serves the evening meal. Finally she cleans up the *bure*, after which time she completes her day by weaving mats.

Tomorrow it will be more of the same. And Eli can expect no help from her husband right now. He has been sick for the past few days, having stayed up all night in his mother's village blowing the *davui* for the dead chief. Lack of sleep, coupled with a rich diet of freshly slaughtered beef and pork was just too much for him.

Tonight a woman from the far side of the island has arrived with two small children and they are staying at Sai's house. The children, both preschoolers, have never seen a person with "white" skin before. When I enter Sai's house to have dinner, the children are so frightened that they simply do not move. They don't speak or even cry. They won't come to the eating mat where I am, so Sai sets up a separate place for them to eat. Still they won't eat—and they won't take their eyes off me. I am feeling hungry and there is lovely fresh fish for dinner. I eat just a little and leave as quickly as I can to give relief to this very distraught and embarrassed mother.

The Price is Right

Tuesday, March 26th—The children staying at Sai's house with their mother are still so frightened when I appear for breakfast that I take my portion of rice and tea and eat on the verandah of my house. Since they will be staying in the village for some time, I attempt to remedy the situation by blowing up a couple of balloons, tying them to a string and giving them to the little ones. It works! By lunchtime, here is the two-year-old sitting right next to me—in full lotus position— eating his fish and taro leaves. However, when the small children of the village learn there are balloons, they come running and crowd the doorway while we are eating. Sai asks them to come back after I have finished my lunch but that doesn't work; a balloon is a very special item and they don't want to chance missing it. In an attempt to have them leave, Tau—who is eating with us— tells them the price of a balloon is 10 cents and sends them home to get the money. The little children believe him and take off running in all directions. By the time they get back, I have finished eating and am sitting on the verandah of my house. Here they come, holding up coins in their little hands! I now have to explain to them that the balloons are free.

The order from the village headman this morning is for the men of the village to cut wood for the copra dryer. The villagers depend on copra for cash income, and much of the coconut that has recently been readied for drying has now spoiled because of the events connected with the chief's death. So the men hack huge limbs off the marvelous *ivi* trees that line the path into the village for the copra dryer. What a pity!

Part of Tau's village health plan concerns hygiene and pure drinking water. Today, the women are cleaning the drain around a water pipe at the far end of the village. I am surprised to see Eli here. She has so much work of her own—and she doesn't even use the water pipe at this end of the village. Here she is, knee-deep in the drain, cleaning it with her bare hands—and she is in such good spirits!

After lunch, Tau shows me a letter he has written to the Island Council, which is composed of chiefs, village headmen and government representatives. In the letter, Tau states that at the last two Island Council meetings, the problems that the villagers brought up were not even discussed; instead the meeting was given over to assigning tasks for the villagers to do. He writes that the government representatives are hired to bring development to the villages and instead of doing so, they use their positions of power to place burdens on the people. It is a very strong statement and I doubt anyone else would dare to write it. I wonder if the letter will get a response.

Tonight, as has been the case a few times recently, there is a video in the village. Someone has come up with a portable generator—it makes a dreadful noise but no one seems to mind—and has managed to secure a video machine and some movies from Suva. So far only religious themes have been allowed in the village: *Ben Hur, Samson, David and Goliath* … Tonight's video is the story of Noah, and people rush to see it. The little sleeping house where it is being shown gets so full that a number of people have to watch from outside.

There is a scene in the movie about the destruction of Sodom and Gomorrah. One of the men asks Tau if the filming of this sequence were done at the time! I keep forgetting how mythical they take the world to be. Tau tells me that when he was a boy, he was taught in Sunday school that Jerusalem is in Heaven.

These teachings really confuse the school children. They ask me to help them with their homework from time to time. One lesson recently was in geography. The textbook explained how the islands of the Pacific were built up over millions of years. I went through the entire lesson with young Josi in Class 8, explaining the geological information. At the end of the session, I quizzed him on the lesson's content.

"How long did it take for the islands of the Pacific to be formed?" I asked.

"Seven days," Josi answered.

Videos are making quite an impact. The children imitate what they see. After the *Ben Hur* film, they went through motions of whipping each other. One night the head teacher from the district school brought in a film as a fund-raiser. He charged 70 cents per adult, 20 cents per child. The men and women crowded into the small house with their children, admission duly paid, only to discover that the film was a James Bond. I wonder what the children will take away from this one!

Hello, Operator?

Wednesday, March 27th—Today I go on the lorry to a village on the northern side of the island to make a telephone call. It is the only village on the island with a telephone; it also houses the island's postal station, and it's a fair distance from here. Tau comes with me. The lorry is really crowded. A number of people are traveling, plus there are bundles of yams, mats, pandanus leaves and kava, not to mention kerosene and benzene drums to be refilled at the supply store.

It's a spectacular drive; I'm always amazed at the beauty of this unspoiled coastline. The road winds through the kind of scenes that are selected for adventure movies in exotic tropical settings. We make stops at villages along the way, picking up and dropping off people and assorted cargo.

Our local Methodist catechist and his wife are with us today. They're on their way to a church meeting on the far side of the island. I'm sitting between them at the back of the lorry. They have a daughter married into a village en route. When we arrive there, she brings her two-year-old son to the back of the lorry so her parents can kiss their grandchild. But it happens again! The little fellow is so frightened at the sight of me—a *kaivulagi* (foreigner)—sitting between his grandparents that they have to abandon the plan and be content to deliver at arms length the treat they have brought for him. There's not much I can do about it because the lorry is so crowded I simply cannot move.

We arrive at our destination. I wait my turn to place the call at the switchboard. Business now completed, I take the opportunity to mail some letters. Then I visit the supply store, and wander about until mid-afternoon, waiting for the lorry to make the return trip to the south of the island.

The vehicle is even more crowded on the return since it is a *Fiji Air* flight day, and we pick up passengers and cargo destined for the airstrip adjacent to our village. In addition, there are supplies for village stores, including a carton of sweetened condensed milk bearing the instruction, "Store in a cool dry place." Almost humorous in this heat and humidity!

By the time we reach our village, the lorry is too crowded for Tau and I to disembark, so we continue on to the airstrip and then walk back to the village. It's almost dusk when we arrive, the entire trip having taken about 8 hours.

Eight hours to make a phone call! It reminds me how patient and good-natured are these people. They have to give over the better part of a day to something I am accustomed to doing in a few short minutes. That they remain for the most part in good spirits never ceases to amaze me—but something deep in the unconscious must be keeping track of it all.

Just Have a Drink

Thursday, March 28th—In the cool of the early morning, some young men are weeding on the outskirts of the village to prevent the breeding of mosquitoes. This project is another facet of Tau's village health plan. After lunch, the headman in charge falls asleep and fails to blow the *davui* (conch shell) to signal the start of the afternoon's work. Some of his relatives get angry with him, and a family feud breaks out. Tau goes over to their house to settle things down, and invites them to drink kava together. It is interesting to see how the sharing of kava mediates social relationships.

At the Island Council meeting today, Tau's letter is read, and the village representatives say it's the first time anyone has ever stood up for them. As for the chiefs and government representatives, they say it's the first time anyone has let them know how they feel.

Show Time

Friday, March 29th—It is very hot today. In the afternoon, I help Tau plant taro as he deepens the drains around the taro patches to prevent the roots from rotting. On the way to the garden, we meet some children returning from school. They are making gestures of shooting each other. So that is what they took away from the James Bond film!

There's another problem emerging with regard to videos, and it's no surprise: the children no longer seem to want to do their homework! The lessons are difficult enough as it is, taught, for the most part, in little understood English. What little homework does get completed takes place in crowded sleeping houses dimly lit with kerosene lamps.

Tonight there was to be a *soli* (fund-raiser) in the village, the money to be used for community improvements, and during the fund-raiser there was to be a choir practice for special Easter music. The choirmaster, who is Tau's cousin, walked here from Nana's village for the occasion. However, just as the event is about to begin, someone arrives and sets up a video in the same location. The villagers immediately give their attention over to the movie, and both the fund-raiser and choir practice go out the window!

Tau is discouraged because he has set up the village work plan—including the fund-raising event—in accordance with what people say they want, and he has put a lot of volunteer effort into it. Now it appears they want something different. He is in a quandary as to what to do. He can let it go: there is no point wanting things for people that they don't want for themselves. Then again, he feels they will grab on to any new thing that comes along without evaluating its effects on the community—and watching mindless videos is not the best new thing for them to grab on to! They do little enough independent thinking as it is; now they are latching onto and absorbing an even larger group mind that will "dumb them down" rather than help them rise above the limiting cultural mindset. Not only that, they are passing it on to the next generation. To deny leadership at this point would be akin to abandoning them. What to do!

The video plays until 4 in the morning.

Part IV

NATURE AND CULTURE

The *Malawa ni Mataka*

Saturday, March 30th—I am awake throughout the night because of the noise from the video. I get up before daybreak and walk with Tau along the beach to watch the sunrise. It is what the Fijians call the *malawa ni mataka* and it is spectacular. The sea is black, the sky is black. Then out of that darkness, a deep red glow bleeds onto the horizon. The glow intensifies, its colour changes from red to orange to yellow to white, and then the brilliant celestial star emerges as though born from a union of sea and sky. It is a brief moment, each phase of the natural spectacle taking only seconds. It is a firm reminder to live in the moment, a perspective immortalized in the lyrics of Tau's song, *Tauri Au:*

> *Au lakova na veibuca*
> *Sirova na veidelana*
> *Vukaca na manawa*
> *Vuravura me'u rawata*
> *Noda bula na malawa ni mataka*

Make the most of life, the song says, because it is as brief as the *malawa ni mataka*. It is one of those perfect moments when time stands still. Tau and I share a drinking coconut, and then we make our way back to the village.

Tau also helps me prepare lunch today. We cook some taro leaves in coconut milk. The Fijian name for the dish is *rourou* and it is one of my favourite local foods. It's a natural green leaf, high in food value, and it doesn't involve violent killing. While we are eating it, Mata tells us that *rourou* is a very special food since Isau sold his birthright for it. An interesting translation the missionaries gave to that well-known Old Testament story in Genesis where Isau sells his birthright to Jacob for a "mess of pottage"! I didn't have the heart to tell Mata there is no *rourou* in the Middle East.

In the evening Tau attends a meeting of the Development Committee he has called to deal with problems associated with carrying out the work plan. He encourages members to express their opinions and ideas at the meeting, but I notice they tend to agree with whatever he says. They do not do a lot of thinking for themselves, nor do they make a connection between setting the work plan and actually doing the work!

They hold the meeting on the verandah of my house. I have set out a clean bucket of water for their kava drinking. I have a second bucket of water nearby with a slight touch of disinfectant in it for cleaning pots and dishes. Someone by mistake pours the wrong bucket of water into the *tanoa* (kava bowl) and mixes the pounded kava in it. Following custom, they serve the person at the "top" of the house first. He drinks the kava.

"This tastes funny!" he says.

They discover they have used the disinfected water, but rather than throw it out and mix some good stuff, they decide to all have a cup just to see how it tastes! There isn't enough disinfectant in the water to hurt anyone; in fact, given the hygienic conditions of kava drinking, mixed as it is with bare unwashed hands, it might do them some good. Nevertheless, I feel badly when I hear about it—which I do, as soon as it happens—along with everyone else in the village.

While the meeting is in progress, I wander across the *rara* (village green). It is a beautiful clear starry night with a bright moon. I can hear the chanting of Psalms by the elderly women who are practicing for the church service tomorrow. So quaint —like a world unto itself, this faraway little island ….

But not really. The rhythm of their ancient chanting is interrupted by the husky voice of a sports announcer on a battery-operated radio, reporting on the international rugby tournament in Hong Kong.

Fiji is winning. Everyone cheers.

Beneath the Surface

Sunday, March 31st—Siga Tabu again. I awake at dawn to take part in the making of the *lovo* (earth oven). It is really fun. We dig a pit near the beach, heat the rocks and, when the temperature is right, fill the "oven" with cassava, taro and yams. Then we close the pit with layers of leaves and palm fronds and cover it all with sand. Only the warmth of the earth reveals that dinner is cooking underneath.

Sai is already up, baking scones in the kitchen hut. She is so patient and hard working, and almost always cheerful. It takes a very long time to prepare breakfast in these limited conditions: a thatched lean-to, an open wood fire, large tin cooking pots with no handles… Here she sits with her husband Mata, stirring the pastry mixture, shaping the scones and rolling them in flour. Mata helps her manage the pots over the open fire; I can see that he has burned his hand in two places.

After breakfast, we uncover the *lovo*. It has taken only two hours to bake the root crops. Then to church. I am always amazed how a village of native people engaged in subsistence activities can transform so quickly into a Sunday best-dressed congregation. I wonder how long they will continue to give over precious hours to monotonous prayers and boring sermons. It must act on the conscious mind at some level—or on the unconscious at another.

Maybe the diversion itself is energizing enough, but the church is such a cultural intrusion and so money oriented. One of the things I find particularly offensive is the way they read out the offering each family contributes right in the middle of the worship service. As if that were not enough, today the treasurer brings a big chart with him listing the annual contribution of each sleeping house. It must be embarrassing for those families who have little means since the required allocations apply across the board. A man who works at the airstrip, for example, can earn $60.00 per week while Tau's brother is paid weekly only $3.80 for tending the village store.

In the middle of the day Tau and I sneak away from the village and enjoy a cool swim in the nearby river. I need this chance to be one with nature, a chance to just "be here now". While I am gone, Tau's cousin arrives with the newly stitched Fijian dress for me. On my return, I try it on. It fits perfectly, a remarkable feat since she took no measurements and did no fittings!

April Fools

Monday, April 1st—A whole month has now passed since I arrived back in Fiji, and I am still trying to make sense of the clues. Right now, my next-door neighbour, Tiwa, is sick. She has been lying down for a number of days now, and on Friday, her husband Saki arranged for her to leave here and go up to Tau's mother's village for some folk medicine. She is staying with Nana there. This morning, I go with the women from Tiwa's clan to Tau's mother's village to visit her.

We gather inside Nana's thatched hut. Tiwa is asleep, and Nana says it is the first time she has slept since she arrived so we do not wake her. We make our presentations and then the wife of the local church leader speaks about the love of God. Here is Tiwa, lying on the mat underneath a mosquito net. She is a very large, overweight woman in her early fifties, sick from an improper diet of sugar, flour, salt, tea and tobacco—not to mention a conspicuous lack of exercise. Now she is surrounded by a group of kinswomen who show their concern by praying, and by bringing her gifts of sugar, flour, salt, tea and tobacco.

We return to the village in the late afternoon. For dinner, there will be *rourou* again, and I'm looking forward to it … until someone, in typical Fijian style, adds a tin of fish.

Oh, well!

Tonight Tau chairs another village development meeting. It is held in a palm frond shelter beside the house of our clan Chief. From this vantage point, I can see children inside the house doing their homework with the aid of a kerosene lamp. The lighting is so poor they must keep their eyes very close to the paper. Little Mili complains of headaches much of the time and I suspect this to be the reason.

The village development meeting is an interesting blend of traditional Fijian culture and Western intervention. It takes place around the *tanoa* (kava bowl), with the chief and elders seated prominently. They serve the ceremonial cup of kava in hierarchical order. Then the business part of the meeting begins: first, a prayer from the local church leader; next, a speech from the *Ratu* (Chief), and finally, the agenda of the meeting, carried out in the spirit of participatory democracy straight out of the British parliamentary system.

It is interesting to observe the proceedings, like how articulated goals get subverted to other agendas, and how being seen as "doing the right thing" and looking good in the eyes of others can circumvent and obscure the original purpose. For example, there is a big problem brewing with regard to the building of the new community centre. The deal was that some men from the main island of Viti Levu who have kinsfolk here would come over and construct the building for the cost of their maintenance. They arrived at Christmas time and up to now, the beginning of April, they have managed to complete only post and beam construction. Their expenses to date have totaled more than $2,000—no small sum in a subsistence economy. What's more, problems have surfaced in the clan with whom they are staying.

The builders came to Tau before the meeting and asked if they might be relieved of their duty. Tau appreciates their dilemma. He also knows the village does not have resources to take the project further at this point, so he calculates the costs and presents the figures, along with the builders' request to leave, to the gathered assembly.

But lo and behold! A spokesman for the builders now says they do not want to leave until they have completed what they came here to do. Someone else says the expenses to the village should not be publicly announced as this might embarrass their guests. All this, in spite of the fact that there is an audible gasp when the villagers learn how excessive these expenses really are!

So the builders will stay to finish the community centre—and the village will continue to support them *carte blanche*. The builders don't really want to stay, and the villagers don't really want to keep them, but this way, everyone comes out looking like they're doing "the right thing." I see that Tau is getting really frustrated. It's like he's pushing against a river when he thought he was flowing with the stream. I fear he is ready to give up on them.

Vakadraunikau (Sorcery)

Tuesday, April 2nd—Tiwa is still sick and her family is taking further means to protect her. They think there is some kind of *vakadraunikau* (sorcery) being done and the most likely spot for it, in their minds, is the big tree beside their house. It has large sprawling limbs and thick green leaves. So they cut it down—which is really too bad because it was the only large tree in the area, and family members used to sit beneath its wide shady branches to avoid the heat of the day. Tonight, all the branches lay on the ground and only the short bare stump remains.

Last night one of the elderly ladies in the village told Tiwa's daughter not to leave any clothes on the line overnight as whoever is doing the sorcery might use one of the articles of clothing to work their black magic. Tonight, the *Ratu*, the village elders and the men from the sick woman's clan gather inside her house to make an offering of kava in an attempt to reverse what they suspect is going on. Through all this, Tiwa remains in the next village with Nana, who by now has had to borrow money from Tau to feed the patient and the visitors who come to see her.

Tonight, while the men are busy with their rituals next door, the young children come as they often do to the veranda of my house. They sing songs and do traditional Fijian dance just for the fun of it. They are so healthy and spontaneous at this young age, and I sense they do not want to be alone when fears of sorcery abound.

The Waterfall

Wednesday, April 3rd—Today Tau and I set out early in the morning to make an excursion to a waterfall about twenty kilometers from the village. We go with the children as far as the school compound. They are so cute. The little girls are in yellow dresses, walking quietly on the road and smiling the whole time. The little boys are running and jumping along the embankment, sliding in the dirt. They would arrive at school looking not at all clean but for the fact that the colour of their uniforms is precisely that of the reddish brown soil. I suspect this to be no coincidence.

Beyond the school, we get a lift on a passing lorry that takes us to the end of the gravel road about half way to our destination.

From here it's on foot along jungle paths and stretches of beach. The scenery, once again, is spectacular—like sets from a Tarzan movie. At times, we make our way through thick jungle by clinging to the leaves and vines. We see no one apart from a few women from a far village diving for shellfish. We stop to drink some young coconuts, then continue along the beach until we come to a homestead. It belongs to a family that is related to Tau and whose members have decided to live outside the village system. We visit and have our noonday meal with them. They are having fish but, according to custom, they cannot serve it to us. Why? Because Tau belongs to a clan that is *kai-wai* (people of the water; in other words, fishermen) while his cousin here belongs to the *kai-vanua* (people of the land, hence, farmers). It is taboo for a *kai-vanua* to serve fish to a *kai-wai*. Where is it written! It doesn't apply to crustaceans, however, so they serve us crayfish chowder instead—which is okay by me.

We reach our destination sometime after mid-day. I have no record of the actual time. The space I find myself in now is like a mythological Garden of Eden … a fresh water river winding through the jungle over rocks and waterfalls on its way to the sea. The flowing stream is embanked on one side by deep rock walls dripping with moisture, on the other by thick dense leaves and vines. Not a tree or anything else in the area has been disturbed. There is something so primordial about it that it seems possible in this instance to exist again in a state of pure innocence. Without culture, without belief systems, without "knowledge of good and evil"…We take off our clothes and jump in the water.

It's so pure, so translucent. In every direction, natural contours, glistening shapes, deep shadows … everything is creative, like Nature giving life to itself. There's Tau, with his tall brown body, slim waist and muscles toned to perfection. Genuine warmth flows from his smiling lips and deep brown eyes. I see him, not as clansman or fisherman, not as Fijian or Polynesian, not in any of his roles or statuses or categories. He is life, the perfect completion to this natural environment.

Time is suspended ….

I know it can't last forever. I know we must return to a place where people preach and pray, "break fast" with processed white flour, engage in rituals to ward off sorcery, use their best and softest mats to comfort the dead ….

It's a long and silent walk back to the village. We arrive just in time for evening prayers. The same words, the same gestures…

From Nature to culture … from the primordial to the ideological … from spontaneity to ritual….

Life ceases to be a joyful play of consciousness.

Let Them Eat Bread

Thursday, April 4th—I learn today that my sick neighbour Tiwa was taken yesterday to the island's nursing station. The nurse who attended her says she has "sugar disease and salt disease". They will send her to the medical station further up the coast today so a doctor can examine her and make arrangements, if necessary, to send her to the hospital in Suva on tomorrow's flight, but the nurse expressed concern that it may already be too late to help her. Not a good sign! Nana said Tiwa had a dream the night before she left to go to the nursing station: in it, she saw the women from our village bringing new mats for her bed. Really not a good sign!

Just after breakfast, news gets around the village that an old man from another clan has gone crazy and wants to kill himself. He keeps banging his head against the posts of his sleeping house, and people are trying to constrain him. They are talking about sending him to a mental hospital because he is mentally ill.

Tau goes to the man's sleeping house to talk to him. Because of traditional relationships, Tau cannot bring up the subject, so he begins the conversation on another level. Very soon the old man starts telling Tau he is upset because he is being condemned by a chief for taking on the role of a titled person in an exchange ceremony yesterday. He explains he was asked by someone else to assume that role and now he just can't handle the criticism coming from so high up in the village hierarchy, so he wants to put an end to his life. Such is the power of institutionalized culture!

Tau listens to his story and that seems to have a calming effect on the poor fellow. He's not mentally ill; in fact, he's very clear on things. The problem is that, like most of us, he has so thoroughly internalized the cultural norms that he cannot transcend them, even when they threaten to do him in. Tau hears the man out and requests that he not beat his head against the wall anymore because the only thing that will give him is a headache. The old man agrees. Case closed.

Tomorrow is Good Friday. Many of the men and women in the village go circle fishing after breakfast and are away for a good part of the day. They go as far as the reef—close to a kilometer—and arrive back with a huge catch of big fish for the holiday tomorrow. About 5 o'clock in the evening, the lorry returns from the other side of the island and, instead of parking in its usual spot at the end of the pathway into the village, it comes right across the *rara*, the village green. Then I see Saki step from the front seat of the lorry and go over to where Sai and some of the other women are cleaning fish near the kitchen hut. After a few seconds, the women start crying really loud so I know Tiwa has died. They have brought her body back in the lorry with them.

Immediately all Easter plans are given over to death ceremonies. They take Tiwa's body to a sleeping house and the older women prepare it for viewing. They place the body on three nicely decorated mats at the upper end of the house, and cover it with tapa cloth. While this is going on, the men hastily construct a shelter of palm fronds outside the house. This is the place where the funeral delegations will be received and the exchange ceremonies carried out. It's also where the men will drink kava throughout the days of mourning. They set up a second shelter of palm fronds beside the clan chief's house for communal cooking and eating. Then the clan chief, Mata, Saki and Tau have a meeting to arrange the four days of ritual mourning and feasting.

The most appropriate contribution I can make is a bag of flour. This I do with more than slight hesitation because it's processed white flour, and I know that in so doing I am contributing to the very thing that has taken the life of my next-door neighbour. I know they are going to cook up at least one full bag of the stuff in any case, and they'll struggle to find the $30 to pay for it if I don't—so a bag of flour it will be.

The mourning rituals for Tiwa are really different from those for the chief of Nana's village. When the chief died, no one was allowed to cry; now, everyone is supposed to. Each time a new delegation of women comes into the "house of death", they immediately begin crying really loudly. On some occasions, perhaps when an especially close relative arrives, the wailing takes on a heightened intensity and gets very high-pitched. No *davui* (conch shell) this time either; instead, there is singing. About 11 p.m., the choir from Nana's village arrives and stays in the "house of death" to sing hymns throughout the hours of darkness.

I leave the "house of death" about 2 in the morning and go over to the palm shelter where the women are mixing and baking huge pans of bread, buns, scones and pancakes. All this processed white flour will be ingested into the bodies of these people tomorrow morning while they prepare to bury one of their kin who died from more of the same.

Good Friday

Friday, April 5th—Despite the date, there is little sign of Easter. All the people of the village eat together because of Tiwa's death. In addition, there are a few hundred people from other villages on the island here to feed. Adults from our village, and especially those from our clan, are busy in the kitchen hut cooking up huge pots of fish, cassava, pork stew and rice. During the early part of the day, delegations continue to arrive and there are more presentations of mats, pigs, whales' teeth, kava and root crops. The *vale ni mate* (house of death) is continually crowded with mourners. Most of them are women, and the wailing wafts over the village in waves, announcing their arrivals.

A coffin is flown in today on the scheduled flight that was to take Tiwa to hospital in Suva. When they lift her body from the mats to place it in the wooden box, it is a particularly emotional scene. They kiss the corpse as they view this wife, mother, sister, cousin, auntie and friend for the last time. In late afternoon, they carry the coffin into the church and, after a short service, take it to the graveyard on top of a nearby hill. They place the coffin on some mats and lower it all into a prepared grave.

One person … and so many kinship ties severed. Tiwa, who was married into our clan, came from another clan in the same village. She was wife to Saki, sister-in-law to Tevi and Nasa, sister to Luga, Tusi and Seli. Here at the burial site, these kinsmen sit around the open grave. In response to the words of the Methodist catechist, they pick up handfuls of the rich red earth and drop it on top the coffin. It is a touching sight and so symbolic of the kinship network within which people wrestle with individual versus communal interests.

Only one day after her death at the medical station on the far side of the island, Tiwa's lifeless body now lies silently in her grave. The remaining dirt is unceremoniously returned to the hole. When it is completed, signaled by laying a sheet of tapa cloth over the new mound, the kinsfolk crowd around the spot to have their picture taken.

Let Them Bake Bread

Saturday, April 6th—A third day of feasting and mourning for the entire village. They kill another cow and hand out the raw flesh in the *burua* (food distribution) to those from other villages who have come for the funeral. In the *vale ni mate*, the older women spend the day in *bikabika* (the "pressing down") while the men drink kava and make exchange presentations in the palm shelter just outside the house.

Mata has put the supply of whales' teeth in my house for safekeeping and, throughout the day, he comes by to pick up or deposit a few more of them. At one point I count 20 of these valuable teeth in the cardboard box. They are keeping their kava supply in my house as well. The amount of kava being consumed for this event alone is costing a few hundred dollars. Then there are the cows and the pigs, the taro, the yams, the mats, the tapa cloth…Maybe it doesn't cost a lot to live here, but it sure costs a lot to die.

Tonight I spend the evening in a small thatched kitchen hut with a group of women and young girls who are baking bread for tomorrow's breakfast. They cook on open fires with big pots, on the tops of which are burning coconut husks to create the effects of an oven. They mix and bake 24 loaves of bread and at least that many dozen buns and scones. They are using the second half of the bag of flour I contributed for the death feasting. Batch after batch of bread and buns and scones … it takes the entire evening. Eli mixes the bread, Vati the buns and a third woman the scones. The younger girls assist by carrying the water and tending the fires. It's a regular assembly line.

We chat about the process as they work. I ask if they prefer to cook singly or as a group. They say the latter because they have a lot of fun together—and I see that they really do. They laugh and they joke, seemingly unperturbed by the congestion created by so many people jammed into so tiny a space.

"And do you enjoy baking so much bread and buns and scones?" I ask them.

"Yes," says Eli, "but we don't have the money to buy them so we have no choice."

"And would you prefer buying to baking if you did have the choice?"

"No," Eli jokingly replies, "I would bake the bread and keep the money!"

Everybody laughs—but, once again, there is that bitter edge to humour.

Someone arrives with our dinner. It's beef stew from a freshly slaughtered cow, served with boiled cassava. The meal sits here until the last of the mixing is done. By this time—about 10 o'clock in the evening—the stew is cold, revealing its extremely high content of saturated fat. It doesn't seem to matter to these women. Beef is very special. They divide the stew into equal portions and eat it with delight. I consume only the lean pieces of my portion, leaving the chunks of fat and the gravy on my plate. When I am finished, they quickly take my dish and divide the leftovers among themselves.

The men who drink kava into the late evening have their suppers taken to their sleeping houses. Kava does not sit well on a full stomach so men often eat their evening meal very late and alone. It is after midnight when I walk past Saki's house on my way to the water pipe. He is preparing to eat his meal. He is saying grace—and he is praying for a very long time. I feel for this new widower. He did what he could to save his wife, but all his efforts were fruitless. Now he sits alone, praying over a plate of cold beef stew. In an attempt to assuage his deep sense of separation, I bring him a dish of *vakasoso* (bananas cooked in coconut milk) that I prepared earlier in the day.

A gracious thank you … a faint smile….
It will take time.

Easter Sunday

Sunday, April 7th—No resurrection to celebrate this time— it's the fourth day of mourning for Tiwa. After a morning prayer service—I don't go—there's a white flour breakfast in the communal feasting shelter.

It's a bit difficult for people at this end of the village to get ready for church today since the one Seventh Day Adventist family—for whom this is not *Siga Tabu*—decides to do laundry at the water pipe precisely between breakfast and the morning church service when everyone else must take their baths. The husband and wife do the washing together and they occupy the total area, seemingly oblivious to the people waiting in their bathing *sulu* (lavalavas) with towels over their shoulders. More than that, the water pipe the couple is monopolizing is not even the one designated for their use. They've come over to our end of the village to do their washing because their own water pipe is dirty. Rather than clean it, they're using the one Tau painstakingly scrubbed while everyone was in church this time last week.

The water pipe is the source of drinking water as well as the place for cleaning food and washing dishes. It also serves as a laundry and a public bath. Even more problematic, it is the "watering hole" for pigs, dogs and chickens that wander unattended throughout the village. There is even a horse that has learned to turn on the tap with its mouth! (It hasn't learned how to shut the tap off again.) Given these multiple functions, coupled with the heat and humidity of a tropical climate, the water pipe becomes the ideal breeding ground for disease and bacteria. I witness villagers unnecessarily sick with nausea, respiratory infections and boils—so many boils—and, apart from Tau's personal campaign, nothing is being done about it. They bring their wounds to the water pipe for cleansing and, in the process, trade them in for more.

Now it's time for church. Never mind that it's Easter Sunday or that we've been through a horrendous death experience the last few days, the service today is just more of the same. There is Taku, in the first week of his new fiscal year as treasurer, collecting the offering in his usual manner, household by household, reading aloud the amount each family has contributed. Then, while the congregation is standing for the Psalm chanting, there he is, sitting down in his pew, counting the money. He can't even wait until the service is over. So conditioned into the institutionalized church is he that he fails to make any connection between religion and life: before church this morning he beat 7-year-old Samu with a leather belt for taking his bath in the ocean. Being in the ocean is not allowed on Sundays! The poor child was crying and thoroughly confused about it all because his Seventh Day Adventist cousins were playing in the water right beside him, undisturbed.

Then there's the new widower Saki whose task it is to keep children in line during these long worship services. I have often wondered why anyone would agree to such a task, and I would have thought that, especially today, he would have deeper thoughts on his mind. But here he is, busy as usual, stalking the aisles with his long stick, tapping children on the shoulders when they get restless or fall asleep. He even wakes up a sleeping member of the choir! Life must go on, yes, but at this petty pace! For a few minutes I am almost afraid he will discover that the book I have with me in church is neither the Holy Bible nor the Methodist hymnal but a paperback copy of *If You Meet the Buddha on the Road, Kill Him*.

The communal mid-day meal follows the usual pattern: titled people eat first, then the rest of the men, the children, and finally, the women. The food choices correspond to the same hierarchy so that by the time the children eat, the choice protein has already been consumed. The women eat whatever is left, often having to settle for a too large portion of starchy root crops. It is still very much a male-oriented society with age commanding both respect and selective treatment. Little girls lose out however you stack it while little boys need only wait their turn.

It is also the first Sunday of a new month, and that means there will be a special combined church service this afternoon for the three villages under the leadership of our paramount chief. It is in the far village this time and many from here do not go because of the death ceremonies.

I remain in the village and spend part of the evening with the women who are doing the *bikabika* in the house of death. There are 17 of them and they come from villages all around the island. It is the kind of sitting around that I would find unbearable—four days and four nights, just sitting there, "pressing down" when there's nothing to press down. These women stay inside this house the whole time. They eat, sleep, talk—the conversation is not profound—and wait out the time, developing headaches and backaches in the process. As usual, the villagers bring them candies, tobacco and chewing gum, adding toothaches to their list of miseries. Some of them ask me for *vunikau* (medicine). I bring them some headache tablets. Then everybody wants one. Even the men outside drinking kava start asking for pills as though they were candy.

What to do! I figure they are so thoroughly conditioned by this time that the wisest thing is to simply part with a few more tablets. Except for one young man, still in his twenties, who also wants one!

"Do you have a headache?" I ask him.

"No, but I might get one," he replies, adding that he does seem to have some pain in his neck and shoulders.

I don't feel like feeding pills to such a young person so I advise him to do some yoga. But for those fortunate—or unfortunate—enough to get one or two of the little chemicals off of me, they will dull their aches for a few short hours while they continue to sit and drink and smoke and chew.

The hypnosis of social conditioning—like in Tennyson's *Ulysses*: "Life piled on life, were all too little ..."

Easter Monday

Monday, April 8th—The four days of mourning has ended and there is a distinctly different feeling in the air. The women who have taken part in the *bikabika* prepare to leave after morning tea. They are laughing and joking as the mats are taken from the house of death and spread on to the village green to dry in the sun. A group of women goes out circle fishing as the men gather to drink kava. I hear some pigs squealing; there will be fresh pork for dinner again tonight.

Not for me! It is my last day in the village for a while. I clean up the house, roll up the mats and pack my things. After lunch and a round of handshakes, with ritual requests to leave and promises to return, I depart with Tau for the airstrip; he will come to Suva with me to record another album of our Fijian music. Two young boys run after us and, without speaking a word, gently take my bags from me and walk alongside. It is a typical expression of the deep sense of connectedness I will soon be missing again. We take the route along the beach and cut up through the jungle path on Tau's piece of land. It is lovely as usual and I want to linger this one last time, but the little *Fiji Air* Cessna appears out of the horizon and zooms over our heads. We run for the airstrip.

Passengers disembark with the familiar bundles and cartons and bags and boxes. Like a circle in a circle…Some more good-byes, hugs and kisses for the children—oh, the children—and we're boarded for a quick take-off down the gravel runway. I peak out of the window. Sai is standing there, smiling and waving. How did she get here in time to see us off! Only minutes earlier she was squatting in the feasting shelter scooping out multiple portions of stew.

The little plane lifts into the air. We fly alongside the village and then head out over the reef. The view is magnificent. It looks like a paradise down there ... a hidden treasure in the heart of the South Pacific, this tropical island, nestling inside its garland of coral, surrounded by deep blue ocean....

Thirty-five minutes in the clouds and we're back on the main island of Viti Levu. Tau and I head directly for a pizza and a glass of wine. I cannot remember pizza ever tasting so good!

Part V

INTO THE DARKNESS

Cannibals

Tuesday, April 9th—I awake in Suva to a breakfast of fresh pineapple, muesli and, best of all, whole-wheat toast with butter and marmalade! Fascinating how food choices become so exciting after being in the village.

And a newspaper! The front page features an article about the *Vunivalu* (paramount chief of Fiji and former Governor-General) who is returning to Fiji and his chiefly island of Mbau after seven weeks of medical treatment in Australia. And then there's a tiny item about a Fijian child who died after being given a transfusion of the wrong blood type.

Life is not fair!

Page 2: "2,000 Fijian citizens living illegally in Australia." I wonder if it has anything to do with lack of medical care ... or telephones ... or death ceremonies ... or chiefly privileges ... or the power of the church ....

Or perhaps something much darker and more disturbing —something from the primordial Fijian culture. Something in Fiji's dark past that leads Fijians to say—even today—that there is "something wrong with the people". I decide to go in search of it by making a fieldtrip to Taveuni, an island in the north of the archipelago infamous for its cannibalism. I am hoping that there, in that deeply historical setting, I might uncover lingering remnants of Maugham's

85

"strange and secret life" which "suggests something aboriginal and darkly cruel".

Taveuni, historically called Somosomo, from its principal town of that name, is twenty-five miles long, and consists of one major mountain that rises gradually to a height of 2,100 feet. Clouds generally cover its summit, hiding a sizeable lake from which cascades a stream that provides a good supply of water to its chiefly town below. The lake itself sits in the crater of an extinct volcano. However wild the appearance of this island might once have been, it is today the image of nature at its best, covered with luxuriant foliage.

But it is not for the natural beauty that I am attracted to Taveuni. It is to witness the interface between Fiji's present-day culture and its cannibalistic history. Even in other parts of Fiji, the cannibals of Somosomo were greatly feared. What happened when the first Methodist missionaries came here? What atrocities did they witness? What were they able to do about it? And what does it say about human potentiality? Interesting that the paramount Chief of this area is currently the Governor-General of Fiji.

To prepare for my virtual foray into cannibalism, I take up Volume I of *Fiji and the Fijians* written in 1858 by the Rev. Thomas Williams, one of the first missionaries to Fiji. Williams offers a graphic account of a custom about which even anthropologists are reluctant to give credence. Page 205:

> *Until recently, there were many who refused to believe in the existence of this horrible practice in modern times; but such incredulity has been forced to yield to indisputable and repeated evidence, of which Fiji alone can supply enough to convince a universe, that man can fall so low as* habitually *to feed upon his fellow-men. Cannibalism among this people is one of their institutions; it is interwoven in the elements of society; it forms one of their pursuits, and is regarded by the mass as a refinement....*

Williams writes that human bodies were sometimes eaten in connection with the building of a temple or canoe, and that chiefs were known to kill several men for rollers, to facilitate the launching of their canoes, the "rollers" being afterwards cooked and eaten. A chief would kill a man on laying down a keel for a canoe, and add one for each new plank. These men were afterwards eaten as "food for the carpenters." It was also common to murder men in order to wash the deck of a new canoe with blood, and this was done on a large scale when a large canoe was completed at the chiefly village of Somosomo on the island of Taveuni.

Fewer than 150 years have passed since these cannibalistic practices were in place. I wonder what remnants of this depraved past one can see or feel there now. Not that Taveuni was that much different from the rest of Fiji. For example, I find this information about Ngau, the island where "my" village is located, on page 209:

I never saw a body baked whole, but have most satisfactory testimony that, on the island of Ngau, and one or two others, this is really done. The body is first placed in a sitting posture, and, when taken from the oven, is covered with black powder, surmounted with a wig, and paraded about as if possessed with life.

It's time for dinner. In fact, it's well into the evening—but I'm not hungry! I take a break from my reading and walk down to the main business area of the town. The walk restores my appetite, so I look for something "appropriate" to eat, and settle on vegetarian food in an Indian restaurant. Then I return to my reading.

I'm still on page 209. According to Williams, revenge was the main cause of cannibalism in Fiji. He gives this example:

A woman taken from a town besieged by Ra Undreundre, and where one of his friends had been killed, was placed in a large wooden dish and cut up alive, that none of the blood might be lost.

But there were many cases where revenge could not have been the motive. Cannibalism was an ingrained cultural practice.

Williams says that some of the chiefs hated cannibalism, and he knew of several who could not be induced to taste human flesh. But these, he adds, were exceptions to the rule.

No one who is thoroughly acquainted with the Fijians can say that this vitiated taste is not widely spread, or that there is not a large number who esteem this food a delicacy, giving it a decided preference above all other.

Cannibalism, the missionary writes, did not confine its selection to gender or to a particular age. Williams witnessed the elderly and children of both sexes headed for the oven:

I have laboured to make the murderers of females ashamed of themselves; and have heard their cowardly cruelty defended by the assertion that such victims were doubly good—because they ate well, and because of the distress it caused their husbands and friends.

"Would that this horrible record could be finished here!" he adds, "but the *vakatotoga*, the "torture" must be noticed."

Nothing short of the most fiendish cruelty could dictate some of these forms of torment, the worst of which consists in cutting off parts and even limbs of the victim while still living, and cooking and eating them before his eyes, sometimes finishing the brutality by offering him his own cooked flesh to eat. I could cite well authenticated instances of such horrors, but their narration would be far more revolting than profitable.

Definitely enough for one day! I'll sleep on it … and hopefully dream of something more cheerful.

Missionaries

Wednesday, April 10th—It's a lovely sunny day. I have some tropical fruit beside the swimming pool. I switch from Volume I of *Fiji and the Fijians* and turn to the Mission History written by the Rev. James Calvert in Volume II:

> *In the entire annals of Christianity, it would be difficult to find a record of any of its enterprises so remarkable, or followed by such astonishing success, as the Mission to Fiji...The truth is just this, that within the many shores of this secluded group, every evil passion has grown up unchecked, and run riot in unheard abominations...Constitutional vigour and mental force aided and fostered the development of every crime; until crime became inwrought into the very soul of the people, polluted every hearth, gave form to every social and political institution, and turned religious worship into orgies of unsurpassed horror. The savage of Fiji broke beyond the common limits of rapine and bloodshed, and violating the elementary instincts of humanity, stood unrivalled as a disgrace to mankind.*

That's the first paragraph!

As reports about Fiji's cannibalistic culture became known to Methodist missionaries serving in the Friendly Islands (Tonga), two of their number agreed to go to Fiji. One of them was the Rev. William Cross who had already served for eight years in Tonga. The Captain of a schooner calling in at the port of Vavau in northern Tonga agreed to take the missionary party to Fiji; the two families reached the island of Lakemba in the easterly group in 1835. Page 7:

> *Early in the morning, the two Missionaries went ashore in a boat, the schooner, in the meantime, lying off without coming to anchor. Deafening shouts along the shore announced the approach of the vessel, and drew together a great crowd of wild-looking Tongans*

and Fijians, armed and blackened according to custom, to receive
the strangers.

I've just started this Volume but already I feel the need for a
break!

The Darkest Chapter

Thursday, April 11ᵗʰ—I return to my reading in Volume II of *Fiji
and the Fijians* as I lounge beside the swimming pool, and discover
the story of the mission to Somosomo. I'm on page 34 now.

> *One of the new stations to be supplied with a Missionary was
> Somosomo. The place is a town of great importance, situated on
> Taveuni, an island lying off the southeastern point of Vanua Levu,
> or the Great Land ….*
>
> *In the year 1837, not long after the first arrival of Missionaries,
> Tuithakau, King of Somosomo, accompanied by his two sons and
> some hundreds of his people, visited Lakemba, where he saw the
> Mission Station and its inmates. What chiefly struck the royal
> visitors was the supply of knives, hatchets, iron pots, and other
> useful things, which the Lakembans were able to procure from
> the Mission-house; and it seemed a very unbecoming thing that
> so unimportant a people should be enjoying such great advantage,
> while they, who were so powerful, were without it. Very strongly
> was their plea for a Missionary urged ….*

"The earnestness shown by these Somosomans to have a
Missionary was certainly not of the most encouraging kind," writes
Calvert, "but there were many things that made it seem right to
comply with their wish." The King's territories were very extensive.
His two sons were not only of high rank on their father's side, but
their mother was a Mbau lady of highest rank, which made them

vasu (related) to all the chiefs and dominions of small but powerful Mbau. In addition to their influence, the Somosomans were desperate characters, and feared throughout the islands. And so it was resolved that missionaries should be sent to Somosomo.

In 1839, two missionaries arrived on the island. Here they witnessed all the horrors of Fijian life, for even in the other islands, Somosomo was spoken of as a place of dreadful cannibalism. The King had urgently pleaded for missionaries, but now that they had come, no one welcomed them. Indeed, they were regarded with indifference. The old chief's house was given up for the use of the two families, but beyond this no one paid any attention to them. Trying as it was, more severe troubles awaited them. Calvert relates this disturbing incident beginning at the bottom of page 35:

> When they arrived, they found the people expecting the return of Rambithi, the King's youngest son, who had gone with a fleet of canoes to the windward islands. After the Missionaries had got all their goods landed, and before the vessel in which they came had left, tidings reached Somosomo that Rambithi had been lost at sea. The ill news caused terrible excitement in the town and, according to custom, several women were at once set apart to be strangled. The Missionaries began their work by pleading for the lives of these wretched victims. The utmost they could affect was to get the execution delayed until the schooner should have gone to search for the young Chief, and bring back further information. The vessel returned, but not with any more favourable news. Now a greater number of women were condemned, and again the Missionaries pleaded hard that they might be spared; but the old King was angry with the strangers for presuming to interfere with the affairs of his people, and indignant at the thought of his favourite son dying without the customary honours. Once more, however, the strangling was put off. Canoes, which had been sent out to search, at last returned, bringing the intelligence that all

was true. It was generally known but not openly talked about, that Rambithi had drifted on his wrecked canoe to the island of Ngau, where he had been captured and eaten by the natives…Sixteen women were forthwith strangled in honour of the young Chief and his companions, and the bodies of the principal women were buried within a few yards of the door of the Missionaries' house.

Thus began the mission to Somosomo! The missionaries and their families suffered greatly there, for cannibalism, widow strangling and the like became dreadfully familiar to them by daily occurrence. "All the horrors hinted at, rather than described, in the first part of this work," writes Calvert on the following page, "were constantly enacted in their most exaggerated forms of cruelty and degradation in Somosomo."

I go to the Tourist Bureau to find out how to get to the island and where to stay when I get there. Apart from a couple of tourist resorts and a guesthouse, there appears to be little in the way of accommodation. I inquire about the location of the guesthouse; they don't seem to know. I ask for a map of the island; they don't seem to have one. *Air Pacific* flies there, they tell me, so they might know.

I go to the *Air Pacific* office and ask the fare to Taveuni. They tell me *Air Pacific* does not fly there, and send me to *Fiji Air*. Now I'm at the *Fiji Air* office: they fly on Fridays. That's tomorrow. I ask the whereabouts of the guesthouse.

"They were supposed to send some brochures," the agent responds, "but they're all out of them."

"But do you know where the guesthouse is?" I repeat.

"I haven't been there," he replies.

Fijians will often answer a question in this indirect way, perhaps because they are not clear about the question but, more likely, because they are reluctant to acknowledge they do not know the answer. I buy the ticket anyway.

To the Garden Isle

Friday, April 12ᵗʰ—I take the early morning *Fiji Air* flight to Taveuni, along with my two Volumes of *Fiji and the Fijians*. In Volume II, page 37, the author James Calvert includes this account by the missionary Rev. John Hunt in Somosomo.

> *On February 7ᵗʰ, 1840, Mr. Hunt writes:*—"*Last Monday afternoon, as soon as our Class-meeting was over, a report came that some dead men were being brought here from Lauthala. The report was so new and so indefinite, that at first we did not know what to make of it. Almost before we had time to think, the men were laid on the ground before our house, and Chiefs and priests and people met to divide them to be eaten. They brought eleven to our settlement, and it is not certain how many have been killed but some say two or three hundred, others not more than thirty. Their crime appears to be that of killing one man, and when the man who did it came to beg pardon, the Chief required this massacre to be made as a recompense. The principal Chief was killed, and given to the great Ndengei of Somosomo. I saw him after he was cut up and laid upon the fire, to be cooked for the cannibal god of Somosomo.*

Rev. Hunt goes on to describe the treatment.

> "*The manner in which the poor wretches were treated was most shamefully disgusting. They did not honour them as much as they do pigs. When they took them away to be cooked, they dragged them on the ground: one had a rope round his neck, and the others they took by the hands and feet. They have been very strange with us ever since. They refuse to sell us a pig; and have threatened us, and treated us in such a way as to give us reason, as far as they are concerned, to expect the very worst …*"

It's a one-hour flight through the islands of Lomaiviti—Ovalau, Ngau, Nairai, Koro—then the coastline of Vanua Levu ("Great Land") leading to the Taveuni airstrip.

I continue reading in Volume II. "Every day the position of the Missionaries became more trying and more dangerous," writes Calvert on page 38 …

> *The ovens in which the human bodies were cooked were very near to the dwelling; and when the cannibal feasts were held, the blinds were closed to shut out the revolting scene. But this greatly offended the natives, who also felt much annoyed at the interference of the strangers, and their faithful reproof of the wickedness of the land. These bold and faithful servants of God were now plainly told that their lives were in danger, and would soon be at an end.*

I get a taxi from the airport and follow a winding dirt road along the coastline. Much of the land in this area today is taken up with coffee and copra plantations, owned by Europeans. The scenery is marginally beautiful, but lacks the coral reef that makes Ngau so picturesque. After passing through a couple of villages, we come to historic Somosomo. Nothing, of course, remains to suggest its infamous past. In fact, the village appears to be quite European with wooden houses, many neatly painted. And the beautiful stream is still there, flowing from the lake atop the mountain.

The most striking feature in the village is the construction of two large meeting-houses for the *Bose Vanua* (the Council of Chiefs) to be held later this year. The buildings are modified Fijian *bure* (thatched) in design, quite beautiful architecturally. The Great Council of Chiefs meetings take place annually in the home villages of the paramount chiefs in Fiji: here in Somosomo, home of the *Tui Cakau*, the current Governor-General; in Mbau, home of the *Tui Viti* (King of Fiji); in Tubou on Lakemba, home of the *Tui Nayau*, the Prime-Minister; in Rewa, home of the *Tui Dreketi*, paramount chief of the Macuata district in northern Vanua Levu and home of the current Prime-Minister's wife. The buildings constructed for the one-week meetings are afterwards turned over to the host villages to be used as community centres and the like.

I find the mysterious guesthouse. It's just outside the village of Somosomo. Owned and operated by Indians, it is flanked on either side by small, family-operated general stores, also Indian-owned.

Taveuni may be called the garden isle, and well known for its rich soil, but there is a striking absence of fresh food here. The stores are well stocked with tinned food, even frozen goods, including chicken and ice cream, their refrigeration maintained by portable generators. And there's beer available. Lots of it! I stock up on food and cook myself a chicken curry. Then I read a bit more about the Somosomo mission. Page 39:

> *Every opposition was made to the work of the Missionaries. The Chiefs forbad their people to become Christian, declaring that death and the oven should be the punishment for such an offence. The health of the Mission families was suffering through confinement to the town; for the King's promise to build them a house had never been fulfilled. Early in 1840, Commodore Wilkes, with two ships of the United States Exploring Expedition, visited Somosomo, and expressed great sympathy with them, placing at their disposal one of his vessels, if they chose to go to any other part of Fiji, and undertaking to remove all their goods, without allowing the natives to molest them. The great kindness of the United States officer was much valued by the Missionaries; but their work had begun, and they were resolved not to leave it.*

The New Mission-Station

Saturday, April 13th—Today I take a local bus to the end of the northern route. As a tourist destination, Taveuni has little to recommend it, compared with Ngau, for example. It has no offshore reef, and while it has lovely rivers, the relief is a single central high volcanic cone which slopes down both sides of the island to a mixture of estates or, as the tourist information describes it, "cute little labour settlements". They have nothing to match the sixteen authentic Fijian villages—or the variety of hills and valleys—one finds on Ngau.

In 1842, new Mission-houses were built on the northern side of Taveuni. As a result, the refreshing influence of the trade wind was lost, and the health of the missionary families suffered in consequence. In that same year, Rev. Cross, serving in another part of the archipelago, got leave to go to New South Wales, believing that another year in Fiji would kill him. But it was not to be. Before he could depart, news reached him of another missionary's death. Rev. Cross, feeling how few missionaries there were left to do the work, consented to remain, on condition he could transfer to Somosomo to be with the Rev. Dr. Lyth who had professional medical training. But the exhaustion of moving, added to that caused by his disease, proved too much, and in spite of Dr. Lyth's medical attention, Rev. Cross, the first missionary to Fiji, died. Page 45:

> *A house was built, in native fashion, over the grave of the Missionary; and beneath the same thatch were several tiny graves, where the devoted men and women of that Mission had laid their little ones who had died early in the land of strangers.*

The bus goes as far as a place called Bouma, then turns around, passing through a few Fijian villages and offering a lovely view of the coastline and Gamea Island. I make notes as I move about, looking for clues from the past infamy of this place. And I read on ….

By 1843, the state of affairs at Somosomo worsened. Much labour had been expended there, but with little visible result. The missionary Journals made clear that to abandon the Station just then would be to imperil the safety of several infant churches in other parts of Fiji, where the influence of Somosomo was strong. It was also felt that Somosomo was not the place for a solitary missionary, so Rev. Thomas Williams, the same missionary who wrote about the early Fijian culture, joined Rev. Lyth. Still they realized little success, in large part, because of native fear. In 1845, Rev. Williams writes:

> *Indeed, the people do not fear without a cause, the King having publicly repeated his determination to kill and eat any of his people who may profess and interest themselves in the religion of Jesus … As the King's authority here is absolute, the people do not dare to oppose themselves to him in such a matter as religion.*

Nearly two more years would pass before the missionaries could persuade themselves to leave Somosomo. In 1847, at the Methodist district meeting, it was resolved to finally forsake this mission.

A Ritualized Feast

Sunday, April 14ᵗʰ—I hear the *lali* (wooden drum) beating at 4 a.m. for an early morning church service. It seems to be only minutes after a lively fundamentalist congregation right across the road ended their service last night. There are three churches within a short distance of each other. The early missionaries would be pleased—and very surprised! Page 48:

> *The people were dark and bad beyond other Fijians, of haughty disposition and diabolical temper, and exercised great influence at Mbau, Lakemba, and almost all parts of the great adjoining island of Vanua Levu. Thus, though the Missionaries made but little*

visible impression on the Somosomans themselves, yet all that was done among them told upon this work through a great part of the group ....

After the giving up of this Mission, two French priests made an attempt to establish Popery on the island, and settled on the spot where the Mission premises had formerly been.

Early afternoon I hire a car—there are no busses today because of the rain last night—and drive the short distance outside Somosomo village to the spot where the new mission station had been.

There is a cathedral here now, sitting on a hill near the coast, with twin flanking towers and stained glass windows. Inside there is a decorative altar and the stations-of-the-cross, but no furnishings, not even pews. Such a massive structure appears overly opulent and strangely out of place in this tropical outpost.

There are a few people about. A Fijian woman guides me the short distance from an overgrown path to the cemetery. There are many old graves here, including those of a number of early missionaries. I am drawn to one of them, that of a Catholic priest, who was buried here in 1886. Such a silent tomb! There is no way to hear his story now. What did he witness? What did he achieve? And did he plan to die here? A grand cathedral in so distant a place may well be the greatest witness to his intention.

And what did the Fijians of Somosomo make of a Roman Catholic presence with its emphasis on the celebration of the mass? There they were, a handful of Europeans, insisting on an end to the killing and eating of human flesh, this same insistence embedded in a ritualized feast of the body and blood of Christ.

A Christian Burial

Monday, April 15th—Early in the morning, I make a last visit into Somosomo village. There has been abundant rainfall in recent days, and the stream from the mountain is flowing vigorously. A few women are sitting on the black rocks, worn smooth by the actions of the water, while they wash their clothes. Some small boys are laughing and splashing about as they take a morning bath. I pause awhile to chat with them and to admire the magnificent setting—and then I move on.

Further along the road that winds its way through the centre of the village, I chance upon an elderly gentleman. I stop, tell him my name and state my purpose: I have come to find the gravesite of the Rev. William Cross.

The old gentleman takes me to the spot where the grave had been. He says that the Wesleyan Methodist Church was later erected on the site but the church was destroyed in an earthquake in 1980. At that time, the grave of William Cross was dug up and his bones placed in a wooden box. A new church is now being constructed; it's one of the two new buildings being readied for the meetings of the Great Council of Chiefs. During the proceedings to be held in October—the same month the missionary died—a funeral service will be conducted, and the bones of Rev. Cross will be buried inside the new church.

"Do you want to see the bones?" the old man asks. I say that I do. We walk a few short paces to a modest building which houses the administrative office of Taveuni, situated alongside the site of the old church. There, inside an office, in a tiny crate rest the bones of the dead missionary. Beside the crate sits a small coffin, the size one would normally use for the body of a child: there is so little left of the man.

I convey my thanks and appreciation to the old gentleman and make my way back to the guesthouse just outside the boundaries of the village. Only then does the significance of this incident sink in. Think of it! The bones of the first missionary to Fiji, now, finally, in the hands of the *Tui Cakau*! It was the old *Tui Cakau*, King of Somosomo, who publicly repeated his determination to kill and eat any of his people who converted to Christianity. Now, more than a century later, the bearer of that same title will give the missionary a Christian burial.

I pack my things and arrange a taxi to the airstrip for the return flight to Viti Levu.

So that's the story of the Rev. Cross. But what happened to the old king? Rev. Williams provides a chilling and detailed firsthand account; put simply, the old king grew feeble and was buried alive, and a number of his wives were strangled and buried with him. Moreover, the scourge of the father was visited upon the son, Tuikilakila, now the Tui Cakau, who was also the real ruler of Somosomo even when his father was alive. Rev. Calvert writes this on page 50 of Volume II:

> *There seemed to be some encouraging signs in the case of Tuithakau; but at heart he hated the Christians still, and allowed and encouraged his sons to persecute such of them as lived on islands, near Lakemba, subject to him...In the meantime, the King found himself in trouble at home. Being often reproved, he had hardened his neck, and one night in February, 1854, he was murdered while asleep on his mat, at the instigation, if not by the hand, of his own son. That son was also killed, to revenge the father's death, by his brother, who himself was soon assassinated. Then the town of Somosomo, where the Missionaries had laboured so long, and where that people of proud wickedness had despised their word, soon became utterly deserted. Civil war, in which brother was set against brother, cousin against cousin, in deadly defiance, made the land desolate, and many fell.*

I board the tiny *Fiji Air* plane. We taxi down the gravel runway and make our ascent over top the coconut trees of the "Garden Isle". The aircraft circles and follows the coast for a short distance alongside the village of Somosomo. We head out over the deep blue ocean, southward, toward the islands of Lomaiviti—Koro, Batiki, Nairai, Ngau, Ovalau…Lush jungle covers all traces of their sordid past, too. As we pass along the eastern shore of the main island, Viti Levu, we skim over the tiny island of Mbau. I now know the darkest chapter of Fiji's cannibalistic past. But to learn how cannibalism finally came to an end in Fiji, one needs to know what transpired on this powerful little island.

The mission history of Somosomo comprises only 18 pages of Volume II. But the chapter dedicated to Mbau and the nearby island of Viwa is 127 pages long. This gives some indication of the importance of Mbau to the missionary endeavour as well as the enormity of the task they faced. Mbau was—and still is—the chiefly island of Fiji, and until the missionaries could make inroads here, their work in the rest of the island groups would have only marginal success. And progress was not forthcoming, in large measure because of the young Chief Cakobau (Thakombau), the real power behind the throne. Rev. Cross had first gone to Mbau in January of 1838. And now it is January of 1850—twelve years later. Volume II, page 299:

> *As yet, every effort to establish a Station on Mbau had failed. The place was frequently visited, and Thakombau had promised to build a Mission-house, confessing that Christianity was true, and would become universal in Fiji; but he must wait until peace was established by the conquest of his enemies.*

Two more years passed and the missionaries pressed on. Then, in December of 1852, a long awaited and much dreaded event approached as the old King Tanoa grew feeble and was nearing death. Fijian custom demanded that many of the wives of so powerful a king should be strangled. In that there was no mission station on Mbau, it fell to the missionaries Watsford and Calvert stationed on the nearby island of Viwa to plead for the lives of Tanoa's wives. As the old King grew more feeble, the missionaries became more earnest in their pleadings, not only warning of the enormity of the crime, but offering, among other things, the highly prized traditional wealth of whales' teeth. Calvert, following Fijian custom, even offered to have a finger cut off, if the lives of the women might be spared. Volume II, page 321:

> On the 6th of December, Mr. Calvert was called away to Ovalau, by intelligence of sickness in the Mission family there. The next day Mr. Watsford went to Mbau alone, and found all the women in the King's house weeping. The selected victims were pointed out with their friends weeping over them…Passing into the principal house, he was still more shocked to see Thakombau's wife and some more women preparing the dresses for the others to wear on the day of their death, whereby he knew that some were to be sacrificed. Mr. Watsford went at once to the young King, and found him among his assembled Chiefs, where, once more, the solemn warnings were faithfully spoken; but in vain. The Missionary then returned to Viwa, but soon crossed over again to Mbau, where he remained till midnight, trying to save the women. Before leaving, he backed his last appeal by offering the new whale-boat belonging to the Mission, twenty muskets, and all his personal property; but still in vain. Early next morning, he went back to Mbau, and found that Tanoa was dead. Hastening on to the house where he lay, Mr. Watsford saw six biers standing at the door, from which he knew that five victims, at least, were to accompany their lord to the grave.

I am enthralled by the account of what happened next.

> Within the house, the work of death was begun. One woman was already strangled, and the second was kneeling with covered head, while several men on either side were just pulling the cord which wound round her neck, when the Missionary stood on the threshold, heartsick and faint at the ghastly sight. Soon the woman fell dead…The third was now called for, when Thakombau caught

sight of the Missionary, and, trembling with fear, looked at him in agony and cried out, "What about it, Mr. Watsford?" Mr. Watsford, with great difficulty, answered, "Refrain, Sir! That is plenty. Two are dead. Refrain; — I love them!" The Chief replied, "We also love them. They are not many, — only five. But for you Missionaries, many more would have been strangled." Just then the third victim approached, who had offered to die instead of her sister, who had a son living. She had sat impatiently; and, on hearing her name, started up instantly. She was a fine woman, of high rank, and wore a new liku. Looking proudly round ... she pranced up to the place of death, offering her hand to Mr. Watsford, who shrunk back in disgust. When about to kneel, she saw that they were going to use a shabby cord, and haughtily refused to be strangled, except with a new cord. All this time the assembly gazed at her with delight, gently clapping their hands, and expressing, in subdued exclamations, their admiration of her beauty and pride. She then bid her relatives farewell, and knelt down, with her arms round one of her friends. The cord was adjusted, and the large covering thrown over her; and while the men strained the cord, a lady of rank pressed down the head of the poor wretch, who died without a sound or struggle.

I guess they found a new cord....

Five women were strangled in this manner to honour the Vunivalu, Chief of Mbau and to accompany him to another world. Tanoa had had an unusually long life, and through all of it, he had remained a determined and unchanged cannibal.

Tanoa's son Cakobau (Thakombau) now succeeded to the title of *Vunivalu*, although he had been supreme for years. For some time he had been styled *Tui Viti* (King of Fiji), a distinction which, though really unfounded, he and his people worked to advantage.

The investiture, attended by Tuikilakila of Somosomo and his retinue, called for an elaborate cannibal feast, the victims being held in the Lasakau (Fishermen's) quarter of the island. Once again, the missionaries tried to intervene. Page 327:

> *As the Missionary approached the great temple a dead stillness rested upon Mbau, which was suddenly broken by a loud shout, proclaiming that Thakombau had just drunk the yaqona (kava) of the Vunivalu, during the preparation of which none were allowed to move about. Another shout from the Lasakau quarter made known that the bodies were being dragged; and soon the horrible procession came up—the dead and the dying, dragged along by their hands, naked, with their heads rattling and grating over the rough ground. As each approached the temple, the head was violently dashed against a great stone, which became stained with blood.*

I saw that stone when I visited Mbau a few years ago. I went with Tau and another young man who lives there. We crossed from the "mainland" in a boat, and they took me on a tour of the tiny island. No temples now, of course, but a big church, neatly kept and situated prominently in the village. Inside the church, placed beside the baptismal font, is the "great stone", serving as a reminder, the young man told me, of the darkness in Fiji's past.

The missionaries pressed on. Eventually, one by one, the paramount chiefs succumbed and adopted Christianity—but not Cakobau; he stayed firm. Then he became quite ill, and, at the same time, heard about the assassination of Tuikilakila of Somosomo who had just visited him for his investiture. That was the final blow. A few days later, he made up his mind. The death drums were sounded. Ten days before, they called people together for a cannibal feast. Now it was a signal for his conversion to Christianity.

There were a few hundred people present. Cakobau stood before them with all his wives and children. It must have been difficult for him to stand in front of them ... the widows whose husbands he had slain, some of them husbands of his own sisters. Many who were present had relatives who were killed by his orders. Some of them had friends who the old King had eaten. And there were children there who were the descendants of those he had murdered.

"I have been a bad man," an emotional Cakobau said to his assembled countrymen. "I have scourged the earth." He dismissed all his wives save one. The couple was baptized and publicly married. The missionary, who had waited so long for this day, was so emotional he could scarcely conduct the service.

Now the way was open for all Fijians to convert to Christianity— and they did. But if the Fijians were delivered from their hell of cannibalism, widow strangling and the like, their mass conversion did not propel them to paradise. Like Pilgrim in Dante's *Divine Comedy*, the road from *Inferno* did not lead to *Paradiso* but took the hero to *Purgatoria*, a place of struggling toward the light. Now the Fijians find themselves at a similar threshold.

Fijians—even today—bear the imprint of their past as a collective disgrace. It is as though the darkness resides in the memory of the cells, inherited and passed on through the generations. The emotional residue lingers in the collective psyche, seemingly encoded in their DNA. Psychologically, they are still cannibals….

But is it just the Fijians? No, I am beginning to see that cannibalism—human beings, consuming and being consumed by their fellow human beings—is deeply ingrained in all of us. Just as assuredly as Cakobau had to die to his old ways, we, too, must travel that road. The question is how…

Part VI

LEAVING "PARADISE"

The Man on the Street

Tuesday, April 16th—There is one thing I have left to do before leaving Fiji: record a tape of Tau's Fijian music. Today I am with Tau in an all-day recording session at a studio just outside the city. We tape a number of songs, including *Lutu Na Yakavi* (Sunset) that appreciates the good things about life in the Fijian village. "At sunset," the lyrics say, "the old men collect together for kava drinking. Because they have neither kava nor the money to buy it, they bring a smile as offering."

Once the musicians and engineers get into position—they are about three hours late—the taping begins. *Vuravura au Dau Vakaloloma* (The Fate of the Earth) ... about people looking for peace outside rather than within, expecting someone or something else to deliver it to them. *Vaka Na Tadra Wale Ga* (Just Like a Dream): "Don't waste your time living in the past; haven't you noticed it is always now?"

This tape of Fijian music is the second one I have recorded with Tau. The first one we did two years ago, when I returned to Fiji on a post-doctoral fellowship. I was trying to get an analytical perspective from Tau on a particular subject and could not get him to think critically about it. Matter of fact, I couldn't get him to think critically about anything. Critical analysis is not a Fijian thing to do. In fact, there isn't even a word for "analyze" in the Fijian language. The term that most closely approximates it is *vakasama*, which is taken to mean both "to think" and "to feel".

Not ready to give up, I asked Tau to write a song on the subject and sing it to me. He is a fine guitar player and has a lovely singing voice. He wrote the song; it was good. Then he wrote another and another … song after song, with deep penetrating ideas that seemed to be inaccessible to him through the medium of rational discourse. We took to singing the compositions together in the evenings when the day's research was done. That's how the songs came into being. But how we came to record them is the interesting part.

There is a man who lives on the street in Suva. He is one of the most frightened people I have ever met. People shun him, and there are those who deride him. I don't know why—perhaps because he is such an easy target. He never retaliates, nor does he ask help from anyone. He pays his way by collecting and selling bottles, and he rests content with what he can salvage.

I saw him often the year I lived in Suva, as he canvassed the garbage bins of the city in his silent world. I determined, with Tau's help, to befriend him. It was difficult at first even to get near to him; he would cower whenever we approached. We gently persisted, with a *"Bula"* (Hello) and an extended hand in which we held out a bit of pocket money. He would accept it, with that chilling look of fear on his face. We would smile at him and continue on.

We kept this up, month after month, until eventually we were able to engage this man in small bits of conversation. Then one day he smiled when he saw us approaching. It was truly exciting.

Some weeks later, while Tau and I were having lunch at my flat in the city, we were listening to a homemade recording of Tau's songs we had sung together. There was a knock on the door, and to our amazement, it was this man from the street. He must have followed us to know where I was living, and he had now mustered enough courage to come to the door and ask for empty bottles. We gave him some. He smiled and turned to leave. Then he stopped.

"That is nice music. It should be on the radio," he said. Then he left. It was so unlike the man even to approach someone let alone speak his mind. He was like a messenger, so Tau and I took the tape to the Fiji Broadcasting Centre. FBC steered us to a recording studio and the music immediately blossomed into a professional tape.

From that time on, Tau's iconoclastic music has been daily "on the radio"—music that flies in the face of the church and the chiefly system … like *Lotu Dina* (True Christian). "When the church bell rings," the lyrics say, "the 'true Christians' come running. Men, with their neckties blowing in the wind; women, all dressed up and smelling of powdered perfume. All the while their poor brothers and sisters are praying on the street, 'Please, Lord, help me' …"

And *Tuberi Ira Na Gone* (Teach the Children). "Teach them to think freely," the song says, "so they will be able to thrive. Otherwise they will grow up to be followers, and will contribute to their own demise."

Through the medium of music, Tau managed to transcend the cultural idiom and embrace the contemplative life, like these lyrics from *Fulusiviti* (Full Speed): "They tell me to rush or life will pass me by. The place, the people, everything is telling me 'Go full speed'. But where will this rushing take me? The world will always be here long after you and I are gone. Look at the lilies of the field, the rivers flowing slowly, the green trees, and the birds flying overhead. None of them ever says, 'Come on, let's hurry'."

We leave the studio about 5 o'clock in the afternoon. There is a bit of graffiti scrawled on the exterior wall of the building; it reads: "Trespassers will be eaten!" There is that bitter edge to humour again.

Say it with Words

Wednesday, April 17th— Today I confirm my return flight to Canada and make arrangements with *Air Pacific* to connect to the *CP Air* flight in Nadi. A marked sadness comes over me whenever I think of leaving this island nation that is such a paradox to me.

I do some shopping for items that Tau will take back to the children in the village when he returns. Interesting, when I asked the children what they wanted, they listed very practical items: pencils, pens, erasers, rulers, pencil sharpeners, and exercise books. Then again, they have little experience of anything else.

They also asked for shoes because, they say, the concrete on the floor of their classrooms is cold in the early mornings. Before leaving the village, I took some paper and traced the sizes of their feet. Now I go to a shoe store run by a lovely Indian man whom I have come to know over the years; we match the paper drawings to his stock of children's shoes.

Tau is with me. I notice that these two men religiously call each other "brother". It's very common to see indigenous Fijians and Indians address each other this way. For the Melanesian Fijian, "brother" is connected to the respect/ avoidance relationship—and it may well be for the Fijian Indian too, for the respect/avoidance relationship is at best a compromise solution for accepting one's position of inferiority. Both sides have reason to feel the underdog: the Fijian Indians, who end up without rights to land, and the indigenous Fijians, who score low on the economic ladder.

Something has got to give!

Say it with Music

Thursday, April 18th—Today Tau and I have a meeting at the recording studio regarding the engineering of our tape and the design of the cover. For the title of the tape, Tau chooses a love song we recorded yesterday. It is called *Noqu Tadra* (My Dream).

It's a wish for an unknown time,
A dream that I hope will come true
Listen to the need of my heart
Let me share my life with you....

The one thing he really wants and cannot have, for I cannot stay here with him. I cherish him and his kin and the natural beauty in his tropical paradise, but I am irrevocably European. Nor can I take him with me; he belongs to these South Sea islands with their green hills and glistening reefs.

Say Good-bye

Friday, April 19th—Tau and I pack up our things and head to the downtown terminal to get a bus to the airport. I am flying to Nadi to connect to my flight to Vancouver; Tau is returning to Ngau about the same time. We wait here, along with a number of other passengers. We wait a long time, but the airport bus does not show up. The timing gets really tight and we cannot wait any longer. We flag down, then pile into two taxis—all twelve of us—alongside numerous suitcases, cartons, bags, boxes and two guitars, and speed to the airport.

We pull up and stop in front of the departure area. There are some people from Ngau there, sending cartons to the island. They grab my bags and usher me to the *Air Pacific* counter. My flight has already boarded! Tau heads for the *Fiji Air* counter to check in for his flight. I am quickly processed and rushed to the waiting aircraft. There is not even time to say good-bye.

Aboard the *Air Pacific* turbo-prop, I fasten my seat belt and peer out the window as the engines engage. I see the little *Fiji Air* plane boarding for Ngau. There is Tau, my loyal research assistant and dearest friend, now returning to the village alone. Part of me longs to be there with him. As we push away from the terminal, that part of me cries.

At the Nadi International Airport, I am alone now. I check my bags for the *CP Air* flight to Vancouver and proceed to the departure lounge. The young Immigration officer stamps my passport.

"Did you have a good time?" he asks me. I don't know how to answer. He asks if I will be coming back someday.

"Of course I will be coming back," I respond. But how could he know ....

It's a long wait in the departure lounge. They are showing videos about Fiji—the sort of thing they think a visitor should or would like to know about this island nation. The Ministry of Information produces the videos and they showcase Fiji's landscape, history and cultural diversity. I've spent many hours in this departure lounge over the years, most of them waiting to board this same flight to Vancouver. The thing that intrigues me once again about this "info-tainment" is the emphasis given to the traditional inherited leadership. We see, again and again, footage of paramount chiefs and, of course, the highly venerated members of the British royal family. The illusion is solid ... not a trace of insight into the inequality of inherited wealth and privilege.

Now there is a new video, one I haven't seen before. It's called "A New Generation of Power". Could it possibly be about the need to transform the present cultural institutions? About the inequalities that exist within and between the two major ethnic groups in Fiji? About the kind of social and political changes that are going to be necessary if Fiji is to avoid an ethnic showdown?

Not at all! It's about a multi-million dollar hydroelectric power project. Any new generation of power—apart from the hydroelectric variety—is likely to bring more of the same, and woe unto them who try to change it.

The chiefs shall rule in Fiji!

I board the *CP Air* jumbo jet bound for Vancouver. As I buckle my seat belt, I see Rev. and Mrs. Vale walking down the opposite aisle. What a coincidence that I should see them here. They are missionaries from Europe who were sent to Fiji to help the Methodist Church determine its direction for the future. Their three-year assignment has now come to an end.

I first met the Vales on their way to the Fiji Islands. They traveled through Vancouver en route, and had contacted me since I had recently completed a doctoral dissertation on Christianization and development in Fiji. The dissertation was not yet bound so I gave them a loose-leaf copy of the 400-plus-page document to help them in their new endeavour.

The Boeing 747 takes off. Comfortably in flight, I make my way to the rear of the aircraft to say hello to the Vales and to see their final report. Like the dissertation, this report is also unbound. They offer to let me read it—all 100-plus pages of loose-leaf copy. I take it and return to my seat, eager to learn firsthand where the Methodist Church of Fiji will head in the upcoming decades.

I guess I shouldn't have been surprised that a lot of attention in the report is directed to administrative issues, especially the compilation of statistics. I learn that only 7% of all Melanesian Fijians are actually members of the church. This has never seemed to be a concern for the Fijians; they show up anyway—three times every Sunday! However, it seems that the institutionalized Methodist Church would like them to be a bit more "confirmed".

I want to know what the report says about psychological and spiritual issues underlying the economic, social and political inequalities. I read on with anticipation. It mentions unemployment, increase in crime, even radiation from nuclear testing in the Pacific, but I cannot find any corresponding ideas about how the Church sees itself involved in these cultural matters. Indeed, there is one statement that seems to encapsulate the whole paradox of the study. It reads,

"The church should just be involved in social action and have nothing to do with politics." As though you can have one without the other!

The bottom line is that the report is about "the surface drama"— the organization of the church, the social issues and economic trials— while "the truly significant drama" playing out in the depths below goes completely missing. And the drama is this: bounded by culture, the Fijians live out their lives as "persons"—the way psychologist Carl Jung uses the term. "Person", he says, is nothing real; it is a compromise between individual and society as to what a man should appear to be. Indeed, person derives from *persona*, the name given to the mask worn by an actor to indicate the role s/he is playing.

If the Fijian is to "strip away the mask" and enter into the ongoing process of individuality, it will require an enormous psychological and cultural shift, for widened consciousness and self-awareness are stages beyond where the *persona* can go. That it is a risky venture is recognized well enough. In Biblical scripture, it is represented as the deadly sin that brings about the fall of man. It's there in Genesis 2:17: eating from the tree of knowledge of good and evil becomes the taboo infringement for which man (sic) is expelled from paradise. If the Fijian is likewise to rob the gods and the traditional order of their mysterious powers, the paradise of his collective psyche goes as well.

And go it must! For, as psychoanalyst Eric Fromm states, the concept of mental health is characterized by the emergence from incestuous ties to clan and soil, and by a sense of identity based on one's experience of self as subject and agent of one's own powers.

Bound to blood and soil, the Fijian is restrained from developing widened consciousness. The traditional culture discourages it in any case, for institutionalized personality is so vital to the social order that anything likely to disturb it is seen as a danger. Fijian culture safeguards itself through the ascribed relationships of respect and avoidance, joking and deference...It requires alliance to the clan, obedience to the chiefs, and fear of the gods. A difficult chain to break, but break it they must in order to get from clan alliance to self-reliance, from chiefly obedience to independent thinking, and from fear of God to love of fellow human beings.

The chain won't break easily. Collective thinking and feeling are far less a strain than individual functioning and effort. There will remain that temptation to allow collective functioning to take the place of individuation. It masks as the paradise of the collective psyche, but it contains the seeds of its own destruction.

I return the report to the Vales. We exchange pleasantries and I go back to my seat. The jumbo jet makes its way toward Honolulu. We are somewhere between the equator and the international dateline, that marginal space and time where I picked up my pen a few weeks ago.

Time to put it down again … for now.

BOOK II

A Coup in Paradise

June, 1987

Part I

A DIFFERENT WORLD

The More Things Change

Sunday, June 7th—Some illusions never change ... like the equator and the international dateline ... all those meridians that carve the world into little sections. It is now two years since I left the Fiji Islands, and I am a few kilometers above the earth, jetting toward a destination of 20 degrees latitude, 180 degrees longitude on this fragmented little planet.

Other illusions do change. *CP Air* has become *Canadian Airlines International*. It seems they have been bought out and don't get to keep the name. Interesting, this new title, because "Canadian International Airlines" has a better ring to it. But then they would inherit the initials "CIA"—and that tends to strike an uneasy cord in people.

And another grand illusion has been shattered—that of a tropical paradise inhabited by noble savages, a culture out there in the middle of the South Pacific that is somehow free from the violence that ravages every other part of our confused world. Three weeks ago, the 6 o'clock World News jarred that North American fantasy. "It seems no place on the planet is safe anymore," stated the anchorman of a major American television network. "Today there was even a coup in paradise."

It happened on Thursday, May 14th, just after 10 o'clock in the morning. Lieutenant-Colonel Sitiveni Rabuka led ten soldiers of the Royal Fiji Military Forces into the parliament chamber of

119

the Government Building in Suva. There, fifty-two duly elected parliamentarians were sitting in the House of Representatives listening to an address by a conservative opposition member. Ironically, he was speaking about the conversion of the Fijian people to Christianity in the late 19th century. "Peace and harmony is the governing principle on which Fijians have been running their lives ever since," he was saying. "This is in contrast to what Mao Tse-tung believed, that political power comes out of the barrel of a gun." At that moment, Colonel Rabuka, dressed in civilian attire while his uniformed accomplices smarted pistols and gas masks walked across the floor of the chamber to the speaker's chair. He boldly stated his purpose: "This is a military takeover; stay down and remain calm."

So ended a post-colonial experiment in democratic government— and just when it looked as though Britain could walk away from this one with clean hands: a gracious ceding of a piece of the Empire with on-going ties to the Crown, along with membership in the British Commonwealth of Nations. Elizabeth—with her handbag—would still be the Paramount Chief of Fiji, with an indigenous high-ranking local chief as her Governor-General. It was all too perfect.

Except for one thing.

The Indians. Those loyal subjects lured from "The Jewel in the Crown" to make yet another British colony pay its way. Willingly they boarded the ships bound for what at least some of them had been told was an island in the Bay of Bengal. Weeks later, they arrived in Fiji as indentured labourers, to convert their human energy into the lifeblood of the sugar cane industry. And when their period of indenture was over, most of them stayed on, painstakingly creating for themselves and their descendants something better than the conditions that had made leaving India an easy choice.

By the time 1970 rolled around and Prince Charlie arrived in Fiji with the papers, the stage was set for a showdown. The Indian population, by this time firmly entrenched in the commerce and industry of the country, now outnumbered the *i taukei* (indigenous Fijians) who had their grip on political power and a privileged ownership of the land. There they were, a majority with economic supremacy and inferior rights alongside a minority with political supremacy and inferior means. Partners now in the subtle art of nationhood....

A great way to start a country!

It's well after midnight and we're all pretty tired but the airline attendants serve us what they describe as "a substantial snack" and encourage us to eat it. The reason given is that "due to the situation in Fiji", they are not servicing the aircraft in Nadi and, therefore, cannot pick up a breakfast meal. Most of the passengers are continuing on to New Zealand. So we eat—mine is vegetarian, which, in this case, is fresh fruit—and I settle in once again for the unrealized promise of sleep.

We arrive right on schedule: 4:10 a.m. I am one of only a few passengers getting off here. I disembark and proceed to Immigration. The official matches the information in my passport with that on the landing card and motions me on. Customs—no check at all—and then through the doors that take me once again into the Fiji night.

Tau ... he came. He's standing there—right in his usual spot. He doesn't see me yet. I fix my gaze on him to make eye contact. Now he sees me—but he doesn't move. I walk over and very gently put my arms around him. He grins.

Tau's sister is married to a man from this part of Fiji, and the two of them with their children live in a village just outside Nadi town. His sister is expecting another child, and Nana, her mother, has come over from Ngau. Nana will be staying with her daughter until the baby arrives. We take a taxi to the village. Nana is very surprised to see me; she didn't know I was coming.

"*Luvequ! Luvequ!* (My daughter! My daughter!)" Nana cries, and she hugs and kisses me.

It is interesting to meet her in what is now one of the trouble spots of the world because when I went to her village to say good-bye to her after my fieldwork was completed a few years ago, she said, "No, don't go; you'll get killed in the war!" Violence: that is what she thought the rest of the world was about. And for good reason: her only information on life outside Fiji was a brief nightly bulletin of world news—and the news was often about violence. Now the violence is here.

We visit for a short while. Nana sits beside me on the mat smoking her hand-rolled cigarettes. She tells us she dreamed about Tau last night so thought he might be coming soon. Tau's sister smiles as she makes tea and cuts pineapple. Her little son is sitting beside her. On the radio, the usual Sunday hymns are playing. It's like nothing has changed.

But a lot has changed. The duly elected government of Indo-Fijian Dr. Timoci Bavadra, in power for only a few weeks, was terminated at gunpoint. The Prime Minister, his eleven Cabinet Ministers and sixteen Members of Parliament were arrested. The Constitution was suspended, along with the army commander, the army Chief of Staff, the Police Commissioner and his deputy. The reason? Colonel Rabuka described his actions as a "pre-emptive" measure to avoid violence arising from Fijian opposition to the newly elected Indian-dominated government. The chiefs will rule in Fiji!

I would like to get to Suva today but there aren't enough tourists for the hotel coach anymore, so back I go with Tau to the airport and arrange to make the three-hour journey in a van. There are five of us—only one other a visitor, who goes as far as a hostel on the Coral Coast. The others are ethnic Fijians. We pass by major resorts along the way and it's the same story: they are all next to empty—and they are usually at capacity this time of year. We stop at the Hideaway Resort for lunch. I have some fresh tropical fruit in the midst of splendid South Sea island surrounding— literally a hideaway this time.

Suva … with its grey hills that stretch mysteriously into a blue distance. It's looking even quieter than it usually does on a Sunday. I settle into the hotel, we get some lunch and take a walk along the seawall. Then tonight, we go for dinner at our favourite restaurant. Scallops with ginger and green onion, chicken with green peppers in black bean sauce, some local beer and a bowl of steamed rice. All this for $10 … and almost no one around to enjoy it.

"Wonderfully Silent"

Monday, June 8th—I take an early morning walk with Tau to watch the city come to life. Fijians and Indians are setting up their stalls in the public market and making their way to offices and shops along the downtown streets. They are mingling together as always, and they are still addressing each other as "brother". Whether or not they adopt the kinship meaning of the term with its avoidance/respect restriction in Fijian society is uncertain, but it is an appropriate mask for resentment nevertheless.

And resentment there is. One week into the coup, when a crowd of about one hundred Indians gathered outside the Government Buildings for prayer and a protest meeting, they were attacked by an equal number of Fijian men. Then twice as many indigenous Fijians marched along Suva's main street, striking Indian vendors, and destroying their stalls in the public market. About thirty Indians were badly injured and admitted to hospital. That was less than three weeks ago.

To the indigenous Fijians, constrained within the social order, the world has come to be perceived as hostile and threatening. They feel the hostility—it is a part of them—but they deny its source and, instead, project that source onto someone or something else. In this case, it is the Indo-Fijians, and so they attack. The Indians have become their scapegoat. And so the surface dramas play on—while the truly significant drama is playing out silently in the depths below: frustration and repression leading, as it must, to projection and attack.

After a lunch of taro and leafy vegetables, I telephone my mother in Canada to assure her that it is safe to be here. She's not entirely convinced, I can tell, but she knows she doesn't have a choice. She speaks with Tau. She asks him to take care of me; he says he will.

I leave the city centre and spend a quiet afternoon reading on the patio of the hotel. It is a lovely setting, in the midst of a garden of pink and yellow hibiscus flowers, sweet-smelling frangipani and tall coconut palms.

When night creeps into the air, Tau and I opt to have our dinner here. "The night is wonderfully silent," wrote Somerset Maugham of this part of the world in 1916.

The stars shine with a fierce brilliancy, the Southern Cross and Canopus; there is not a breath of wind, but a wonderful balminess in the air. The coconut trees, silhouetted against the sky, seem to be listening.

Such natural beauty—and almost no one here to wonder at it!

Nine Critical Days

Tuesday, June 9th—Tau joins me for another early morning walk, this time along Victoria Parade and onward up to the Governor-General's residence, currently occupied by the *Tui Cakau*, paramount chief of Taveuni. It is a stately mansion in typical British colonial style and it crowns a spacious piece of prime real estate a short distance from the Government Buildings. The grounds are neatly manicured and the lane from the front gate to the portico is lined with ornamental palm trees.

On the day of the coup, Ratu Sir Penaia Ganilau issued a statement from this majestic setting in which he deplored Colonel Rabuka's actions, declaring a state of emergency and ordering the troops to return to their barracks. They didn't. Nevertheless, the Queen's representative in Fiji proclaimed himself to be Chief Executive.

That didn't stop Rabuka. The following day, *Radio Fiji* broadcast a statement in which the spunky coup leader named a Council of fifteen ministers with himself as chairman. Very confusing for the listening public because just one hour later the station broadcast a recording in which the Governor-General condemned the coup and announced that he had assumed control of the government. However, troops went immediately to the radio station and seized the tape. And just to be doubly sure that people were clear on who's the boss, Rabuka made a statement to the press later the same day claiming the military regime was in full control of the country.

That was day two of the coup. On day four, Rabuka was sworn in as head of the government by the same Governor-General ... until day five, when Ganilau issued another statement saying it was impossible for him to recognize the regime. Never mind: on day eight, Rabuka declared to an enthusiastic crowd, "We have won!" Only one day later, the Governor-General announced the appointment of a nineteen-member advisory Council to help him run the country until fresh elections could be held.

Those were nine critical days in May.

It is only now that I learn I had inadvertently played a part in the coup! It seems that when the coup leaders took over the Fiji Broadcasting System, one of our recorded songs was repeatedly played on the radio that first day. The song is called *Vuravura Au Dau Vakananuma*, (Thinking About the Fate of the Earth). "People say we're in trouble," state the lyrics, "Others say it is too late to do anything. Many are asking, 'When will there be peace?' The Church preaches that peace will come tomorrow. They are putting their faith in an empty dream." The thing is, neither Tau nor I can figure out whether the song was used by the coup leaders to reinforce their control, or by a resistant *Fiji Radio* disc jockey trying in a subtle manner to encourage a counter-coup. It could be read either way! So whom were we supporting?

The guard is still here at the front gate to the mansion. He stands at attention and routinely goes through a series of ritual motions even though there is no one around. He wears the traditional white pocket *sulu* with a red tunic, and he carries a rifle. A decorative touch, I used to think, but it takes on added significance now. For the Governor-General is calling at least some of the shots: the deposed Prime Minister has "gone to London to visit the Queen" but she, on the advice of her representative in Fiji, will not be receiving him.

One of the victims of the coup is air service to Ngau. Tau tells me the Ovalau ferry will leave for Koro and Ngau on Friday night. We decide to make the overnight trip, offering us a few more days for preparations and to enjoy amenities not available on the outer islands … like pizza and wine on the patio of the hotel.

"The night is wonderfully silent …"

Nei

Wednesday, June 10th—A day of calm in the city, and the relationship between ethnic Fijians and Indians is respectful, even warm. Tau and I spend the day in sundry activities in preparation for our trip to Ngau.

In the late afternoon, I go with Tau to Nairai to visit his auntie who has come to Suva for medical reasons. Nei is married to Tau's mother's brother and lives in Nana's village on Ngau. She has been here for a few weeks now and is staying with her married son and family in their subsidized housing unit outside the city centre. Like Raiwasa, where we visited two years ago, it is a densely populated area of poor Fijian city-dwellers. The units are tiny single room cubicles with a living room/sleeping space and a food preparation area; the shared toilet and shower area is adjacent. So many people—and so many small children—in such a congested area. It seems the perfect breeding ground for discontent … but I see no outward signs of it.

My arrival creates a minor stir. Europeans do not generally make an appearance in these parts. The children stare; the adults defer. Tau's cousin walks to the street to meet us and ushers us to the appropriate unit. Children follow and peer inside the doorway until they are instructed to leave. We sit down on the mat and present our *i sevusevu* (kava offering) along with gifts of food: six double loaves of whole meal bread—(they customarily eat white bread but I won't give it to them)—with plenty of butter and jam. It will get well used.

Nei is sitting on the mat resting against a pillow. She is a thin elderly lady with beautiful hands and long slender limbs. She still looks striking despite her weakness and weathered skin. She has been in hospital for some medical tests and is awaiting her surgery. Then she can return to her husband and family on the outer island.

Tau has a *vasu* relationship with this family, meaning that he can enter their house and take anything he wants—food, clothing, a cane knife, a radio…Appropriately enough, the joking relationship exists between cross cousins, minimizing the chances that this culturally sanctioned theft can lead to violence. If the mother belongs to a chiefly family, the *vasu* extends to the whole village. Our village lost some goats and a church bell that way. Both valuable items—and all we could do was laugh.

We have a nice visit. They invite us to stay for dinner and I suspect they may have prepared special food. But there are so many of them—and they have so little. It's different in the village where people have gardens; the Fijian city-dwellers must purchase all their food. We decide to take our leave and stop at a restaurant on the way back to the hotel.

Wanting to Stay, Wanting to Go

Thursday, June 11ᵗʰ—It is raining. After breakfast I go to the Immigration office to get my visitor's permit extended. There is a long line-up of males applying for passports. In fact, the line-ups have been so long since the coup that the office now closes its doors at noon each day in order to process the huge number of applications. While I fill out my forms and wait for the bureaucratic procedures to be completed, I gaze at the despondent faces of those quietly standing in the queue. No excitement, not even apparent anxiety … and all of them are Indians.

I'm granted my extension, and I leave the building by easing my way through the crowd. Here I am, wanting to stay, amid so many people wanting to go. But I have the comfort of a Canadian passport and an onward ticket to Australia while they must wait for bureaucracy and opportunity to grant them something better. That they are able to remain so pacific is remarkable.

I take up the rest of the day with preparations for an extended stay on Ngau. I shop for a new pair of flip-flops and rations of rye crackers, bran cereal and peanut butter ….

Part II

COMING "HOME"

Showers of Blessing

Friday, June 12ᵗʰ—I sleep in this morning in anticipation of our long overnight trip to the island tonight. Finally, at 9 p.m. Tau and I set out in a taxi for the pier at Walu Bay on the outskirts of Suva to board the *Ovalau* for the passage to Koro and Ngau. Our boarding time is 10 p.m. with sailing time an hour later. We arrive about 9:30. There are others here already and soon a number of chartered buses arrive. By 10 p.m. there are at least 250 people at the dock—but no ship! We wait. People greet each other, laugh and chat away. We continue to wait— 11 o'clock … midnight … 1 o'clock in the morning….

By this time it is raining. There are no shelters, no seating and no washrooms—just a gravel dockside. People gravitate to an umbrella or perch under the overhang of the roof from one of the locked warehouses—and they sing! "Showers of blessing, showers of blessing I see …" pours forth from their splendid voices, and then in beautiful four-part harmony, "One people, one nation; praise ye the Lord!" It's powerful in its stark spirituality. All the time, I hear no complaints, and sense no upset or anxiety. After a few false alarms— ships that appear out of the horizon then sail on by—we spot the *Ovalau* and up goes a big cheer. It ties up to the dock at 2:15 a.m.

The *Ovalau* fills quickly, and people stretch out on the benches to sleep—a good idea because it will be a long trip and we are already tired from many hours of waiting at the dockside. We set sail at 3 o'clock in the morning.

I find myself seated next to a young Indian girl in her early twenties named Madeline. She is very talkative and shares a great deal of her life with me in only a few short minutes. Next to her is seated a Fijian woman whom she tells me is her sister-in-law. It seems Madeline's brother has married a Fijian girl—marriages between Fijians and Indians are rare—and Madeline lives with them. She works as a nurse at a mission hospital as does her sister-in-law. They, along with 200 other nurses, are on their way to a conference on Koro Island.

Madeline tells me the solution to the political problem in Fiji is prayer. She is very religious and talks a lot about relationship as a healing factor in nursing. She is Anglican and informs me that some Catholic sisters will be leading sessions at the conference.

We chat on as the ship pitches and rolls. Her sister-in-law grows weary; she lays her head on Madeline's lap and falls asleep. A while later Madeline gets tired and, without request or reservation, lays her head on my lap and falls asleep.

It is quiet now, silence interrupted only by the rhythmic splash of water brushing against the windowpanes. All around me, people are sleeping. But sleep evades me; there is something about this moment that won't let me be. This dear Indian girl with her Fijian sister, their combined weight now pressing against me: if I cannot stay awake to hold them, they will both lose their balance and fall. It's like a symbolic plea, these silent human forms, for someone to resist the darkness, to stay conscious and keep together two vulnerable ethnic groups in one precarious nation. Is there the vision? The will? The time? A couple of hours later, Madeline is hopelessly seasick.

I watch the sun creep onto the horizon and paint the black water with glistening silver tones. A silhouette of the island of Ovalau arises into view. We sail on by. Dawn gives way to daylight and we pass through the tiny islands of Lomaiviti. At midday, we arrive at Koro Island.

Koro arises abruptly out of the sea. It is a pretty island with mangrove swamps at the shoreline and a few sandy beaches. It looks lush and tropical—and inviting. Almost all the passengers are disembarking here. When we near the dock, I awaken Madeline who by this time is weakened to the point of exhaustion. Her sister-in-law helps her from the vessel, and the last I see of them, they are walking arm-in-arm to a waiting lorry.

The Arrival

Saturday, June 13th—The passage from Koro to Ngau takes five more hours. We sail through the open waters passing alongside Batiki and Nairai, two small volcanic islands dotted with small villages. Not many people call these islands home. Soon thereafter, I spot majestic Ngau. I say "majestic" because it is tropical and green almost beyond description, and it rises out of the sea in the centre of a turquoise lagoon. The closer we get the more excited I feel, not only because it is such a breathtaking scene, but also—and primarily—because I am coming "home".

We dock at a point on the island about 20 kilometers from the village. The doors of the vessel swing open—and there they are, those familiar welcoming faces, waiting all these hours with a lorry to take us to the village. There's Mata and Rewa and Pita. It's just like old times. No questions … no reservations … just big smiles and vigorous handshakes. They grab my luggage and away we go.

Pita is driving the lorry. He's about 35 years old, and I especially want to talk to him because his wife has recently died of leukemia. She was the mother of six, the youngest only five months old at the time. I tell him I heard the news about Tila and that I am sad. He says nothing. He doesn't seem to know how to respond. It is as though there is no cultural instruction for dealing with death and loss once the mourning rituals have taken place. I shake his hand again and pat him on the back. His face, bearded now to announce his widowed status, shifts into a shallow grin. There he stands, strong and handsome, with the physique of an Olympic athlete, but at this moment fragile as an abandoned child. It is too soon to talk about it—and too late to cry.

I get in the back of the lorry amidst cartons, crates, food and Fijians and we set out for the village. It's so wonderful that I find myself laughing. The others pick up my mood and return the sentiment. Not that I haven't been through all this before—but just to be back on this island and to be with these people again, it's exhilarating.

Once in the village the scene is familiar. People, especially children, gather around the lorry to see who and what has arrived. There is the usual round of handshakes, and the children lean their faces forward to get their kisses. Without hesitation, they pick up my bags and head in the direction of my little house. Here we go again…

Inside the house, Mili has already set out the mats in preparation for my coming. Little Mili … she is twelve years old now. I've known her since she was three. I was doing my fieldwork here at the time. One day she simply arrived with her blanket and moved into my little grass hut with me. She stayed for about three months until one day her mother came and took her home. I cannot get a sense that children miss not being with their mothers, but then again, in this extended family system, they have many mothers and they appear equally at home with all of them.

It makes for a wondrous sense of security, this extended family system. On an earlier visit to Fiji, I took Mili to Suva. It was the first time she had been off the outer island and the world of electricity and refrigeration was amazingly strange to her, like when she tasted ice cream for the first time and exclaimed, "Oh, it's cold!" I took her to see her first movie. The film was the hit musical "Annie". To put the story in context, I explained that Annie was in an orphanage because she did not have a mother or a father.

"Then why doesn't she just go to her village?" Mili replied without hesitation.

I've seen most of the villagers by this time and I'm really looking forward to seeing Mili—but she's nowhere about. This puzzles me a bit because she has made such preparation for my coming. I inquire and find that she has gone fishing. It seems she waited here all afternoon but the *Ovalau* was so many hours behind schedule that work could wait no longer. That is another thing about village life. Children from quite a young age take part in the daily routine alongside adults—and there are few exceptions made. When she finally arrives back, wet and happy, it is a joyous reunion.

Dinner time: *ika vakalolo* (fish cooked in coconut milk) and yams. Tau isn't all that excited about it but it tastes wonderful to me. After food and conversation, I'm longing for sleep. It's too cool and I'm too tired to have a bath at the water pipe. I light the kerosene lamp, make a little bed on the sleeping mat and drift into sleep.

Life-Giving Food

Sunday, June 14th—Siga Tabu—Sunday. I even think about not going to church because I find it so out of place here to the point of being exploitative and oppressive. However, I know it has a lot of meaning to the people and it is at church that their fellowship is expressed in scripture and in song. After a breakfast of yams, lemon tea and cassava fritters, I have a bath, don my Fijian dress and make for the church building.

The service is boring as usual. The sermon is much too long and it has so little cerebral quality, but the singing is magnificent, and it is wonderful to be here with everyone. They still have that annoying and embarrassing practice of calling out the amount each family contributes at offering time. In fact, the church committee has now set the figure of 70 cents so it's more like a tax than an offering— and the church building is still the grandest structure in the village. They've even hooked up electric lights in here by means of a portable generator. I don't know why because they don't have services at night. I'm sure if their Jisu Karisito could see this he would throw up—and if these people were to encounter him, they would probably dismiss him as an aimless hippie.

Sunday dinner: the most special meal of the week. There is fish, baked taro and yam. Delicious, and I encounter the lovely custom of food exchange again. Today at breakfast and now at midday, people send special dishes to the house where I am eating. It is customary to do this the first Sunday after a visitor has arrived in the village. This morning, it was cassava cakes, and now, fish dishes and prepared root crops. Usually a small child brings it, and the hostess sends back something from our meal as a gift in exchange. It creates a lovely warm feeling and it binds the community together. Indeed, food nourishes in more ways than one.

In the afternoon, I go with Tau for a walk along the beach and then up to Tila's grave. Two months after the event, the tapa cloth still covers the spot where her body was interred. It is torn and faded now, but it still declares that death has claimed a recent victim. Underneath it, the earth is settling down again, gradually consuming the remnants of what was not long before a vibrant woman…Whatever it is that breathes life into us, it has ceased to be generous to Tila, and it will cut each of us off in its own time.

Happy Holiday

Monday, June 15th—It's a holiday today. I ask Mili why and she tells me it's the Queen's birthday.

"Silly queen stuff," I say.

"Don't say that," she replies.

"Why not?"

"Because she's the Queen."

I laugh. Mili looks puzzled, even shocked, then adds, "Don't you like the Queen?" I explain that it has nothing to do with not liking the Queen, that I'm sure she's a very nice lady. It's the idea of regarding some people as more important than others that I do not accept.

"Oh," she replies. And that is that.

After morning tea, I go with Tau to the bush to clear a spot for a vegetable garden. We have brought seeds with us from Suva: tomato, lettuce, cabbage, carrots, cucumber, green pepper, and green beans—vegetables that can be eaten raw. It's not part of the cuisine here despite the fact that these kinds of foods grow quickly and easily in this tropical climate. The standard diet is sadly lacking in roughage.

Clearing the land is difficult. The jungle is dense with leaves and vines and I'm not used to swinging a cane knife. We get the job done but not without a few blisters. I'm glad for a break of fresh oranges and a cool bath under the water pipe when we get back to the village. Then I retreat to a palm frond shelter and have my own kind of holiday … some time alone, with a good book.

The Coffin

Tuesday, June 16th—In the early morning Tau and I walk up to his mother's village so he can get a new blade for his cane knife. Since Nana is in Nadi with Tau's sister, we go to his Uncle Momo's house. Tau is very fond of these relatives. Aside from Momo—his mother's brother—who is quite elderly now, there is his auntie, Nei, currently in Suva for medical treatment, and their sons and daughters, all of whom are married, apart from the youngest son.

I've been coming to this home for years now. I've taken food here, rested here. I feel a real sense of kinship with this family and I like being with them. But there is one thing I have always found disconcerting: the presence of a coffin resting on the upper crossbeams inside their house. I remember the first time I saw it. It was some years ago now, when, after a meal, I was invited to rest awhile. So I stretched out on the mat and let my eyes gaze upward—and there it was, the coffin, balancing on the poles directly above my head. I think I was very, very silent. When I left their home that day, I asked Tau what that coffin was doing there. He said it was for the old woman who lives in that house.

"Where is she now?" I asked him.

"Oh, she's out fishing," he replied.

Years passed, and the old lady went right on living. Then finally, just last year, I received a letter from Tau saying she had died. I thought how pleasant it will be to visit this family without having to look at that coffin anymore. Now here we are once again in this same sleeping house. We have breakfast —*ika vakalolo* and cassava. Then I rest, my eyes gazing upward, and there is another coffin right in the same spot. After we leave, I ask Tau whose coffin *this* is. He says it's for his uncle. I inquire if it perhaps disturbs the dear man to have his coffin right in his house where he must sit under it by day and stare up at it at night. He answers no, that the old man is 78 years of age and knows he will soon die, and that it's a good idea to have his coffin ready.

Coming of Age

Wednesday, June 17th—This morning Mili was arguing with her little brother, which is most unlike her. Then before she left for school, she burst into tears. She got very little comfort, just *"Kua dula* (Don't cry)". I gave her a hug and comforted her as best I could. After she left for school, I asked Sai if Mili has started her menstrual periods. She said yes, that on Friday she left for school, but came back frightened.

I guess no one had prepared her for it. So when Mili returned from school today, I talked to her about it, using the Fijian expression *"mate ni vula* (monthly sickness)"* as do the women here. But Mili did not know what I was talking about. I tried to explain, and used the phrase *"na dra* (the blood)"*.

"Io, period! (Yes, period!)"*, she replied, using the English rather than the Fijian word, so she must have been told about it in school. As I talked to her about it, she showed great interest and no embarrassment or shyness whatsoever. Yet sometimes if I ask her a simple question about what she thinks or how she feels about something, she can remain completely silent. I guess she has no cultural instruction to express her thoughts and feelings, that it's not a part of her coming of age.

I spend some time today cleaning up my little house to make it more attractive and comfortable, and I reflect on my visit to Momo's sleeping house yesterday. I am intrigued by the ease with which Fijians seem to accept death. It would appear that they have achieved a yogic-like state where you "die before you die". Yet that hardly seems to be the case as Fijians are "culture bound" in the *persona*, and there is scant room inside the social system to get beyond it. But there must be some entranceway into the "gap" for them, some way to experience that space where the cultural mind is quieted and the chatter subsides. There must be a real coming of age…

"No, Thank-You"

Thursday, June 18th—Given the cultural constraints within which these villagers conduct their lives, there is something strangely disconcerting about waking up in the morning with the full knowledge that I can choose whatever I want to do with my day. I almost feel as though I should be asking their permission, for they tell everyone where they are going. And when they return, someone is bound to ask, *"Lesu mai vei"* (Where have you been?)".

When I first came to this village to do my fieldwork, the men would return from the gardens and say something to me about drinking kava. I understood very little of the language, so would politely smile and say "No, thank you" in Fijian. After witnessing this a few times, Tau gently explained to me, "Pamela, they are not inviting you to drink kava with them. They are just telling you that is what they are going to do."

Tonight, the men bring over the big *tanoa* (kava bowl) and, without asking, set up their kava party on my veranda. No, thank you? Once again, it would be an entirely irrelevant response!

Body Language

Friday, June 19th—Today there will be a *sogo* (feast) in the village because the head teacher of the district school is leaving the island to take up an administrative post in Suva. He has been in the capital for the past while, and is returning today to collect his family and household belongings; they will be sailing out tomorrow. Today the villagers put aside their regular tasks and make preparations for the feast.

In the early afternoon, people begin to arrive from the neighbouring two villages served by the district school. The women form themselves into cooking groups and the men get an early start drinking kava. Tonight we will eat together in the new—finally completed—community centre.

By the time I enter the building, the place is packed with a few hundred people, and the party shifts into full swing despite a major hitch: the guest of honour is not present. The government boat, which is bringing him back from Suva to collect his family and belongings, has not arrived; the party must proceed without him.

The villagers make presentations—gifts of mats, coconut oil and the like, every sleeping house having been "requested" to contribute one item. It falls to the head teacher's wife to make the acceptance speech in her husband's absence. I am directed to sit with her at the upper end of the room. I don't really want to but, once again, I need to be sensitive to their request. I compromise and take a position a few seats *ra* (lower) along the eating mat. We sit quietly as she speaks. Her demeanor is appropriately sad with tears running down her face. I notice that most people are not even looking at her; for some reason, they keep their heads down. I sense they don't buy the display of unhappiness, knowing all too well she is more than happy to leave, as would any of them should the opportunity for a well-paying job in the city become available.

As soon as the speech is ended, the platters and dishes of food are placed down the long row of eating mats. Now it is time to enjoy the feast—or almost. Someone hushes the crowd, including all the children, for the singing of a hymn and the saying of the grace. An indigenous ordained clergyman is on hand for the occasion. He prays over the baked taro, yam and cassava, the goat meat curry, the baked fish, the prawns cooked in coconut milk…The smells are tantalizing— and the blessing goes on forever. I watch the children, sitting there patiently, not daring to reach for the food as the clergyman keeps right on praying. Such emphasis on ritual matters—and such somber piety ….

Finally the feast is underway. I take some taro, prawns and watercress stew. It's lovely—except for the watercress stew; there's something in it that puzzles me. It looks like seafood so I bite into it. It's not seafood: it's fish eyes ….

After dinner the women and young girls clean up the eating area, and make their way to their sleeping houses with small children. The men stay behind and once again drink kava into the early hours of the morning. It's all such a lovely expression of community spirit but there is something vaguely unsettling about it ….

Moving Up and Out

Saturday, June 20th—I'm still unsettled about the feast last night. I watch these villagers contribute so much to someone who is moving up and out while they themselves cannot do so. I wonder if it creates an unconscious discontent in them. Their subsistence life is one of "habitual ritual": the daily gathering of food, preparing and eating it, washing dishes and washing clothes—until Sunday comes and then it's preaching and praying….

Is it enough for them? Do they want nothing more out of life? They appear to be happy, in spite of the fact that even their joking is culturally prescribed.

The government boat arrives with the head teacher to pick up his family and belongings. The people of the village spend most of the day assisting him with "moving up and out". When the boat pulls away from its moorage and sails away, the villagers stand along the shoreline and watch it fade into the distance. Do they wish they were going too? Do they even think about it?

In the evening I am feeling ill. Must be something I ate—or something that is eating me! These villagers are becoming great teachers for me, allowing a glimpse inside culture in a way I could never see in my own surroundings back home. I know I don't "belong" here—but I don't belong there either. What it really means to "come home" is far more mysterious and elusive than I had thought.

Part III

GOING "HOME"

Momo

Sunday, June 21ˢᵗ—I never cease to be amazed at the continual drama of life in the village. Tau's cousin arrived at 5:30 a.m. from his mother's village to tell us their uncle died about 4:00 this morning. Momo, Tau's mother's brother, the dear man with whom I had breakfast just five days ago … now he will get to use his coffin.

For 78 years Momo lived what his culture prescribed as a good life. In that sense it is not so sad an occasion, but his wife Nei is still in Suva and is scheduled to have her surgery on Wednesday. She left without knowing she would never see her husband again, and now it's unlikely she'll even be able to come to his funeral. The same with his sister Nana; she's still in Nadi waiting for her daughter to give birth. She will not be able to get here in time to bury her brother.

It's strange. As soon as Tau saw his cousin this morning, he knew right away what had happened. When we were in Nadi just a couple of weeks ago, Tau's sister told him she kept dreaming about Momo and feared that he would die. As for the old man himself, just two days ago, he requested his eldest son to ask all his children to come and visit him. He was not at all sick but I guess he just had a sense that he would die very soon.

After Tau and Iliki were informed, their cousin went to a further village to send a radio message announcing the death. It will be heard by wife Nei in Suva, sister Nana in Nadi, two sons on Koro Island

and a daughter living in a far village on this island. What a way to find out you have lost your father, husband, brother … but such is the necessity here, given the distances and difficulties of travel and communication. Fijians have grown accustomed to listening to radio broadcasts in order to find out if the bell tolls for one of their own. Today, for Tau's family, it does.

The other news is that Katu, who is in charge of the Sunday school program, has now instructed that each child contribute 20 cents per week. That's in addition to the 70 cents minimum per family at the morning worship service. For Iliki, that's $1.70 every Sunday. Iliki has no income apart from collecting a bit of copra that yields only a few dollars a week. With that limited amount he must pay for kerosene, sugar, flour, tea, salt and matches, not to mention clothing and school fees. Why do the Fijians support an institution that makes such demands? It's oppressive, and I feel like boycotting the church. Yes, I'm going to stay here in my little house today while they are preaching and praying.

In the afternoon I go for a walk with Tau. It's peaceful to be alone with him, and I want to give him a chance to share his feelings about the loss of his uncle. After we return to the village, he calls a meeting of the clan in Tomisi's house to plan the funeral presentations from this village. As Tau is the closest relative to the dead man here, he must organize and head the delegation.

The meeting goes on for a few hours. Mili comes over to my house. When there is a death, Fijians like to feel safe and do not want to be alone. She settles in and stays the night.

Momo's Funeral

Monday, June 22nd—In the early morning I go with Sai and Eli to take our contributions to the head of the clan. They bring mats; I bring kava. We put them on the floor without any ritual. Then we have our baths and get ready to go to the dead man's village.

We climb into the back of a lorry that Tau has rented. It's really crowded; almost all of the adults from the village are coming. Then they pile in the mats, tapa cloth, taro, yams and pigs (still alive), and, of course, out of sight, a supply of whales' teeth. It is pouring rain and very windy, despite the weather forecast. It's almost as though the heavens are crying out for the loss of this human life that breathed for nearly fourscore years on a remote little island, nurturing offspring of his own as well as those of his brothers, and being a *vasu* to Tau for all of their shared existence.

When we arrive at Nana's village, I go with the women to a specified sleeping house to await the presentation of our *magiti* (wealth). As we wait, the women prepare the mats and tapa cloth for our entrance to the house of death—the *vale ni mate*. They chat away, showing little evidence of sorrow.

When we join the men from our delegation outside the palm shelter where the presentation will be made, Sai puts aside two large blanket-size sheets of tapa cloth and hands them to me. I am now involved in all of the rituals. We present the mats, pigs, taro and yams, the kava, the whales' teeth and some other pieces of tapa cloth. While the men remain there to drink kava, the women, as well as Tau and Iliki, go to the entrance of the house of death.

Following tradition, all the furnishings and personal effects have been removed from the interior of the house. A very large sheet of tapa cloth is spread across the top front of the house, extending from the crossbeam to the floor. Behind it is an empty space reserved for the storage of new mats and tapa cloth as they are received. In front is Momo's body, lying in his coffin, which has been placed on a pile of new mats. Around the body sit his daughters, resting against the coffin, sometimes laying their faces on its lid.

We enter and go forward to share our grief and as we do so, those inside the house burst into tears once again. Sai now drapes Tau and Iliki in the sheets of tapa cloth I have been holding. They approach their dead uncle's body, removing the tapa they are wearing to place it on top the coffin. Then they sit quietly nearby. Everyone is crying. After a few minutes, Tau goes to the head of the coffin and his female cousins remove the lid so he can kiss his uncle. The wailing intensifies with this gesture. Iliki follows suit and the intense wailing is repeated. I am glad for all of us when the two of them leave to join the men who are drinking kava outside.

Delegations from around the island continue to arrive and ritual wailing marks each entrance. Eventually a group arrives from the far side of the island, bringing with them Momo's daughter who is married into their village. She enters, wearing the traditional tapa cloth and goes directly to view her father's face through the glass window on the lid of the coffin. She cries, along with those who have come with her, and they are joined once again by the women already seated inside the house … deep mournful wailing that continues for 20 long minutes. When it finally subsides, the daughter continues on unabashedly, for at least an hour more.

Time passes, and eventually Momo's two sons and only remaining brother enter to see their relative for the last time, accompanied by the pallbearers who will remove the body from the house. Final good-byes are said, and the pallbearers step forward to begin their duty.

What happens now is outside the ritual expectation. The daughters will simply not give up the body. They wail and scream and hang on to the coffin so it cannot be lifted. A scene of near pandemonium ensues and no one seems to know what to do. The eldest son intervenes and gestures for the body to be removed; the pallbearers persist and manage to ease the coffin away from the daughters and remove it from the house. Now their youngest brother joins his hysterical sisters. He is the only unmarried offspring of the dead man, still living at home with his mother and father. He accompanied his father almost everywhere. It is as though he suddenly realizes that his father has left his house for the last time. He screams and cries and pounds the floor. His sisters try in vain to control him, and the intensity of his grief ignites the other mourners inside the house. I sit motionless, along with the others who are not sure what to do.

After a half hour has passed, Sai leans over and asks me if I want to go up to the grave. I peer outside the door and see that the funeral service is already over and they are taking the body to the burial plot. While we were sitting here in the dead man's house, the funeral was going on in the church nearby—and most of the family missed it.

We leave the house and join those who are already in the procession. We walk along the road, then up a hill a short distance from the village. By the time we arrive, the graveside ceremony is already in progress. Each of the daughters finds a spot where she can be alone. They sit here, not really watching the proceedings. They don't need to; they know the ritual all too well ....

The coffin rests on mats stretched across the opening in the earth. The local church leader reads the familiar words, "soil to soil, sand to sand ..." There is a short prayer, and the coffin, wrapped in pandanus mats, is placed into the grave. Only the men attend to these duties, the women remaining a short distance away.

The gravediggers stay behind to fill in the earth as we make our way back to the village. There is no wailing now, just a subdued atmosphere, and by the time we arrive, all attention has shifted to the feasting. There appears to be no grief either; I guess they are all cried out.

I have never learned to grieve on cue. I was the only one who did not cry, and I am now suddenly feeling very sad that Momo is gone. I'm standing there, in the midst of all these people bustling about me—and I burst into tears.

They don't seem to mind. By this time, they're busy with the pig kill. I find it a most deplorable sight, not only from the point of view of sanitation but also cruelty. I watch one pig being cut down the middle before it is fully dead. I see Tau's brother's son transporting a large handful of intestines in his bare hands and another youth carrying a stomach. I feel ill.

Twenty pigs meet their death in this fashion. Then there are the cows … those gentle animals, magnificent in their anatomical structure, patiently standing there, awaiting the spear. Iliki will do the "honours". It is one thing I have never been able to fathom about him. He is otherwise so gentle and loving, and I get the impression he would not be able to bring himself to hurt anything. But here he stands, alongside this magnificent living creature, with spear in hand. He fixes his gaze on the neck of the animal and then, without hesitation, drives the spear into its jugular vein. The animal falters and rich red blood oozes from its body. It staggers some more and the pool of blood grows deeper. Then it collapses and falls to the ground.

The freshly slaughtered animals are the feature of the noonday feast. I am ushered to the head of the eating mat, accompanied by Sai. There is a choice of beef soup or pork curry. I opt to have only root crops and dine on cassava. After the meal, I go back to the *vale ni mate* to sit with the women while the men present the *burua* (food distribution) to the delegations that have attended the funeral. Gradually the day wears on and people depart in hired lorries. We stay into the afternoon where the pig killing and cooking continues, and when I finally go back to the village at dinnertime, Mata has already arrived and has cooked up a huge chunk of beef for the evening meal. I cannot bring myself to eat it; I have some green leafy vegetables instead.

So Momo has departed from this life, and Tau has lost his uncle. I understand some ritual things need to be done before we can bring ourselves to put a human being into a hole in the earth, but I am intrigued that killing would need to be one of them.

The Mourning

Tuesday, June 23rd—As they are the *kai-wai* (people of the water), Tau's clan by tradition provides fish to his mother's village during the ten-day mourning period. Today, the men go to the reef with spear guns and return with a lot of fish. The weather is quite cool; Tau is chilled when he gets back.

After lunch, the men walk up to the dead man's village to take the fish. Tau goes with them and stays for the remainder of the day, drinking kava and keeping company with his kin. Iliki, Eli and their children have actually moved there for the full ten days of mourning. Tau is torn as to what to do. He knows it is expected of him to remain there for the full period, but he doesn't want to spend ten days sitting there doing nothing apart from drinking kava and making conversation. He is caught in a cultural bind, not knowing whether to fulfill his kinship obligation or choose what he wants to do with his time. I'm really feeling for him; while he is away, I clean up the house—and I organize his meager belongings, which are in a terrible mess.

The Party

Wednesday, June 24th—Today is the *bogi va* (fourth night) since the death of Momo, and there is a "coming out" party associated with it. In preparation, the men from Tau's clan once again go out fishing and, after lunch—it's fish—we all take a lorry to the dead man's village.

When we arrive, I go with the women to the *vale ni mate*. The house remains empty, the furnishings not yet replaced. But the mood has changed. The *bikabika* (pressing down) by the elder women, which has been going on for the past four days, is over, and now it is time to party. Our delegation brings tobacco, matches, chewing gum and candies, and places them together on a mat in the middle of the floor. Then someone from their group separates the items into smaller piles. I am fascinated with the deliberation involved in deciding just which items should fall into each lot. The women sit around smoking, talking, eating candies, and laughing—a lot of laughing. Meanwhile, the men drink kava in the palm frond shelter constructed outside.

The partying continues until 7 in the evening. Then there is silence and people shift to singing a hymn and saying a prayer. They do this at 7 o'clock every evening. Now it's time to eat. I'm with the *kai-wai* (fishermen) women so we are served pork. They give me fish since by now they have noticed I don't eat pork. They are also intrigued that I don't eat salt. In fact, they continually talk about how slim and healthy I am and how they would like to be likewise, but they don't seem to make any connection between what they eat and how they look and feel. Interesting, Tau also does not eat pork; it makes him sick to his stomach. Yet on this occasion he is given pork just the same—and he eats it—because he is *kai-wai*. It's a good example of the subtle domination of culture.

After dinner, it's back to the *vale ni mate* with the women. At this point, they all lie down and go to sleep. I don't want to sleep and right now, I am feeling incredibly bored. I sit here, leaning against the wall, hoping like hell that Tau will come and rescue me.

I look around the room: silent bodies, passing away their time as though they will live forever. At least the daughters of the dead man are resting now. One of them is wearing a *sulu* (lavalava) with that popular slogan: "Fiji: the way the world should be". It is more out of convenience than conviction, I surmise, since the T-shirt worn with it sports the inscription, "Country Pride: Farm Fresh Chickens". Her young daughter is making a fashion statement of a different sort; the T-shirt on this little one reads, "Jesus is alive". The evidence is scarce.

The women invite me to lie down. I know I'm not fitting into the plan and it's upsetting the way things are done and, as a result, they don't know what to do with me. I just don't want to lie down and go to sleep, and I'm having just about the most boring day I have ever had in my whole life!

It seems like an eternity before Tau comes to the door. He asks me if I would like to go back to the village with him or wait and come later with the women. I'm out of there so fast I don't even take the time to answer his question.

It's a relief to be away from all that and revitalizing to be with Tau. We set out in the dark of the night for the village. It's wonderfully beautiful even though the darkness reveals only faint silhouettes. The contours of the hills … the rustle of the palm trees … the sound of the ocean: such a contrast to what has been going on for the past few days.

What a paradox: a lush tropical island, a village beside a white sand beach, swaying palm trees, waves crashing over a reef, a turquoise lagoon. Everywhere there is life. So much life! Yet there they are, indulging death by killing living creatures and sitting for days inside an empty house!

Death obsesses them while life eludes them.

Maybe it's the same for all of us.

The Photograph

Thursday, June 25th—I return with Tau to his late uncle's village, this time to take a picture of Momo's grave for his aunt Nei in Suva who has missed her husband's funeral. The site is beautifully decorated now with leaves and flowers strung on poles around the mound. Momo's female relatives come with us to pose for the picture. When this task is accomplished, Tau and I walk back to our village, stopping to work in the garden.

This evening Tau stays home despite requests from his relatives that he return to Momo's village. It's not just a casual invitation; they firmly expect him to remain there with them for the whole of the mourning period.

"Tau, your uncle has been dead only a few days and your kin are here. You should be staying here with us," they said to him this morning. Kinship first and foremost—like Iliki and Eli who fulfill the cultural expectation so well … shifting their whole family there, killing animals, cooking food and washing dishes, talking together, sleeping together….

Tau can no longer give his life over to all that.

The Aftermath

Friday, June 26th—By now I have a cold, and Tau has an upset stomach from eating freshly slaughtered pig meat. I know we need raw food, especially foods rich in Vitamin C. There is no fresh fruit in season in the village right now but a few kilometers away there is an independent farmer who grows watermelons and sells them locally. It's something rare in these parts. He is *Kai-Vitu* (Seventh Day Adventist) and, in keeping with that tradition, is vegetarian. After a breakfast, Tau and I set out for the farmer's homestead. On the way, we stop once again in Momo's village to check on all the kin. They seem to be doing well enough without him.

From there the road follows the beach and is nothing short of spectacular. Jungles of palm, *ivi*, vine, mango and breadfruit trees, the turquoise ocean with the crashing reef, white sandy beach with black stones, deep blue sky with spots of small fluffy white clouds … A travel poster!

We arrive at the homestead. A nicely cut path leads from the roadway to a traditional thatched hut. It is a beautiful setting. The compound is spotlessly clean, a striking contrast to the village where natives share their living space with pigs, dogs and chickens. In addition to the watermelon patch, there are gardens of vegetables and flowers. A fast moving brook runs alongside the hut, providing plenty of fresh, clean water.

I'm intrigued why it does not occur to others to do this kind of thing. Instead, they give their resources and energies over to the chiefs and to the church. They plant the crops that can be used in ritual feasting. They make pandanus mats for ceremonial exchange and raise pigs for honoring the dead. In this way they move in ritual cycles until their days are ended.

The *kai-Vitu* and his wife sit down with us on a bench made from a coconut tree and we eat a beautifully mature watermelon. We buy a second one to take home. Before we leave, the owner shows us his garden—cabbage, tomatoes, carrots, and the watermelon patch…He knows Tau's land and my interest in the natural environment.

"You build your house on that piece of land," the man says to me as I am leaving.

Tau's land, stretching along the beachfront, is even more beautiful than here. It has coconut palms, mango trees and plenty of vines, and borders a fresh water river. It is the perfect setting for a project Tau has in mind. He wants to build traditional grass huts there and plant lots of fruit trees and flowers. It would be a place for people to come so they could learn about "the Fijian way of life" without interrupting the privacy of the villagers as they now do. It's a timely idea, because foreigners are beginning to arrive on the island with no place to stay. Because Tau's village is nearest to the airstrip, the villagers take the visitors into their homes, yet realize no income or other compensation for the food and facilities they so graciously provide. Tau's project would change all that. Moreover, it would also provide cash income for the village, thereby helping people meet their financial obligations.

Tau and I have dubbed the project "Encounter Culture". It's a great project, an idea whose time has come! Only one problem: the chiefs will not grant permission for Tau to do it.

Little Mili

Saturday, June 27th—Tau goes fishing with members of his clan to Yaciwa. His oldest brother, Tomisi, with the help of the children who tag along, will go ashore on the little island to roast cassava while the others fish on the reef. They are gone for hours. Mili doesn't go; she stays behind and spends the entire afternoon with me. She is in a talkative mood and gives me a very competent massage as she chatters away.

Mili is a complex little girl. She is only 12 years old but is in many ways like a grown woman. She cooks, sews, washes clothes, goes fishing, collects firewood … often undertaking these tasks by herself. In other ways, she is very much a child, still unable to assert herself or to let me know how she feels. Sometimes I cannot detect her mood at all; she can assume a blank expression and go for long periods without saying anything. Either she is displeased about something and afraid to express it or there is simply no cultural instruction for her to do the kind of thinking that I am asking her to do. I sense it is the latter. And, in retrospect, I now think it's also a gender thing. I remember when I was doing my anthropological fieldwork here a few years ago; I tried to include both male and female perspectives about changes taking place in their village as a result of a foreign aid program I was researching. The women, without exception, had absolutely no opinion about it.

The Drama Goes On

Sunday, June 28th—Hymns on the radio … church three times a day … the usual routine. I decide not to take part this week; the exploitation is too much for me. When the children ask me for their Sunday school offering this morning, I give them some—but not the specified amount—and I tell them why, though I doubt they understand it.

It's a lovely day. I skip the communal food and eat some fresh new vegetables from our garden. The carrots, green peppers and beans taste wonderful. Tau attends the afternoon church service, and then prepares to go to his mother's village to take part in the ten-day mourning ceremony for his uncle. Just as he is about to leave, word arrives in the village that one of Tevi's relatives in a farther village has died. Another death —and Tau is called to the house of the chief of the clan instead.

So the ritual will begin again. The cousin will come to the meeting with a bundle of kava root, followed by his brothers. He will present the kava to the chief of the clan, explain that a relative has died, and request the assistance of the clan in meeting the costs of the funeral. The chief of the clan will respond in the affirmative. With the request ritual completed, the men will get down to practicalities: how many mats, pigs, taro and yams, how much tapa cloth and kava, how many whales' teeth … and the drama goes on.

The First Born

Monday, June 29th—What a lovely day! The order went out this morning for the men of the village to cut wood for the copra dryer. They hacked more huge branches from the big *ivi* tree on the path into the village. What a shame! It provided such shade from the heat while walking to and from the village.

Today Tau is called to another clan meeting—not about a death; it's a birth this time. Tomorrow is the first birthday of an *ulu matua* (first born). The mother is from Tau's clan, the father from Matuku in the Lau group of islands and is related to one of the other clans in our village. The whole village—160 people—will eat together tomorrow to celebrate the event. We will bring gifts—mats, tapa cloth, soap, money, cloth…The women will prepare huge pots of *ika vakalolo* and pork curry, and there will be baked taro and yams. The first birthday is the only one traditionally celebrated in this way.

Tonight, I help Mili with her homework again. It's Math this time. She is having difficulty with it since the teacher neglected to demonstrate the concepts and the answers he gives in class are sometimes wrong. What to do! The children are suffering because of adult incompetence! My dilemma: how to help Mili without making her teacher wrong! It is critical because Mili must pass examinations this year in order to move on to secondary school on another island next year. So I press ahead and teach her how to calculate the diameter and circumference of a circle by the dim light of a kerosene lamp until late into the evening.

A Nourishing Gift

Tuesday, June 30ᵗʰ—It's time for the Ngau *vula tolu lailai* (church quarterly meeting) and it will be held in our village today. Early this morning Tau joins a group preparing the root crops for the *lovo* (earth oven). Others are involved in cooking up huge pots of food while still others go out fishing.

By mid-day, the delegates arrive. They hold their meeting in the church building while village members lay out the feast. Some of the men weave baskets of palm fronds in which to present the food. It is really lovely. Once the meeting and feast are over, the delegates take their leave. All that preparation—and I wonder what really got done!

Attention now shifts to the birthday party for an *ulu matua* in our village. I have my bath in late afternoon in preparation for tonight's event. While I am at the water pipe engaged in this very public ritual, 8-year-old Samu arrives and interrupts my bath to show me an egg that a chicken has laid.

"That's nice," I say to him, or something to that effect, and he goes away. A minute or so later he returns and interrupts again, this time to wash a small cooking pot. When it is clean, he fills it half full of water, puts in the egg and leaves. I finish my bath and return to my little house to towel dry and get dressed. Not long after I'm comfortably inside, Samu arrives to interrupt me now for a third time. What could he possibly want now! There in his little hands is a tin plate on which is sitting one boiled egg. He has cooked it for me!

That was the meaning of all the interruptions; he was indicating that he was doing it for me. Not a word was spoken and the act was motivated by no reason that I can ascertain … just the simple gift of a boiled egg. The event so touches me that I stop what I am doing, and sitting here, wrapped in a wet towel, prepare to eat the egg. He stays to watch, noticeably delighted with his achievement. When I break the shell, I discover the egg is only slightly cooked! The white of the egg is transparent and runny, the yolk barely warm. I struggle to swallow it, much like someone coming to terms with his or her first raw oyster. It's not exactly appetizing—but the kindness nourishes me well.

And now the birthday party….

While I continue to resist, Fijians continue to insist that, on these special occasions, not only do I eat at the first sitting but I also sit at the "top" of the mat. Tonight I think I have figured a way around it. I will simply stay in my little house until those who occupy the top roles in the hierarchy have eaten.

But it is not to be. When the food is ready to be served, a delegation arrives at my door to collect me, and they escort me once again right to the top of the eating mat. Now I'm sitting with the *Tui* (Queen) of the village and the grandmother of the birthday child. From this vantage point I can look down the long line of extended kin networks spread on either side of the eating mats to where the women at the far end are poised and ready to dish out and serve the food.

These people are remarkably handsome with their brown bodies and prominent facial features. The children, with their big eyes, radiant skin and quiet anticipation are especially engaging. It reminds me of that scene in *The King and I* where the numerous offspring of the polygamous patriarch of Siam are displayed to their new tutor from Wales. At this moment, there is something so endearing about them, so wonderful, that I suspend my reserve for their blind adherence to cultural norms and teeter on the edge of falling into their paradise of the collective psyche.

I have some fish cooked in coconut milk and a chunk of taro—plus a very tiny piece of the birthday cake which I share with the grandmother since there is not nearly enough to go around. After an appropriate length of time has elapsed, I express my thanks and beg my leave.

Mili escorts me back to my house at the far side of the village. She is carrying a two-year-old boy who has fallen asleep and is much too heavy for her. I take the child and the three of us make our way in the darkness across the village green. The sky is lit with millions of stars, brilliant against the winter night of the southern hemisphere. It is very, very lovely. We come across a group of small boys who are sitting in a circle, singing. It is a most exquisite moment, and I begin to question whether or not there really is that Hindu "purpose of the universe" underlying all this surface drama. Because this moment—well, the surface drama is pure bliss ….

Then the sleeping child starts drooling all over my nice clean blouse. What's more, I'm in my bare feet, and I step into something that is definitely not mud. Stark reality jars me back to the sensual world. I deliver the child to his sleeping house, wash my feet at the water pipe and go to bed.

Part IV

THE ENDLESS CYCLE

All in a Day's Work

Wednesday, July 1ˢᵗ—Today I accompany Tau to a village about 8 kilometers away to make another phone call. It's the nearest telephone—now a second one on the island. Tau wants to phone one of his clan members in Suva to ask that he meet the ferry when it arrives from Ngau tomorrow to pick up the clan's outboard motor. Some time ago one of the young men in the village took the motor without permission and used it on a boat without proper fittings. As a result, he lost it overboard. The men went diving and found it, but it hasn't worked since and all local attempts to fix it have been in vain. There is no recourse now but to send it to Suva for repair.

The reason I want to go with Tau is so that I can view the magnificent scenery on this westerly side of the island. We set out on foot early in the morning. There will be no lorry available for a few hours and the telephone service does not extend past mid-day. There is some overhead cloud, which makes the walking bearable; otherwise, the heat of the sun would be intolerable along the stretch of road that is not shaded. I take along some of my precious supply of crackers and peanut butter, as well as a new biography of Margaret Mead so I will have something to read while we wait for a return lorry.

It is lovely walking along the road. First it meanders at sea level through palm-fringed jungle, *ivi* and breadfruit trees, and vines so

157

thick one cannot see the ocean only a few hundred meters away. Tau cuts some jasmine flowers from a bush as we walk along; the fragrance is exotic and enchanting. Not far outside the village, we come upon young men weeding in their taro gardens; they chat with each other in rhythm to the movements of their cane knives.

Further along, the road becomes hilly and then ascends abruptly, revealing the physical relief of the island. Higher we climb, to the summit from where we have a spectacular view of the coral reef with its turquoise waters surrounding the island. It is an experience of which some can only dream.

But it's getting hot—and the hills are steep. Tau cuts a coconut from a low-hanging tree; we rest and drink the milk. I see a passage through the reef from up here, and beyond the reef, deep blue ocean as far as the eye can see. It is such a magnificent prospectus that I want to linger, but we need to get to the telephone before the service shuts down for the day.

We arrive in the village before noon and Tau places the call to Suva. His relative is not there and will not be back in the city until Monday. We have just walked 8 kilometers along a hot and hilly gravel road to make a phone call only to find the other party not there. The outboard motor repair will have to wait. Such is life here in the outer islands!

So here we are. It's about 12 noon. God knows how many hours it will be before a lorry comes along. We sit by the roadside, eating our crackers and peanut butter until they are gone. Our conversation somehow shifts away from the magnificent setting to the frustrations of living on an outer island: poor transportation … inadequate communication … not to mention a boring, repetitive diet … constraints of the church … the chiefly system…

All of a sudden I want pizza and wine … and ice cream— and I want them right now. Tau too—which makes it worse. The strong desire for these items grows out of all reasonable proportion. There is no way to satisfy the desire, and all we can do is wait for a lorry. So we wait—but there is no lorry. By now we're in the heat of the midday sun, and mosquitoes are hovering around us. We are not having fun.

We have two choices: we can wait here for an unknown period of time for a lorry to chance along, or we can set out on the 8-kilometer trek back to the village, chancing that a lorry will pick us up somewhere along the way. The scenery would be equally beautiful in the return direction, but we would have to climb those hills again and we've already done that once today. What's more, it's much hotter now. Then again, it would beat sitting here along the side of the road swatting mosquitoes and waiting for a lorry that might not even come.

So back we go. In the midday heat, the hills seem higher, the valleys longer…Just past the mid-way point, Tau spots some papaya and guava; we pick and eat them as we walk along. Then he tells me there is a lovely brook inland that is not all that far from here. We head along a half-beaten path and there, in a most glorious tropical setting, is a swimming hole of clear fresh water. It is too good to be true in the heat of the day! We take off our clothes and jump in the water, and we linger in this exquisite setting until the day nears an end.

It is glorious. At moments like these, all the setbacks and inconveniences seem worth it just to be in this exotic setting with this lovely man who wants nothing more than to be with me. I know I cannot stay here—and I cannot take him with me. He knows it too. But right now, we relish in the moment.

Eating and Sleeping

Thursday, July 2nd—Today I work in the garden with Tau preparing seedbeds and digging mounds for yam. It's hard work but we've chosen to do it ourselves rather than take part in the communal gardening, which, by this time, has become an imbalance of labour and reward. By doing the yam garden ourselves, we can plant the other vegetables on the same piece of land, and we can transplant the cabbages into the yam mounds. I'm learning a lot about surviving on a piece of land.

I'm feeling really hungry when we arrive back in the village from the garden, and I'm glad that Sai has prepared a huge pot of eggplant curry for lunch. I eat a big bowl of it and within an hour feel dreadfully ill. It's difficult to stay healthy here; I cannot control the conditions that lead to repeated illness. Pigs, goats, chickens and dogs roam the village, eating scraps in and around the kitchen huts and drinking at the water pipe.

I plan to skip dinner but am so hungry after losing all my lunch that I'm glad to see *rourou* (taro leaves cooked in coconut milk) on the dinner mat, but decline it when I see leftovers from dinner plates being put back into the pot. They are very comfortable with this kind of eating arrangement; I have yet to get used to it.

Tonight I take a late bath at the water pipe. It's very cool by this time but refreshing nevertheless. Mili, as she often does, comes over to do her homework and stays the night. Meanwhile, Tau, as he often does, conducts a clan meeting on the verandah. I fall asleep before either of them is done. I remember Tau shutting off the kerosene lamp and asking me if I want a blanket so I won't be cold. And I remember him lying down on his sleeping mat beside me.

Coconut Candy

Friday, July 3rd—A good time to beautify the compound surrounding the house. I weed the area around the papaya and banana trees, and plant some frangipani. Tau is busy with some of the men of the clan; they are cooking *vakalolo*, a treat made with brown sugar and coconut syrup. There will be a rugby tournament at the school compound tomorrow and they will sell the *vakalolo* as a fund-raiser.

Iliki is in charge of the "candy" and puts it in our house for safekeeping. After dinner tonight, I feel like having something sweet, and I just can't resist the temptation to taste some of it. Tau also. We pour a little of the thick syrup onto some brown rice crackers and it tastes like caramel popcorn. That's only enough to make me really want some, so I drink it straight from a cup—rich coconut milk and brown sugar rendered into thick syrup. The taste is exquisite—like eating very fine toffee. I can't stop eating it! Neither can Tau. As a result, I feel very uncomfortable the whole night.

Perfect Moments

Saturday, July 4ᵗʰ—This morning Tau and I are both up before dawn, mostly because we are sick from eating so much *vakalolo* last night. I walk with him along the beach to see the *malawa ni mataka* (daybreak). It is difficult to describe the beauty. First, Venus, the morning star against a dark sky, the silhouetted palm trees fringing the beach of an endless ocean. Then the red outline of an approaching dawn, and slowly, very slowly, a brilliant ball of fire breaking onto the horizon. A new day has begun ....

It is so perfect a setting that I could not possibly prefer to be anywhere else. I don't want to return to the village. I don't want to return to Suva—or even Canada. I just want to stay here on the beach where the river meets the sea.

We walk in the sand to the point where the breakwater from the airstrip interrupts the view. By the time we turn back, we can see that the village has come to life. It is low tide, and women are on the beach looking for bait for today's fishing. Young boys are scouting for coconuts; they will sell the copra to get money for buying the *vakalolo* at the rugby tournament today. Little eight-year-old Samu who (partially) cooked me that egg the other day has found a choice spot on the beach. There he sits, on that white coral sand nestled by palm trees, feasting on fresh young coconuts. I gaze at him as he quietly sits there by himself, and I wonder if he realizes how perfect a moment is his.

Tau and I arrive back in the village about 6 a.m. The men in his clan are pounding cassava to go with the *vakalolo*—what's left of it! The women are preparing breakfast. Tau and I opt instead for hot water with lemon to offset the richness of the candy. Then Tau cooks a breadfruit and the two of us eat it together.

Most of the villagers—including Tau and all the children —head up to the school compound for the rugby tournament. It is an opportunity for me to be alone in my little house. For lunch I have fresh vegetables that Tau collected for me before leaving. There are green beans, carrots, and green peppers. I steam them lightly, and squeeze fresh lime juice on them for added Vitamin C. It is such a refreshing change ….

In the evening, the villagers drink kava on the verandah once again. It's warm and comfortable here in the cool winter evenings. I have my bath and fall asleep inside the house while they drink and clap and sing outside. It is paradise!

The Vula Vou

Sunday, July 5th—In the early morning I once again walk with Tau along the beach to his beautiful piece of land. Like before, the experience is so peaceful and wonderful that I just want to stay here forever.

Today is the *vula vou* (new moon)—the first Sunday of the month, so there will be a *vanua* (confederation of villages) church service, this time in a far village. Most of the people of this village, Tau included, leave after lunch to walk the five kilometers to the host village.

For dinner tonight, there are just the five children with me. We have tea and scones left over from breakfast. Tea to them is very special and they do not take at all to vegetables! We enjoy some time together, waiting for the adults to return. The children stay with me and fall asleep around 10 in the evening; still the adults have not returned. It turns out that the lorry that was to bring them back never showed up, so after waiting the better part of the evening, the adults decided to walk home. They arrived back about 3 in the morning.

Some days start out paradise and end up paradox!

Hired "Help"

Monday, July 6th—As we are finishing breakfast, one of the young men in Tau's clan asks if he can work in Tau's yam garden to earn some money. There is no cash income apart from copra, and people have ongoing financial obligations. Tau tells him to come to the garden this afternoon and invites Iliki as well. I go on ahead with Tau. We roast breadfruit and eggplant for our lunch, and have some drinking coconuts. As we are eating, the two young men arrive—accompanied by a third! Here they are, the three of them, working in Tau's yam garden to earn money. It's fascinating to watch the dynamics of all this. They have a great time, joking and laughing—but they really aren't doing any work! Tau and I accomplish much more than these three men together in half the time. Somehow it doesn't seem to matter; they just need some money.

Tonight Tau has organized a fund-raising program at the community centre. There will be rugby videos and a movie as well. Lots of people show up, but at the last minute the event gets cancelled because one of the chiefs of the island arrives and calls a meeting in the same venue to tell villagers the results of the latest Island Council meeting.

The chiefs still rule in Fiji!

This Land is My Land?

Tuesday, July 7th—Early this morning I walk the beach alone to the end of Tau's property and follow the jungle path inland. It is, once again, like wandering in a magical piece of wilderness of storybook magnitude. One part of me feels like supporting Tau in his plans for this land; another part says to just let it go. This choice piece of real estate is designated by the clan for his exclusive use. But because Fijian land is tied to the *vanua* (chiefly system), it is the chiefs who will decide what he gets to do with it.

It's very disconcerting—and it puts me in a very critical mood. Tau works so hard at everything but ends up with nothing. The chiefs usurp his community development work. The yields from his taro and yam gardens get appropriated for ceremonial exchange. He cannot realize his dreams for this beautiful piece of land without permission from the Island Council, which never gets around to making a decision about it. His life is an endless cycle, going nowhere. He sees through all the structures but remains bound by them….

What do I do? Or refrain from doing?

Lunch is Served!

Wednesday, July 8th—I was planning to go to Yaciwa island with members of our clan today but it's cool and windy, so I go with Sai to the school compound instead. Three times each month it is her turn, along with one other woman, to prepare the midday meal for the school children from this village. The district school serves our chiefly jurisdiction—called a *vanua*— composed of three villages; the other two villages similarly have a two-woman team preparing food for their children.

We arrive at the compound about 11 in the morning. The other women are already here and have huge pots of cassava cooking on an open fire. (The children each bring one raw cassava with them when they walk to school in the mornings; the women collect and cook them communally.) The outdoor cooking area is adjacent to a "dining hall" which consists of a wooden frame covering three long crude tables with benches on either side. There is one table for each of the three villages and the one for our village is situated so close to the wall of the shelter that the children have to climb under (or over) the table to get to the outer bench.

Sai and Eti—the other woman from our village—are preparing fish and cabbage to go with the cassava. Eti is 19 years old and is one of twelve children. She has two children of her own, one age 3, the other an infant seven months old. Both children are with her today and she is attending to them while preparing the food for the 40 school children. Poor woman: the baby is crying most of the time and the three-year-old is very uncooperative. I take them for a while in order to give the distraught mother as well as those trying to work around her a much-needed break.

The women from Tau's mother's village are preparing soup with tinned fish, cassava and a variety of shellfish found on the reef. I notice there is a small pot of *ika vakalolo* being cooked as well. I ask Sai why a second dish is being prepared and she tells me that two of the children from that village are *kai-Vitu* (Seventh Day Adventist) and they are not allowed to eat shellfish. It seems a particularly incongruous rule for people living on a tropical island surrounded by a coral reef!

The children from the third village will be having curry. I cannot identify exactly what kind of curry it is. There's cassava in it and bits of prawn and other shellfish, and I see some fish bones—though I cannot see any fish.

I watch the preparation; it takes considerable time, and given the cooking conditions, represents a remarkable feat. When the work is done, all three of the huge pots of food look appetizing, especially the soup from Tau's mother's village with its rich coconut cream.

The lunch bell rings. It's time to eat. The children line up at the water pipe to wash their hands. Then they line up again, this time at the entrance to the dining shelter: boys first, then girls—and short to tall. When the cue is given, in they run and all semblance of organization ceases. The children scramble for seating at their respective tables. Samu abandons his lot and joins the group from the village getting the soup with the rich coconut cream!

The "meal service" begins. Some of the older girls assist. A woman from each of the villages scoops the soup. One student adds a piece of cassava and a second student passes the dish to the children seated at the table. No waiting: the children eat as soon as the food is placed in front of them.

It's all over in a few short minutes. In fact, most are finished before the total number is even served. Then away from the table they run, handing their plates to anyone they can con into taking them—the girls are particularly vulnerable —and off they scurry to the playground, to divest themselves of an enormous excess of energy.

A few of the students are assigned to "clean-up". Their task is to scrub the plates with sand and rinse them. Then the women soap, wash, rinse and dry the dishes, and put them back on the shelves immaculately clean. It's a lot of hard work by my count: Sai alone washes at least 50 plates. Then they turn their attention to the pots, scrubbing them inside and out with sand and ash until they too are spotless. By 2 o'clock in the afternoon it is done. All in all, about 3 hours of cooking and cleaning for 3 minutes of eating—and tomorrow it will be the same.

Tennyson … life piled on life…Is it all too little?

Kinship, Kinship

Thursday, July 9th—Some of the villagers go to the north of the island on the lorry today; there is a ceremony of sorts connected with the payment of provincial taxes. Last night they held a fund-raising in preparation for the get-together today. Each male is to contribute $30.00. People are really excited about the outing. Excited about paying taxes!

Tau and I go to the garden. We take our taro, *ivi* nuts and breadfruit and find three small wild yams en route. We make a *lovo* (earth oven) in the garden. While the food is baking, we clear land and plant yams. When the food is done, we take it to the village to eat along with some fresh seaweed. The meal is delicious, wholesome, clean … and private.

Well, almost private. When Tomisi's wife, Vati, sees us entering the village, she immediately calls us to have lunch with her family. We decline, indicating we will be eating at my little house—so she sends the food here. It's *ika vakalolo*!

It's another example of the close kinship ties. Vati knows Sai is away and, as the wife of Tau's eldest brother, she automatically assumes responsibility for Tau's food—and by association, mine as well…We're one big extended family.

After lunch I go with Tau to collect food and firewood. When we get to the bush, Iliki and Eli are here working in their vegetable garden together, transplanting cabbages. It is a lovely scene. The garden—taro, cassava, yam, and cabbages—is set beside a stream and shaded by coconut trees. When they see us, they beckon us to come over.

Of course, as brothers, Tau and Iliki observe the strict avoidance relationship, so all the communication is channeled through Eli and me. Tau asks Eli if he can have some taro from Iliki's garden since his own taro is not yet mature. She says yes, and tells him to take all he wants. So Tau goes ahead and digs taro from his brother's garden. While this is going on, Iliki comes over to me, hands me his cane knife and asks me to cut the roots from some mature cabbages he has just pulled. He tells me he doesn't want to do it because his hands are dirty. I cut the roots for him, then ask him where he wants me to put the cabbages. He instructs me to put them in my *su* (a basket woven from pandanus used by women for carrying food and firewood); the cabbages he pulled are for Tau and me.

It's very touching. Here he is, a man in his early forties with a wife and six children, and no income apart from the periodic sale of a bit of copra. They have so very little, this couple, but they are resourceful and waste nothing. They have beautiful children. The *ulu matua* (first born) is a boy who is now in secondary school on the island of Ovalau. Next is Nitai, pretty and petite, who dances as she walks … then another little girl with big eyes and a ready smile, another little boy … and another little girl. The sense of kinship that is extended to Tau is lovely to watch. There's something almost spiritual about it. To be here in this most natural setting witnessing so strong a sense of kinship is to be drawn once more into the security and comfort of the collective psyche.

By sundown Sai has not yet returned from the north of the island so little Mili cooks dinner—cabbage and cassava—and Eli sends over some fish. A few minutes later, while we are eating, one of Eli's daughters appears, asking for cassava. Food freely requested, food freely given … yes, one big extended family.

In the evening, when I return from my bath, I see that a number of children have collected on the verandah, together with their blankets and school bags. We do their homework together and eat coconut Tau and I baked in the earth oven earlier in the day. Then they settle in for the night!

Why not! I well know that my private space is never really my own. Sleeping houses, like most everything else in the village, are communal property. I learned this early on when I was living in my little grass hut during my years of fieldwork. On any given night, there might have been ten or more children sleeping in that tiny space with me. They never asked permission or waited for an invitation; they simply arrived. They would be either all girls or all boys. They never mixed; whichever group got there first asserted their sleeping rights. Sometimes one or the other would arrive early in the evening and "hang out" with me so as to prevent those of the other gender from claiming the space.

The Hundredth Night

Friday, July 10th—Today is the *bogi drau* (one hundredth night) "party" for Tila. She died 100 days ago today. Once again, all regular activities cease and energies are given over to the death ceremony. Some of the men from Tau's clan go out fishing while others head to the gardens to get taro and yams for the earth oven. People from neighbouring villages begin arriving early in the day, bringing food and making ritual presentations.

At mid-morning I am called to have tea with the women in the community centre. I decline as I'm avoiding as far as possible the white flour food they consume on these occasions. I skip lunch also, opting to have some seaweed which is highly nutritious and which otherwise will go to waste.

As I am finishing lunch, some of Tau's kin from another village come by. First to arrive is his mother's brother's son with whom Tau carries on a lively conversation. They are classified as cousins and therefore have a joking relationship. A while later his mother's sister's sons appear; they are classified as brothers and, following tradition, Tau does not speak with them. I carry on the conversation until Fijian vocabulary and mutual interests are exhausted. Then they amuse themselves by playing my tape recorder and eventually all of them fall asleep. It's interesting to me how comfortable they are in Tau's presence without talking to him. It's all just programmed in there and accepted without question. It has nothing to do with choice, and I am convinced they don't even think about it.

Tonight the people of the village, along with those who have come from villages around the island, enjoy a feast in the community centre … another of those not so rare occasions when everyone eats together. It's the familiar setting: men at the upper end, drinking kava; the women cooking up huge pots of food and serving it to their kin networks seated on either side of a long row of eating mats. There is fish—lots of it—and taro and cassava and yam, and they have killed nine pigs so there are also pots of pork curry and pork stew.

I eat a piece of fish and some taro, managing this time to take a seat *ra* (below) that of the *Tui* (Queen) of the village. The men drink kava, and sing and chat until it is nearly dawn. The women set aside plates of food for them and deliver it to their respective sleeping houses. For Tau they leave pork and taro. Tau doesn't like pork and everybody knows it, but he's *kai-wai* (fisherman) and they cannot serve fish to him so, once again, pork is what he gets.

Tau says nothing. Neither does he eat it. The pig stays in the pot and the man stays hungry.

"Sabbath" on Yaciwa Island

Saturday, July 11ᵗʰ— It's a lovely day today … beautiful sunshine after lots of rain during the night. I take an early morning stroll along the beach. It is very high tide so I walk up to the airstrip and then follow the jungle path down to the sea. It is wonderful! The thick green leaves and vines are bathed with glistening drops of water and streams of sunlight. The coconut palms are swaying softly and the waves are breaking quietly on the shore. Giant *dilo* trees spread their huge branches, many large enough to support a sturdy tree house, and their roots create driftwood-like patterns in the sand.

It's the perfect day for a trip out to Yaciwa island, but the outboard motor belonging to Tau's clan is now—finally—in Suva for repairs. There is one other motor in the village, and it's not in use today because the owner is *kai-Vitu* (Seventh Day Adventist) and he won't be fishing on the Sabbath.

Tau and I go to rent the engine from him—but he won't rent it to us because it's the Sabbath! Not Sabbath for any of us, mind you, but that doesn't seem to matter. He says he doesn't think it is moral to use his property on the Sabbath! As if the damn motor is *kai-Vitu*! All these villagers who wanted to go out fishing with us—a free trip because I was paying—to get food for their Sabbath tomorrow will now have to walk out at low tide or pole the heavy boat through the shallow waters. Now that's Christianity in action. Praise the Lord!

Two women and the smallest children start off in the boat with some of the stronger men moving the vessel with a pole and a couple of makeshift paddles. The rest of us walk to Yaciwa at the lowest point in the tide. We will all come back by boat together at the end of the day.

It's a fair trek—and a difficult one at points because the current is very strong. On the up side, the sea life, the corals and the fishes are in brilliant and abundant display, and being in the midst of it all is exhilarating.

Yaciwa island is beautiful. It's a coral cay situated on the sheltered lee side of the reef. Over a long period of time, coral rubble and sand have been deposited by the wind and the waves to form a sand pit, and eventually it has developed into an island. Plant seeds have floated on to the cay, and bird droppings have provided fertilizer for the plants to grow. Now, dense vegetation covers the area and it has become an ideal place for sea birds to nest and lay their eggs.

There are twenty people at Yaciwa by the time Tau and I get there. Some are out on the reef collecting shellfish. Some are fishing with handmade spears in the shallow water on the lee side of the reef. Others are swimming with masks and spear guns. Some of the small children are walking at the very edge of the reef where the waves crash over the edge; they are in their bare feet and appear neither uncomfortable nor afraid. They learn at a very young age to survive in this environment.

I'm amazed how quickly the women "set up camp" and I'm fascinated how closely they have replicated the village pattern, complete with mats, cooking pots, coconut scraper, and dishes … Once this is done, they attach baskets to their backs and head into the water with fishing lines. Iliki goes diving with Tau's spear gun.

The spear gun arrangement is interesting. Iliki, who is a good spear fisherman, has only very crude diving equipment. Tau has a new spear gun and I figure Iliki would like to use it. I know too, given their strict avoidance relationship, that he cannot ask Tau for it; neither can Tau offer it to him, so I become the intermediary. First I ask Iliki on Tau's behalf if he would like to use the spear gun. He indicates he would, and now it is time to tell him how the mechanism works. In the presence of Iliki, Tau explains it to me, step by step (in Fijian), and asks me if I understand. I repeat it, step by step (in Fijian), asking Iliki if he understands. In this manner, it gets done, all without a word or even a glance between the two brothers.

The women are line fishing, Iliki is spear fishing, Mili is scraping coconuts, Nitai is preparing the taro leaves, and Tau is making the *lovo*. We spread the root crops in the pit on top of the hot rocks and cover them with leaves and earth. The women come ashore with their catch. They clean and scale the fish, then build a fire and prepare to cook them. It's noon by now and getting very warm; I don my snorkeling gear and head into the cool water along the inside edge of the reef while the food is cooking. There are magnificent corals in a variety of shapes and patterns, "home" to countless species of brightly coloured fish. It is ... paradise...

Lunch. Tau gets the head of the biggest fish; I get a generous portion of its midriff along with a big plate of taro leaves cooked in coconut milk, some taro and breadfruit. When the meal is over, the women strap the baskets to their backs and head into the water once more. This time they are fishing for tomorrow's food. Tau and Iliki each find for themselves a spot in the shade and fall asleep. Some of the children are back in the water; others explore the island.

By late afternoon the sun falls low on the horizon, and we begin to feel cold and tired and hungry. It's time to return to the village. We pile into the boat—all 22 of us—and start pushing our way back to Ngau. Two men, one at the front and the other in the rear, guide the vessel with poles through the shallow water of the lagoon. It's a long way, moving at this speed, and it will get more difficult as the water becomes deeper. Vati has a better idea: she takes two *sulu* (lavalavas) and ties the corners with vine to a couple of the long-handled spears. It creates a crude but effective spinnaker and we position the boat so the wind will fill the cloth.

It works, and the breeze carries us at a steady pace in the direction of the far shore. A short while later, two more *sulu* are surrendered, this time from male bodies already suffering from exposure, and a second sail is rigged and put into place. This time it needs to be hand-held, and able-bodied youth are shifted into position. A paddle now becomes a rudder and we make our way, slowly, quietly...

It reminds me of that scene from the film *Bounty*, just after the mutiny, where Captain Bligh, in his little boat with his little crew and his little stores, with the aid of a hand-rigged sail, is searching for a safe place to land. They have stopped at the island of Tofua but have had to make a quick getaway because the natives aren't very friendly. They're tired, they're thirsty, they're hungry and they're suffering from exposure. Just off the horizon are 300 of the most beautiful islands in the whole of the South Pacific. Fresh water, taro, breadfruit, coconut, mango, papaya … in short, everything they need to sustain life ….

But they can't stop there. Why? Because, according to the beleaguered captain, the Fiji Islands are "the most savage islands in these waters … where cannibalism is perfected almost to a science."

A scene or two later, one of his crew is dying and he says, "Captain Bligh, when my spirit is gone, there will be nothing but flesh remaining. I beg you, use that poor flesh to save the others."

"No, no", replies the English Captain, "We're civilized men, not savages, and as civilized men we shall die."

When Bligh made it safely back to England and was exonerated of the actions for which he lost his ship, he tracked down his mutineers in Tahiti and had them hanged.

How civilized! And now we are sailing near the Bligh Waters— they named it after him—twenty-two of us, in a little boat, with a little food and a hand-rigged sail. We're cold, we're hungry, we're tired and, by this time, we're suffering from exposure—in the most civilized islands in these waters, the Fiji Islands … where Christianity has been perfected almost to a science!

Breaking a Taboo

Sunday, July 12th—Early this morning we make a *lovo* and bake taro, coconut and *ivi* nuts. Little Samu puts some cassava on the fire as we are heating the rocks so we have roasted cassava as well. Meanwhile, Sai is baking fresh buns in the kitchen hut for our breakfast.

Tau and I break a taboo today. We have no leaves to put on top of the root crops for the *lovo*. So while the rocks are heating, we go to the bush to cut some *ivi* branches and palm fronds. It is the first time Tau has ever done such a thing and he is a bit anxious about it. In fact, he asks me if I would like to stay behind while he does it. I say no, of course, because it doesn't represent a taboo to me. Together we go to cut the branches and bring them to the village—and the sky does not fall down!

Any work associated with food collection on Sunday is considered a serious taboo infringement. But now something happens unexpectedly that seems to override the taboo. Our breakfast of freshly baked buns with guava jam is abruptly interrupted when we are informed that someone has died in a village further up the coast. Villagers immediately make plans to attend the death ceremonies, and they go at once to their gardens to get food for the feasting without any apparent apprehension or concern.

Fascinating! People can go without while they are alive. In fact, sacrifice is the in thing—unless you're a chief—but when you die, you get the full treatment. Why does death seems to matter more than life!

Part V

TROUBLE IN PARADISE

To the "Mainland"

Monday, July 13th— Sai told me last night that the funeral will be today and that a group of people from the dead woman's village on the main island will be chartering a plane to Ngau. The flight will arrive sometime in the morning. It's a good chance for Tau and me to get to Suva on the return flight. We want to visit the office of the Ministry of Fijian Affairs there to find out how Tau can make some progress on the plan to develop his land.

Early this morning Tau and I check with the *Fiji Air* agent in the village. He doesn't know what time the plane might come and says he will go up to the airstrip at 8 a.m. to phone the Suva airport in Nausori. Tau and I arrive at the airstrip by 8:30. The agent—just off the phone—has been told there is no special flight. As he is communicating this to us, a little *Fiji Air* plane appears and lands on the gravel runway! Out step an Indian pilot and a group of Fijian women bearing mats and tapa cloth. The pilot says he is returning to Suva so the agent asks Tau to help unload the plane while he prints us up a couple of tickets. I pay the agent our standby fare; we board the aircraft and fly away.

Ngau is so beautiful from the air … the high jungle-laden hills, the coconut palms, the coral reef, Yaciwa island…So inviting it looks from this magnificent prospectus … truly a tropical paradise. We soar out over the deep blue ocean spotted by the islands of Lomaiviti, past the powerful little island of Mbau to the coast of Viti Levu and touch down on the airstrip at Nausori.

There's no ground transportation to meet an unscheduled flight so we take a taxi to Nausori town from where we catch a bus into Suva. The bus driver, an Indian man, plays Hindi music through a loud speaker. An image of the goddess Kali holding a head dripping with blood in one of her many arms adorns the front of the bus. It is an image not easily accommodated by the Christian Fijian view of things, in spite of the fact that institutionalized Christianity itself is premised on a blood sacrifice.

The bus station in Suva is adjacent to the public market. I buy some papaya and bananas, and enjoy a breakfast of fresh tropical fruit. Before the day is out, I have added pizza and wine. The taste is so wonderful that I am forced to question whether I would sacrifice paradise for a pizza!

Telling Nei

Tuesday, July 14th—In the early morning I walk with Tau along the seawall in front of the Governor-General's residence. I'm always fascinated to watch the guard who stands there, in Buckingham Palace style, at the entrance to the driveway. Every five minutes or so, he goes through his changing of the guard routine. As usual, there is no one in view to watch him. With eyes front and exaggerated movements, he swings his arms, stamps his feet...I've watched this routine many times over the years. The only difference now is that just inside the gate stands a soldier in full battle dress carrying a rifle!

There is "trouble in paradise"....

Tau and I go about things as usual, enjoying these few days in Suva. We head to the Methodist church office to see Tau's cousin who works there. He is the son of Tau's late uncle Momo. We want to inquire about his mother Nei's health. He tells us she was still in hospital when the radio message of her husband's death reached Suva so they decided not to tell her at that point in time. She had her surgery, recovered and was discharged from hospital. Then they arranged to have some mourning rituals for her benefit among relatives in a village just outside Suva.

They took her there. When they arrived in the village that day, there was also a wedding ceremony going on. When she inquired about the ceremonial occasion, they told her of the wedding but not of the death. They would break the sad news to her in the morning. That night, in that village just outside Suva, Nei celebrated the wedding. It was still quite early but she was tired from the surgery and all the excitement so she went to bed. And she had a dream. In the dream, her husband told her he was leaving now, that it was time for him to go. It was a very vivid dream and, upon waking, Nei told it to her hosts. She said she didn't take it to mean anything. It was then they told her that her husband had died and had already been buried. How she took this shocking news I can only imagine. She did not go back to Ngau … and is still on the main island outside Suva, with relatives from her village in Ngau who are supporting her in her grief.

"Encounter Culture"

Wednesday, July 15th—Today Tau and I set out on a series of meetings to further the "Encounter Culture" program for the use of his land. Visitors would live in modified Fijian thatched huts adjacent to the village, hence, preserving the privacy of the villagers and preventing uninvited outsiders from arriving on their doorsteps. The program would introduce visitors to the indigenous culture, not only to aid in international and cross-cultural understanding, but also to explore the role of culture in the formation of our perceptions about ourselves and the outside world. Participants would have a chance to discover how cultural perceptions are formed, and how they are maintained and reinforced. With this insight, they could free themselves from their own conditioned ways of thinking. "Encounter Culture", in a very adventurous and exotic way, would be an anthropological rite of passage. We talk to people at the Economic Development Bank and the Visitors Bureau. The meetings go well and Tau is encouraged. He feels confident that the program will be a big success, offering great rewards to visitors and villagers alike.

No Opinion

Thursday, July 16th—Tonight Tau and I are invited to the home of a Fijian family living in a small unit of a subsidized housing development in the Suva suburb of Nairai. The wife works in a hotel coffee shop; the husband is a draftsman. They have relatives in Tau's village on Ngau.

When we arrive, two Fijian men are present, drinking kava. We join in and, after some preliminary conversation, they ask what I think of the political situation. I tell them it's a bit like wishing the earth were flat and then proceeding as if it were so. I don't think they get it. I expand somewhat, putting the situation in historical context: the culture of the Fijians, the plight of the Indians…I still don't think they get it. I ask them what *they* think of the political situation. They respond that it is up to those in power to do something about it. They have no opinion as to what. In fact, there appears an almost total incapability to think about it. They willingly relegate responsibility to "higher-ups".

As we are about to have dinner—and they have prepared special food—a family of six arrives unexpectedly from Nadi to spend the night. Once again, kinship ties prevail. The mother of the family from Nadi is a cousin of the wife we are visiting. The hostess seems not at all perturbed to have six unexpected guests. In fact, she appears to be thrilled to see them. I take only a bit of food so that it can be shared around. On the way home, we stop at a restaurant to have dinner.

The Enemy Within

Friday, July 17th—Early this morning Tau and I have our planned and critical meeting with a key civil servant from the Ministry of Fijian Affairs, the government body whose task it is to see to the needs of the indigenous Fijians. Tau wants to consolidate his plan to develop his land. He has presented his proposal before the island chiefs for approval on more than one occasion, and despite the passage of many months, they have yet to respond in any manner. Tau asks for assistance from this Ministry to get things moving.

Beside the doorway in the office of this civil servant is a wall hanging on which is written a statement from Pope John Paul II. It reads:

The admiration which I feel for the people of Fiji existed before I came to your country. In a very visible way, you are a symbol of hope in the world. You have something to teach the world about solidarity and loving respect for every person.

The message seems to have fallen on deaf ears—both inside and outside the office, for the psyche of this deeply acculturated Fijian civil servant reflects the cultural wound. The problem is not with the Fijians but with everyone else around them, he expounds. And no one—except the Fijians themselves—can possibly understand Fijians. The solution to the problem is simple: everyone else is to get out of the way, because, as he puts it, Fijians are different. "We are ruled by our chiefs. We act only if and when the chiefs say so."

"We are very patient people," he elaborates. "We are good at waiting." In short, he—and his Ministry—will do nothing to assist Tau to get permission to develop his own land.

I watch this man who occupies a rather prominent post in the government hierarchy, constraining the very people it is his task to advance. He is an example of the culture *writ large*, a prisoner, in love with his own chains. In this manner, he has become the enemy, preventing the Fijians from competing successfully within their own country. Like him, the Fijians internalize the constraints, then repress and project their frustration onto an unwitting victim, in this case the Indians, who are advancing for the very reason that they are not caught in the same cultural bind.

The enemy: not "out there" to be controlled and defeated but "the enemy within", controlling, defeating, and feeding upon its own hostile imagination.

Following this very uncomfortable—and unproductive— meeting, it takes us a while to settle our minds and get things back into perspective. I feel I no longer know how to make good things happen for these people. The knowledge that their own chiefs and administrators are holding Fijians back from competing successfully in their own country weighs heavily on my mind. I feel like it is time to turn my attention to deeper things.

We have not yet had breakfast so we get something to eat. Then we pack our bags and make our way back to Nausori airport. It is here that we meet a newly married young couple from Israel, wearing *sulu* with packs on their backs, headed for ... guess where? To Ngau. In the course of conversation with them, I learn that they know no one on the island and do not know where they will stay. They have tent and camping gear with them and feel no need to get permission to camp on someone else's land. These are the very tourists who are looking for and would benefit from Tau's "Encounter Culture" experience. There is no program to offer them now, but they are coming anyway—and the villagers will not benefit or be compensated for the unauthorized use of their island.

We board the *Fiji Air* Cessna for the short flight. Once again, we fly in over the coconut palms and touch down on the gravel runway. We take a lorry to the village; the Israeli couple comes with us. I take them to my little house to park their luggage while Tau asks the appropriate ritual permission for the two foreigners to camp on their land. The villagers are curious, of course, to know who these foreigners are.

Sai comes to the veranda and introduces herself. She immediately assumes they are with us and, therefore, invites them to dinner. As soon as the couple heads out of the village to the piece of land Tau has arranged for their use, I quickly tell Sai the couple is not with us so she does not feel she must prepare meals for them. Would she have minded in any case? Would she simply see it as her duty? Or does she even think about it at all! Who knows!

The couple pitches a tent on the piece of land just outside the village. The villagers immediately go to them, bringing drinking coconuts, inviting them to take their meals with them and stay in their sleeping houses. They find it strange, even unfriendly, to have these foreigners in their midst and yet have them remain outside the village.

Once the visitors are attended to, I turn my attention back to my own affairs, and to the big papaya tree beside my little house. It had a number of very large unripe papayas on it. I had been watching them carefully for weeks, anticipating the day they would be ready to eat. One was just beginning to ripen the day I left for Suva last Monday. Tau thought it would be ready by the time we return. When we arrived in the village, one of the first things I did was check the tree to see if the big papaya was ready to eat. But it was gone—that one and four more large unripe ones. When the family who took them saw me looking at the empty tree, they came and told me that the papaya were ripe so they picked them.

Tonight for dinner we have *ika vakalolo* … and cooked unripe papaya. Guess whose!

A Farewell Party

Saturday, July 18ᵗʰ—Today we go to Yaciwa island, a kind of farewell party since I will be leaving the village on Monday to go to Australia. I want to offer the outing to the members of our extended family. I know that Saturday is a busy day because of the preparations for *Siga Tabu*, so I am pleased that all of the nine children, plus Iliki and Eli and Sai come with us. We also invite the Israeli couple.

We were planning to take the village boat but discover it has a hole in it. So there is only Sele's boat—and, once again, it is his Sabbath. Lucky for us this time, it happens that he is going by boat up to Tau's mother's village for his Sabbath church service. He agrees to drop us off at Yaciwa island on the way and pick us up in the late afternoon on his return.

It takes a while to get things ready. We cut firewood for the *lovo*, and get some taro leaves for *rourou* from the garden. The children are really excited as they collect the leaves for the *lovo*. Mili gets the coconuts, Iliki the taro and breadfruit. We leave about 9 a.m. and the trip to the island takes 20 minutes. Once again, the women and girls "set up camp" and replicate the village pattern, complete with mats, cooking pots, coconut scrapers, dishes and the like.

Immediately upon arrival, Sai and Eli and a third woman who come with us attach baskets to their backs and go out line fishing while the children play at the edge of the reef. Iliki goes spear fishing. Little Mili starts scraping coconuts, her younger "sisters"—Iliki's daughters—cut up the taro stems and Tau makes the *lovo*. We put in the root crops and cover them with leaves and earth. It's a familiar pattern now, even to me. The women return from fishing with a very good catch; the reef is full of fish! They clean and prepare the fish as the girls prepare the *rourou*. Iliki, back from spear fishing, builds a fire, and the fish and *rourou* get cooked.

I'm watching all this and by now it is midday. I don my snorkeling gear and once again head into the cool water to view the coral and fishes. By the time I am back, the meal is ready. There is fish—lots of it—and taro and breadfruit and *rourou*. The Israeli couple waits for the women to eat.

"No, you eat now. We eat after," Eli says to them in English. I didn't even know she could speak English!

The meal over, I give the children some treats of peanuts and rice cookies I have brought from Suva. Now that their work is done, I think perhaps the women can rest and join the party, but they strap their baskets to their backs and head into the water again. This time it is for tomorrow's protein. Iliki and Tau, as before, find a spot in the shade and fall asleep. The children are in the water again and are exploring the island.

I sit with the two Israelis who are eating some roasted coconut and *ivi* nuts. We chat. They tell me they really wanted to camp rather than stay with a family in the village because this is also their Sabbath and there were some things they wanted to make sure to do, like lighting a candle, taking unleavened bread and wine. It was very windy, they tell me, and they had a terrible time trying to light the candle. All this discussion got sparked, actually, when Iliki offered them a piece of a giant crab he caught and roasted on the fire. They, of course, could not eat it, observing strict Jewish dietary laws.

"To what sect of Judaism do you belong?" I ask them, knowing that there are varying degrees of strict observance.

"There are no sects in Judaism," they respond.

"Well, in Canada, we have Orthodox, Conservative and Reformed, for example."

"That only applies to Jews outside Israel in order to maintain some Jewish identity," the woman states, and then adds, "To be a Jew is to live in Israel."

"Is there a consensus among Jews in Israel about how to resolve the Palestinian issue?" I ask her.

"There is," she replies, "but it doesn't fit with that of people in other parts of the world." I deem it wise to change the subject.

As promised, Sele returns with the boat to pick us up late afternoon. The women are still out line fishing and I notice they do not come ashore. I wonder if they realize he is here waiting for them. Or is he "waiting"? He doesn't appear to be. He is just sort of "here now". It is an hour longer before the women have their catch, after which time we climb in the boat and motor our way back to the village.

Praying or Preying?

Sunday, July 19th—Sai bakes scones early this morning and sends some to the Israeli couple. I skip breakfast; Tau and I go out to the garden where we find a ripe papaya high in a tree. Tau cuts a tall pole and knocks it down. We eat it in the garden, truly a Garden of Eden—and the people are not even allowed to come here today!

At the worship service this morning, on the instruction of the Methodist church office, there are to be prayers offered for a peaceful solution to the current political crisis in Fiji.

"O God, give peace to each individual in Fiji, and fill us with love so that a peaceful solution can be achieved," they pray. After the service, these same villagers react to news on the radio about Fijian youths breaking into Indian shops in Raiwaqa.

"They deserve the kind of treatment they are getting because they're impossible," offers one, referring to Indians. "To make it easy for themselves, they should just surrender."

"What Butadroka (founder of the Nationalist party) said is what they deserve," adds another. "'Just give me one hour to lead this country; I'll take them all to the wharf'". He goes on. "Well, the punishment would be that they can't swim. So just push them off the wharf and that's the end of them."

"There's a saying that Fijians have been saying from way back and it's turning out to be true," adds a third, "that there's no good Indian except a dead Indian."

Frustration … repression … projection … attack … Frustration at ending up in an inferior economic position in their own country … Repression of their feelings, masked by a façade of brotherhood … Projection onto their Indian compatriots as the source of their problem … Attack as a solution to their woes. It is the essential dynamic of thwarted individuality playing itself out. Praying inside this mindset isn't going to get them through this one.

Tonight there is choir practice. Tau's cousin has come from his mother's village to lead the singing. He tells Tau that his uncle Momo kept a daily journal right up to the time of his death. On the day his wife went to Suva for medical treatment, he wrote, "Today my heart is very heavy. Nei went to Suva to the hospital. I feel that we will never meet again." He put a $10 note on that page in the diary to be given to her when she returns.

Tau takes the Israeli couple to the community centre tonight and presents some kava as their *i sevusevu*. Then they drink kava and listen to the choir practice. That the couple is from Israel is really exciting to these villagers; they truly see Israel as the Holy Land, if not right up in Heaven. The Israeli couple sings a song in Hebrew; the villagers are enthralled. It is a lovely cultural encounter but I find it an interesting and disconcerting parallel … Fijians scapegoating their Indian compatriots who were unwittingly transplanted on their land while embracing Israelis who willfully planted themselves on the land of the Palestinians.

Leaving "Home"

Monday, July 20ᵗʰ—Today I will once again leave my little island home. I get up early to help Tau plant the yam seed that Mata has already cut. If the seed is not used soon, it will rot. I see our little vegetable garden sprouting away: lettuce, carrots, corn, cucumber, green peppers, tomatoes…They will grow into healthy plants and provide good nutrition for Tau after I have left Fiji.

After breakfast back in the village, I tidy up the house and hastily pack my things. Once again, Tau will come to the main island with me. We make our way to the airstrip, weigh in, buy our tickets and then sit for a while with Sai and Mata who have come to see us off.

The little *Fiji Air* plane appears in the sky and touches down on the airstrip. Before too many minutes have passed, the pilot signals he is ready to leave again. I shake hands with Mata who says he will be slim the next time I see him. I kiss Sai in Fijian style; she tells me to come back soon.

Tau and I board the flight. I can see Sai through the tiny window. She waves and smiles as we taxi to take-off position. Then the little plane speeds down the gravel airstrip and I see her no more. The coconut palms, the long sandy beach and the turquoise sea … out over the reef to the blue ocean dotted by the islands of Lomaiviti … the coast of Viti Levu and we are once again back on the "mainland".

The Great Council of Chiefs is meeting in Suva today. The delegates are in the Civic Auditorium adjacent to Sukuna Park on the main street called Victoria Parade. Members of the right wing *i Taukei* (indigenous Fijians) movement are holding a rally in the park. There is a huge crowd of Fijians here; they are listening to music and making speeches. Excitement is running high; inside the Civic Auditorium, the Council is hearing submissions from the fourteen Provincial Councils to consider whether or not to allow representation in tomorrow's meeting by the *i Taukei* movement and the deposed Coalition government.

The crowd is getting caught up in the rally. At the edge of the park, along Victoria Parade, Indian shopkeepers stand quietly in their doorways, taking in the scene. Later in the evening, we come across police and army personnel at one of these same Indian shops; the windows have been smashed.

Disparity … dissatisfaction … tension … violence: the surface drama playing out in the physical world.

Frustration … repression … projection … attack: the psychological drama playing out in the depth below ….

"Fiji for the Fijians"

Tuesday, July 21ˢᵗ—This morning after walking up to the Governor-General's residence and back, Tau and I go for breakfast. The restaurant is on the rooftop of a hotel, which itself is situated on a hill overlooking the city. From here one has a marvelous view of the ocean and islands in the distance.

From this vantage point, we can also view the Civic Auditorium below and see members of the Council of Chiefs heading for the second day of their meetings. They look so educated and professional in their shirts and ties, pocket *sulu* and suit jackets. Yet most of them have probably not had the opportunity to graduate from secondary school. They have little knowledge of economics and the wider political process, little or no understanding of Indian culture or history … and here they assemble to decide the political future of a divided nation.

There is an unusually large contingent of police and military around today, and the military are armed with rifles. Understandable in these circumstances—but not the image one is accustomed to see in this docile South Pacific nation. I go about things as usual, enjoying these last few days before leaving Fiji. I stop to chat with the Indian merchant whose shop was damaged last night. He shows me a hole in the glass door and says nothing was taken; the police and army arrived very soon after the break-in occurred.

It seems the Coalition supporters asked for a permit to meet at Sukuna Park today and were denied. As for the *i Taukei*, their permit was given for one day only—which was yesterday—but today their supporters are here again in large numbers. They bear signs that read "Fiji for the Fijians", and declare that they want Fiji to become a republic.

A number of demonstrators take the podium and make impromptu speeches; the sentiment is largely anti-Indian.

"We have been led to believe that Fiji is owned by the Fijians," shouts one supporter, "but it is not. Just look around. Indians own all the businesses. None is owned by Fijians."

One Fijian woman braves the crowd and speaks into the microphone. "We Fijians are known for being loving, so why can't we show love to the Indians. They work hard."

The crowd shouts her down. "Do you belong to the Indians?" they heckle. And the surface drama plays on ….

Tonight after dinner, when Tau and I walk along Victoria Parade, we see that all the Indian shops have wooden timbers covering their storefronts, the kind of fortifications normally put in place for a pending hurricane. It is a hurricane indeed, but this time of a very different nature.

Shattered Windows, Shattered Lives

Wednesday, July 22nd—In the early morning I walk with Tau to the seawall beside the Civic Auditorium where we can enjoy some fresh oranges. There are a lot of military personnel about, and the building itself is roped off. There are military on the roof as well. The tension is palpable.

We go to the public market. I buy two lovely papayas and some passionfruit from an Indian vendor. He is happy and smiling, and says it is nice to see me again. I ask him how his business is doing; he replies that no one is shopping at the market this week.

The Council of Chiefs meeting goes into its third day of session at the Civic Auditorium. The crowd outside, mostly *i Taukei* supporters, keeps vigil. They have their signs again: "Fiji for the Fijians".

Sometime in the early afternoon, a number of Indian shops become the target of the mounting tension. One shop is an up-market jewelry store; the windows and glass counters are smashed. Immediately the store is locked and metal shutters placed over the exterior windows. Other shopkeepers follow suit until all the duty-free shops are closed.

Later in the afternoon, Tau and I return to the public market to buy some fruit for tomorrow's breakfast. It is a very strange experience. Most of the stalls are closed and covered with canvas. Then I realize there are *no* Indians in the market at all. Out of fear, they have simply closed their shops and gone home. One can feel the tension, like the calm before a hurricane. We leave the market without buying anything.

We go to the post office to get some stamps. Even here the windows have been covered with metal reinforcements. Inside, where there are usually lineups, the building is almost empty. A young Indian teller informs us that many of the clerks are afraid to stay downtown; they have left their posts and gone home. Outside, I see that other establishments are boarding up their windows: a travel agency, the office of *Air New Zealand*—even the Pizza Hut ….

Oh, no, not the Pizza Hut!

Time to Go

Thursday, July 23rd—I am awake very early to catch a taxi to Nadi with Tau. There are three other passengers, all of whom—plus the driver—are of Indian origin. I greet them when we meet and they respond but, apart from that, they do not speak at all with us during the three-hour trip.

The driver is in a very foul mood—not surprising, given the events of late. He drives like hell—which is not unusual for taxi drivers in any case—but there is more than making good time on his mind. He is angry. At one point along the open highway, three Fijian men are sitting along the border of the pavement. There is plenty of room, with no traffic in sight, and the driver can easily steer out a bit and go around them. Instead, he blows his horn and drives straight toward them, missing them by only inches. We make a brief stop at the halfway mark—the public market in Sigatoka. It is a chance to get some food. I find something, but the tension inside the vehicle is not conducive to digestion so I decide not to eat.

Upon arrival in Nadi, Tau and I go to the village just outside town to visit his sister. The new baby has arrived now and Nana is still here.

"*Luvequ, luvequ,* (My daughter, my daughter)" she repeats as she hugs and kisses me.

We chat for a while and give Nana some tobacco money. Then we leave. She walks with us as far as the village edge to say good-bye. Minutes later, when we reach the end of the straight stretch of road before it turns toward Nadi town, I look back and see that she is still standing there.

Please ....

Friday, July 24th—A lot of international flights pass through Nadi in the middle of the night. My check-in time is 3 a.m. for a 5 a.m.

departure. I question the wisdom of sleeping for only 2 or 3 hours and decide to stay awake. A few other hotel guests, also catching flights in the night, are partying in the hotel bar. They are happy. Of course they are happy: they are flying out of here.

Tau comes with me to the airport. After the check-in procedures, we sit down for a last few minutes together. He grows very quiet and says nothing. I want to reach out to him and I don't know how. I take a piece of paper and write on it "Please ..." followed by a number of blank lines and ask him to complete the sentence. He takes the pen.

"Please ... help me get out of here," he writes.

What do I do! I cannot take him with me. I talk about returning to Fiji, about how much I care about him, about how much his friendship means to me. But they are empty words of comfort and I know it ....

The *Canadian Airlines* jumbo jet is sitting on the tarmac now. It completes the refueling on its short stopover between Honolulu and Sydney. The passengers will be in the departure lounge and I know it's time to join them there.

We stand up, look at each other and silently fall into a warm embrace. Before passing through the glass doors, I look back at this lovely man, so ready to share whatever life and fortune he has with me. I love him dearly, this acculturated *i Taukei* whose fate it is to belong to these "cannibal isles".

I feel numb—and helpless. I board the flight—a DC-l0 bound for Sydney—and settle into my seat. The jet taxis down the runway, then its engines roar and we fly out of the Fiji night.

Yes, it seems there is no place on the planet that is safe anymore. There was even a coup in paradise.

BOOK III

The Reluctant Republic

November, 1987

Part I

THE SECOND TIME AROUND

Boxes, Little Boxes

Saturday, November 7th—Air Pacific: the only international airline from which I have never felt tempted to steal the cutlery. I'm bound once again for the Fiji Islands. As I take up my pen, we are as far northeast of Sydney, Australia as a jumbo jet can travel in one hour.

Only a few months have passed since I left Fiji, but in that short time a lot has happened. For the first while, things were looking up. Governor-General Ratu Sir Penaia Ganilau, who was head of the country's emergency government when I departed at the end of July, was searching for a formula to solve Fiji's ethnic and political problems. The principal means was Constitutional reform. He set up a review committee to recommend changes to the 1970 Constitution that would assure political supremacy for the ethnic Fijians. That seemed to be what coup leader Sitiveni Rabuka was demanding.

The Constitutional Report was due at the end of July. By mid-August, when it was already two weeks overdue, the eagerly awaited report suffered another setback. The problem: "a faulty photocopier delays Fiji's Constitutional Report". That was the headline in an Australian newspaper on August 15th alongside a picture of Colonel Rabuka signing a contract for his autobiography!

There's a little old lady sitting across the aisle from me. She's wearing a blue print dress with matching glass bead necklace and earrings. Her hair is soft white as is the crocheted short-sleeve sweater covering her thin shoulders. She is sitting by herself and is noticeably anxious. I watch her completing her landing card for Fiji Immigration; her hand is shaking so badly she cannot fit the letters into the tiny square boxes.

"Are you traveling alone?" I lean to ask her.

That's all she needs. She confides how terribly nervous she feels and confesses she doesn't know what to do. She asks me to check her landing card. It's correct, apart from the fact she has neglected the part about nationality.

"A-U-S-T-R-A-L-I-A," I direct her to write.

The Australian lady tells me that her sister lives in Fiji and will meet her at the airport. In the meantime, she is on her own. She takes daily medication for high blood pressure and insomnia, and she obtained a letter from her physician so the authorities in Fiji will not think she is importing illegal drugs. In her haste to get to the airport, she has brought the letter and forgotten the medication.

"All this pressure," she laments, "is too much for an old person." I assure the dear lady that I will stay with her until we meet her relatives and that I will assist her with whatever needs to be done. This seems to greatly relieve her anxiety. It is then she tells me she has brought along two dogs and a cat. She's going to be staying in Fiji for a few months and she couldn't possibly leave them behind. They are tranquillized and riding in a separate compartment, of course, and she says it has cost more for their passage than for her own. I find all this quite astounding considering her age and medical condition. I'm beginning to wonder just what I've gotten myself into—and then she adds that one of the dogs is blind.

So the long-awaited report of Fiji's Constitutional Review Committee was delayed because of the breakdown of a photocopying machine! No matter, for there was another and even more promising development taking place during these intervening months: the move by the Governor-General to set up a "conference of national unity" as a step toward restoring an elected government. By mid-September, both the defeated and deposed Prime Ministers had agreed to be part of it, quite an achievement since the two had not even met since the May 14th coup. Not only that: they were reconciled that neither would be leader; instead, the Governor-General would continue to exercise executive authority.

Not that a conference of national unity would solve everything. On the contrary, its task would be to achieve the near impossible: getting Fiji's Indian population to accept Constitutional amendments that would relegate them to a permanent position of political inferiority. At least it would restore the country to some level of respectability in the international community, and it would buy time: time for ethnic Fijians to placate their fears of Indian domination, and time for Indo-Fijians to be assured a meaningful role in the economic life of the country.

Breakfast—a fascinating texture to the eggs—and I plug into some classical music for a while. Through the window of the aircraft I can see cloud formations over the vast Pacific Ocean. Across the aisle the little old lady is busy doing a crossword puzzle in the flight magazine. Now the letters fit neatly inside the tiny square boxes. It's like a metaphor for what is happening in Fiji. At first you find the boundary too   constricting, but with time, you get comfortable inside it.

So a way out of Fiji's political crisis seemed to be at hand. And history might even be kind to Rabuka. The record would show that just one week after the coup, in which no one was killed, and in which the arrested members of the deposed government were released, Rabuka had handed power right back to the Governor-General. And a little over a hundred days after the coup, the leaders of the two most important political parties in the country were ready to sit down together with the intent of forming a national government under the direction of the Queen's representative. This new bipartisan government, whose task it would be to return the country to parliamentary rule, would itself be guided by democratic principles.

It was past mid-September when the Governor-General made the welcome announcement, and it was the single most hopeful development since the May 14th coup. But then—just when you thought it was safe to take pictures—a second military coup! At 4 p.m. on Friday, September 25th, Rabuka once again resumed control of the government of Fiji. His rationale this time: recent developments would not achieve the aim of the coup, which was to assure ethnic Fijians control of Parliament and of the nation.

Events now moved in quick succession. Politicians, civil servants and judges were arrested. The two daily newspapers and a commercial radio station were closed. Soldiers rounded up foreign journalists for deportation. Phone links with the outside world were cut, and an 8 p.m. to 5 a.m. curfew was imposed. Twelve days later, in a midnight radio broadcast, Rabuka read a proclamation declaring Fiji to be a republic.

We prepare to land. The dear old lady across the aisle grows nervous again.

"Do you realize," she says as she secures her seatbelt, "that we are putting our lives in the hands of one man!" I tell her there are at least two people up there in the cockpit plus a computer.

"A computer?" she exclaims. "What will computers do next! They'll be running our lives before we know it." I'm beginning to think that might be a distinct advantage.

Rabuka staged the first coup with the assumption that he enjoyed the support of most ethnic Fijians. That covers about 46 per cent of the population, and the record shows that he did have powerful support, including that of the Great Council of Chiefs and the former Prime Minister. But this time things would be different. Rabuka had now opposed not only the majority population of the country and the duly elected government but also the Governor-General who by now had the support of both the former and deposed Prime Ministers. The only people left are the ethnic extremists of the *i Taukei* movement and the military forces; in short, an ethnic minority—and all the guns.

Once again, critical days lay ahead for Fiji.

I accompany the little old lady through Customs, help her retrieve her luggage—three large suitcases tied with oversized blue plastic bows for identification—then deliver her to equally anxious relatives beyond the sliding glass doors. There's a sister and her husband, their son and the Fijian girl to whom he will soon be married. They all embrace their visitor and welcome her to the republic of Fiji. Then off they go together—in search of two dogs and a cat.

Tau is waiting for me as usual. While I convert some currency, he looks for transport to Suva. The exchange rate is very good. For the first time in my 17 years of coming to Fiji, the Canadian dollar is worth more than its Fijian counterpart.

We take a cab to the Nadi bus station from where the Indian driver finds us a running cab to Suva. We debate the wisdom of making the trip on a Saturday night because of the curfew and the fact that we have made no preparations for food on Sunday; no restaurants are open because of the military rules. But there is no transport on Sunday, and we don't want to stay in Nadi until Monday, so we set out in a private cab with two Indian guys.

We have a nice time, chatting in English along the way; they tell great stories and express opinions about the coup. They find the Sunday laws particularly irksome, forced to sit at home all day doing nothing, not even being allowed to play in their yards … no jogging, no swimming, no picnicking…Their home taxi station is beside the military camp. They know many of the soldiers—including Rabuka—and they like them. In fact, they describe them as "nice people". But they say that some of the army recruits are not clear about their role, and are quite taken with their sudden power. One story they tell is of a young boy sent by his father to buy something. The child did not make it back before the 8 p.m. curfew so was taken by the military to a cell. Then they waited outside the boy's home for the father to go looking for him, which he did, and found his son crying in the lock-up. The soldiers then arrested the father for breaking the curfew, and both father and son spent the night in jail!

To help us through the Sunday restrictions—there is no restaurant at the Suva hotel where I will be staying—the cab driver stops along the way so I can buy some mangoes. And when we get to Sigatoka town, about the halfway mark, the young driver stops at a mosque to pray while a second man drives us through the police checkpoint to get to the public market. I find some eggplant, sweet potatoes and squash. The hotel in Suva has a small kitchen facility where I can cook vegetables. Then it's back through the police checkpoint to pick up the driver at the mosque and onward to Suva.

I drop my bags at the hotel, and Tau and I hastily make our way downtown to eat so as to be back before the curfew—now extended to 11 p.m.—goes into effect. We are walking to the restaurant at 8 o'clock on a Saturday night through the heart of town—and there is hardly anyone around. Shop windows are boarded and padlocked. Street signals are not working—they have been turned off to save electricity—and above all, there is no activity. It is like a ghost town. The restaurant too is almost empty.

We take a cab back to the hotel because of the darkness and eerie silence.

Walk, Don't Run

Sunday, November 8th—Sunday in Fiji is quiet enough in any case but especially so after the second military coup. In the afternoon we go for a walk. You can walk—probably even speed walk—just so long as you don't run. So walk we do, down along the harbour, then

Victoria Parade as far as the former Governor-General's residence beside the Botanical Gardens. Once again, we see very few people—not more than a dozen the whole time—aside from police and military personnel.

I am interested to know if the "Buckingham Palace" style guard at the President's mansion is still at his post. I figure he will no longer be there, given the fact that Fiji has now been declared a republic and the role of Governor-General no longer exists. But there he is, in formal dress of white *sulu* and red tunic, with rifle at the side and eyes straight ahead, pacing through the ritual movements with the formality that only royalty can command. Fiji is a reluctant republic.

We walk back along Victoria Parade to the hotel. There are two soldiers posted near the Fiji Development Bank. Two young Fijian women across the street are calling words to them. The soldiers are noticeably pleased with the attention. They grin nervously. It all seems such a paradox to me, these tough soldiers in full battle regalia sporting loaded rifles, distracted by a few sweet words and suggestive glances from the opposite sex. How vulnerable they are, how cliché—yet how formidable. It reminds me how easy it is to mould people into just about anything you want them to be.

Wholly Communion

Monday, November 9th—Radio Fiji used to sign on at 6 a.m. with "God Save the Queen". This morning they play a few bars of "Blue Spanish Eyes" before the Fijian national anthem. I don't get it.

I take an early morning walk along the beachfront with Tau. The city has not yet come to life and there are few people about. Two trucks loaded with army personnel pass along the main street. In the second truck a soldier waves excitedly to Tau. The soldier is a chief from his island, just one of many Fijians who have rejoined the army because of the political crisis. I guess it offers meaning and excitement to those who support the coup.

We want to send some treats back "home" to the village—bread, jam, peanut butter—but there are so few passengers traveling to Ngau that I cannot find anyone to take them, so we must send packages by air freight. We buy the goods and wrap them securely, then head to the freight office to fill out the forms and pay the fee. Decorating the walls inside the building are scenic Fiji travel posters with catchy slogans:

"Fiji: the way the world should be."

"Fiji: so much to share."

"Smiling faces, friendly people"

"We play all year."

Packages duly registered, Tau heads to the Ministry of Education to see about a UNDP (United Nations Development Program) position that is being set up to offer grass roots community development to islands in the South Pacific. The Ministry has recommended him for the post in view of his university education, community development record and overseas experience. There are to be twenty people hired and a one-week training program is to be held this month to choose and prepare the successful candidates. He's feeling quite hopeful and is clear that this is the kind of work he wants to do. However, when he arrives at the Ministry office, they inform him the project is being taken out of Fiji in view of the political instability here. He is very disappointed. He wants to work actively in social welfare and is eager to break out from the village at the same time. I feel badly to see his hopes dashed yet again. It's just another example of how wide-ranging is the effect of one man's political actions.

We go to the public market. There is an area where kava is sold, and where an Indian merchant who buys kava wholesale from Ngau owns a stall. Over the years, I have often seen men from Tau's island there; it's one of the places they like to gather when they come to Suva.

I have always felt uplifted watching Indians and Fijians sharing a cup of kava together.

We approach the spot—and there they are, just like before, swapping stories and opinions as they drink together. They call us over to join them and offer the customary kava.

I lift the cup and drink. It is like the shared wine of communion, this ground root of the pepper plant mixed with water and served in a coconut shell. I feel a sense of oneness with them, an authentic fellowship achieved without the sham and pious pretence of organized religion. No rituals, no vestments—just a wonderful sense of unity. One of the ethnic Fijians is wearing a T-shirt that seems to say it all. It reads, "Take a good look at me. I'm a Fijian. So what?"

So What ... is the Goal?

Tuesday, November 10th—I'm awake at 4:30 a.m., probably because I went to bed so early last night. It is so quiet here in the evenings with the curfew, and the city is dead after trading hours finish for the day.

I sit on the patio of the hotel. It faces a rock cliff garden, framed by coconut palms. Beautifully coloured birds are singing as they move about the tropical landscape. The scene is truly peaceful.

After some morning fruit, I go to the post office to get stamps—and there it is: an oversized reproduction of that now famous engagement picture of Charles and Diana. It's the one where Charles is standing on a box to make himself appear tall and the bride-to-be is tipping her head to make herself appear shy. Two illusions that time would shatter—and another example of Fiji as the reluctant republic!

In the early evening Tau and I take a bus to Raiwaqa, a densely populated Suva suburb of largely ethnic Fijian city-dwellers. We have been invited to a Fijian home there, with a request that I offer information and advice about the future career of an eldest daughter currently completing Form 6. The daughter is not present; she is in a Catholic boarding school ready to sit for her final exams. In the home at present are her parents, her maternal grandmother and two younger sisters. The grandmother I met before, they tell me, while I was doing my fieldwork on Ngau. The elderly lady reminds me that I gave her a necklace at the time—I don't remember—and she still has it with her.

The tiny house has been neatly prepared for our visit. There are freshly ironed pillowcases and a new Fijian mat on the floor. The family is dressed up in Sunday attire. They seat us on a coach with pillows pressed against our backs and then proceed to sit on the floor. I beckon the grandmother to sit on the coach beside me; she does.

We exchange greetings and I am introduced to the family. There is the usual kind of reserve one feels when meeting people for the first time so we begin with customary chitchat. When did I arrive in Fiji? When would I depart? Where was I staying? Would I be going to the village?

The family makes its living selling kava, and Tau's clan is the supplier. They buy the root by the kilo and package it into $1.00 size packets. It is at this time each day that people come by for their evening supply, and in a few short minutes, they sell $10.00 worth. The father tells us the men drink kava in the Catholic hall across the street and the coup has inadvertently provided them with a unique opportunity. If they are not home by the 11 p.m. curfew, they dare not leave the hall—and no one dares to come fetch them—so they get to stay out the whole night!

"And Sunday?" I ask.

"Well," he says, "these habits are hard to break in spite of the Sunday rules. So we meet—and we drink—but we don't exchange money for the kava on that day. It's drink now, pay later!" And he laughs.

The purpose of the meeting has not yet come up. I see the father beckon a daughter to prepare a table in front of us; they want to serve us tea. We quietly follow the course they have set for us, but Tau wisely suggests we have our tea on the mats in the customary Fijian manner. It is agreed, and they spread a red and white tablecloth and bring two cups of tea, a plate of cabin crackers and some butter. Only the two of us will partake; the others will watch and attend. I don't think I shall ever get used to this custom.

The tea is very hot; it takes me a long time to drink it. They sit quietly as I sip, and then we get to the task at hand.

"Well, where do we begin?" the father asks shyly.

"What is the goal?" I ask in reply.

My question shocks him. He says he doesn't know the goal, and I can see that he wants me to tell him what to do. I ask him what his daughter would like to do. He replies that his daughter says she will do whatever her parents want her to do. He then tells me the guidance teacher had suggested she become a teacher, but the daughter said she didn't want to become a teacher, and then later said she would. I ask if his daughter is aware of other career choices. He doesn't know. I suggest she not be rushed, that she be given some time to look into this. I ask about her interests and with what age groups she is most comfortable.

"Your questions are very complicated," he replies.

Now the conversation gets very interesting, and I see a depth in this man that seems to have been denied expression for a very long time. He tells me he was educated by Catholic priests, and that they really cared about the lives of their students. They imparted spiritual values as well as academic training, and that is why he sent his daughter to the same school. Now the priests are gone, he says, and the teachers, though academically qualified, do not seem to care about the students. Teaching is just a job for them, a way to get money. So we talk about all this, about what happens to people when they feel alienated from the product of their labour. People, not liking what they do, yet spending most of their active time and energy doing it. About education as a means to fitting people into slots in the labour market....

By this time, the kava bowl appears, and others join us. Tau buys two packets of his own kava and offers it as our *i sevusevu*. We shift into the ritual words and gestures of the ceremony. Then we drink: Tau first, then me; they give me my own coconut cup, as is the custom for a chief. Then the others drink and we carry on our discussions ... about love, about human relationships, about the quality of life and the things that so easily distort it ....

It grows dark. The kava bowl empties. Tau and I beg our leave. The daughter will probably become a teacher.

Bananas!

Wednesday, November 11th—At the public market, people are setting up their stalls for the day. It is alive and bustling at 6 in the morning. I am amazed at the abundance and variety of natural produce: truckloads of bananas ... mangoes and pineapples and papayas ... lettuce, cabbage, watercress, and cassava ... taro and yams ....

A banana vendor raises a canvas covering for shade over his temporary stall near the street. He swings a rope over the high branch of a tree to secure the covering, but the weight of the rope is not sufficient to bring it down the other side. He ties a banana to the end of the rope and tries again. It works! So ingenious! Bananas are the one commodity this man has plenty of—and he has figured out more than one thing he can do with them.

I watch an Indian lady inside the market opening up her stall. Neatly dressed in a freshly ironed sari, she stands on top of a counter reaching high above her head. Across the aisle, a Fijian man notices her effort and, without hesitation, climbs up to help her. Not a word is spoken … just a sense of their being in it together.

I wander among the stalls. There is a beautiful fragrance here and there lifting into the air, from tiny altars to Vishnu or Siva or whoever they take their god to be. Incense and flowers are offered to the gods in exchange for life and a new day.

Later in the morning I go downtown shopping with Tau. The stores are noticeably low in supplies of imported goods, and prices are high. I feel for these people. They have, for the most part, little disposable income. In the daytime it is business as usual—what there is of it, that is—and one almost forgets the unusual political circumstances, apart from the military presence. Even this has a decidedly Pacific flavor if not a sense of outright comedy about it. Like today, we are walking along the street and a truckload of military personnel approaches. The men are dressed in typical army camouflage with rifles and it all seems serious enough—except that they are smiling and waving vigorously to people they recognize as they pass. It's got to be the friendliest little coup in the history of the planet. Yet it is not to be taken lightly. These same smiling and waving people are ready and capable of violent action, if only the word is given.

We walk back toward the public market to get some fresh water clams for lunch; they taste great with butter and lime juice. We see a government jeep from the Ministry of Rural Development approaching and the driver is moving along at a respectable speed. Two policemen on motorcycles move up behind him and turn on their red lights and sirens. I cannot figure out what rule of the road the driver has possibly violated. Then I see what the fuss is all about. Behind the motorcycle is a limousine with darkened windows. Behind that, there is a second police motorcycle—an escort for some big wig in the military government. The jeep pulls off to the side and the entourage makes its way. For some reason, it strikes me as humorous. It's bananas!

On our return to the hotel, we meet a Fijian lady who spots Tau and immediately asks him—actually tells him—to give her some money. He laughs.

"Don't laugh. Come on, give me some money," she says. They joke for a bit and Tau gives her $5.00.

I don't recognize the woman and I cannot make sense of the exchange. Afterwards, he tells me that this lady had taken care of him once when he was three years old. His father was sick in hospital and his mother had gone to visit him. On that occasion, Tau was left with this woman. That was almost thirty years ago—and she has been collecting on it ever since.

Bananas!

Howdee!

Thursday, November 12th—In the early morning I go for a swim in the hotel pool. The setting is magnificent with leaning palm trees overhead, and the water is cool and refreshing. Birds are chirping away as they look for their breakfast. After my swim I have papaya. What a magnificent invention is a papaya. I wonder what the recipe can possibly be. That's one thing you can say for God: She sure can cook!

In the afternoon I go downtown with Tau to do some shopping for our trip to the village. There are so many things I want to take the children, including school materials for their exams next week. They will need pencils and rulers, erasers, pencil sharpeners, mathematical sets…Then there are practical items like towels, and shirts for the school uniforms. And then treats like Indian spiced peas and peanuts—and, of course, copious loaves of bread and jars of peanut butter.

The shopping is challenging because many items are now in short supply. In some shops I feel a reluctance to look over items unless I am prepared to purchase since the mainly Indian clerks appear so desperate to make a sale. I'm really feeling for them, but I know there is not a lot I can do to help them right now.

Tau does some shopping for the clan. He wants to buy a new fishing net for them. Like most other items, fishing nets are also in short supply, and rather than return to the village with none, he settles on two that are less in size and strength than he was hoping for. They can be stitched together.

We get what items we can find and make our way back to the hotel with the bags and bundles. All this sounds like a straightforward procedure, but to move along the streets of Suva with Tau, one must allow a great deal of time for what can best be described as a traditional Fijian social ritual. It is this customary habit Fijians have of conducting conversations on the sidewalks; in fact, it would be considered most unfriendly for people who know each other to pass on the street without engaging in this kind of ritual exchange.

I say ritual because, in most cases, nothing of substance is communicated and the dialogue follows a definite pattern. It goes something like this:

"*Bula.* (Hey, there.)"
"*Io.* (Hi.)"
"*Cava vou sa i rogo?* (What's new?)"
"*Sega soti ni dua na ka levu.* (Not much.)"
"*Kivei oqori?* (Where are you off to?)"
"*Au sa lako mada va'qo.* (Just heading there.)"
"*Cava ko la'ki cakava?* (What are you up to?)"
"*Sega, se cageta ravi mada na veva e sala.*
(Nothing, just kicking the paper on the street.)"

I've always been fascinated with this ritual as it can occupy a fair bit of time that, to my way of thinking, might be put to better use.

I'm thinking it to be peculiar to Fiji or to the South Pacific or perhaps traditional societies, and mention this to Tau. He informs me there is a similar European ritual and he relates a conversation he heard during one of his trips to Canada a few years earlier. I had taken him to the small prairie town of Vauxhall, Alberta. I knew a family there and thought it might be an interesting place for Tau to visit, especially since the only thing he remembers learning about Canada in school is that it is a breadbasket! We drove into the prairie town and before we got to our destination, a member of the family—whom I had not yet met—hailed us down on the street.

"You must be Pamela," he said as he jumped into the car. I asked how he knew we were in town. He said the man in the hardware store had told him. I asked how the man in the hardware store could possibly know about us.

"There aren't many Volvos with British Columbia license plates on them in Vauxhall, Alberta!" he replied.

He proceeded to show us around town—the community centre, the curling rink, the Catholic church, the grain elevator...Like Tau in Suva, this guy knew just about everybody in Vauxhall, and when they would meet, the conversation went like this:

"Howdee."
"Howdee."
"What d'ya know for sure?"
"Not much."
"Where are ya headed?"
"Oh, here an' there."
"What are ya up to?"
"Oh, a little bit o' this and a little bit o' that and gettin' nowhere fast."

I remember encountering something similar when I was a sixteen years old girl, embarking on my first "anthropological fieldwork" in the small French village of L'Ardoise on Cape Breton Island in Nova Scotia, one of Canada's east coast maritime provinces. I was hosted by a family with very limited means, as were most other families in the village. The church, by contrast, was magnificent and very beautiful. On Sunday morning they took me with them to Mass, the first I had ever attended. What struck me was how often members of the congregation moved from a seated to a kneeling position—up and down, up and down ... but I said nothing.

Later that day, a teenager from the village accompanied me across the Canso Causeway to the mainland to attend a Protestant worship service—the first he had ever experienced. After the service ended, I asked him what he thought of it.

"Up and down!" he responded. "Up and down!"

It reminds me that we are more alike than we know. But, in this latter case, it also harks back to something even more fundamental. The human mind, in its incessant need to know, to understand and to control, confuses its perception of an event with the event itself. Indeed, perception becomes reality.

Part II

LET IT BE

"Black Friday"

Friday, November 13th—It's Friday the 13th—"Black Friday" as the Fijians call it. Interesting that Melanesians—*mela* means "black"— would designate that colour as inauspicious, and it reminds me how deeply ingrained are my own superstitions, for I'm thinking twice about the wisdom of taking a plane trip on this ominous date.

Just a few more supplies to get this morning and then we pack up our bags and bundles and boxes for the trip to the outer island. We board the transport bus for the ride to the airport and find an empty seat near the back just over the rear wheel. I soon see why no one was sitting here: there is a hole in the floor and every time Tau puts his foot down, it presses the broken floorboard against the fast moving wheel and it makes a terrible noise. It's not very safe at all, but it goes with the territory. I hope the aircraft is in better condition.

The roadblocks en route seem routine by now. Then we turn into the airport lane and get stopped by the military again. A soldier boards the bus and, standing at the front near the driver, utters some words. He is a very young man and so soft-spoken that we cannot hear what he is saying. Passengers look at each other in an attempt to get an accurate reading on the situation. The driver asks the soldier what he wants and then communicates to us on his behalf.

"Everybody must get off the bus," the driver says in a loud voice. I know this is a military dictatorship and all that, but there's

215

something about the situation that is just plain funny. There are some Indians sitting behind me; they grin and make comments. I start to laugh. Tau cautions me not to dare laugh, but that makes it even harder to keep a straight face. We disembark, the bus is checked, and we get back on again. Whatever they're looking for, we haven't got.

We arrive at the terminal, only to find that all the bags and boxes and bundles have to be searched. There is a huge lineup because everybody has lots of bags and boxes and bundles. One by one, the packages are opened, examined and resealed. It takes a fair bit of time given that the bags and boxes and bundles, for the most part, are secured with tape and bound with rope. More humorous still, most of the contents turn out to be bread.

After check-in, we are sent to the international departure lounge for a final security check, this time with the aid of a metal detecting machine. Then we wait for our flight to Ngau.

We wait a long time. A *Fiji Air* plane boards and departs for the island of Kadavu, followed by an *Air Pacific* jet destined for Labasa on the big island of Vanua Levu. Meanwhile, a passenger from Ngau walks into the lounge unchecked; the security guards are taking a break at the time. Then, with the jet engines roaring just outside the open windows, the passenger is spotted and taken back to the lounge entrance for his security check. The noise level is so high at this point that I'm sure no sound could be heard from the metal detection machine. When the check is finished, the passenger—wearing a *sulu* (traditional Fijian wrap-around male skirt), T-shirt and sandals— returns to his seat. This time, everyone—including Tau—bursts out laughing.

There are only five of us remaining in the international lounge by this time and we are all bound for Ngau. When the flight is finally announced, we pass through the designated departure gate and board the tiny *Fiji Air* plane. After all the waiting and the security precautions, we five now find there are seven passengers on the flight! So much for security!

If one wants to experience how very beautiful are the islands of Fiji, a flight on a small *Fiji Air* plane is a must. One can maneuver under, over or around fluffy white clouds, and there is a magnificent view of the intricate patterns in the reef. It is truly magical.

Friday the 13th—and the only reading material aboard the aircraft apart from the safety brochure is a religious tract entitled, "Have you got what God wants?" Here we are, riding around in the clouds and I'm reading, "The right time has come and the Kingdom of God is near …" A few minutes later we come down to earth over the gravel airstrip on Ngau.

It's so wonderful to see all the familiar faces. There are big smiles and hearty handshakes. I hope I can always return to this place. Paradoxically, it is "home", as much by default as design. We take the lorry to the village and dump our bags and boxes and bundles inside the verandah of my house.

After the greetings, I am left alone to settle in. The place is a mess. While I would usually set about to make it cozy, clean and attractive, my intuition this time tells me to just let it be.

Except for one thing.

"Do you know there are two eggs on your sleeping mat?" I say to Tau.

"Yes," he says, "and there are three more in the cupboard; I've been saving them."

"But they'll go bad in this heat," I protest.

"No," he says, "have a look at them."

I open the cupboard door. There I discover three rotting eggs emitting enough hydrogen sulfide to stock a chemistry lab. I shut the door again and I laugh. It's my house—but what the hell! Just enjoy the people and accept how things are. While I am laughing, Tau quietly removes the rotting eggs.

I air out some blankets and sweep the mats on the floor while Tau gives the two fishing nets to members of his clan. They immediately start stitching them together in preparation for tomorrow's fishing.

For dinner there is cassava and *rourou* (taro leaves). Then, after a cool bath at the water pipe under a beautiful star-lit sky, I fall to sleep in my little house to the strains of Christmas carols from the choir practice in the community centre. The melody I last remember hearing is "On Christmas Day in the Morning".

Collecting Seaweed

Saturday, November 14th—I miss the *malawa ni mataka* (daybreak). When I wake up, it is already daylight and Mili, in the village for Christmas break, has come to tell me it's a good time to collect *nama* (seaweed) while the tide is low. Off we go along with one of her "mothers"—her *Nana Levu* (Big Mother). *Nana Levu* is her father's oldest brother's wife.

The three of us head up the beach, then out to the tidal flat. *Nama* is a very nourishing seaweed found in abundance in this part of Fiji. We gather a few kilos of it in less than an hour.

I watch the two of them, how they bend from the waist rather than crouch, and how they remain in this position for sustained periods of time. The water is only a few centimeters deep so that cannot be the decisive factor. It is conditioning. Before the hour is up, I find myself doing the same thing! It is so subtle, this process by which we acquire culture.

Our carrying bag already full, *nana levu* instructs Mili to remove her *sulu* to hold the remainder. She obeys, and walks back toward the village in her shorts and halter-top. Now I see that her *nana levu* has left another *sulu* hanging from the low limb of a *dilo* tree outside the village. She instructs Mili to put on the *sulu* before entering the village. It is another subtle instruction, acquired without awareness, and Mili is one step further into her enculturation. Good/bad, right/wrong: it's all in place before too many years have passed.

I skip breakfast as usual. I eat some mangoes instead and seem to have appetite for little else. It's mango season in Western Fiji but the ones on Ngau are not yet mature. I've brought some from Suva but my supply is fast dwindling because the children are snitching them. They don't see it as snitching; they just see them hanging there in a basket on the verandah, and take them when they feel so inclined.

It's only 9 o'clock in the morning and it's already hot. Mili comes over and enters the house, turns on my radio, and then joins members of Tau's clan who are sitting under a tree preparing the fishing net. I go to the verandah where Tau is busy fixing something. While we are sitting there, a chicken enters, walks past us into the house and heads for a sleeping mat, presumably to lay another egg. Tau gets up from the verandah and goes inside the house. I assume it is because of the chicken, but instead, he turns off the radio, leaves the chicken where it is and then goes to work on the fishing net. Mili returns. She walks into the house, turns the radio back on and chases the chicken outside.

Let it be ….

Tonight Tau conducts a clan meeting on the verandah to discuss upcoming Christmas events, kava business and other clan matters. He has a number of small projects going now, and wants to prepare clan members to carry on without his leadership. It's a question of timing because if he steps aside too early, the projects might come to a standstill; if he waits too long, the members will not learn to do things for themselves. They don't yet get the connection between not achieving financial goals and blaming the Indians who do.

Lost Christianity

Sunday, November 15ᵗʰ—The church bell rings and the drums beat early for the morning prayer service. After a white flour breakfast there is Sunday school, the main church service, the mid-day meal—*ika vakalolo* and root crops—an afternoon rest, afternoon church service, an evening meal—*ika vakalolo* and root crops—then choir practice … the typical Sunday routine. I skip most of the food and all of the church. Tau's cousin brought me a lovely big papaya this morning so I eat it throughout the day.

In the afternoon, I retreat to a palm frond shelter that Iliki has built— attached to the back of my house—for storing the clan's kava business. Yes, there is no private property! Right now it's still empty, and the woven palm leaves make it very cool inside.

The villagers are worshipping; there is no doubt in their collective mind that Christianity is the one true religion. They do not have the spiritual heritage of India to enlighten them, and I am forced now to reflect on what might have transpired in my life had I not had that advantage. Indeed, so convinced was I of Christianity that very early in my life I decided to be a missionary. More paradoxical still, I was going to take the Christian message to India.

It was an early childhood experience that pointed me in that direction. I remember it vividly. It happened one Sunday morning in rural Nova Scotia when I was eleven years old. A missionary was guest speaker at our village church that day. He had just spent six years in India and was home on furlough. He told us about all the false gods they have over there and about their very primitive notions of medicine. For example, there was a local healer, he said, who grew the nail of his small finger on the right hand about three inches long so he could reach down and clean out the throats of people with respiratory infections. I never forgot that. Then he said the benediction in Hindi and that really blew my mind.

The missionary was encouraging people to go to India, and I was sure that was the path for me. Years later, when I graduated from high school, I studied Theology as part of a Bachelor of Arts program in Psychology and Religion, and in the course of translating the Bible from Hebrew, I "read between the lines". I discovered that the Old Testament is an anthropological monograph about a group of pastoral nomads in the Middle East. At the same time, I was studying Comparative Religion and quickly realized there's a lot to be said for other great traditions like Hinduism and Buddhism.

Of course, by then I knew I couldn't be a missionary—but I was still concerned about the guy who put his finger down people's throats, so I chose a more practical path and took a graduate degree in Social Work, concentrating on international development. I traveled to Southeast Asia and the Pacific islands, looking at foreign aid programs run by governments and international voluntary agencies. When I saw what was happening, I knew I couldn't do development either. The aid programs were perpetrating in the secular world what the missionaries had done in the name of religion. In both cases, they were destroying indigenous patterns of living and pulling local populations into the vortex of Western culture.

Interesting. First I was going to India to convert them. Then I was going to go there to help them. When I finally got there, I found it was the Indians who were "converting" and helping me. I discovered in India the perennial wisdom of the very religion I would have tried to dissuade.

And what of that wisdom? The *rishis* (holy men) looked upon a world in motion—the wind and the waves, birth and death, growth and decay…But, they asked, is that all there is? Is there nothing that stays the same and could therefore be experienced as real, in contrast to the things that change?

Yes, answered the *rishis*, there is something. And that something they called *Brahman*—God.

On the one hand there is *Brahman*, taught the *rishis*, and on the other hand, there is the universe. *Brahman*: the indwelling life, the light, the force, the energy. Universe: that which *Brahman* fills or that in which *Brahman* resides. The universe is therefore the same substance as *Brahman*. At the same time, paradoxically, *Brahman* is also distinct, a kind of subatomic energy operating at its own level of consciousness, residing in or pouring itself into a multitude of forms.

The Hindu *Upanishads* tell the story of a student who says to his master, "Teach me the nature of *Brahman*." The master does not reply. When the student asks a second, then a third time, the master answers, "I teach you indeed, but you do not follow. His name is silence."

If the *rishis*, looking outward, saw a world in motion, so also did they when they looked within. Within themselves, they saw a world of change—thoughts, emotions, images and sensations—one following another, like restless waves upon a sea. But was that all there was? Did nothing in the midst of this ceaseless motion stay the same? Once again, the answer was affirmative. Somewhere within or behind the tumult, apart from it, superior to it, they proclaimed, there was a silent and constant witness. This they called *Atman*—the Self.

Endless change without, and at the heart of the change an abiding reality—*Brahman*. Endless change within, and at the heart of the change, an abiding reality—*Atman*. Were there then two realities? No, answered the *rishis*, *Brahman* and *Atman* are one and the same, and they summed up the affirmation in the words *Tat Tvam asi*—That Thou art.

This philosophical statement is perhaps the best-known and most succinct verse of the *Upanishads*. And despite the fact that the *Upanishads* represent for the Hindu what the New Testament represents for the Christian, it is such a departure from the Fijian understanding of spirituality.

Church is out! My reflective "retreat" is over! The palm frond shelter is soon filled with children ….

I will be leaving the village tomorrow, so tonight I accept an invitation to drink kava at Tau's eldest brother's house. I always enjoy being with this family. There are twelve children, many of them still at home, but the sense of family extends well beyond the nuclear unit since this head of the family is also chief of the clan. During the few hours I am in their home, at least sixty people pass through. Some come to sleep here for the night, some spend the evening drinking kava and chatting, others drop in briefly after choir practice. People move about the house with such ease; they seem to feel equally at home here with the chief of the clan as they do in their own sleeping houses.

I remember the European man who set up the community development program that I came to Fiji to research. One of the "teachings" he gave to the Fijians was "People matter more than things." I have always thought it peculiar that he felt the need to teach them that. It goes without saying here: things matter not at all! In fact, I would be hard pressed to find any "thing" in good condition while the people, tough and seasoned to survive in these rugged conditions, are as robust and handsome as I have seen anywhere.

I take my leave near midnight but not before one of the sons asks me to buy him a new part for his spear gun when I get to Suva. Fair enough: it's his livelihood. I bought him the spear gun back in 1979. That it is still functioning is marvel enough; it has new wooden parts, a new steel rod, and new rubber but sports the original metal frame. With a new trigger mechanism, it will qualify as the "same old axe that has had two new blades and six new handles".

It's all part of the circle of life ….

Part III

LET IT GO

Leaving "Home"

Monday, November 16th—I am awakened early to say good-bye to Mata and others who are leaving in the lorry for a wedding (this time!). Iliki and Sai are going too, along with the local church leader. By the time they are back, I will have left the island.

Tau is feeling ill today—too much kava, too little sleep and too poor a diet—so this morning I clean up the house for him as best I can. Then I pack up my things. For some reason, I feel as though I will not be coming back here. I take one last look around the little one-room cottage I have called home. Everything that is here—the hand-woven mats, the linen and dishes, the guitars, even the hut itself—I can leave behind.

But one thing catches my eye. It is a cloth hanging of the Desiderata I hung on the wall the day I moved in here a few years ago. These wise words of counsel seem to be speaking directly to me now....

> Go placidly amid the noise and haste, and remember what peace there may be in silence ....

Should I take it with me or leave it hanging here on the wall?

> As far as possible and without surrender be on good terms with all persons. Speak your truth quietly and clearly; and listen to others, even the dull and ignorant; they too have their story ....

No, leave it here. Leave everything here. Just take the words and emblazon them on the mind.

Keep interested in your own career, however humble; it is a real possession in the changing fortunes of time....

I am feeling really unsettled. The words trigger waves of emotion. At the same time, they are especially comforting right now.

Beyond a wholesome discipline, be gentle with yourself. You are a child of the universe, no less than the trees and the stars; you have a right to be here. And whether or not it is clear to you, no doubt the universe is unfolding as it should ....

I say my good-byes and walk up to the airstrip. Mili comes with me. She sits quietly beside me while we wait for the little *Fiji Air* plane to arrive.

Therefore be at peace with God, whatever you conceive him to be, and whatever your labours and aspirations, in the noisy confusion of life keep peace with your soul....

People stand about, joking with each other, laughing at things that I do not find even marginally funny. The checking-in process goes on all the while with lots of people getting into the act. Mili takes a red felt pen and paints her fingernails. Eight-year-old Samu and some of his gang take a black felt pen and paint beards and moustaches on their faces. They look like miniature middle-aged men and I get a glimpse of the upcoming generation. They will assume their adult roles and life will go on.

With all its sham, drudgery and broken dreams, it is still a beautiful world ....

The plane arrives. Only the local *Fiji Air* agent and his daughter are on board; there are no paying passengers this time. I say another quick round of good-byes, give Mili a big hug and a kiss—she stands motionless—and I board the plane. It skips off down the gravel runway and we fly away. Away from the dirty water pipes and the diet of fish and yams, away from the church with its boring sermons and its confused morality, away from the little house that was so generously given to me, away from the chief of the clan and his beautiful family, away from Iliki and Sai and from Nitai who dances as she walks, away from Mata (who gained all the weight back) and away from Mili who said nothing as she watched me go. But not away from Tau—I have brought him with me. I am not yet ready to say good-bye to him.

The reef is beautiful from the air. I can see the coastline of the island and its high volcanic interior. Over there to the right is the village where the wedding is taking place. They will be killing pigs about now; tradition calls for it. Mata and Iliki and Sai ... are they having fun there? Meeting obligations? A little bit of both? Who knows ....

We fly away out over the turquoise of the reef once again to the deep blue of the South Pacific Ocean, over the islands scattered here and there in their volcanic irregularity, then back to the "mainland" of Viti Levu. We take the airport bus into the city. Along the way we pass an army unit of young recruits marching along the highway in the rain. It's like a scene from "Full Metal Jacket".

It's a holiday today—Prince Charles' Birthday—again! One more paradox in this reluctant republic! The shops are closed but there are some open stalls outside the public market with lots of mangoes. I buy three heaps of them and settle into the hotel where I can eat them at my leisure; the children cannot snitch them this time.

It's pizza and wine for dinner tonight, definitely a tradition now when returning from the village. But somehow it all feels different this time ... like it's completed, like I'm going through the process for the very last time. It's confusing and unsettling. I feel a sense of sadness mingled with relief.

"Go placidly, and remember what peace there may be in silence," I remind myself. But I'm glad for a tropical shower that gives expression to my unrelenting sense of grief.

Human History

Tuesday, November 17th—There is another tropical shower this morning. I watch the raindrops splash and disappear into the swimming pool: individual droplets surrendering their distinctiveness by merging with the water below … like *Brahman-Atman* ….

I walk down to the market to get some more mangoes. I don't sense any tension now. Things seem to be a lot more relaxed, in large part, perhaps, because the curfew has been lifted. I watch an Indian man trying to wheel a heavy cart of produce through a narrow aisle. It is cumbersome and necessarily holds up the flow of people making their way among the stalls. A Fijian man comes by, hits him on the back and complains that he is blocking the way. The Indian man is taken aback and turns to face his accuser. Then he notices that the Fijian is joking with him, and the two of them burst into laughter. It is a wonderful moment and such a contrast to the oversensitivity between the two ethnic groups a few weeks earlier.

The headline in the *Fiji Times* today announces that the former Governor-General has accepted the post of President of the new republic. Things are really moving quickly: lifting of the curfew, demobilization of the army, now the Governor-General becoming the President…Will that get the Fijians through their social conflicts, economic trials and political upheavals? I don't think so; they are still bound by their traditional culture—and will remain so.

Today I see a Fijian man wearing a T-shirt that reads: "Fiji: living naturally". If only….

No Myth-Dream

Wednesday, November 18th—Another beautiful day in the paradox that is Fiji: clear blue sky, sunshine, chirping birds, palm trees, hibiscus flowers, sweet smelling frangipani…I sit on the patio and take it all in, then enjoy an early morning swim.

The housemaid comes by to tidy the room. She says there are too many problems in Fiji now, and they are caused by the coup. The biggest problem is unemployment.

"No work, no money; no money, no food!" she says as she busies herself about the room. She lives on the fourth floor of a subsidized housing unit in Raiwaqa. Married with two children, she now gets four hours of work per day at the hotel and says with such a small family she can manage on that. But what of others, with no work and many children, she laments, who have no income with which to buy food.

"So much *kerekere* (borrowing)," she says, "flour, sugar, matches … children crying because they are hungry and there is just no food to give them. Villagers are luckier because they have their gardens, but it is a very big problem for the Fijians who live in the city.

"Rabuka," she goes on, "doesn't realize it. He has lots of money and there is plenty of food in the military camp. He doesn't know how the people are suffering; he doesn't realize the problems he has caused …"

I walk downtown in the early afternoon. The cruise ship *Fairstar* has docked with a "cargo" of Australian tourists. For a few short hours it is almost like old times. The duty free shops open on Cummings Street, and the tourists leave the premises with bags and boxes. The temporary souvenir stalls once again spread out along the dockside selling everything from woodcarvings to coral necklaces. Where they get the stuff I don't know—not much of it is Fijian handicraft.

It doesn't matter. The tourists are buying it like crazy—wooden swords with their names carved on them, and "grass skirts" made of plastic…The city has come alive, and at least some of the citizens in this reluctant republic will eat better tonight.

My prize pick of a T-shirt I see worn today is one of a lush tropical island scene with the words "Another lousy day in paradise". A fitting description of the paradox that is Fiji!

The Sound of Music

Thursday, November 19th—It is a beautiful sunny day with soft white clouds in the sky. I start the morning with a swim in the pool and have my daily fix of mangoes. It's anything but a lousy day in paradise.

I do some banking and go shopping for Fijian handicrafts to take home to Canada. I buy some beautiful handmade bags of woven pandanus and tapa cloth. Then I make my way to the recording company that produced our first tape of Fijian music. The company has "gone under", one of the many casualties of the coup, and I want to make one last visit to the owner. His office is adjacent to the recording studios on the second floor of the building. The retail outlet on the ground floor is locked and empty. Upstairs, sitting at his computer, I find this gracious Indian man who, after thirteen years in the music recording business, is closing shop.

It is a lovely reunion; I am very fond of him. He confirms that he is going out of business, and that there is no point pressing on. He is bitter and openly so.

"I believed in this country, Fiji," he says. "I have traveled to many parts of the world and have always returned here, telling people everywhere that Fiji is the best place to live.

"Thirteen years of investing all my wealth back into the business. And now, for what?" he laments. "Not a dollar to my name." He no longer trusts the Fijians and is convinced that Indians will not have a chance to succeed here. "I used to like Fijians," he confesses to me, "but now, when I see one, I feel different."

He asks me if I would like to have the master copy of our tape. Symbolic, I think, because it is a kind of Fijian/Indian artifact; it took the cooperation of both ethnic groups to produce it. I offer to buy it from him and then he includes the labels and the stickers for the tape covers, and I offer to pay for them too. Then it extends to throwing in the retail copies of the tape remaining in the storeroom. Yes, I'll buy those too; it becomes one of those impromptu things you do without thinking twice. We make up a price on the spot, and by this time, we're both laughing because, after all, it doesn't really matter. The transaction completed, our shared professional history comes to an end. I ask him what he will do now.

"I'm too emotional right now to make decisions about the future," he replies, and then he adds, "Oh, well, God will take care of it all."

"But which one?" I ask him.

"Oh, any of our 108 or their one Lord Jesus Christ!" he replies. We laugh together. Then I bid him farewell, knowing I will probably never see him again.

Tonight Tau and I go for dinner one last time at our favourite restaurant. There are about twelve people in the dining room now and, by contrast, it seems almost crowded. After dinner, when we are looking for a taxi, we find our friend from Naiqaqi—the family that lives in that tiny space next to the American Embassy. We hire his cab for the ride to the hotel.

As we near our destination, he once again reiterates how much he likes our music. He says he bought the second tape but the first one was never available when he looked for it. Well, I just happen to have sixteen copies of it on me so I hand him one. He's more than a bit surprised by this—and I must admit it is rather synchronistic. I guess one of those sixteen tapes was destined for him because this family is part of the history too.

Leaving Paradise

Friday, November 20th—My last "lousy day in paradise"; I am flying out of this reluctant republic tomorrow. One more day of blue sky, sunshine, hibiscus flowers and tropical fruit beside the swimming pool ....

After a morning swim I go downtown to do one last bit of shopping—a trigger mechanism for that spear gun. Tau comes with me. We try four shops; only one has any spare parts. The replacement, usually $20, now costs $30, and the new ones coming in will be more expensive still given two devaluations of the Fijian currency. Both parties suffer: the Indian storekeeper who cannot afford to be with the item—and the Fijian coastal villager who cannot afford to be without it.

I cannot get a connecting flight to Nadi tomorrow. The remaining choices are the local buses or a "running cab", taxis that make the trip over and back in one day and leave as soon as they fill all the seats. Tau and I choose this option and decide to make the trip to Nadi today.

Upon arrival, we drop our bags at a hotel near the airport and catch a local bus into town, where we get some food items to take with us to Tau's sister in the nearby village.

The visit is predictable and uneventful as usual. Nana has left and the new baby is a few months older now. The mother breast feeds, and then hands the baby to me as she quickly goes outside to bring in the clothes ahead of an approaching downpour. We visit for a while and then say good-bye.

It is late afternoon when we walk back into Nadi town. It is very quiet and there is almost no one around. Most of the duty free shops are closed, and those that remain open have few or no customers in them. Other storefronts are bare, a testimony to the difficult times these people are now facing. We buy some Indian snacks and make our way back to the hotel.

Tonight is our last evening together. We go for dinner at a popular Indian restaurant. Unlike so many establishments, it is filled with people. The atmosphere is festive and the food is excellent. We agree it will be a happy occasion; tomorrow will take care of itself.

Go Placidly

Saturday, November 21st—It rained last night—really hard. It's in time for the cane fields but too late for the burned pine forests that I saw on the ride to Nadi yesterday.

After a breakfast of tropical fruit, I pack up my things and Tau and I head to the airport. The taxi driver is in a wonderful mood, and it seems to be because of the much needed rain.

"The trees are happy, the plants are happy," he declares with enthusiasm. "See, look at the grass; it's happy …"

Once we arrive at the terminal, we discover that the running cab on the return trip to Suva is leaving straightaway. So I must say good-bye to Tau right here and right now, and am forced to bid a hasty farewell in front of the peering Indian taxi driver. Then they speed away. It is all too sudden and it feels incomplete ….

I enter the terminal and check in. There is a long line-up at the Immigration checkpoint. Most of them are Indians. These are the ones whose visas have come through. The males are stoic; the females, for the most part, are crying.

I step into the air-conditioned comfort of the international departure lounge. I watch carefree tourists waiting to board their flights, most of them oblivious to the pain of local people who compete to lure them onto their beaches and sell them their duty free goods and plastic souvenirs.

I board the aircraft and take my window seat in a non-smoking section. The plane lifts into the air and we jet our way to Australia.

There is an Indian man sitting in the next row, filling out the questionnaire on the Australian landing card; he's another of the lucky ones who gets to leave.

Across the aisle is an indigenous Fijian man. During the safety demonstration, when they tell us that there's an oxygen mask in the toilet and if you're in there when the masks are released, stay in the toilet and use the one in there, he looks at me and starts to laugh. He's typically casual about things, lighting up a cigarette in a non-smoking section, seat back when they are already into dinner service...It's so easy to forgive them with their handsome faces ... their innocence ... and their cheery dispositions....

Then there's the European woman sitting next to him. She doesn't notice any of this; she's lost inside a book entitled, "Go Slowly, Come Back Quickly".

Go slowly, and come back quickly? Or go placidly, and remember what peace there may be in silence?

I put down my pen, somewhere in the sky over the South Pacific Ocean. For whether or not it is clear to me, perhaps the universe is unfolding as it should.

BOOK IV

Piercing the Darkness

November, 1988

Part I

THE LIGHT OF HINDUISM

Diwali

Wednesday, November 9ᵗʰ— I'm aboard an *Air Pacific* Boeing 737 traveling from Port Vila in Vanuatu to Nadi in the Fiji Islands. The cutlery has *QANTAS* markings on it; they are serving us a mid-morning snack. The man sitting across the aisle from me is the owner of my favourite Chinese restaurant in Suva. Business must be picking up, I imagine, so I ask him.

"No, very slow," he replies. "Too much unemployment. People can't afford to eat in restaurants."

"But you can stay in business?"

"I don't know how much longer," he responds. So he took a little holiday—ten days in Australia. "Take things easy," he adds. "What else can I do?"

Sitting beside me is an Indo-Fijian girl, returning home after an extended absence. After the coup, she quit her job and took off looking for better opportunities. Now she is coming home to a calculated uncertainty. Her parents, both teachers, have since emigrated and are now living in Australia. She was 21 years of age at the time and therefore could not be included on their application. Now she will make an application of her own, and expects she might be able to emigrate in about two years.

"We're not comfortable in Fiji anymore," she laments. "We don't know what to expect. And we don't feel we will be allowed to succeed. So many Indians getting pushed out of their jobs." Her life has become one of fear and uncertainty. No way to live—whether real or imagined ….

It was 33 degrees in Port Vila—a hot, dry, piercing heat—so the slightly overcast sky and hint of rain is a welcome relief when we land in Nadi. I'm struck again by the humidity and by the decidedly Third World feel inside the airport terminal. It's pervasive, right down to the roughness of the toilet paper in the washroom.

And now the moment I have been looking forward to: a reunion with Tau. He is there, as always, standing off to the side so that I have to look for him. This time he walks to meet me, a warm smile on his face. He reaches out and puts his arms around me. Ah, it's good to be back in Fiji.

One of Tau's "brothers"—his mother's sister's son—works at the Gateway Hotel, situated right across the road from the airport, and Tau has already reserved a room for me. We grab a cab despite the rather short distance since I've brought some bulky items with me. We pack the suitcase and boxes inside the trunk of the taxi and prepare for the trip to the other side of the road, but the car—a run-down American model—won't start. The Indian driver makes repeated efforts, but the starter continues to grind and the generator light repeats the warning.

"It's a good thing we're on the ground," Tau says to me with a devilish grin. It strikes me funny, but it is unsettling at the same time, because this visit to Fiji will be a short one, and there is an air of finality about it. I am returning to Canada this time, since my consulting work in Australia is completed, and I have no ongoing anthropological research in Fiji. Reality sets in: this is my last chance to answer the question of India.

There are secondary goals as well. I want to help Tau find meaningful employment that will offer him a productive and joyful life after I have left, and I want to visit and say farewell to members of Tau's clan with whom I lived in the village. Luckily, I will not have to go far to find them. A number of them are currently on the nearby island of Ovalau, while Sai and Mata, along with little Mimi and Toni, are in Suva.

As for little Mili, she is right here on this side of the island. Last year I arranged secondary education for Mili at a school near Nadi. She lives with Tau's sister who is happy to have the company of a relative from Ngau. I thought it a good plan too since the alternative was a boarding school in Ovalau with dubious adult supervision. Put another way, I was concerned Mili might end up with a baby before she ended up with a school certificate. She has been here almost a year now. So after dropping my bags at the hotel, Tau and I take a local bus to Nadi from where we walk the short distance to his sister's village.

I'm really excited about seeing Mili, but I am hardly prepared for what I find. Little Mili, the tiny girl who moved into my grass hut with me ten years ago, who woke up much too early in the mornings and proceeded to sweep the mats in my *bure* while I would have preferred some undisturbed sleep. Mili, who in typical Fijian style would take my teakettle to the water pipe, fill it to overflowing, and then tiptoe across the one room grass hut to the kerosene stove, spilling the contents on the nice dry mats. Drip … drip … drip … but she was trying so hard to please me—and she was so tiny. Now here she is, a teenager, playing with her new friends on the village green, bigger and taller than I am. She displays reticence when she sees me, almost as though she's not quite sure what to do. I beckon her to come inside Tau's sister's house. This she does, and sits down on the mat beside me.

It has been a year since I have been inside this house, but apart from the fact that each of Tau's sister's three children is a few centimeters higher, nothing has changed. The large living/dining area of the house remains devoid of furniture while Fijian mats cover the area in traditional style. There are electrical outlets but no electricity has yet been connected. We sit together on the mats as daylight turns to dusk. We chat—about school, about life—and then Tau and I leave.

It's a holiday today … Diwali, the Hindu Festival of Lights. According to Hindu tradition, Diwali falls on the 15th day of the dark fortnight in the Hindu month of Kartik. In our western calendar, that occurs sometime in the month of October or November. As Tau and I walk along the road back to Nadi, Hindu families greet the dusk by placing lighted candles along the borders of their houses, in their courtyards and beside the walkways. The tiny white candles emit a yellow glow, illuminating chalk drawings on the sidewalks as offerings to a Hindu god.

Tau stops to watch an Indian man who is lighting candles along the balcony of his two-story house. The man pauses and looks at him for a moment.

"Happy Diwali." he says to Tau, cautiously.

"Happy Diwali," Tau responds, and the cautious man relaxes into a smile.

The spiritual heritage of India…It is one of the world's greatest— what should I call it—awakenings. The great scholar of religion Houston Smith said that Hinduism would rank as one of the world's greatest human achievements except that "achievement" isn't really the right word—because it wasn't achieved. It was more like a direct reception, an opening through inspiration to persons who were able to receive this enduring "Breath of the Eternal". Not acquired, as we are accustomed to think of knowledge, it was knowledge that seems to have arrived "full-bloom", imparted by advanced souls who had cultivated what might be described as a kind of "night light", a night vision of the spirit.

We continue into Nadi. By now, darkness has set in, and along the main street of the town, in front of their shops, Indian families are lighting firecrackers. The sparklers and fireworks reach into the sky, and the air turns misty from the smoke. And everywhere there are candles—in the homes, on the streets, along the pathway into a Hindu temple ... the lights of Diwali, symbolizing spiritual vision, and now, the enduring light of Hinduism put to the critical task of piercing the darkness of the Fiji night.

Hinduism is not the correct word, of course, and India never used it. The *rishis* knew better than to try to put a name to ultimate reality because it is indefinable and includes everything. The *Upanishads* (spiritual treatises) might shed some light on this philosophy, as the name itself points to its grand purpose; literally, "sitting near devotedly". It is the idea of a disciple sitting at the feet of the master, as in Christianity, the disciples drawing forth to hear the teachings of Jesus, a master of Wisdom, *moshel meshalim* in Hebrew. The *Upanishads* have also been referred to as secret teachings; secret, perhaps, because they would be transmitted only to those spiritually ready to receive and profit by them. It was truly "knowledge of God".

And what of that knowledge? In the *Chandogya Upanishad* is written: "We should consider that in the inner world *Brahman* is consciousness, and we should consider that in the outer world *Brahman* is space." Once again, it is *Brahman-Atman*, and, as in the parables of Jesus, this truth is sometimes revealed in stories like this one:

> *There lived once a boy, Svetaketu Aruneya by name. One day his father spoke to him in this way: 'Svetaketu, go and become a student of sacred wisdom. There is no one in our family who has not studied the holy Vedas and who might only be given the name of Brahman by courtesy.'*
>
> *The boy left at the age of twelve and, having learnt the Vedas, he returned home at the age of twenty-four, very proud of his learning and having a great opinion of himself.*
>
> *His father, observing this, said to him: 'Svetaketu, my boy, you seem to have a great opinion of yourself, you think you are learned,*

and you are proud. Have you asked for that knowledge whereby what is not heard is heard, what is not thought is thought, and what is not known is known?'

'What is that knowledge, father?' asked Svetaketu.

'Bring me a fruit from this banyan tree.'

'Here it is, father.'

'Break it.'

'It is broken, Sir.'

'What do you see in it?'

'Very small seeds, Sir.'

'Break one of them, my son.'

'It is broken, Sir.'

'What do you see in it?'

'Nothing at all, Sir.'

Then his father spoke to him: 'My son, from the very essence in the seed which you cannot see comes in truth this vast banyan tree. Believe me, my son, an invisible and subtle essence is the Spirit of the whole universe. That is Reality. That is Atman. That thou art.'

That thou art—*Tat tvam asi* in Sanskrit—that is the essential truth of Hinduism.

"Truth is one," proclaims the *Rig-Veda*, the most ancient of the Hindu scriptures, "and sages call it by various names." Sri Ramakrishna stated, "So many religions, so many paths, to reach the same goal." And from the *Bhagavad-Gita*, another Hindu scripture:

Whatever path men travel is my path
No matter where they walk it leads to me.

Indeed, it would seem that the supreme gift of India has always been to reconcile differing faiths and differing beliefs to advance the unity of humankind. What an irony that the people being attacked as a result of the traditional Fijian mindset are the very people who are holding the key to its deliverance.

"You're not celebrating Diwali?" Tau asks the Indian taxi driver as we head to a restaurant for dinner.

"No," the man replies.

"So you are celebrating the money instead," Tau jokes.

"I don't celebrate Diwali," he replies. "I am a Muslim."

Hindu, Muslim, Sikh—Indians from the Aryan north and the Dravidian south: not a single Indo-Fijian community but fragmented units of historically displaced people, united only in the minds of the indigenous Fijians. But there, within that dispersed and displaced Indian population, lay Hinduism's exceptional ability to see the unity of all things.

Diwali calls for Indian cuisine. We savour dhal soup, spicy chicken with yoghurt sauce, steamed rice … served with plenty of local beer. For dessert, it is lychees with ice cream. I assume it will be vanilla ice cream so I don't bother to inquire. It arrives—succulent lychees atop artificially flavored pink ice cream. When will I learn!

A Good Thing for the Children

Thursday, November 10th—I awake to a beautiful sunny day, and it is remarkably hot for 7:30 in the morning. I go with Tau by bus into Nadi town to buy some mangoes at the public market. At this early hour, school children, in their neatly pressed uniforms, are boarding the bus. Some are in blue and white dresses, some in grey skirts/ pants and white blouses, still others in an all-white garb with head covering, each group going to its respective public or private school. The children, with deep brown eyes and glowing skin, have such innocent faces. I wonder if they are learning unity or diversity ….

The bus gets very crowded, and before we reach Nadi town, there are four of us sitting in a space designed for three. Next to Tau and me is a little Indian boy whose school bag, strapped to his back, exceeds his depth by a wide margin. When a little Fijian girl slides into the same seating space, we can accommodate her only by shifting the little boy sideways and resting his school bag on my lap. Symbolic, I think, how a simple shift can allow two ethnic groups to comfortably share the same space.

I get some mangoes—four varieties—as well as bananas and papaya, and we make our way back to the hotel to enjoy lush tropical fruits in a lush tropical setting. At midday I return to Nadi once more, this time to invite Mili to have lunch in town. We settle on Indian food, though midway through the meal she informs me she prefers Chinese!

When I return Mili to school after the lunch break, I find myself engaged in conversation with a remarkable Indian gentleman. He is the headmaster of the school. In fact, he built it. Well educated—the first to hold a doctorate in Fiji—he has laboured for 37 years to educate the youth of this island nation. Now, with white hair and beard and leaning on a cane, he shares the depth of his disappointment. He has lost one-third of his 24 teachers since the military coup, including all his better-educated ones and all his Department heads.

"I cannot ask them to stay when there is no future for them here," he laments. Many of his Fijian students have left as well since their parents can no longer afford to pay the fees.

"Might you also go?" I ask.

"Oh, I am 61 years old. Too late to start a new life now," he responds quietly. "Anyway, I have done a good thing for the children."

The school offers Forms 3 through 6 (equivalent to North American grades 9 to 12) as well as the foundation year for university. The classrooms are sparse and in need of repair, but that will have to wait. Textbooks too, are old and tattered, not to mention out of date. I sit in on a Form 3 English class bravely taught by a young Indian woman whose training is in basic science. She had taken over the class less than two weeks ago when the English teacher swiftly vacated the post. It's English grammar. She reads from the textbook and asks the students to supply the correct answer:

"One of the most famous (woman, women) in the world is Mrs. Gandhi."

"Women," the students reply.

"Right," she says. But even the right answer is wrong. Mrs. Gandhi was assassinated a number of years ago.

"If you want a job with a challenge," the principal says to me, "come teach in my school. And send me teachers; we are desperate."

I beg my leave at mid-afternoon and walk down the hill into Nadi town. I cannot rest my mind from thinking about this dear Indian man. He has conviction and purpose. He has thought about education and has given his best. At the end of it all, he sees his beloved school crumbling before his eyes.

"Do think about what I suggest to you," he had pleaded as we parted, "although I can only pay $4,500.00 per year. There are flats behind the classroom complex. You could stay there."

The voice of this aged Indian man continues to haunt me throughout the evening. Like the candles of the Hindu Diwali, he endures and, in his deeply human way, attempts to pierce the darkness of the Fiji night.

Right Education

Friday, November 11th—Tau and I take the early morning tourist bus to Suva. It's operating again although there are almost no passengers; there are only three of us aboard on this trip. The bus makes its scheduled round of stops at the resorts along the coral coast as we wind our way to the capital.

Suva: hot, overcrowded. We disembark at the Travelodge in the midst of police and security personnel. The Prime-Minister of Singapore is here, we discover, and at a press conference he makes the point that the new Draft Constitution has not resolved—and will not resolve—the basic problem that led to the coups, because the root cause of the problem is the economic disparity between indigenous Fijians and Indo-Fijians. To right this inequality, he says, indigenous Fijians must become part of the modern world—and this can only be achieved through right education.

Right education: the very thing that Indian schoolmaster can offer to the children of Fiji. The very thing the spiritual heritage of India can offer to the adults of Fiji. The very thing the indigenous Fijians are removing from their midst.

Eerily Silent

Saturday, November 12ᵗʰ—Tomorrow is Sunday. Neither shops nor restaurants will be open—and Monday is a holiday. I must stock up on food supplies to get through the weekend. Sunday it will be Indian food; Monday, it will be Fijian. Off I go with Tau to the public market and the food section of an adjacent department store.

It is so crowded! Everyone has the same idea. At least the department store is air-conditioned. I get a shopping cart and stock up on the basics: brown rice, curry powder, garam masala, butter, peanut butter, blackberry jam, chicken, and plenty of local beer. Then to the outdoor market: mangoes, pumpkin—for the curry, tomatoes and cucumber, seaweed, clams and lemons, yams, coconuts and cooking bananas. Some fresh bread and muffins from the Hot Bread Kitchen round out the food-shopping venture.

In the evening Tau and I go to dinner at our favourite Chinese restaurant. The owner is here, standing in his usual spot at the front entrance. Quite a few tables are occupied. Things are looking up.

We have a drink and order our choices: braised scallops with ginger and green onions, chicken with green peppers in black bean sauce, stir-fried vegetables and steamed rice. Simple … inexpensive … delicious ….

After dinner, we walk along the harbour. It is silent—eerily silent. And without the streetlights, darkness closes in. It's too dark to walk so we catch a cab back to the hotel. From this vantage point, there is a good view of the harbour, defined now by the light of fishing vessels and cargo ships resting in port. The sea is calm, stretching to the horizon. The sky is clear, with dazzling stars defining distances further than the mind can easily imagine.

Light … universal light—literally. If only it were also figuratively so ….

Religion, Religion

Sunday, November 13[h]—I take an early morning walk with Tau to the summit of a hill from where there is a commanding view of the city with its fine and spacious bay "surrounded by grey hills that stretch away mysteriously into a blue distance", as Somerset Maugham put it.

But there is more to be seen than the splendid natural setting. Before us is a feast of religious ideology. First we pass the national headquarters of the Assemblies of God, a fast-growing fundamentalist sect of Christianity that will give the nearby Dudley Methodist Church a run for its money.

Further along, on the flat of the summit stands a Hindu temple. Chants of "Hare Ram", sweet-smelling incense and an image of Sri Satya Sai Baba add to the mix. Just down the street, heading back toward the harbour, stands a mosque. The first haunting call to prayer echoes from its modest minaret, breaking the silence of Jubilee

Hall—the first principal Methodist Church in Fiji—with locked doors and boarded windows, directly across the street.

Further down the hill there is a second Hindu structure—the Sri Laxmi Narayan Temple—with open doors but no one yet inside. In its neatly groomed courtyard stands a post on which is written in Hindi and in English, "May Peace exist on Earth".

Across the street, not yet open for the Sunday rituals, sits a Baptist church. We walk on and come to a stately mansion with portico and well-groomed terraces; it is the Catholic bishop's house, and between there and the Roman Catholic cathedral at the foot of the hill, one gets a grand view of the spacious Anglican cathedral off in another direction.

Hinduism, Islam—and enough brands of Christianity to warrant a World Council of Churches … all professing to be in the peace and good will business—and all unwittingly reinforcing the ethnic and religious divisions that keep peace and good will at bay. Each of these religions is premised on some aspect of the Divine, but over time they have managed to cloak that divinity in beliefs and rituals that obscure the essential spiritual teachings. In the process, they have become barricades rather than bridges.

At the close of the day, we take another walk. The narrow crescent of a new moon signals the onset of night. Down the hill toward the harbour, the streets are empty. It is silent, so silent that Tau feels afraid, and wants to turn back. Our return route takes us past the main Methodist church. It's a few minutes before 7 p.m., the scheduled hour for the regular evening service, but the church is empty. No evening worship is possible without public transportation as most worshippers come by bus from the poorer suburbs. At the hotel we hear, over the airwaves, a broadcast of a Methodist sermon in place of the real thing.

But what is the "real thing"? I 'm reminded of the words of India again: "Intellectual knowledge is easily acquired, and, intellectually, the answers have always been there. Intellectual knowledge must be transformed into personal and emotional experience in order to be permanently imprinted on the subconscious mind."

Transformed … into personal and emotional experience. Organized religion continues to be the principal vehicle for spiritual transformation, but little if anything here would appear to be getting through to the subconscious mind.

Mind over Matter

Monday, November 14th—Prince Charles' birthday—still a holiday more than a year after Colonel Rabuka declared Fiji a republic! Shops and offices are closed, so I make an excursion with Tau to Pacific Harbour to spend a day on one of the finest beaches in Fiji. It's about an hour's drive from the capital, and the setting of a lovely resort complex. Once here, I swim out into the waves. The water is slightly cooler than tepid but it is not cold. It's wonderfully refreshing. Then I join Tau on the beautiful soft white sand beach. It is exquisite, but very soon after we move to a shaded area; the summer sun is far too intensive. What's more, Tau doesn't need to sun bathe.

"What am I doing, laying here on the beach?" Tau jokes. "I'm already dark!"

I look out into the Pacific. The scenery from this vantage point is magnificent—deep blue water lapping along the shore, and in the near distance, the island of Beqa, famed for its fire walking.

It seems it was the people of Dakuibeqa village in Beqa who started the tradition of walking on white-hot river stones. They believed their fire walking powers were conferred on them by a legendary chief called Tui Namoliwai, and that these powers would remain with them so long as they maintained their faith and had no fear of fire.

But it's not as simple as that. There is a lot of preparation involved in fire walking, including a four-day period where the participants refrain from eating coconuts or indulging in sex. Violate the taboos and you lose the immunity from fire. And it would appear that some do, for the villagers are also believed to be able to heal people who have suffered burns. The fire walking itself, accompanied with dancing and the recitation of sacred hymns, is supervised by a member of the warrior clan.

Interesting, when you come to think of it, because another culture associated with fire walking is India. Hindus believe that the Goddess Kali intervenes with her *shakti* (power) to protect the firewalkers from injury. In this case, the ritual involves a ten-day fast to attain purity of mind, during which time the participants abstain from sexual relations and the eating of meat. They meditate in isolation, overseen by a Hindu priest. The mental preparation of the rites helps to achieve a balanced and spiritually evolved life, while the fire walking itself is believed to be a means of becoming one with the universe.

More interesting still, both cultures practice the ritual in Fiji. Two vastly diverse cultures, originating from two very different parts of the world thousands of miles apart, share the same traditional ritual. And through historical coincidence, they end up doing it right next door to each other!

Fire walking—on hot coals—and they do not burn their feet. I've seen them do it a number of times. And I actually did it myself once—not in Fiji but in North America—at one of those corporate seminars. At the culmination of a four-day program, I had only four hours to get into the proper state of mind to walk on fire. But it was no ordinary four hours; in fact, I did not even realize that four hours had transpired between the beginning of a deep meditation and the walking on red-hot coals. I did not get burned—nor did I feel the heat. It is a matter of overriding fear by activating the subconscious mind.

What is the difference, I now wonder, between believing fire-walking is accomplished through mind over matter, and believing it is facilitated by the supernatural forces of Tui Namoliwai for the Beqa islanders and the Goddess Kali in the case of the Hindus. The boundary line between spirituality and rational science is fading. We now know that the atom is not the smallest particle, and that subatomic particles do not behave in accordance with the laws of time and space as we currently understand them. Viewed from this perspective, it may all be simply energy transformation, called by different names: the gift of Namoliwai … the *shakti* of the Goddess Kali … the power of the subconscious mind…If we could find a common language, perhaps we could better understand the mystery of our shared human experience. Perhaps that would help these two ethnic groups in Fiji walk through the political hotbed together.

Matter over Mind

Tuesday, November 15th—It is overcast this morning and by noontime the clouds burst forth into a fresh tropical shower. I put my abstract deliberations aside, and dedicate myself to a *concrete* matter: Tau's seemingly perennial task of job-hunting, critical now since I have no ongoing work for him. Given the political crisis, there is little employment available, but Tau has found an advertised community development position that appeals to him. It's matter over mind this time.

We update his curriculum vitae—he has a Certificate in Community Development from USP (the University of the South Pacific) in addition to his years of rural development work in Fiji and experience abroad—and then make our way to an office that offers a typing service. We explain how we would like the document prepared and the young Fijian girl responds to everything in the affirmative.

"Would you like it typed with black ribbon?" she asks.

"I assume so," I reply, "but what are the choices?"

"We don't have any black ribbon," she says.

"So what ribbon do you have?" I ask.

"Only brown."

"Well, what does the brown ribbon type look like?"

She scans through a stack of files but cannot find anything that has been typed with brown ribbon.

"Well, will it photocopy?" I ask.

"Very light," she replies.

"So in the whole office here, you have only brown ribbon, is that it?"

"Yes," she replies, "someone took the typewriter that has the black ribbon in it."

"Well, is there any other place we can get this document typed?" I ask her.

"Yes, just down the street." She names the establishment. We thank her kindly and proceed there.

"Can we get this document typed, please?" I begin again.

"Oh, no, we don't do typing," the girl replies.

"Do you know where I might get it typed?"

"Yes, a few blocks from here." She gives the directions. We walk the few blocks and enter the premise.

"Can we get a document typed, please?" I ask again.

"No, we do not do typing here."

"Do you know where we might get it done?"

"There is a place on the second floor that does typing." Up the stairs, a young Fijian girl sits behind a typewriter.

"Can we get a document typed here?" I ask her.

"Well, I'm busy right now."

"No, I don't mean right this minute. Like in due course, say, tomorrow."

"Yes," she says.

I show the young girl the rough copy and explain how we would like it done. She then tells me she cannot do it for a number of days since she has a big stack of typing to do. A number of days will push us past the deadline for submission of the application. So we leave, no closer to our goal!

Okay, maybe it's not matter over mind; maybe the position doesn't matter—or won't even "matter"! So what to do? Well, let's go to dinner.

We choose a different restaurant. It is well patronized on this occasion since the employees of a large business are having a social gathering here, occupying the whole of the main floor. Tau and I are ushered upstairs where only one other table is occupied. The two Europeans—who have not yet been served—sit quietly. We order: fish in black bean sauce, Mongolian hot pot, stir-fired vegetables, rice…Then we wait—and we wait. A long time! It would seem the meager restaurant staff is not accustomed to serving so many patrons at once, for dinner does not arrive, not for us nor for the couple at the adjoining table.

A full hour passes and still we wait. We make eye contact with the other couple; the man simply smiles. We continue to wait. The couple is visibly unperturbed by the situation. In fact, the man is so present and radiates such a sense of peacefulness that I cannot resist engaging him in conversation.

"What brings you to Fiji?" I ask him.

"Just hanging out," he responds with a smile. To him it just doesn't matter.

Mind over matter!

The food finally arrives. It is very good.

We leave the restaurant and head toward the taxi stand adjacent to the public market where people are drinking kava. Tau hears someone call out his name. He looks in the direction of the sound and recognizes a woman from a far village on Ngau. The family has come to Suva to sell kava. They shout for us to come drink with them. Kava does not mix well with food, and Tau responds that we have just eaten. The woman then asks Tau to come closer and bring "the woman who sings on the radio" so she can meet me. They have heard our music over the years but we have never met. We proceed there.

"Oh, she's just a tiny little girl!" the woman exclaims to Tau when we arrive. I guess she had visualized a much larger woman—Fijian woman tend to be rather full figured—and my light frame and less that 50-kilo weight did not meet with her expectation. Once again, mind over matter! In Nepal, they perceived me to be very tall!

We chat awhile, and then beg our leave. A taxi pulls up at the stand and we hail it, only to discover it is our friend from Naiqaqi who lives in that small flat in the shadow of the spacious American Embassy. During the short ride to the hotel, we agree to visit the family the following night.

God With Us

Wednesday, November 16th—The day starts with another attempt to get Tau's curriculum vitae typed. We locate a typist who says she can do it this morning. Tau explains how it is to be done and we are to collect it "after lunch". We return after lunch, but it is not ready. We take another break, and return in the late afternoon. The document is typed—but unreadable: no breaks between the categories, inconsistent spacing, and many typing errors…We go through the vitae with the young girl once again, page by page, outlining how it is to be done. We will collect it "tomorrow".

In the early evening we arrive at the home of the family in Naiqaqi and are ushered into their small two-room flat. Since we were here a year ago, some furniture has been added: a single bed, a chair and a small table inside the room where we will drink kava. On the wall hang pictures of the now elderly couple, displaying the youth and vigour of their bygone days. The wife, then a striking woman in her twenties, is now 57, and grandmother to eleven children, some of whom live with them in this confined space. Attached to the wall is the poster of a Fijian man, posing in an army T-shirt in the style of a Hollywood teen idol. At the top of the poster, in bold print are the following words: "FIJI: GOD IS WITH US", and the poster is autographed in neat handwriting: "Siti Rabuka". To these Fijians, the coup leader is a hero, and the bold print affirms that God is on their side. It is a world of good and evil, right and wrong … in short, a world of "us" and "them".

Tau presents our kava. He talks about caring and about the importance of relationship. Our hosts speak about how happy they are that we have come to see them again. The grandmother beckons one of the children peering into the crammed doorway from the adjoining room to climb on the bed and remove two shell necklaces from where they adorn the photographs. The child complies, and the woman places them around our necks. We belong in the "us" category.

We drink the kava. For ten years I have been coming to Fiji, and in all that time I have never grown to like the stuff, which has the consistency and appearance of mud. But as a mediator of social relationships it is unsurpassed. The rounds of drinking around the kava bowl from the shared coconut cup, interspersed with conversation, allows our time together to flow smoothly. After a few hours, when the large kava bowl is emptied for a second time, we beg our leave.

But the visit leaves me unsettled … lovely people, thoroughly conditioned in a narrow ethnic mindset, thereby reinforcing the discord in their own nation. I'm reminded of a statement made by Vivekananda, a monk of the Ramakrishna Order in India. "One atom in this universe cannot move without dragging the whole world along with it," he said. "There cannot be any progress without the whole world following in the wake, and it is becoming every day clearer that the solution of any problem cannot be attained on racial, or national, or narrow grounds. Every idea has to become broad till it covers the whole of this world ..."

God Within Us

Thursday, November 17th—After a breakfast of mangoes and toast, we set out to collect the curriculum vitae. It has been retyped—and a considerably improved job the young woman has made of it. We correct the few remaining errors, sign the cover letter and mail it to the appropriate address.

This afternoon has been set aside to visit Sai who is here in Suva. She came three months ago because of illness, and brought Mimi and little Toni with her. Her husband Mata will arrive tonight on the weekly ferry. I go with Tau to visit the family. For our *i sevusevu* (offering), we bring, along with traditional kava, some food items: a half dozen double loaves of whole meal bread, a couple jars of jam, a can of Ovaltine, a chicken, a bag of rice, packages of noodles, a large cabbage ... items that would be expensive for them to acquire in the city.

We take a taxi because the address is obscure. Toni runs up the lane when he sees me; he jumps into my arms and holds on tight in spite of my attempt to remove my sandals before entering the house. Mimi, who is big and tall now, grins and says nothing. Sai, in the company of her relatives, is sitting on the mats in the main living area. We greet and kiss in Fijian style.

The house is a tiny unit with a living/dining room, and a sink and cupboard. There is a sleeping area and toilet upstairs. To the rear of the house on the main level is an exit leading to a cooking area constructed of roofing iron. The house, in typical Fijian fashion, is sparsely appointed. Over the main doorway is hung a family portrait, flanked on either side by cloth tapestries, one of Jesus as the Good Shepherd, the other of the Last Supper. God with us ….

Tau places the box of food in the centre of the room. Its contents are examined, and removed to the appropriate place. The kava bowl appears. Sai and the other women take their positions and mix the powdered root with water. When its consistency is deemed correct, they make the appropriate gestures and utter the ritual words.

"*Vakalailai* (Just a little)," I urge as they dip the coconut cup into the kava bowl for me. I take the cup and, as is the custom, drink its contents in a single swallow. Now that I have participated in the first round of drinking, I can henceforth politely decline. The conversation carries on, interrupted at appropriate intervals with "*Taki* (Pour)" after which each in turn shares the cup of kinship.

Kinship … it's lovely. But will they ever get beyond it. It would take a cultural education of a new type, one that would foster the development of a global consciousness—indeed, one that would give a soul to that consciousness. It would be a movement from "God with us" to "God within us" ….

How do you communicate that to people who experience themselves as separate? If they could get below the surface, they would find there is unity between ethnic groups. If they were to go deeper still, they would discover that the culture they are dismissing is indeed a variation of their own.

Day turns into night and the kava bowl empties. We beg our leave. Just as we get to the street, a taxi pulls up bearing Mata who has arrived on the ferry. So back into the house we go—Tau and I, the entourage from the household that has followed us to the street to say good-bye, Mata—and the taxi driver. The taxi driver is a very big man, an appearance that is remarkably suited to his joviality. He is related to Tau's mother's family somehow, and refers to Tau as "uncle". When introduced to me, he calls me "auntie". I find it most amusing, in large part because he is so much bigger than I am.

The kava is mixed again. Same routine—but this time, the women retreat to the side of the room and the men assume the key roles. *"Vakalailai,"* I urge again, as the cup is dipped into the kava bowl for me.

The ritual goes on. I watch the predictable gestures and conditioned social behavior. There is much in this culture that is admirable and good, much that is worthy of preservation. But a nation cannot rest in unresolved discord. At such times, it must strive for adjustment, achieved by a series of integrations leading to the formation of a deeper harmony. When any integration is found inadequate to new conditions, of necessity it breaks down and advances to a larger whole.

Finally the kava bowl empties again and we beg our leave. The taxi driver leaves too, and brings us into the city. None too soon, for it is very late, and tomorrow I will set out on an expedition to the old capital of Fiji. There, in that quaint historical setting, I shall endeavor—literally and figuratively—to go to the top of the mountain. One and a half centuries ago, something happened on that mountaintop that might shed some light on the Fijian situation. But tonight it is the darkness that prevails.

Part II

ON THE MOUNTAINTOP

The Old Capital

Friday, November 18th—Tau accompanies me as we wind our way along a dirt road on the northern coast of Viti Levu. It's hot and the bus we are on is very crowded. Three hours it takes us to get to a dock, from where we take a ferry for a half-hour crossing to the island of Ovalau.

It's another hour-long bus ride from the dockside into Levuka town. It is still hot and the bus is still very crowded, but this time the winding dirt road is bordered by splendid stretches of dense rainforest. We arrive at the quaint old town at 5:30 in the evening.

Levuka is the old capital of Fiji. It was here that the self-styled *Tui Viti* (King of Fiji) ceded the islands to Britain in 1874. Fiji remained a British colony until its independence in 1970. During that century, the capital of the island nation was shifted from Levuka to Suva.

Levuka has a delightful setting, with its small frame single storey buildings stretching out along the waterfront. The town has changed little in the ten years since I was last here. I imagine it looks today much as Suva appeared to Somerset Maugham in 1916. But while Suva is no longer just a trading station, a trading station this sleepy little town remains.

Forming a backdrop to the historic buildings of this old capital, a magnificent mountain rises to a steep precipice, a volcanic cone of immense beauty and grandeur decorated by jungle growth of

259

deep forest green. A number of narrow lanes wind up the mountain. Stemming from these arteries, a series of paths with concrete steps stretch high into the mountain to reach houses perched along the hillside.

Members of our clan from Ngau are here in Levuka, and I look forward to meeting them. First and foremost, I want to see Mela. She is from Tau's brother's family, the daughter of the chief of the clan. Mela was only a little girl when I did my fieldwork in the village in 1979. Like many of the young people of Ngau, she came to Levuka for secondary schooling. After it was completed, she moved in with a family here, working for her keep in their bakery as well as holding down a fulltime job in the fish packing plant at the edge of the town.

The bus drops us off on Beach Street. I'm not sure where to begin looking for Mela but I needn't have been concerned, for there she is, standing on the side of the street, right in front of me. It is a joyous reunion after so many years. Her face lights up with excitement and anticipation. She's so much bigger now, but there is a spark about her that reveals something eternally childlike. It takes me back a decade, to the site of her scraping coconuts and washing dishes at the water pipe in the village.

It is dinnertime and darkness is fast falling. I invite Mela to dine with Tau and me, but for some reason she declines and agrees to meet me tomorrow after she finishes her shift at the fish-packing plant. It's a Friday night so I figure she must have plans with her friends, and do not press the matter.

Tau and I take a local bus to a beachside resort about three kilometers away. It is a beautiful establishment with attractive little cottages in a natural setting beside a black sand beach. I will set up here for the weekend so that we have a place to entertain our clan members during our stay.

Killing the Messenger

Saturday morning, November 19ᵗʰ—Before 8 in the morning, Tau and I take a local bus into Levuka town. The bus is filled with women on their way to another day of cutting and packing fish at the canning factory. Three hundred women make up a shift, and more than 400 women are employed there altogether.

Once in town, we walk along Beach Street to where some fishing boats are tied up along a dock in the distance. One of them is a boat recently purchased by Tau's clan. Some of his kin are here on a fishing expedition! As we draw closer, we see them walking to meet us. There's Tau's brother Iliki, his brother's son Tiki, also Seli, Solo and Veli. It is another joyous reunion.

The visitors take us to the boat to show us their new business acquisition. They are excited about the purchase; it offers them freedom and a source of income. The boat is not very big, but sufficient for its purpose. There is sleeping space for three, and it is equipped with a small cooking stove. There is no washroom facility—they manage without it. Indeed, that is something I had to learn while doing my anthropological fieldwork on Ngau. On one occasion, I was aboard a similar boat on the long sail from Ngau to Ovalau. There was no on-board facility. When I could wait no longer, two members of the clan simply held me over the side of the boat! Along with privacy, modesty is one more thing you need to forego if you want to do fieldwork in the Fiji islands.

Our visit to the boat completed, I express my interest in going to the top of the mountain. There is a village there, nestled in the crater at the summit, where a renowned warrior chief named Verani was killed over a century ago. As a warrior, Verani had put many people to a violent death, but he converted to Christianity, taking the name Elijah. There was strife between the people on the islands of Mbau and Ovalau at the time, and Verani Elijah agreed to go to the mountaintop village of Lovoni as a peace messenger. He, with two of his brothers and four others, landed at Ovalau by night, and made their way through the bush up the mountain. At daybreak, after pausing many times for prayer, he and his small party reached the village where he presented *tabua* (whales' teeth) as a peace offering to the local chief. The *tabua* were graciously received and drums were beaten in acknowledgement. But when the Christian chief walked past a temple, a lesser chief attacked. Verani Elijah fell dead beneath the blow of a Fijian war club. All the party but one perished, and several were eaten. It was a major setback in the cause of inter-island peace.

I read about this historical incident in the mission history of Fiji, and now I want to go to the place where it happened. Solo tells us that the bus to Lovoni leaves at 10 a.m. and says he will come with us, so the three of us board the bus and head to the infamous mountain village. It is a long, winding road, interspersed by villages and thickets of rain forest. When we get to the crest of the high inland mountains, the rain begins to fall. On we drive … as far as the village of Bureta. Then the bus turns around and heads back to Levuka.

Tau and I look at each other. Solo says nothing. So as not to embarrass him, I let the incident pass. When we arrive back in Levuka town a couple of hours later, I ask the driver why we did not go to Lovoni.

"Busses do not go to Lovoni," he replies. "Only transport trucks go to the top of the mountain."

I have only one more day on Ovalau and it falls on a Sunday: my chances of getting to the top of the mountain are slim. Under the military restrictions, no public transport is available on that day. Even business vehicles cannot be used for private use on a Sunday. There are few private vehicles in these parts in any case and none at all to which I have access. I sort through all the possibilities and figure my best bet is to see if we can get a permit to use the van from

Mela's business to make the trip. Tau comes with me to the police station to seek a permit.

We talk to the officer on duty, a very pleasant man whose official uniform cannot conceal a placid nature. We state our interest. He replies that we cannot arrange that since the van is registered as a business vehicle. We explain that we have no business purpose in mind; we simply want to drive to the village. He refers us to his superior who says we can only get a permit if we want to go there in order to go to church.

Fair enough! The superior instructs us to indicate this is the purpose of the request and to put the request in writing. Tau writes the letter, and the superior types the permit in response.

```
"Levuka    Police    Station.    Sunday    Permit.
Application approved. This vehicle will only
be used for the purpose intended for and not
otherwise."
```

Tomorrow, I shall "go to church" on the top of the mountain.

On the Path

Saturday afternoon, November 19th—I meet up with Iliki at the close of the afternoon to visit his son Josi who attends secondary schooling at Levuka Public School. Established in 1876, it is the oldest school in Fiji, once attended by some of Fiji's prominent leaders. The name is deceiving because Levuka Public School is a Roman Catholic institution, nestled in the steep slopes of the mountain behind the Catholic church which sits prominently on Beach Street and whose green neon cross on the tall steeple can be seen far out at sea, a beacon to small fishing vessels plying the waters of Lomaiviti. We climb up the mountain on steps of concrete in the direction of the dormitories.

The setting is as magnificent as I have seen anywhere, and the beauty alone is enough to captivate. But there is something about this place that makes me exuberant. I don't know what it is but I feel that I am drawing very close to something, as though some great mystery were contained herein, or some great wisdom or insight is here to be gained.

Up, up we climb, through luxurious foliage and coconut trees. Eventually Iliki indicates in his shy manner that we have arrived at the dormitory where his son is boarding. The steps continue up the mountain and I want to follow them, but we head to a side path and enter a white wooden building.

The dormitory is very spartan: ten beds in this young boy's room, most with mattresses covered by sleeping mats. There is also a simple dining room with wooden tables and benches. We find young Josi.

Like his father, Josi is a very quiet boy. He initiates no conversation, and answers a simple "*Io* (Yes)" or "*Sega* (No)" to my queries. We chat about school, about living on this island, about his studies…His father Iliki says almost nothing the whole time. In fact, it is difficult for me to register this as a visit, but I guess they are simply being here together; conversation is superfluous. Close to an hour passes, and Josi's dinner hour approaches.

"Would you like to go now or would you like to stay longer?" I ask Iliki.

"It's up to you," he replies.

"But he's your son," I protest. Then I remember where I am. "Yes, we can go now," I say to him.

We bid good-bye to young Josi and return to the path. I see the steps leading further up the mountain. I still want to follow them, but Iliki has no interest in that. The purpose of his climb is over and he is ready to return to the boat to drink kava with his kin. But something in me cannot let it pass.

"What lies beyond the dormitories?" I ask.

"The teachers' quarters," he responds.

"Just the teachers' quarters?"

Iliki nods.

We make our way down the mountain, retreating from the stunning backdrop that makes the old capital of Fiji such an exquisite little town.

Breaking Bread

Saturday evening, November 19th—Tonight is my time to be with Mela. We have arranged to go out for dinner, but first she must bake bread and cook dinner for the people who live in the home where she is staying. She offers me tea as I wait.

"I was really excited when I saw you arrive yesterday," she begins, "and all day today at work I was really excited. I wrote you a letter. I asked for your address in the village. But they never sent it over."

"What did you say in that letter?"

"I want you to help me with my life."

"And why did you think to ask me?"

"Because my mother said when you come to the village, you always ask about me."

"Your mother told me you were getting married."

"Yes, she wanted me to get married because that man was in business. But I said I'm not ready for that. I don't want that."

"So tell me what you do want."

"I want to help the gang, you see. All the ones coming up. To pay the school fees, the books, the food. And *Tata* (Father) is getting old now. To look after him. I'm saving up my money to buy paint and things to finish the house."

"The house in the village?"

"Yeah, I want to help the gang."

"That is what you want for all of them. Now, tell me, what do you want for you?"

"Yes, I need to do something good for myself, too."

"Yes, what do you want to do?"

"I don't know. You tell me what to do."

"You know what is good for you. It's what feels right. What feels right for you?"

"Some kind of work where you help people. I don't know what kind of jobs there are but I want to help people. I don't like business. Like this place here, I don't like working here. It's only business. Just mixing bread and selling bread."

She places some newly baked buns on the table along with a plate of butter. She is engrossed in her thinking and neglects to provide a knife. And she tells me about her life. She works a day shift in the fish packing plant. At night she comes home and works in the bakery. She has little free time, except on Sundays. And then she is confined to church and to "rest".

"On Sundays I stay in my room and sleep," she tells me.

For six years Mela has lived in this environment. But she has not succumbed. She is filled with discontent—and that is a good sign. I determine to help her create a new life for herself.

Tau arrives and the three of us leave for dinner at the Old Capital Inn. The menu consists of a mix of standard Chinese and simple European fare. If you want to have your evening meal there, you place your order by 5 p.m. so they can remove the critical food items—chicken, beef, fish—from the freezer. The clientele and the profit margin are both too meager to make educated guesses. Now I realize why Mela declined my dinner reservation last night; she knew we had missed the 5 p.m. deadline. So today I placed our order in plenty of time to assure the food would be defrosted, having asked Mela earlier in the day what she would like.

"Oh, anything that's edible," she replied.

"No, what would you like?"

"Anything. You choose for me."

"No, you tell me what you would really like. Do you want beef or chicken or fish?"

"Yes, any of those."

"Okay, here's how it is. There's beef chop suey, chicken with cashew nuts—"

"Chicken with cashew nuts! I love chicken with cashew nuts! Can I have that?" Her big eyes sparkle.

"Yes, I will order you chicken with cashew nuts."

The three of us have dinner together. Tau tells Mela about his Community Development education at the University of the South Pacific, and about the kinds of helping jobs there are to do. Mela is keen—she wants to pursue this—and decides to come to Suva with us on Monday. It is exciting to watch her come alive. She is only one—but there is no limit to what one person, given a proper education, can achieve.

Breaking Breadfruit

Sunday morning, November 20th—We begin early to prepare a midday feast. It will be a grand gathering of the clan: Iliki, Seli, Tiki, Solo, Veli, Mela, Tau and myself—eight of us, bound together by shared history and kinship. Tau and Seli did much of the preparation yesterday: digging the pit for the *lovo* (earth oven), collecting rocks, and gathering leaves and coconuts. And yesterday Tau and I purchased the food: chicken, yams, taro, seaweed….

The setting is really lovely: a beautiful compound dotted by coconut palms alongside the ocean. The clan members arrive early. Tau and I light the *lovo*, and begin to prepare the root crops. Then we assemble the leaves to wrap the chicken and two big parrotfish that Iliki and entourage have brought with them from the boat. There is a large breadfruit tree sitting right beside our *bure*, and it's full of ripe breadfruit.

"Let's get a couple of breadfruit to bake in the *lovo*," I say to Tau.

"We can't; it's Sunday. It's against the military rules to gather any food on Sunday."

"Bullshit!" I say to him. "The breadfruit are sitting right there on the branches, and you can't take them because it is Sunday?"

"It's the military rules," he repeats.

Seli is mixing kava on the veranda as we prepare the food for the *lovo*.

"Seli, look at those breadfruit sitting in that tree," I say to him. "How about we put a couple of them in the *lovo*."

Seli jumps up, climbs the tree and, without hesitation, twists off two beautiful mature breadfruit. Chicken, fish, taro, yams—and breadfruit! We place the food on the hot rocks and cover them with leaves and sand. Dinner is in the oven.

As soon as Mela arrives, she starts cooking. I tell her to rest today but she says she likes to do it. She prepares *rourou*, that wonderful dish made from the leaves of the taro plant, along with some seaweed.

Dear Mela, she asks me if I remember the time we partied on Yaciwa island in 1979. I remember it well. I took Mela so that she could have a day free from her daily chores of preparing food, washing dishes and clothes, and caring for her younger siblings. She was very tiny then, and I placed a mask and snorkel inside the boat for her so that she could swim and enjoy the fish and corals. But as soon as we arrived at Yaciwa, she immediately went ashore on the little coral quay and set up to prepare food for our small group. The whole time we were there, she worked, much as she would back in the village, and at no time did she play in the water. Now, a decade later, she has taken over my little kitchen and is puttering away, preparing food and washing dishes.

The feast is soon ready. We open the *lovo* and remove the baked chicken and the fish, the breadfruit and the root crops. The smell of the freshly baked food is tantalizing.

Mela takes a mat from inside the cottage and spreads it on the veranda. I get some plates and serving dishes. Cutlery is not used. Mela dismembers the chicken while Tau cuts the root crops. We gather around the mat—Mela directs us where to sit—and Veli preambles the grace with a spontaneous statement of his feelings.

"We are the members of a clan who are away from our home island," he says. "But we have gathered to share food together, and in so doing, we have strengthened the bonds of love and kinship among us." Then he prays. "Bless those who have brought us together and who have prepared this food for us. Take care of us, O God, and keep us safe." The sense of oneness I feel at this moment is indescribably lovely.

When the meal is over, the male members of the clan find a quiet space and fall asleep. Mela is so quick at doing the dishes that she has soaped them up even before I can finish eating. When I offer to help her, she protests. I judge it better just to let her do it. When she is done, she finds an empty bed and falls asleep. They are all so comfortable, here in my rented space. And they never treat me as an outsider. A year may pass between visits but always they are the same. Kinship, seemingly indestructible, in the face of time and distance, of economic disparity, of military rule…Oh, that we could realize this for the whole of humanity!

On Holy Ground

Sunday afternoon, November 20th—It is time for our trip to the top of the mountain. Our police permit goes into effect at 3 p.m. There will be four of us: Tau, Mela, a driver and myself. We dress for church, Mela and I in long Fijian dresses, Tau in his Sunday *sulu*. With police permit in hand, we head out for the long drive to the summit.

To get to the mountaintop village we must follow the coast road about half way around the island. From there a narrow winding road heads into the high interior. Up we ascend, into the thick green forest covering the rocky hills. Further along we can see the rock cliffs that define the top of the mountain. It is spectacular. Then the steep climb levels off, and there, nestled in an area surrounded by peaks, sits the infamous historical village. A quick glance is enough to realize that we are inside the crater at the top of the volcano.

We drive to the end of the road. It's a typical-looking Fijian village apart from the spectacular setting. Crowning the settlement is a Methodist church with a brightly painted red roof. It is 4 p.m. The church is filled with people, and, as if on cue, at the very moment we shut off the engine and step outside the van, the choir begins to sing.

Our Father, which art in heaven
Hallowed be Thy name
Thy kingdom come, Thy will be done
On earth as it is in heaven ….

Oh Verani Elijah, what a contrast to your entrance into this village! And what a transformation! Indeed, you brought the Christian counterpart to the light of Hinduism. You used *your* vehicle to higher consciousness to redefine kinship and seek a new harmony. You broke down an integration that was inadequate to a new condition, and, in the process, advanced the Fijian culture to a larger whole. Like *Brahman-Atman,* you were a spark of the divine, and I feel that I am standing in your presence on holy ground.

I look at the mountain peak at the far end of the village. It is strangely familiar, yet I have never been here before. There are a few men sitting inside a corrugated iron shelter near the church. I go to them and express my interest in Verani Elijah. They show me the place where the Christian chief was killed. They confirm that his body and those of other members of the mission were delivered to the missionary and taken to Levuka where they were properly buried. Then they point out the mountain peak that Verani Elijah ascended to gain access to the village—the same peak that looked familiar to me.

"What is on the other side of that mountain peak?" I ask.

"Levuka Public School," a man replies.

Yes, of course! When I walked up the mountain yesterday, not only was I closer to the mountaintop village than I knew, but I was walking in the footsteps of the man who came in the dark of night to bring peace to a warring tribe. A powerful chief himself, Verani Elijah redefined kinship to include those outside his own group. In so doing, it took him—literally and figuratively — to the top of the mountain. And that is what the Fijians need to do now—stand on "higher ground".

We beg our leave and return down the mountain, then follow the coastline around the island and make our way back to Levuka town. It grows dark and it is past dinnertime, but I do not want to eat. I just want to wander into the Fiji night. The stars are brilliant and propel me into a kind of infinity. I see Sirius, the "three in one" that guided the Polynesians in their canoes, and mighty Canopus.

The universe—unfolding as it should….

Part III

CULTURE BOUND

Chiefly Speaking

Monday, November 21ˢᵗ—The taxi arrives at 3 a.m. to take Tau and I into Levuka town to catch the bus to the ferry to get back to Suva. Mela is coming with us, and her little brother Tiki is here to see us off. Three o'clock in the morning and he is standing there smiling! How lucky I feel to be a part of this extended family. We board the bus at 4 a.m. and half an hour later we leave the quaint old capital.

It's a five-hour trip back to Suva. I'm tired. I fall asleep on the ferry, but once on the main island, there is no place to rest my head; the bus is crowded and the seats are narrow. The road is dusty and so bumpy that it would entice even the most ardent supporter of the women's movement to revert to wearing a bra. By the time we reach Suva, I feel sick. We get a taxi to the hotel and I fall asleep once again.

The Great Council of Chiefs is meeting this week. They are holding their sessions at the military headquarters on the outskirts of Suva. It is an interesting—and very telling—choice of venue! The critical items on the agenda are the Draft Constitution and the proposed new structure of the Great Council of Chiefs. There are about 270 chiefs from all over Fiji attending the meetings.

This morning marks the first of the round of meetings, and it is expected to be a stormy one. The Draft Constitution is, at best, contentious. How can the Council of Chiefs dictate that one of their number will be elected Prime Minister within a democracy? After all, the political crisis was triggered by the fair and democratic election of an Indo-Fijian Prime Minister. And even if the chiefs of Fiji were to recant on that contentious issue, would the military stand by and allow an Indo-Fijian to assume the role of Prime Minister yet again? I don't think so!

No. Their deliberations are designed to guarantee more of the same: narrow communalism ... obedience to chief ... fear of God: in summary, ethnic prejudice and collective fear embedded in an inferior Constitution—and not a lot anyone can do about it.

"Go placidly ..." I remind myself. So tonight Tau and I decide to take in a movie—a light comedy—as a respite from the chaos of political imaginings. A good idea, we think, but it turns out that the projection system is as shaky as the Constitution. When the system breaks down altogether, the impatient audience resorts to shouting. While all this is going on, I remind myself, the 270 Fijian chiefs are being entertained as the honoured guests of military ruler Colonel Rabuka and his officers. If these agitated theatre-goers could see "the real picture", they would really have something to shout about!

A Voice in the Wilderness

Tuesday, November 22nd—I am still thinking about the cultural dilemma in Fiji as I have my breakfast of mangoes and toast on the patio beside the swimming pool. Mela arrives after lunch as scheduled, and I set my work aside and go with her to learn about furthering her education. She has her New Zealand School Certificate—though her marks are not great—so we begin to explore sub-degree programs at the University of the South Pacific here in Suva. A Certificate program would seem to be the most appropriate, allowing her to do Social Work. We go to USP to get information, then to the Ministry of Education to find out what kind of financial assistance might be available. Mela is excited and highly motivated.

It is hot and very humid. The sky is overcast and the clouds are holding in the sultry heat by the time we complete the round of meetings. But there is one more gathering I want to attend: a meeting about the Draft Constitution. Submissions are being made to the Commission from various parts of Fiji, and in Suva today, a women's organization whose members represent different ethnic and religious communities in Fiji is meeting to finalize their proposed submission.

A room on the first floor of the building has been reserved for the meeting. As it turns out, an office might have sufficed since only ten women have shown up.

They read through the proposal paragraph by paragraph.

We view with deep reservation the substance of the Draft Constitution of Fiji and the process by which it has been formulated and imposed on the people of Fiji ….

I have brought Mela with me. She is a bit bewildered by it all, but I think it is important for her to realize what is happening in her country.

A most disturbing feature in the Draft Constitution is the proposed entrenchment of the military in civilian and political institutions. The militarization of civilian life is a singular act of oppression and will only increase the use of violence by the state against its citizens ….

Given that there is precious little critical analysis on the part of women in political matters such as these, their proposed submission is remarkable—and encouraging.

The 1970 Constitution, although it may have had certain deficiencies, can be said to have contributed immensely to the building of trust and good will amongst the different communities of Fiji….

Mela sits quietly beside me. She listens intently.

After 17 years of peaceful coexistence that made Fiji a "symbol of hope" for the world, we could have taken a bolder step towards strengthening the bonds that had been forged between the different communities during this period to further advance Fiji ....

The proceedings are in English. "Do you understand what they are saying?" I ask Mela.

"Yes," she replies.

We believe a new generation is emerging in Fiji which, having experienced ... growing up in a multiracial environment, is not handicapped by the previous generation's narrow communalism and prejudice ....

What are the chances, I wonder, that this nineteen-year-old girl will grow up in a Fiji free of narrow communalism and prejudice.

The Draft Constitution is a seriously retrogressive step for Fiji as it threatens to undermine the unity and strength of our nation and betrays the hopes of young people for a better Fiji ....

Mela is the epitome of young people who want to live and work in a better Fiji—and she belongs to the generation that will have to alter the cultural and political dynamics that have brought Fiji to this crisis. But what of it does she understand!

The submission is adopted, and the meeting comes to an end.

"Do you know why there was a military coup in Fiji?" I ask Mela as we leave the building.

"No, not really," she says.

The overcast skies break into a raging thunderstorm, and there is violent downpour of rain. Fitting—and it gives me time to consider just how much I should tell her.

Part IV

HOMEWARD BOUND

Spiritual Anthropology

Wednesday, November 23rd—Today is my birthday. It brings up that perennial question again: What are we doing here? Allan Watts once said the most amazing thing is that there is anything happening at all! Life *is* the ultimate cosmic mystery.

A *birth day* marks the appearance of a mere individual for a cosmic moment on the planet. Not that we have arrived here from somewhere else; we are not born into the world—we are born out of it. Whether we are born to a purpose is arguable, but if you set out on a mission, the universe will conspire to help you. And now for me all the pieces are falling into place.

I enjoy a quiet day: breakfast on the patio, lunch with Sai and Mata, dinner with Tau. And I reflect, for today is the day I have chosen to formulate an answer to the question of India in the context of my own discipline, Anthropology.

India gave me a deeper understanding about what we as humans can potentially be. Human history, I learned in that ancient setting, is not a series of secular happenings without shape or pattern. On the surface, we see only "social drama"—economic trials, political upheavals, institutional conflicts—while the truly significant drama— the tension between the effort of human beings and the purpose of the universe—is playing out silently in the depths below.

In my sojourns in Fiji, I have witnessed economic trials, political upheavals and institutional conflicts. This world of "social drama" represents one side of the equation: the effort of human beings.

I have also witnessed the enduring light of Hinduism in this island nation with its conception of the spiritual oneness of all things. The growing to conscious awareness of this unitive state of being represents the other side of the equation: the purpose of the universe.

But what of that "truly significant drama"—the tension between the effort of human beings and the purpose of the universe—playing out silently in the depths below? How does one uncover that?

"Not in the world the eye can see, but in the mysterious centre of thought," stated Gauguin, in his attempt to capture the Polynesian psyche on canvas. And to the extent that he was able to achieve his goal with images, now, through the discipline of Anthropology, I shall attempt to interpret that "truly significant drama" in words.

Anthropology: from the Greek *anthropos*—human. That is the discipline I chose to understand the place of humankind in the world. Anthropology had its origins in the natural sciences and there was a tendency early on to understand human culture as acting in accordance with natural laws that could be empirically observed. Anthropology may have come a long way since then, but culture is still (correctly) understood as a blueprint for survival and, following from this, an attempt to operate within—or to transcend—the limitations imposed by nature. But it has always been nature with a small "n" and culture with a small "c".

Anthropology has acquired a vast body of knowledge about culture that has served to advance our understanding of our human being-in-the-world. Like the ethnic conflict in Fiji, as world geopolitics thrusts us headlong into clashes with both nature and culture, our choice is now between creating one world—or no world at all. The development of world-consciousness is the new blueprint for survival. Once again it is about culture acting in accordance with natural laws. We have come full circle. But this time it is Nature with a capital "N" and Culture with a capital "C". This new reality requires an Anthropology that speaks not only of the cultural body and the cultural mind but also of the cultural Spirit. In short, we need a spiritual Anthropology.

In our "normal" cultural state, we experience ourselves as egoic beings, taking the material world—the one that is knowable to the senses—to be our only reality, while, in fact, there are two states of being: the egoic or lesser self from which we derive our personal and social identity, and a higher Self of pure awareness that is observer of the egoic being. In short, the "I" we take to be ourselves, this entity that lives out its days in the world as a social being, is not who we really are at all. This smaller self co-exists alongside the higher Self, knowable only through higher states of consciousness.

This theoretical stance makes "scientific" sense only recently—in the wake of quantum physics, which recognizes matter as a form of energy. Now, energy can be understood as psychic force and, following from that, Spirit as an even more subtle form of energy.

Spiritual Anthropology would recognize subtle energy as part of a continuum throughout creation, extending from the solid mass of rocks and sand to the subtle awareness of intention and pure consciousness. Human beings would mirror this continuum, depending on their level of consciousness. The outward expression—the cultural world— would be a reflection of the collective consciousness.

Every culture provides a vehicle in some form whereby its members can experience higher states of consciousness. It is a mixed blessing that organized religion has traditionally been the vehicle for this experience, because its spiritual teachings have been too often mired in ritual and dogma, in institutional infighting, exploitation, even war. Spared of institutional trappings, spiritual growth would give rise to a very different experience of being-in-the-world. It would illuminate the whole spiritual struggle of the human soul: the conflict between the cultural self (who we think we are) and the Universal Self (who we really are). The "really significant drama" is the push and pull between the two, the one pushing toward unity and compassion, the other pulling back to separateness and fear.

The place of a culture along the continuum could be read in terms of its dominant outward expression. For example, Greek ideas about social and political organization led to the establishment of the city-state. Roman ideas about law and order led to advancements in administration and the practice of law. In general, when these cultural institutions no longer express the underlying ideas, they either transform or the culture dies.

The dominant expression in Fijian culture is chieftainship. And the idea that underlies the expression of chieftainship is kinship. Fijians believe that in order for kinship—the basis of their social organization—to survive, their chiefs must rule. It is through their chiefly system that they have come to know who they are and what they are to do. But given the present cultural reality, the attempt to express kinship through the vehicle of chieftainship is no longer viable. In fact, instead of it being the *expression* of their cultural life, chieftainship is now creating *repression*, which has led to projection— making the Indians their scapegoat—and culminating in attack.

Very sad! All the more so because the Indians brought with them *their* dominant expression—which is Hinduism— and the idea that underlies the civilization of India is, in a word, spirituality. For the devout Hindu, the chief aim of life is spiritual realization through purification of the mind, and this pursuit leads to the discovery of the spiritual oneness of all things.

Two opposing cultural expressions! But what if they were to integrate the two defining ideas that underlie them? What if they were to redefine Fijian kinship (as did Verani Elijah), this time in light of Hindu spirituality? They would come to realize the kinship—the oneness—of all the people in Fiji. And they would be doing what every successful culture does when its current expression is found inadequate to new conditions: strive for adjustment by advancing to a larger whole—in a word, integration—in order to seek a new harmony.

Fijian culture, in spite of its dark history, was authentic to the past. But the past is no more, and the chiefs of Fiji are trying to force their old ideas onto a new reality. If the Fijians could use Christianity—their vehicle to higher consciousness —as did Verani Elijah, Fiji could once again become a glowing example to the world. Indeed, Fiji is a microcosm of the world since there is no place on the planet any more where cultures with competing ideas have not run up against each other.

Spiritual Anthropology: that's my answer to the question of India. But there is one thing more—how to transform this intellectual knowledge into personal and emotional experience in order that it be permanently imprinted on the subconscious mind. I'm sure that, in due course, the universe will offer up the requisite personal and emotional experience ....

The Heavens Rejoice

Thursday, November 24th— My flight out of Fiji is one day away, and I will once again depart from Nadi. There are things I need to do before leaving Suva: banking, shopping, booking seats on the bus to Nadi...Along with Tau, Mela will be coming with me so she can have a visit with her "sister" Mili, classified as sister because the fathers of the two girls are brothers. Mela is very excited about the trip; she has little opportunity to travel.

It is still early in the day when I go to reserve the bus seats, and I'm still thinking about that idea of a unity state of consciousness. In practical terms, how is it to be realized? It would not appear to be a function of the brain because the brain is primarily concerned with thinking, and I know one cannot get to higher states through rational thought alone. Then again, I'm not even sure the brain is used primarily for thinking ….

I arrive at the appropriate office but the desk is vacated. I inquire, and learn that the agent is in the building, and that she will sell the tickets again at 5 p.m. I search and find her sitting inside a beauty boutique chatting with a girl who is polishing her toenails. I approach her directly.

"Can you tell me how I can get tickets for the coach to Nadi?" I ask her.

"I'll sell them to you after 5 o'clock," she replies.

"But doesn't the coach leave at 4:30?"

"Yes."

"Well, won't it be too late if you sell them to me after 5?"

She stares at me with a blank expression on her face. I can almost see the neurons firing in her brain.

After a long pause, she asks, "You want to go today?"

I nod.

She looks at me and says nothing. Then I witness a most marvelous display of coordinated bodily movements that I can only surmise are being synchronized by the human brain. She jumps up from the chair, walks over to her desk, sits down, and proceeds to sell me three bus tickets.

Yes, the brain is not used primarily for thinking!

There is one person I have not yet seen on this visit to Fiji. It is the man who lives on the street, making his way in life by collecting and selling bottles, the same man who encouraged Tau and I that day some years ago to get our music "on the radio". I asked Tau about him and he said the old fellow is still in business and that he spots him walking along the street from time to time. Then today, as though to complete everything, within an hour of the time we are scheduled to leave Suva, I see him, slowly walking along Victoria Parade with his sack of bottles.

When the man spots me, he stops and stares for so long that I question whether or not he remembers me. I walk up to him and extend my hand. He says my name and then he asks a number of questions about where I have been and where I am going. He is so open, so unafraid, so unreserved….

Oh God, it is wonderful! In the scheme of things, of what consequence is the growth of this homeless man? Yet I cannot help but feel that the heavens resound with joy over it.

I leave Suva with a profound sense of completion.

Fiji, Ever Fiji

Friday, November 25th—A final breakfast of mangoes at the hotel near Nadi, then a local bus into town to invite Mili and Mela to lunch. After we eat, I bid them good-bye, not knowing if or when I will see them again.

I return to the hotel, pack up my things and head to the airport. Tau comes with me. My *Air Pacific* flight turns out to be a *QANTAS* 747. I check in and manage to book a window seat in a non-smoking section.

The weather turns sultry and soon the clouds burst into a thunderous downpour of rain. The terminal, by this time, is filled with principally Fijian Indians gathered to bid good-bye to departing family members. Many relatives are present and have dressed up for the occasion. I cannot decide whether it is to impress or depress because it makes for an unbearable emotional scene.

It's time to go. Tau accompanies me to the Immigration checkpoint. People are crowded about the area, their heads leaning to catch one last glimpse of a departing relative. I look into the eyes of this lovely

Fijian man. What does the future hold for him? I give him a card. It
reads simply:

Heart for heart
Soul for soul
Let us be
Forever friends

"When are you coming back?" Tau asks me.
"I don't know."
"When will I see you again?"
"I don't know." What more can I say…What more can I do…A
warm embrace … he turns and walks away. I pause a moment to see
if he will look back. He does.

I choke back my tears and make my way through the formalities,
then board the flight. I find myself seated next to a young Indian
woman wearing a muted pink sari with burgundy trim. The colour
accents her beautiful dark skin. On her lap is a very large portrait of
Sai Baba in a gilded golden frame. She periodically looks straight at
me and flashes a broad smile. Soon after, she begins to speak.

Nitala is her name. She is 22 years old and comes from a town on
the northern island of Vanua Levu. She is the second of five children,
all of whom are in Fiji except her sister who is five years her senior
and lives in Australia. It seems that two months ago Nitala married
an Australian man of European descent, the marriage having been
arranged by her older sister. The couple had not met before the
wedding; the match was decided on the basis of photographs and
the older sister's recommendation. Two months ago, the prospective
husband came to Fiji to claim his bride and the two were joined
together in a customary Indian wedding. After the ceremony, they
spent one week together in Fiji, then the groom returned to his native
Australia and began the process of obtaining a visa for his new wife.

It took two months; the visa has just arrived, and today is the big day: Nitala is immigrating to Australia.

"They didn't want to give me a visa," she confides. "They didn't think it was a real wedding but I told them they could see the photos if they wanted."

"Did they think you were getting married just to get out of Fiji?"

"Yes, that's what they think. They gave my husband a difficult time, but he made them give me a visa. He said, 'This is my wife'."

"And you are happy to go to Australia?"

"Yes, I want to go. Now I want to get my mother and the rest of my family out of Fiji."

She tells me that her father died only six months ago. He had a heart attack, and was only 45 years old. When he had the attack, the family took him right away to the hospital but the doctor there said they were busy and told them to wait outside.

"My brother got into a real fight with that doctor," she says, "trying to get some help for my father. But no help—and he died." Her flashing smile disappears for a time and her brown eyes moisten.

After a while, she speaks again. "I'm wearing this sari because my husband wants his friends to see that he has a real Indian wife."

"He wants them to see you as an Indian?"

"Yes, because he's a European man."

"So he wanted you to wear a sari. And what did *you* want to wear?"

"Jeans."

"So why didn't you wear jeans?"

"Because I have to please him now."

"And for how long do you have to do what pleases him? Your whole life?"

"Yes, my whole life. He likes this colour. It's his favourite sari and he told me to wear this sari."

"And what colour do *you* like to wear?"

"Yellow," she replies.

She has strong black hair, not straight, yet not curly. It is rolled into a bun on top of her oval face. Now she removes the comb and lets the hair fall down her back.

"Oh, everybody is happy about my marriage. All my relatives are happy," she continues.

"And are *you* happy about it?"

"I'm too happy," she says in her Hindi accent as she beams another broad smile at me. "Everybody likes my husband—because he is very funny. And my sister, she says he is good. He lives next door to her and she knows him about a year. She says he is good."

On her left hand, she is wearing rings on the three middle fingers: a combined wedding and engagement ring on the traditional fourth finger, a decorative gold ring on the index finger, and a ring bearing the image of Sai Baba on the middle finger.

Sai Baba. One of his statements I have always thought particularly poignant: "Politics without principle, education without character, commerce without morality, are not only useless but dangerous."

"I see you have a picture of Sai Baba," I say to her.

"Yes, he's my god," she replies.

"What does he teach?" I ask.

"I don't know."

"Your parents, were they born in Fiji?"

"Yes."

"And their parents?'

"Fiji."

"And your great grandparents?"

"I don't know. Maybe India."

"Do you know from what part of India your family came?"

"I don't know."

"Do you know how they came to be in Fiji?'

"No, I don't know."

"Do you know about the indenture system, the history about how the Indians first came to be in Fiji?"

"No, not really."

"You didn't learn about it in school? In your history or social studies classes?"

"I heard some stories about it. But we are Fijians. We just grew up as Fijians."

"Fiji is your home."

"Yes, but not now. Fiji is spoiled. It was so good before but now it's spoiled."

"Because of the coup, you mean?"

"Yes, after the coup, everything changed. We would never leave Fiji before; it was so good. But after the coup, right away, my sister, she left Fiji. And now me, then my mother, and all my family … we just all want to get out of Fiji."

"You don't want to be Fijians anymore?"

"No, no more. It's no good anymore. No good jobs and we don't know what will happen. We don't feel safe. Fiji is spoiled because of the coup."

"Do you know why there was a coup?"

"Because Ratu Mara didn't want to give up his power."

"You think Ratu Mara was behind it?"

"Yes."

"Do other Fijian Indians feel that way?"

"All the Indians think that."

"You don't think Rabuka acted alone?'

"No. It was Ratu Mara."

Poor Ratu Mara … destined, perhaps, to be saddled with responsibility for the current political situation in Fiji. It was this same man who had laboured hard on the original Fijian Constitution. Whatever deficiencies it might have had, it was a far superior document to the one now being forced on the people of Fiji. What a legacy for so distinguished a statesman! I had met and talked with Ratu Mara just a few months earlier when he came to celebrate Fiji Day at the World Exposition in Australia where I was a consultant at the United Nations Pavilion. He was sad and tired; he had been through enough.

"Someone has to be blamed for the political situation," Ratu Mara lamented, "and it's going to be me." And now, back in Fiji, he finds himself standing before the Great Council of Chiefs, undermining his own Constitutional document to placate those who are determined to govern Fiji with a far inferior one.

"It's a big decision to leave one's country," I say to Nitala.

"Yes," she replies. But there is no turning back. Whatever being Fijian meant to her, it is not sufficient to outweigh the disappointment of suddenly realizing that Fiji is for those Fijians who take the motto of Fiji literally: "fear God and respect the king".

"Do you know the words of the national anthem?" I ask.

"What's that?"

"The song they play on the radio first thing in the morning and next to last thing at night."

"Some of it, I know."

"Can you tell it to me?"

She engages the help of a second Indian woman sitting across the aisle from her. Between the two of them, they come up with the words.

Blessing grant, oh God of nations, on the isles of Fiji
As we stand united under noble banner blue
And we honour and defend the course of freedom ever
Onward march together, God bless Fiji
For Fiji, ever Fiji, let our voices sing with pride
For Fiji, ever Fiji, let her name hail far and wide
Our land of freedom, hope and glory

To endure whate'er befall
May God bless Fiji for ever more

Still clutching the photograph of her god Sai Baba, Nitala begins the second verse of her birth country's national anthem:

Blessing grant, oh God of nations, on the isles of Fiji
Shores of golden sand and sunshine….

Fiji: the fragile island nation that Nitala once called home. But it is no longer habitable for her with its boundaries based on class and ethnicity, on colour and religion. She can escape a divided humanity and fly away while Mela must stay behind to create her world anew. On planet Earth, our fragile island in space, we share the fate of Mela for there is likewise no place else for us to go. We too must strive to create the world anew.

BOOK V

A Matter of Life and Death

December, 1993

Part I

GOOD GRIEF

Return to Cannibal Isle

Monday, December 6th—The *QANTAS* 747 touches down at Nadi International Airport and taxis to the gate. It has been more than five years since my last visit. I disembark and make my way through Immigration and Customs, then step through the glass doors.

There stands Mili. She is a young woman now, looking more grown up even than in the pictures she sent me. She has a faint smile on her face and when I walk over to her, she says very little and gives me a hug.

The Melanesian Hotel outside Nadi … the bus ride from Nadi to Suva … meeting Tau's relatives in the city … it's all the same. Everything seems to stay the same ….

Almost everything ….

The preoccupation in Fiji these days again centers on a chief. This time it's the paramount chief, the former Governor-General who is now the President. He's 75 years old and is dying of leukemia. He has been ill for a lengthy time and his death would appear to be imminent. In spite of all that, he has been flown by charter jet to Walter Reed Hospital in the United States, along with an entourage of relatives and attendants. *Fiji Radio* keeps the nation posted on his condition.

As for the locals, there is no longer an air service to Ngau. Not enough village people can afford to fly nowadays to keep the route open. Christmas is fast approaching and a number of people from the village—including secondary school children on their annual break—are returning to the island: Mili, Mata, Iliki's daughters ... so many of Tau's kin. I will return with them on the next overnight ferry. It will be in about one week's time ....

Home Again

Monday, December 13ᵗʰ—A full week has passed quickly. The ferry to Ngau leaves tonight. It is pouring rain—again—when we gather at the Suva dock around midnight. We load the bags and boxes on the ship, trying to keep ourselves from getting totally drenched. It will be a long trip to make in wet clothing.

Once aboard, Tau's kin set out a mat for me in what can be described as the only dry spot on the vessel, right in the middle of the ship, away from the open railings where the rain is beating mercilessly against the thick plastic tarps. The girls crowd on the mat with me while the men and boys crouch on adjacent benches. The ship is very over-crowded, it is wet and uncomfortable—but there is such an overwhelming spirit of kinship that I truly feel a sense of bliss.

"Isa Tau"

Tuesday, December 14ᵗʰ—A long night passes and it is daylight when the ship slides up to the wharf at Ngau. We remain some distance from the village, however, and need to wait a few hours for transport; the high tide has made the road to the villages on the south end of the island inaccessible. We eat some mangos and have tea with kin in a nearby village while the tide recedes. Then we pile everything onto the back of a truck and head out to the village.

I've brought some kava with me for the *i sevusevu*, and after we arrive, I ask Iliki to do the ritual for me. We head to the house of the chief for the ceremony. At that moment, a very strange thing happens. The wind picks up suddenly and starts to howl. It is like a raging hurricane in an otherwise calm and sunny day. As soon as I step inside the door of the chief's house, the women waiting there gather about me in a circle and start crying.

I cannot cry. I never did learn to grieve on cue. I remain there, sitting cross-legged on the mat with my head down, while they hover around me, wailing.

"*Isa, Tau* (Poor Tau)," they murmur between sobs. "*Tau sa mate.* (Tau is dead.)" It is the first time they have seen me since his death and, following Fijian custom, they are reenacting the ritual mourning to give me a chance to grieve.

After what seems a dreadfully long time, their wailing subsides and they release their grip on me. We shuffle into position and proceed with the kava ceremony.

"Pamela has returned because of the death of Tau," Iliki explains as he ritually handles the kava root. "She has come to place a marker on his grave."

The ceremony ends. The wind dies down and everything is calm again. I cannot understand this phenomenon. Is it just coincidence? Or is there some deep connection with the forces of nature? Or Nature? It is just like that scene in Michener's *Hawaii* where the Malama dies and the winds begin to howl.

Months ago, Tau began to feel ill while in the village. He tried to wait it out but his condition did not seem to improve. He wrote to inform me but because of poor transport and slow mail service, it was some time later before I could get funds to him so he could travel to Suva for medical help. By the time he did get to Suva, he was so ill they admitted him to hospital right away.

After a brief stay in hospital, Tau was discharged. He telephoned
me with the news and asked for more help. I sent a bank draft to him
in Suva. He wrote to thank me, and then went to cash the money,
but the bank informed him it would take six weeks to process the
draft! They had to clear it with my bank in Toronto, they told him. He
wrote to tell me, so I sent another letter to Suva with quick cash to last
until the bank draft could be cleared.

Then I got another phone call—not from Tau this time. It was
from someone else … to tell me Tau had died. When my letter arrived
a day or so later, Tau's relatives in Suva opened it, and they used the
quick cash to buy flowers to place on his coffin for his burial back in
the village.

Iliki and his family are now living in the little house Tau shared
with me. I see that my belongings—mats and linens, dishes, even my
guitars—have been distributed around the village. No matter. When
I last left the village, I had a sense I would not be coming back to my
little house again.

A Grave Sight

Wednesday, December 15th—Early in the morning, I ask Vati
—Mela's mother and Tau's oldest brother's wife—to take me to Tau's
grave. She leads me through the jungle growth, up to the summit of
a hill overlooking the deep blue ocean with its turquoise lagoon. The
view of the reef is stunning from here. I find myself silently reciting
the words of Tau's song about the beauty of the reef:

> *The glistening of the reef around the island of Ngau*
> *With its corals of many colours, it's like a garland*
> *Shells and fish of all kinds live in it*
> *From big ones all the way to the little bait-nibblers*
> *I'm just amazed at its beauty ….*

When the grave comes into view, Vati turns and hugs me and starts to cry. There in front of me is a simple mound of red earth supported by porous coral stones. I can't feel anything—and I still cannot cry. I just see a heap of earth ….

Rivers and mountain ranges on the land
Hills that are green and full of life
Wild yams and cultivated yams, taro, prawns, eels
Not to forget the staple supply of seaweed

Vati then points out the graves of others from the clan who were well and alive when I did my fieldwork here. None of them was elderly. Like Tau, they were cut down before their time as life just carried on around them ….

We attend to our daily routine
Women fishing in the rivers with their nets
Men planting taro on the land
And every morning, the children go to school
To be educated for the good of tomorrow

We make our way back to the village. When I arrive at Mata's house, he tells me they have just announced on radio that the ailing President has died at Walter Reed Hospital in the United States. The Fiji government will send over another charter jet with an official delegation to escort the body home.

It is little more than one week before Christmas but all seasonal programming on *Fiji Radio* is immediately cancelled and replaced by hymn singing. The period of mourning will extend throughout the holiday season and into the new year.

The tributes start pouring in: "Ganilau exemplified the qualities of a chief," ushers one statesman (himself a chief), "honest, diligent and kind." Declares another, "Ratu Sir Penaia has assured (sic) a prominent and honourable place in the history of Fiji."

A prominent and honourable place in history … as though that is what it's all about ….

Watch Out for the Sharks!

Thursday, December 16th—There is a taboo against fishing now because of the President's death. The reason given for the taboo is that the shark is the dead President's *mana* (power) and must therefore not be disturbed. All of a sudden people start reporting that they see sharks swimming close to shore! Even if it were allowed, the villagers say they are afraid to go fishing. A pity, no matter what the rationalization, because the people in this village depend on fish for their daily diet ….

Not more than a few hours later, a "request" arrives from the paramount chief of Ngau for the *kai-wai* (fishermen) in the village to provide fish for the feasting ceremonies associated with the President's death. Their fear mysteriously subsides, and they ready their nets to go fishing.

Such is the power of the chiefs….

Grass Houses

Friday, December 17th—Today some members of the clan build three large shelters where we will prepare food and eat together over the Christmas holidays. The first one is made of all natural materials. The second has walls of plaited palm fronds and metal roofing; the third is a tent-like structure with a plastic roof.

As soon as the structures are completed, people gravitate to the first one, the one made of all natural materials, because, like the Fijian *bure*, it is cool in the heat of the day. There are very few thatched huts left in the village now. One belongs to the newly married son of the clan chief.

Do you like living in the *bure*?" I ask him.

"Yes. When it's hot outside, it's cool inside. When it's cold outside, it's warm inside."

It's the same old story. Every Fijian praises the *bure*, but none of them really wants to live in one. This young man does not plan to either. Inside his *bure*, in the spot usually reserved for a picture of Jesus or the Queen, hangs a poster of a block house with a tin roof, on which is written: "Looking for a Home for your Family? Look no further. It's ready now from the Housing Authority. Call us now. We'll take care of you."

The traditional Fijian *bure* will soon be no more. Why? People who live in grass houses … well, they shouldn't.

It was the same story when I came to the village to do my fieldwork so many years ago, and needed a house of my own. I told them I would like a traditional grass hut. They resisted, saying they would build me a nice little wooden one. When I repeated my preference, they made their bias clear.

"A grass hut is not a suitable house for a white woman," they told me. I persisted, and they did build me a grass hut. Then they proceeded to spend half of their time in it!

"Food for the Chiefs"

Saturday, December 18th—A few days ago there were three turtles in a pen and another one on its back at the shoreline. Next day there was another one there and today, still another. Five beautiful live turtles, held there in the blazing summer sun. They are rather easy to catch now because they have been coming ashore to breed.

I find it really disturbing and talk to the fishermen who are holding them. They tell me that the turtles are "food for the chiefs". Chiefs have always been accorded special food; before their conversion to Christianity, that special food was *bakolo*—human flesh. When the missionaries persuaded the Fijians to give up the eating of human flesh, they substituted turtle as the special chiefly food. And in spite of the fact that killing turtles is in violation of the law, the tradition has managed to survive to this day.

"Do you think it is legal to take them?" I ask.

"Yes," they respond.

" I think it is illegal," I counter, and they now admit that it is. I try to impress upon them that turtles are an endangered species, and that they need to be protected. They respond that they need the turtles for *bakolo e liu* (special food for the chiefs) because it is Christmas.

"Is there no alternative?" I press on.

"We have no money," they inform me. "A cow would cost $400 … a pig $70 or $80."

"What about fish?" I ask.

"There are no big fish on the reef," they respond.

I talk to the village headman. He acknowledges that the fishermen's actions are contrary to the law, but is unable—or unwilling—to bring pressure to bear. Why? Because, like the rest of these villagers, he strongly believes in the *sau vanua*, the greatly feared "supernatural" power of the chiefs.

Tau would not let them get away with this. He would not be afraid of the *sau vanua*. So what should I do! It's not my place, I know, but without Tau, who else will try to save this endangered species now ….

All the Way Down

Sunday, December 19th—This morning there are seven live turtles in captivity. One of them has been laid upside down; there is pressure on its head and its eyes are red. When I check on it later in the day, the eyes are bulging.

It is extremely hot! I cannot bear to see the turtles in this condition any longer. I need to talk to someone else about it, but they are all in church!

Later in the day, I state my case to the chief's clan.

"They take too many turtles," the spokesman tells me. "If they took only two, it would be okay." He says he will talk to the fishermen tomorrow, and then follows with a question.

"What punishment will the government yield if this gets reported?" he asks. That's what they really want to know.

Tonight the villagers hold their choir practice in the new palm frond shelter as they drink kava. It is wonderful to hear their singing, but there is something surrealistic about it—like that scene from *The Mission* where the native children have been taught by the Jesuits to play the violin. Christianity: it's such a cultural transplant. How does it really translate to these Fijians? Here they are, sitting cross-legged in a palm frond shelter, singing Methodist hymns in four-part harmony. All the while, those poor turtles are down there on the beach, waiting to be sacrificed for their chiefs.

Not all cultures have such disregard for turtles. Some actually venerate them. I know of one culture that believes the world sits on the back of a turtle. I wonder if it would help if I told the Fijians that. The point, of course, would not be for them to take the story literally but to point to the magnificence of this prehistoric creature. Would they "get it"? Or would they dismiss it as did a Western man who heard it from one of the women of that culture:

"What does the turtle sit on?" the man questions.

"Another turtle," the woman replies.

"Then what does *that* turtle sit on?" the man challenges.

"Your question is no good," comes her reply. "It's turtles all the way down."

Mythologically, of course. But in the Fijian case, it's turtles all the way down to extinction, I fear.

Spirit of the Dead

Monday, December 20th—This morning I see that most of the turtles have "gone missing", and the one remaining turtle has been put back in the cage. I doubt that I have saved its life—but maybe I've managed to relieve it of at least some temporary suffering.

But what am I doing! I have returned too late to save Tau, and I'm trying to save turtles! Why am I doing this? Maybe I feel that I could have saved *him*. Or maybe I'm trying to come to terms with *his* death by preventing the death of something else. If I had been here would Tau still be alive? Could I have made a difference? One of the young men told me that Tau was lonely, that it was as if he didn't want to live anymore. Maybe if I hadn't left at a time when he had no employment, no income … no hope….

They have also started telling me about strange things that happened after Tau's death. One young man says he was sleeping alone in the house where Tau used to eat, and that "Tau" was there all night, from about 10 p.m. until 7 in the morning. Tau's spirit, he says, "left through the window" when he heard his older brother's voice in the morning. And one of Tau's "brothers" tells me that after Tau died, and before he heard about it, he saw the spirit of a young man standing in the doorway of his house, crying.

I wish Tau would send a message to *me* ….

The Schoolmaster

Monday, December 20th —Since I no longer have a house in the village, I am staying in Mata's sleeping house. He is happy for the company since his wife Sai, whom I last saw in Suva where she went for medical treatment, has also passed away. Mata now shares his sleeping house with the schoolmaster.

I have been in the village for a full week and, in all that time, no children have come to the house to visit me. It feels strange because there were always children in my space when I was in the village. Now I am alone in the house a great deal of the time.

But all that is about to change. Shortly after lunch today the schoolmaster leaves for his own village for the Christmas break. I walk with the children as they escort him to the lorry. After the lorry departs, three of the children follow me back to Mata's house, and they come inside. Soon after there are six children here, then ten, then about twenty and by the end of the afternoon, more than thirty. For the first while, they sit quietly, smiling. Then they start to talk, and before too long, they are singing. They spend the entire evening with me.

It is wonderful. It makes me ponder what image these children have of "teacher", and what subtle—or maybe not so subtle—rules have been put in place to constrain them....

Christmas "Passed"

Wednesday, December 22nd—Christmas is fast approaching but one gets no sense that it is near. There are no Christmas carols, no holiday activities ... no cheer ... nothing at all but mournful hymn singing on the radio.

I feel for the children. It should be a lovely time for them, and I want to do something to bring them a bit of joy. I have brought with me the tape of a Christmas carol Tau and I wrote in Fijian and English, and which he recorded with the children in the village a few years ago. The lyrics tell the nativity story:

Shepherds on the hill
All the earth is still
Angel voices fill
The bright and starry sky
Wise men from afar

Following a star
To a manger where a baby lie ....

It is the perfect thing to bring them joy—or so I think. I set up my recorder and play the tape. Some of the older children recognize their voices and grin with excitement. Except for Mili. Tau was one of her "fathers" and she was very attached to him. When she hears his voice on the tape, she starts to cry.

I shut off the tape. So much for trying to bring them joy! Is there no way to find happiness in this dismal scene? Just when I am ready to give up, something wonderful occurs. Some of the young boys are sent out to collect coconuts, and they take me with them. After walking along the palm-fringed beach, we take a flat-bottomed boat up the river that borders what used to be Tau's land. The river is framed by coconut palms, tropical vines and huge trees spreading their branches into a canopy. It is stunning, like a Disneyland jungle cruise—except that it is the real thing. I almost expect to hear a music soundtrack—but in this case, we make our own for they ask me to sing the rest of the Christmas song:

Jesus, Prince of Peace
Was born among the beasts
And chosen from the least
To be the king of kings
Christmas is the day
The Messiah came to stay
So clap your hands and pray
And sing

Soon they are singing along and we are having a positive experience. Yes, carol singing is one thing we can do in these mournful circumstances.

Christmas "Present"

Thursday, December 23rd—Only two days until Christmas. Some of the boys at the far end of the village are lighting small firecrackers. It is the only fun activity I have witnessed so far. While we were in Suva, before taking the ferry to Ngau, Samu had asked me to buy him firecrackers for Christmas. Because I see the other boys lighting theirs, I decide to give Samu's to him today. He is delighted. He eagerly opens the packet, but then he stops and turns to me.

"Do you want me to use them now?" he asks.

There it is again: that inability or reluctance to undertake any action without permission. I saw it again when it came to plans for Samu's schooling. Like some of the other children in the clan, Tau was one of Samu's "fathers", and because Tau was one of the few men in the village to have income, he paid Samu's school fees. In that Tau is no longer here, I will now temporarily take on that role. Samu has relatives in three parts of Fiji, all three wanting him to school with them. In order to set things up with the appropriate group, I ask Samu which of the three relatives he prefers.

"Any of them," he replies, and tells me to ask his older sister. I try one more time to determine his preference. He says he'll talk to his "father", another of Tau's "brothers", and then he'll tell me, adding that he will do what his "father" says.

"You are lucky to have three choices, and to have relatives in all three places," I say to him.

"Yes, and they all like me too."

"Why do you think they all like you?" I ask jokingly.

"Because my 'father' is dead," he says without hesitation.

Kinship … a seemingly indestructible social safety net based on a hierarchical system that is different from love as a value in itself. It is wonderfully reassuring, and functions to safeguard the wellbeing and social stability of its members. But no matter how well the safety net works, it is always just barely working because, in human terms,

it exacts a heavy price. One hint of independent decision-making …
choice … and the whole hierarchy comes tumbling down. Decision-
making may be a necessary portal to individual freedom, but it is not
a door through which too many Fijians are prepared to walk. The
motto of Fiji sums it up rather succinctly: "Fear God and respect the
King."

Christmas Eve

Friday, December 24th—The mournful hymn singing on the radio
overshadows the peaceful ambience of this special night. Previously,
when I was in the village for Christmas Eve, we would go carol
singing, wandering from sleeping house to sleeping house along the
village green. It was lovely, in the cool darkness of the early summer
evening, the skies of the Southern Hemisphere aglow with billions of
stars. But tonight, there are no Christmas carols with their messages
of peace, joy and love.

I wander along the beach. The leaves of the coconut palms sway
gently and seem to whisper in the breeze, and I can hear the waves
crashing on the reef ….

I think of home … I think of life … I think of Tau ….

"Good-Bye"

Saturday, December 25th—Christmas Day arrives. We go to
church … we feast together … and with the help of Mela's father—
chief of the clan—I hand out a copious supply of balloons to the
children ….

In the afternoon, I go alone and quietly up to Tau's grave to
place the marker. Not a bronze plaque—just a natural piece of wood,
beautifully and lovingly handcrafted and engraved for me by my
brother in Canada. I push the attached metal rods into the hard terrain,

step back and take a look. There, protruding from that mound of red earth bounded by porous coral stones, is our perennial message that will echo into eternity.

> Heart for heart
> Soul for soul
> Let us be
> Forever friends

No name, no date … just those few simple words, for I cannot think of Tau as lying beneath this hump of ground. I sense his spirit soars out over that deep blue ocean with its turquoise lagoon, making the reef glisten like a *salusalu*—a garland—like the words in his song. I gaze at the spectacular view and let myself be amazed at its beauty.

I linger a while … I cannot feel any emotion … I take a final look and make my way back to the village ….

I am now ready to leave. There is no regular transport off the island in time for me to get my flight out of Nadi on New Year's Day. Everything seems to be booked. Mela manages to secure passage on a government supply ship that is going from island to island in Lomaiviti collecting tribute for the President's funeral. The ship is to leave Ngau sometime after midnight tonight; Mela will accompany me.

In the early evening of Christmas Day, I say my good-byes in the village—except to Mela's mother who comes with us in the lorry. We ride together in silence, waiting in the back of the truck at each village en route while the local chiefs, with much ritual and kava drinking, present their apportioned lot of taro and mats and whales' teeth for the dead paramount chief. It's after midnight when we arrive at the dock.

Mela's mother has to leave now, for the lorry is returning right away. She hugs me and says good-bye. At that moment, something breaks inside me and I start to cry. I cry really hard and I cannot stop. People are standing about, staring at me.

Mela takes me to someone's sleeping house to wait, since the vessel is moored offshore, and the tide is not yet high enough to access the ship by the dinghy. She sits beside me as I continue weeping uncontrollably. To make matters worse, I have no tissue with me. My eyes are streaming tears and my nose is running. There are a number of women in the house.

"Isa, isa. Tau sa mate," they whisper to each other as they look on with a mix of curiosity and compassion.

I don't know how it happened—or why it happened when it did. I just know that at this critical departure, the rational mind shut down, and surrendered to a deluge of emotions. All the anthropological Journal data I had faithfully and objectively collected over a decade in Fiji culminated in an intensely personal and emotional experience. It was deeply painful and deeply liberating at the same time.

Intellectual knowledge is easily acquired, they taught me in India, and intellectually, the answers have always been there. But in order for it to be permanently imprinted on the subconscious mind, they said, intellectual knowledge must be transformed into personal and emotional experience….

John 19:30: "When Jesus therefore had received the vinegar, he said, It is finished: and he bowed his head, and gave up the ghost."

My homework was done. Now the real work could begin.

Part II

THE LAST WORD

A Dreadful Voyage

Sunday, December 26th—I am grateful for passage on this government supply ship but it is really a dreadful voyage. I might have guessed what would lie ahead when eight of us, crowded into a dinghy overloaded with kava and taro and mats for the President's funeral, embark in pitch darkness at 3 o'clock in the morning. In keeping with the occasion, the chiefs are hushed, even silent. It is an ominous start to a horrendous experience.

On board, there are no seats so Mela spreads a mat on the hard front deck. The sky is filled with stars when we pull up anchor. By daylight, the weather changes. It begins to rain and blow, and it quickly worsens. The navigator beckons us into the steering cabin. There is a hurricane to the north, he tells us, and we are in for a rough ride.

All day it storms. Huge waves toss our vessel as though it were a tiny cork. I stay on deck, trying to avoid seasickness, but eventually I have to get to a toilet—down two flights of narrow steps inside the vessel. I make it only halfway down the first flight, then rush back to the outside railing to vomit.

The Koro Sea is rough at the best of times, but today it is especially vicious. From Batiki north to Koro and east to Nairai, the vessel collects its heaps of mats and kava and taro. Sometimes the winds are too high for the small dinghy to go ashore, and we must anchor and wait while the ship pitches and rolls.

Night falls again and the winds start to quiet down. By this time I am feeling very weak, and fall asleep on the deck. After a few hours, Mela awakens me, pointing straight ahead over the rail. I look out to see the lights of Levuka town on the island of Ovalau. Especially welcoming is the green neon cross on the tower of the old Sacred Heart cathedral, placed there a century ago as a landmark for sailors returning from the sea to this old whaling capital of Fiji. As it did for them, it marks the gap in the reef so that our ship can navigate this dangerous entry by night.

It is an hour to midnight when we dock in Levuka. The chief of Ngau invites me to come the rest of the way with them to Suva. I quickly decline, with thanks, and depart the ship with Mela in hopes of finding a *Fiji Air* flight from here before too many days.

A New Harmony

Monday, December 27th—I wake up this morning in the calm and comfort of Mela's home. She is married now—not to a businessman; her husband works in the Fijian government—and they have two little girls.

I am emotionally exhausted, not to mention weak from the rough sea voyage. Mela takes gentle care of me, bringing me nourishing food and making me comfortable. Later in the day, she takes me for a walk to the village of Nasova about a kilometer away. It is the site where Fiji's Deed of Cession was signed in 1874, and it was the main seat of both the Cakobau government (1873-74) and the British colonial administration (1874-82). And that is where I found the final clue ….

At Nasova, there are what have come to be known as 'cession stones', three inscribed monuments, commemorating key historical events in the political life of Fiji. The first stone was placed on the centenary of the signing of the Deed of Cession in 1874:

THE INSTRUMENT CEDING
TO QUEEN VICTORIA, HER
HEIRS & SUCCESSORS, THE
POSSESSION OF, AND FULL
SOVEREIGNTY & DOMINION
OVER, THE FIJIAN ISLANDS
AND THE INHABITANTS
THEREOF, WAS SIGNED HERE
ON THE 10TH OCTOBER, 1874

The second stone commemorates Fiji's independence just four years short of a century later on October 12, 1970. On that occasion, Charles, Prince of Wales, visited the colony on behalf of the Queen for the formal ceremonies.

The inscription reads:

TO COMMEMORATE THE
VISIT TO LEVUKA OF
HIS ROYAL HIGHNESS
THE PRINCE OF WALES
ON THE OCCASION OF
FIJI'S INDEPENDENCE
12TH OCTOBER, 1970

Prince Charles visits an independent Fiji again just four years later to commemorate the centenary of the actual signing of the Deed of Cession.

THIS STONE WAS UNVEILED

BY

HIS ROYAL HIGHNESS THE PRINCE OF WALES

ON 9TH OCTOBER 1974 TO

COMMEMORATE THE 100TH ANNIVERSARY

OF THE SIGNING OF THE DEED OF CESSION

AT LEVUKA

ON THE 10TH OCTOBER 1874

These stones would appear simply to commemorate three historical events. But read in sequence they reveal something very interesting: the Fijian ability to both peacefully surrender and peacefully reclaim their political sovereignty. What was happening then that is not happening now?

The clue is in the building nearby: the Governor's *vale levu* (Government House), an excellent example of colonial hybrid architecture of the late nineteenth century. What's interesting about it is that the architectural hybrid—half European, half Fijian—represents a cultural achievement on the part of both the colonizer and the colonized. For the colonizer, British dominance was visually downplayed; for the colonized, Fijian compliance was visually elevated. Whether conscious or not, the way was paved for a psychological transformation to take place—an integration to seek a new harmony. In the process, Fiji became part of a larger whole.

Integration … to seek a new harmony…That's what the Fijians need to do now.

Die Before You Die

Tuesday, December 28th—I am able to get a *Fiji Air* flight to Suva tomorrow, so today is my last day to be with Mela and to say good-bye to this historical place. I wander through the lanes of the old colonial capital, nestled here at the base of the steep mountain. Even today, Levuka has the feel of a 19th century whaling town with its weather-worn clapboard buildings and narrow streets.

The mountain beckons as before. From the base at the old Methodist church, 199 steps lead up to some of Levuka's finest old buildings, including Methodist mission homes and a Methodist school. I make the climb to the top of Mission Hill.

From this perspective, the view is magnificent … the islands of Lomaiviti nestled in a deep blue ocean stretching to the horizon. Off in the distance I can see the island of Ngau where Tau's body rests for eternity. But his body was not a cultural body, and his mind was not a cultural mind. He died before he died, and now his spirit forever belongs to that interrelated, interdependent and indivisible whole….

I take a final look. Then, with calm surrender, I retrace my steps down the mountain.

A Cultural Body

Wednesday, December 29th—Today I say good-bye to Mela and board the *Fiji Air* plane for Suva. The flight from Levuka to Nausori airport takes only ten minutes. From there it's a bus ride into the city where I check into a room at the Travelodge on Victoria Parade.

The President's body is now lying in state at Government House. His coffin is piled high with sheets of tapa cloth on top of which is spread a Fijian flag. The *Fiji Times* offers a pictorial of events from the Presidential mourning rituals: European businessmen awkwardly sitting cross-legged at a ceremony, Fijian women draped in black watching over the casket, a soldier with rifle in formal dress guarding the coffin, women engaged in special prayer sessions for the President, "members of the public" on their knees shuffling past the casket, people signing the condolence book … and foreign dignitaries, like the King of Tonga, arriving for the state funeral tomorrow.

For the funeral, workers have constructed a pavilion in the shape of a Fijian *bure* near the Parliament Building in Albert Park. It's quite beautiful and the inside ceiling is lined with large sheets of tapa cloth. Meanwhile, in the President's home village of Somosomo on the island of Taveuni, the clan of traditional conch blowers for the *Tui Cakau*—his official chiefly title there—began blowing the conch on Monday and will continue blowing it non-stop until the dead chief is buried there on Saturday. Gravediggers are rushing to complete the tomb for the New Year's Day burial. According to the *Fiji Times*, the traditional gravediggers are staying up all night to make sure the special tomb is ready. Their leader is quoted as saying it is their traditional duty to see that the body of the *Tui Cakau* is properly buried. He says they are helping army engineers from Suva complete the construction work. On Monday, 50 men were brought from villages on the island of Taveuni to begin preparations of the burial site. They will be clearing the area by pulling weeds with their hands.

A Cultural Mind

Thursday, December 30th—Today is the state funeral in the open park in Suva, and it takes the better part of the afternoon. About 5000 people show up. The Travelodge is directly across the street from the park so I wander over in the sweltering heat to watch the proceedings. Accompanied by a 300-man gun party from the Fiji military forces, the flag-draped coffin arrives atop a gun carriage. Eight warrant officers, who were assigned as pallbearers since the arrival of the body in Fiji last week, place the coffin on the specially prepared platform as a 200-strong choir bursts into a somber funeral hymn. The acting President—who is none other than Ratu Mara—delivers the tribute.

"Like so many here and far away," he states, "I struggle to come to terms with my loss, and my country's loss." His sincerity is not in question; Ratu Mara's daughter is married to the late President's son.

After the funeral, the flag-draped coffin is removed from Albert Park, and the huge funeral cortege makes its way to Princess Wharf for the boat trip to Taveuni. It is very hot and the scores of soldiers and policemen in their formal dress are sweating like pigs. I feel for them, marching along in the heat, while all the big chiefs ride beside them in air-conditioned limousines. A short while later, I watch a flotilla of ships sailing out to sea from Suva Harbour.

So many ships! No wonder we had such difficulty getting a boat from Ngau!

A Message from Heaven

Friday, December 31st—New Year's Eve. The *Fiji Times* is again full of pictures of the President's mourning ceremonies. There's a full-length picture of the Thakaudrove women lining the sides of the road at the jetty on Taveuni, waiting for the ship bearing the dead President's body. The women form two rows, flanking a lengthy "red carpet" of new mats. Dignitaries, military, police, and pallbearers will trample the new mats while the women sit at either side on the bare rough concrete. Then there are the pictures of the heaps of taro, the stacks of whales' teeth, the piles of kava, the mounds of wreaths and flowers ….

In Suva, the crowds have dispersed. I check out of the hotel and prepare to leave for Nadi, from where I am booked on an early morning *Air Pacific* flight to Tonga tomorrow.

I am ready to leave Fiji; I am done with what I came here to do. I take one last short walk before boarding the bus.

"Oh, Tau," I murmur, "please give me a sign."

And that is when I see him: the man who lives on the street, slowly walking along Victoria Parade with his sack of bottles. He stares at me … he smiles at me … and he walks toward me…Oh God, what a mystery that for a second time, in my final moments before departing this place, I should encounter this homeless man. It is such a paradox that one who has so little could offer me so much. But then again, whom better could Tau choose to get through to me ….

Forever Friends

Saturday, January 1st—New Year's Day. My early morning *Air Pacific* flight to Tonga is delayed. Something about the plane being "unavailable". Gee, I wonder why! It will go later in the day, they promise.

While I wait, I read today's *Fiji Times*. Headline: "21-Gun Salute for Ratu Sir Penaia". It continues, "The chief marshal of the funeral ceremony says the army and the traditional gravediggers have both agreed to take part in the rites of the high chief's funeral. A battery of four guns has arrived in Somosomo for the 21-gun salute. They will begin firing immediately after the last prayer and before the gravediggers place the casket in the tomb that the army engineers have constructed. Four detachments of escort troops, each of them comprised of an officer and 60 men, will escort the casket from Ratu Penaia's chiefly *bure* on the hilltop down 200-metres to the sacred burial grounds….

"When told about the weight of the casket and the enormous task the gravediggers would face trying to lift it inside the tomb, (the spokesman) said it was no problem. 'I have brought 50 men from the villages and I will choose the eight strongest to carry the casket', he said."

And on and on…A delegation of women will decorate the inside of the tomb with special mats and tapa cloth. The soldiers will seal the vault. The burial site will be cordoned off and only the soldiers and gravediggers will be allowed to step on the sacred burial ground.

After the entombment, the four detachments of soldiers will march the three-kilometer stretch back to their barracks accompanied by the army band. Special ceremonies will then take place for the gravediggers after they have bathed in the sea.

Then this quotation: "When questioned about what was the distinctive feature of the state funeral, (the spokesman) said it was the fact that the state paid for all the expenses while the army controlled all the ceremonies."

The best possible medical attention, unlimited financial resources, not to mention chartered ships and jetliners, army battalions and police units, stacks of taro and kava, piles of mats and tapa cloth from every island of the nation. All this for a man who dies of leukemia at the ripe old age of 75 while a vital young man, with exemplary talent and ability, dies in obscurity in the same land for lack of money and medical care before he has had a chance to live barely half that time.

Fiji sacrificed Tau. They sacrificed him as surely as they did those victims in the nineteenth century to provide "food for the chiefs" or to grace the cornerstone of a new temple or to launch a chief's canoe… It is culture—with a small "c", and culture is what a separate self does with death.

But culture cannot have the last word. That belongs to Nature—one, whole and undivided—and Nature is what a unified Self does with life.

Now I continue my earthly journey without Tau. But I know that, heart for heart, soul for soul, we will be forever friends. For, at the end of the long journey, I realize what I could not comprehend at the beginning … the day I arrived on that island in the middle of the South Pacific Ocean and encountered a Polynesian man leaning against a coconut tree, half naked, with his mass of fuzzy hair and deep brown skin, brandishing a machete….

It should have felt strange, perhaps even frightening. But it did not. It was as though I already knew him. More than that, it was as though I had known him for a very long time. In retrospect, it was more like, "Well, here we are again; you're a brown-skinned Polynesian and I'm a cultural anthropologist. I wonder what we are to do this time."

I wonder what we are to do next time ….

EPILOGUE

Dr. Pamela Peck left the Fiji Islands and returned to Canada in December of 1993. As a result of the events and experiences recorded in these private Journals, she did not resume University lecturing or pursue an academic career. She continued to travel, to read, to reflect and then to write. Three years later, in 1996, she published a seminal work on the perils of culture, entitled: "The Cannibal's Cookbook: Recipes and Remedies for Human Sacrifice."

"The Cannibal's Cookbook" is a critical and insightful account of how culture shapes our perceptions of reality and gets us to do what we don't intend to do. From Egypt to India, from Paris to Papeete, the anthropologist reveals the rituals of culture that render and keep us spellbound. "We follow the dictates of our social system much as we respond to hypnotic suggestion," she writes. "Robots we are, ready and willing to do and to be all manner of human sacrifice."

"The Cannibal's Cookbook" is available through:

PJenesis Press,
City Square PO Box 47105
Vancouver, Canada
V5Z 4L6

One final and sad note: during the final editing of these Journals for publication, Pamela learned that Mela died of breast cancer.

ACKNOWLEDGEMENTS

To India, for launching me on the spiritual quest, especially Swami Lokeswarananda at the Ramakrishna Mission Institute of Culture, Calcutta who put the right book in my hand, and the summary of Indian Philosophy and Religion compiled by Swami Prabhavananda in "The Spiritual Heritage of India". For her enlightened Christian perspective, I express my debt to Cynthia Bourgeault, an Episcopal priest, who in her succinct book entitled "The Wisdom Way of Knowing" reveals the path to reclaiming the ancient Christian tradition.

To Ken Johnson, contributing editor, partner and best friend, for invaluable and unwavering support in every way, and to Barbara Yearsley for very helpful editing.

To the people of Fiji—native *i taukei* and Indo-Fijian, who shared their lives and their stories with me on my many sojourns to their beautiful island nation; I will not forget you. I especially remember Mili and Mela.

And to Tau, who will forever live in my heart.

ABOUT THE AUTHOR

Cultural Anthropologist Pamela J Peck is an author, composer, playwright and lecturer whose professional interest is education for a global perspective and the application of social science knowledge to the practical concerns of everyday life. Canadian born, she holds the degrees of Bachelor of Arts in Psychology and Religion (Mt. Allison University), Bachelor and Master of Social Work (UBC), and PhD in Anthropology (UBC). She was a Research Associate at the University of Delhi in India and a Research Fellow at the University of the South Pacific in Fiji.

Pamela has traveled in and studied more than eighty countries around the world, and has lived and worked in a number of them. She uses her cultural experiences to infuse and inform her novels, short stories, screenplays and stage musicals. Drawing on the archetypal structure of classic mythology and Jungian psychology, her creative works embody timeless and universal principles. Her stories appeal to people of all ages as she takes us on magical and adventurous journeys to the far corners of the outer world, and into the inner recesses of the human mind.

The present work is autobiographical and is a true and faithful record of her travels and studies not only in the Fiji Islands but also in India.